POISON 2
The Dark Dimension

JAMES G. ZOMCHICK

Poison 2
The Dark Dimension
Copyright © 2024 by James G. Zomchick

Library of Congress Control Number: 2024915089
ISBN-13: Paperback: 978-1-64749-999-0
         Epub: 978-1-965293-00-3

All rights reserved. No part of this publication may be reproduced, distributed, or transmitted in any form or by any means, including photocopying, recording, or other electronic or mechanical methods, without the prior written permission of the publisher or author, except in the case of brief quotations embodied in critical reviews and certain other noncommercial uses permitted by copyright law.

Although every precaution has been taken to verify the accuracy of the information contained herein, the author and publisher assume no responsibility for any errors or omissions. No liability is assumed for damages that may result from the use of information contained within.

Printed in the United States of America

GoToPublish LLC
1-888-337-1724
www.gotopublish.com
info@gotopublish.com

Contents

Chapter 1 1
Chapter 2 15
Chapter 3 23
Chapter 4 31
Chapter 5 41
Chapter 6 51
Chapter 7 65
Chapter 8 75
Chapter 9 81
Chapter 10 103
Chapter 11 113
Chapter 12 127
Chapter 13 141
Chapter 14 155
Chapter 15 167
Chapter 16 185
Chapter 17 205
Chapter 18 215
Chapter 19 227
Chapter 20 239
Chapter 21 251
Chapter 22 265
Chapter 23 275
Epilogue 277

To my wonderful and beautiful wife, Marisol, without whom, I could do nothing!

I would like to thank Kristin Reinders for the wonderful book illustration.

Chapter 1

When I joined the military, my parents were surprised. They were not supportive. I guess in their minds, they thought I would just move on into the farming community of our town. In their hearts, they must have known that I needed more. They must have known that I would leave as soon as I could, not out of resentment or defiance or even to prove myself. It was because I felt that there was a greater need, something I needed to do, and I could never achieve it there. Still, they didn't stop me.

When I joined, I came up against opposition. I'm sure the people there thought that the opposition would stop me, destroy me, and prevent me from continuing, causing me to fail and give up. But no. I had grown up an outsider, an outcast. I was allowed to join the Chinese military only because officially I was a Chinese citizen, even though I was never looked at as such. What they did not realize was that I felt this all my life. Joining the military and being ostracized were no real challenge; if anything, it was easier. For once in my life, I had the chance to show others what I could do, not who I was or who they thought I was.

Soon, I was able to prove myself. To my surprise, those in charge, who were not concerned about how I looked but only about what I accomplished, quickly took notice of me. I began moving up, not because of my heritage or who I was or was not, but because of who I saw myself to be. It was a liberating time for me in the military.

For as long as I can remember, I felt the desire to help people, to protect them. Maybe because I knew what it was to be vulnerable. It was, and still is, something organic, something I cannot resist: the need to keep people safe, to save them. I felt the need to protect as many people as I could. The closest I could come to achieving that goal was in the military. So I joined, not for myself but to help others.

Vicky pauses and looks around the cabin. The room is purposely dimly lit to set a mood, supposedly for relaxation. This does not work for Vicky. "Do you ask all your patients so much intimate details about their lives?"

The doctor pauses and then replies, "No, not everyone. I do find sometimes that doing this helps to ease the tension, and sometimes, they are able to open up. The more the mind is relaxed, the more they can remember. And you, Lieutenant Young, are quite the enigma. Sometimes it's necessary, especially when the experience was so dramatic. Can you tell me a little bit about your teenage life?"

Vicky starts, "I don't remember much about my teenage life." She pauses, squishes her lips, and looks straight into the doctor's eyes. "I'm sorry, I do not mean to be rude to you or your occupation, but if you have everything you need, my crew has just come through a horrific experience. I have people in the sick bay—some may not make it. I have questions that I need to answer, and I won't find those answers here."

"Yes, yes. I apologize. Of course, you are free to go. I have everything I need."

Vicky slides her chair back and gently yet firmly stands up. "Doctor," she announces as she exits the room.

Now, with the door closed, quietly in the dark, the doctor meshes his fingers together and, with his two pointer fingers extended, places them on his lips, allowing his mind to sink into deep, dark thought. Outside his cabin, the hustle and bustle of the crew is a quick reminder of the tragedy they have just undertaken and that the insanity of everything is real. It is up to Vicky and the rest of the leaders to logically gain control of the situation and save the lives of the entire crew and, perhaps, much more than that. All of them, especially Vicky, feel this burden; they know they need to find out what is going on.

Vicky's first stop is the makeshift science department, where she sees Private Rikes, who has been in constant communication with both Doctors Shome and Davis. Before she can approach Rikes from his seated position, looking over instruments, Rikes notices her and rushes over to her. "Madam!"

"Report, what did you find?"

"Well, you know I am not a scientist, but talking to both Dr. Shome and Dr. Davis, between taking care of the injured, we think that they were able to piece together." He looks sideways, trying to complete his statement without sounding overconfident. Everyone knows that there is an abundance of information that they may never be able to completely figure out. Confident that Lieutenant Young understands this, he continues, "It would seem that the organisms found on the planet are microorganisms merged with some sort of advanced nanotechnology. They are almost like cybertronic microorganisms, both living and machine. We hypothesize that they were designed so that each one of these organisms could take complete control of a person, and using some sort of hive technology, they herded the people into the spaceships to be experimented on."

Vicky stares deep into him, her voice slow and sad. "Using this technology, they were able to lead all these people to slaughter without any resistance. They never stood a chance."

Vicky breathes in deeply, shaking her head. The more she understands these alien invaders' actions, the more horrifying they become. "You read Wei's report. Have you got a chance to speak with Miller?"

"No, madam. With all that happened, I haven't had the chance. Do you think that's important?"

Vicky looks away, as if she could see Private Miller from there. "I think that I should speak to him. Maybe there was something that he left out."

Vicky turns back toward Private Rikes. "And what about the mice creatures? Any information on them?"

Rikes looks blank-faced. "I think you should talk to Dr. Shome about them. There's something about the mice that she is refusing to tell me. Again, she is the scientist. She has a far greater understanding than I do. I think you should speak to her. Maybe you can get the truth from her."

Vicky charges forth while Rikes jumps back to complete his previous task. Vicky moves aside a plastic curtain. Shome is over a microscope. "Dr. Shome, we need to talk."

Without looking up from her microscope, Dr. Shome replies, "In a minute, Lieutenant Young, I'm busy—"

Vicky cuts her off. "No, we should talk now! Tell me what you have found about the planet. What's not in the report?"

Shome pauses for a second, lifting her head from her microscope, staring forward. She takes a breath then stands up to address Vicky. In that faint second, Vicky is able to read her expressions. It is not one of confidence or arrogance. Instead, she is full of confusion and sincere concern. Vicky tilts her head ever so slightly to focus on what she was about to hear. "It's the mice," Shome states bluntly.

Vicky inquires, "What is it? What is so special about these mice?"

"That's just it!" exclaims Dr. Shome. "They are not special, not special at all! From the few dead mice that we've pulled out from inside some of the broken spacesuits, these mice genetically match almost identically with typical brown Earth mice."

Vicky, who thought that nothing could surprise her, especially at this point, stands surprised. She responds slowly, confused, "But that's impossible."

"Yes," says Shome as she shakes her head frantically. "It is impossible. I went over this one hundred times with Dr. Davis, and it should not be possible, but so far, this is the best that we could deduce as to what happened." Shome pauses. "Have you had a chance to debrief about the microorganisms?"

"I am informed. Basically, nanocybertronic organisms were used to take control over those poor people to be experimented on."

Dr. Shome sadly shakes her head in agreement. "Well said, tragic but true."

Shome points away with her finger. "We wanted to examine some of the floating corpses, but Captain Reynolds thought that it would be disrespectful to disturb the grave site. Rikes, however, had a good idea. We could get close enough to some of them and scan them from the ship. It worked. From our scans, we found in each victim's head the area which the microorganisms infected in their brains, but no signs of the tech. It would seem that after they murdered each victim, they removed the microorganisms and sent them back to the planet to seek out more victims. It would seem that the organisms were more valuable to them than the people's lives. Eventually, there were more organisms than people. And eventually, no people were left at all. With no people left to continue their mission, their default was to survive. They went feral. They ransacked the entire planet, killing every living creature they could devour. Everything, that is, except for the mice."

Scrambling through some files on her computer, Shome clicks on a file titled "Genetic and Chemical Composition." "There is something in the mice's chemistry that does not allow the microorganisms to infect them. To the best of what I can tell, it's similar to the antiviral sheen that we use to cover the space suits, which is most likely why the organisms could not attack our away team right off. They had to wait for a break in the suit in order to infect our people."

Dr. Shome gestures her finger toward the good lieutenant while she continues to explain her report. "With this catastrophic change in the planet's ecosystem, the mice soon adapted into the alpha land predators, evolving to a state of viciousness. And the only thing that the microorganisms feared. Now, as for them matching Earth mice DNA, that—" Shome opens her hand, as if she were preventing Vicky from moving. In fact, Shome is herself trying to make sense of her own findings. "How is it possible? We cannot figure that one out."

Lieutenant Young loses her patience. Respectfully, she states, "Dr. Shome, this is all fascinating, and I am sure when we get back to Earth, we can analyze this data in greater depth. But for now, how does this affect our position?"

Shome sits down to take a breath and, with one finger, taps her chin. "I see what you're saying. It might mean nothing, but it might mean everything. There's one more thing I need to show you, and then you can decide."

With that, Shome stands up and walks over to a tank. She puts on a thick rubber glove. Carefully she places her hand inside the tank and retrieves the snakelike sea creature. Vicky, fascinated, adjusts her position to get a better look. "Is that the creature brought back from Miller's suit?" asks Vicky.

Shome shakes her head. "Yes. Dr. Davis and I put it through a barrage of tests. It would appear that although this is a unique, previously unidentified species, its DNA is very similar to certain species of sea creatures back on Earth. It makes no sense."

Vicky, very matter-of-factly, states, "So whether we want to believe it or not, we have to agree that the data points to the fact that somehow we are connected to this planet. Right? What about the young lady you and Davis found aboard the ship?"

Dr. Shome's mood lightens. "Poison? Now that is an entirely whole new thing."

Vicky interrupts, "I prefer not to call her that."

Just then, Dr. Davis barges in. Noticing Lieutenant Young, she pauses. "Excuse me, madam." She then looks toward her comrade, Dr. Shome. "We have an emergency."

Shome looks over at Lieutenant Young. Vicky nods. "It is okay, there are a few more people I need to talk to anyway."

With that, Shome quickly retrieves some of her equipment before following Dr. Davis. Vicky turns to leave, then suddenly, as if she remembers something, she stops and quickly, without turning her body, turns her head only toward the direction of the exiting doctor. "Dr. Shome, one more thing!"

Shome pauses. "Yes, what is it?" she asks.

"The information you have from the microorganisms, where did you get it from?"

Dr. Shome quickly runs over and taps a thick test tube. "We were able to remove some microorganisms from out of Private Duncan's arm. He was infected, but due to his quick actions, they never got into his bloodstream."

Vicky nods as Shome rushes off. Vicky walks over to take a closer look at the test tube. Vicky then turns. She knows whom she needs to talk to next. Aboard the *Tiqu-Qi*, there are three prisoners. Dr. Long is on house arrest while he's recovering in his bed. In a small examining room, barely big enough for a bed, is the girl they call Poison with a soldier on guard in front of the door. Lastly, the only prisoner actually in the brig is the grey alien they found aboard the alien ship.

Vicky finds herself standing behind the grey cold bars, staring over the alien's shoulder. Sensing her presence, the alien ever so slightly shifts his eyes to the left, waiting for her to address him. She stands silently, pondering her next move. She never gets the opportunity to finish her thought when Moses' voice interrupts over the intercom. "Planning meeting in the main conference room at 0500."

Vicky checks her wrist; she realizes she has under twenty minutes before the meeting. There are still many things she has to check and information she must retrieve before the meeting. The alien creature finally turns his head, but Vicky is gone.

One of Vicky's many tasks was to visit Poison one last time before the meeting. Outside her door, the private on guard acknowledges Vicky. "Madam."

Vicky nods, and the private quickly responds. Taking the key card from his vest pocket, he turns and swipes it to unlock the door. Vicky opens the door to step inside. She directs her attention toward the private. "I'll be fine."

He nods in compliance and gives her enough room to enter. Vicky shuts the door behind her. Poison, like a captured animal, does not move. She timidly looks over at Vicky. Poison is standing as far to the end of the room as possible. The room, however, is so small it would not take much for Vicky to reach out to touch her if she so desired. "How are they treating you?" asks Vicky.

More like a shy child than an adult woman, the girl nods. "Fine," she whispers.

Vicky asks, "Did they feed you?"

The girl picks up a tray with the food still in it. "They gave me some food. Honestly, I'm not even sure if I can eat or not."

The girl holds back tears; still, great anguish lies within her just off the surface. She does not fully understand what she really is, and this is one of the many things that torments her. Vicky understands that her suffering is far greater emotionally than what was done to her physically. Vicky pauses for a second and gathers her courage, which is something she rarely needs to do. "Have you remembered anything from your past?"

The girl shakes her head and answers, "It's in pieces… I remember quick images of my parents and the feeling of sadness… and fear! As they were taken away from me. I remember being grabbed and dragged, but not much more than that."

Vicky shakes her head. "How about your name?" she says. "Do you at least remember your name?"

The girl looks down shamefully. "No, I do not."

Vicky continues, "Well, I would like to stop calling you Poison. I think everyone deserves a name."

The girl does not respond; in fact, her not responding is an even greater response. Vicky clears her throat and continues, "I was thinking of the past mission, where we found you,… I cannot. help but remember an old story from Earth. It is about a lady who found a treasure box, and curiosity got the better of her, and she opened it. When she opened it, all sorts of creatures came out, and the Earth that was in peace at that time became in peril. The name of the lady was Pandora. It was called Pandora's box."

The girl, drowning in a sea of conviction, looks up. "I am the peril."

"No." Vicky chuckled, surprised that Poison would think that of herself. Vicky ever so gently explains, "I don't believe you are the 'peril.' If anything, you might just help us survive. But on this voyage, I can't help but feel that things were released, set into motion. Terrible things were released! I can't stop thinking that we do not yet know the full measure of the consequences coming. But the name Pandora has some merit. Perhaps a shorter version. I wouldn't want to call you Pan, maybe Pam? Would you mind if I called you Pam?"

Again, the girl looks away. "Madam, I don't deserve a name."

Vicky reaches forward to touch her. This action startles her, and she retreats in fear; her back is up against the wall. Vicky notices her reaction and hesitates. The girl glances up at Vicky's face. She feels a release from her fear. Looking into Vicky's eyes, Poison feels comfort. There is a sense of safety rising from the aura that surrounds Vicky. Maybe aura is not the right word; maybe it is Vicky's spirit. Something unexplainable yet powerful, like the wind or the rage of the ocean. At the same time, there is something calming that causes a calming effect over most people when Vicky is in charge. Perhaps it is the perfect combination of power and caring, sincerity mixed with the ability to cause change. In any event, Poison can feel it. Her guard goes down. For the first time in her life, she feels that she may have some value. Vicky, sensing her understanding, continues her motion forward, placing her hand ever so slightly on her shoulder. "They may have tried to make you a weapon, but you. You!" she emphasizes, "are a person. Whether human or not, I do not know, but you are a person! And you were victimized. There's nothing you should be ashamed of, and everyone deserves to be known as a person."

She looks away timidly then looks back up at Vicky. "Pam sounds good. Thank you."

Vicky smiles. "I'll see you around, but I have a meeting in a few minutes. If I find out anything, I'll let you know. And if you remember anything, tell the guard, and he will inform me."

She nods. Vicky leaves, and for the first time, the girl feels good enough to lie down on the bed. Within moments, she is asleep.

There is one last stop that Vicky has to make before she goes to her briefing. There is a fourth prisoner. Although officially he is not declared a prisoner, he is contained in the cargo area of the ship, unable to enter the rest of the ship freely. There is an armed guard posted, watching his every move. For these past few hours since both teams arrived back, Private Diamond has not moved at all. Vicky enters the cargo area, and as earlier, the private on guard acknowledges her and gives her entry. She walks over to Private Diamond. Ever so slightly, she places her open palm on his chest. She looks up at him. "Things have been crazy around here," she states. "Don't worry, we have not forgotten about you. We will find out how we can help you."

The feeling of unaccepted defeat causes Vicky's hand to slip slightly down his hard metal chest. How can she possibly help him? They don't, can't comprehend what has happened to him! How is it even possible? Is Private Diamond really in there? All these questions and more are circling around in her head. Her wrist communicator vibrates. She looks down. In shock, it causes her to blink and look again, not believing what she sees. The message is from the last person she would have expected: it is from Private Diamond. It reads, "Thank you."

She looks up at him. She has trouble forming words. Finally, she manages to form her words. "How, how is this possible?"

Again, her wrist vibrates. The new message reads, "I am not sure. I am learning more and more about the capabilities of this form."

She looks up, her eyes as large as saucers. Vicky bites her lip and shakes her head. There is hope. "Good! Find out everything you can do, and we will find everything we can do."

She smiles and walks out of the cargo bay.

As usual, Vicky is the first to enter the conference room, her reports in hand. The room is dark. As she enters, the automatic lights turn on. For a moment, she does not realize she is not alone; there is someone sitting at the far end of the round table. Startled, Vicky quickly places her reports down on the table. Lieutenant Young does not recognize the person, and instinctively her hand slides over her sidearm. At the end of the table, on the seat to the far right, sits a young lady barely in her midtwenties, mahogany-skinned and pretty. She has bright dark-brown, almost black eyes. Her hair is straight and falls a good measure past her shoulders. She appears to have on some sort of silky black leotard. Covering most of the leotard is what looks like an ancient tunic. The tunic is badly tattered and shredded. If it was white at one time, it no longer is. It does not look dirty, just old, discolored, and worn. Some of the tunic looks burned, as if it were pulled from a fire or if she was in a terrible accident. The girl sits back in her seat, very comfortable, with her feet up on the table. She has long black leather boots, which reach up just below her knees. In sharp contrast to her tattered robe, the boots look new and shiny. Four sets of straps and buckles run down the outer side of each boot. Draped over her shoulder and across her chest is a strap holding an old brown leather satchel. The satchel has one large flap, and it appears to contain something bulky within, perhaps a poorly folded sheet or something like that. Although the satchel is worn and has an ancient design similar to that of the tunic, it is not as ragged as the tunic.

The unidentified lady's eyes follow Vicky's hand as she places it over her sidearm. Her eyes then return to Vicky's face as she casts a plastic smile over at Vicky. Vicky returns the favor and raises her wrist communicator to her lips. She hails Private Rikes, asking him to join them in the conference room. Just then, the other participants start entering the room. Captain Reynolds is first, followed by First Mate Moses Lean and then Lieutenant Minor, Vicky's immediate superior. Next to enter the cabin is the first navigational officer, Wei, and Jacob Miller, the chief engineer. Both medical officers are in constant demand, caring for the injured, so they gave their reports to Vicky. As the crew enters, the door closes behind them. They are all in deep conversation, Moses with Captain Reynolds and Jacob with Wei. So occupied are they that they instinctively move around Vicky as they enter, heading toward their desired seats, not yet noticing the oddly dressed lady sitting at the end of the conference table. Lieutenant Minor is the first to notice the young lady. However, not wanting to admit he does not know who it is, he is afraid to say anything. Captain Reynolds is the first to say something. Catching a glimpse of her from the corner of his careful eye, he does a double take, first glaring at the young lady then glancing back toward Vicky, who he knew was the first one in the conference room. "Hello? Excuse me."

Then he turns toward Vicky, hoping that she has an explanation for this mysterious uninvited girl sitting comfortably in his conference room, and at the head of the table, no less. "Is she with you?"

Vicky puckers her lower lips and very matter-of-factly shakes her head. "No." She glances over at the captain. "She is not. When I came in, she was sitting there. I was about to inquire of her who she is."

With that, all the conversation in the room stops, and the entire company gives their full attention to the young lady. The door opens behind them as Private Rikes enters. "Madam?"

Vicky, with one finger, gestures for him to stay quiet for the moment. He quickly follows her command. Before Vicky speaks, she taps Private Rikes with the same finger and points toward the lady; understanding what she wants, he quickly takes out his handheld scanner and starts to scan her.

"Okay," starts off Vicky. "Would you mind telling us who you are?"

The young lady replies with a giggle, "Sure." (She says it almost as if she were talking to herself, awaiting her chance to shine.) Her natural voice seems soft, yet she has learned to project it, as someone would who felt neglected and trained themselves to be heard. In fact, her voice is projected so loudly that it almost echoes within the chamber. As she continues to speak, her pitch changes dramatically from soft to squeaky, almost childlike and piercing. She removes her feet from off the table and sits up as tall in her chair as possible for her small stature. "Why, hello." Her words are trailing, almost like a song. She stands dramatically.

"How did you get aboard my ship?" demands Captain Reynolds.

The girl pushes the chair back and stands to her feet with a grin and a giggle. With her hand placed dramatically upon her chest, before replying, she looks at her fingernails as if inspecting them. Finally, she replies very matter-of-factly, "I kind of go where and wherever I want."

Simultaneously, Vicky shifts her attention from the dialogue between Captain Reynolds and the mystery girl to Private Rikes. "What's the status?" she asks in a tone just slightly above a whisper.

He shakes his head in confusion. "Madam, it's difficult. Having trouble reading her, it's as if she's there and then … not. She is there, then it just reads energy, an unidentified energy."

Vicky looks down, pondering his findings. "When it scans her, what is she?"

"From what my scan can make out, she appears to be human."

The captain, whose ears are trained to pick up the quietest conversation, catches the conversation between Vicky and Private Rikes. Both Vicky and the captain realize that this form of questioning may not be the best way to interrogate this young lady. With her hand just below her waist, Vicky gestures to the captain for permission to change tactics. Captain Reynolds, without saying a word, allows it, as Vicky takes one step forward. Vicky walks slightly toward her left, bringing her just a step or two closer to the girl. "So tell me," asks Vicky, "who are you?"

The girl smirks a little smirk. Placing two fingers on her collarbone and then waving her hand out, palm up, as if presenting something. "Well,…I am the daughter of the most powerful being in all of the universe."

Vicky's face distorts in confusion. The rest of the room stare at one another, wondering if they understood her. Wei yells out, "Excuse me? The father of who?"

Lieutenant Minor fidgets nervously by himself. The girl curtsies just a bit. She clears her throat. "As I said, I am the daughter of the most powerful being in the universe."

She pauses and looks up from her stance, very satisfied with herself. Vicky regains control of her appearance. "Very well, and what is your mission?"

Throwing her arm dramatically in the air, she walks around to the back of her chair. Pushing the chair forward under the table, she responds, "I was asked to come here,…to help."

Captain Reynolds and Wei almost respond together, "Asked? By who?"

Vicky motions her hand ever so slightly and respectfully toward them, then she also asks the girl the same question, "Who? Who asked you to come here?"

Vicky's voice is calmer and invites a response. Then the girl giggles, her body crunching up, similar to that of a small child finding something very silly. She waves her fingers in a downward motion as if she were pushing something down. The pitch in her voice goes up two or three octaves. She finally replies as she regains control of her giggling. "It's not like my boyfriend or something like that!" She takes a deep breath and then recomposes herself. "He's just a friend who asked me to come to help you good people." She flashes a huge smile.

"And just who is this friend?" demands the captain, exhausted of all his patience.

The girl puts on a grumpy face. "Well, let's just call him,…Doc. Yes, that's it! Doc sent me to help guide you people."

Vicky moves in front of Moses, who has been quietly strategizing. Vicky asks, "And who is this Doc?"

The girl squints her eyes, as if she were trying to find just the right words to say. "Let's just say that he is someone who has an intimate interest in what actions you are about to take."

Vicky looks back at her comrades; they, too, are baffled. Is she truly there to help, or is she a threat? Vicky turns back toward the girl. "So tell me," asks Vicky, "do you have a name?"

The girl laughs. "I go by many names. I always wanted to say that." She starts over. "I go by many names, but you can call me Bridge."

"Bridge?" questions Vicky.

"Bridge!" questions the captain, more in the form of a command or complaint than a question. "Yes!" She puts her grumpy face toward the captain. Vicky continues, "This Doc—"

She is quickly cut off by Private Rikes. Reaching for his sidearm, he yells out, "Madam, she has something in her bag! Some sort of animal!"

Vicky responds in turn with her sidearm in hand. Captain Reynolds unexpectedly pulls out an old-time revolver. Lieutenant Minor, uncertain what to do, follows the crowd and searches for his sidearm as well. Moses, who has no weapon, changes his stance, ready to attack the girl if need be. Bridge looks at them blank-faced then at her bag. She places a hand on the bag and then places her other hand out as if to say "Stop." Again, she bursts out into laughter, tears rolling down her cheeks. She taps her bag. "Don't worry, he can't harm you!" Bridge cries out between her laughing. "This is just my pet."

She waves them down with her hands as she tries to regain her breath from her hysterical laughing. She straightens herself up as best she can. "This is just my pet, Dead Cat."

Rikes looks over at the others. Bridge raises her hand in submission. "May I?"

Captain Reynolds nods. "Go on."

With one hand still up in submission, Bridge places the other hand over the flap of her bag. She opens it and reaches in. She pulls out a black, obviously dead cat. Then with both hands, she holds him under his arms, facing them. With his eyes shut, he hangs there lifeless. She waves him in an attempt to animate him. "This is my pet, Dead Cat! He has been my friend for years. Don't worry, he won't harm you. Oh, and one great thing about him is he is unbreakable! Yes, yes, his bones cannot break. Look."

With that, she grabs hold of the cat with one hand around his leg and mercilessly slams his head hard against the table, sending shockwaves through the room. The crew jolts back in shock and dismay. Bridge proudly holds his head up. "See?" Then she continues to whack his head three more times against the hard table. The sound echoes through the room until Vicky can take it no more. Now it is she who puts her hand up to stop Bridge as she reluctantly looks away. "Can you please just stop beating the cat?" requests Vicky.

Bridge giggles. "Don't worry, he can't feel a thing."

Noticing the awkwardness in the room, Bridge smiles and gently places the cat back in her bag and closes the flap. A nauseous feeling overtakes everyone in the room, except for Bridge, of course.

Vicky, remembering the urgency and why they are there, resumes the questioning. "So tell us, Ms. Bridge—"

"Just Bridge," corrects Bridge.

Vicky acknowledges the correction and continues, "Bridge, what do you want from us, and what can you do for us?"

Bridge stands tall in an attempt to be serious. "Before I help you, I need something from you."

The crew look at one another, confused. Captain Reynolds blurts out, "What do you 'need' from us?"

Controlling her emotion against the good captain, Bridge replies, "Am I to understand that you have three prisoners aboard this ship?"

"Yes," replies Moses. "That is correct."

"Go on," commands the captain.

Holding her head up, Bridge continues, "Before I help you, I need to see all three of the prisoners."

Chapter 2

The verbal commotion in the corridor is almost violent as the crew argue about what they should do with their "guest." They leave Bridge guarded by Rikes in the conference room.

"By no means possible," yells Captain Reynolds in loud, frustrated whispers, trying to control his volume so as not to concern the rest of the crew, "should we allow this stowaway to roam freely around our ship! She could be any sort of threat, let alone should we allow her to visit the three people who present the most immediate danger to us! She herself should be thrown into the brig."

Lieutenant Minor, who finally got up enough courage or perhaps was just responding to something that aligned with his fear, chimes in, "I agree with the captain, you should lock her up!"

Vicky, Wei, and Moses are not certain; there is something odd, something that they cannot figure out. They need answers that throwing Bridge into prison will not give them. Vicky interjects, "Sir, if I may? I know that this is your ship. However, she appeared here as if out of nowhere. I think it is safe to say that she did not come aboard on Earth. On Rikes's scans, she doesn't appear human. I think that if she wanted to go see the prisoners, she probably would have gone there first. She's asking for our permission."

The captain shakes his head. "I don't know, that seems awfully risky, and we don't give in to terrorists or their demands."

Moses humbly interjects, not wanting to go against his captain, "Sir, she's not demanding, she did ask."

Wei, now on the fence, asks, "Did she?"

Vicky nods, her eyes shifting to Wei. "I think she did. At least, in her perspective, she did. We can all accompany her, and Rikes will continue to monitor her. Maybe there is a strategic reason, as well."

Catching the captain's attention, he says, "Go on."

Vicky continues, "We know that the prisoners are holding back. Maybe there is information that they forgot, or maybe they are purposely holding back. For whatever reason, there are things we still need to know."

Captain Reynolds steps away from them with his finger to his chin, pondering what Lieutenant Young had just said. He comes back, pointing his finger at Vicky and nodding for a moment before talking. "Yes, there's a lot more to those three than what we know! Especially the girl and that alien. We just may have a chance to uncover something. Very well."

Vicky looks at the others. "So are we in agreement?"

Wei answers for them. "Yes, we are."

Lieutenant Minor shouts out, "What?"

The crew all look toward him, waiting for him to complete his comment. When he doesn't, they turn away to enter back into the conference room. Lieutenant Minor gathers his courage and interjects again, "But we don't know who she is. Why should we allow her to walk around? We should just lock her up and proceed to go home!"

Captain Reynolds knows that he is on a very precarious line; here on one side, Lieutenant Minor is the military commander on this voyage. However, Captain Reynolds is in command of the entire ship and, therefore, everyone aboard the ship, a fact that he was sure to inform Lieutenant Minor of before they left port. The captain decides to respond carefully, "With all due respect, Lieutenant Minor, I think that we can properly keep an eye on her and perhaps find out a bit more of this puzzle than what we know."

"Not to mention," adds Vicky, "Bridge has promised to tell us something. I believe that it is something important."

Lieutenant Minor scoffs. "She is insane! She is clearly insane, have you seen her?"

Moses jumps in. "I agree, I believe that your assessment of her is correct. However, that does not mean that she will not provide what she says she will."

Again, Wei asks, "So are we in agreement?"

Moments later, the conference room door slides open as the crew walks in. Vicky takes the lead, walking toward the visitor, who had regained her seat at the far end of the table.

"So," chimes Bridge in a musical, almost-teasing tone, as if she already knows what they have decided, "what did you decide?"

Vicky nods. "We will allow you to see the three prisoners. You will be escorted and under guard the entire time. As soon as we're done, it's right back here, and you will tell us what you promised. At that point, we will then decide what to do with you. Agree?"

The entire room stares, waiting for her reply. Happily, almost giddy, she stands to her feet. "Great."

Bridge moves from her chair and starts to walk around the table toward the door. Private Rikes adjusts his sidearm as he tracks her movement.

"Not so fast," cautions Vicky. "There are some things that we must go over first. One, you will always stay between Private Rikes and myself…"

As Vicky is talking, Bridge comes around the table, bringing her a couple of meters from her. Suddenly the atmosphere in the room grows cold as a chill runs down Bridge's spine. She is overtaken by fear! Like a small creature startled by a hungry predator, Bridge jumps back, sliding on her backside, backward across the table to the other side, panting in what can only be described as a panic attack. Bridge scans her eyes around the room and then stares at Vicky as if Vicky has physically hurt her. Unsure what to do, Lieutenant Minor grabs for his sidearm. Also not knowing what else to do, the rest uneasily reposition themselves, preparing for whatever may happen next. Even Vicky is bewildered. "What, what's wrong?"

Bridge, her eyes as wide as saucers, transfixed by Vicky, her voice trembling, asks, "What are you?"

Vicky, still baffled by her reaction, asks, "Pardon?"

Bridge shakes her head nervously then slowly scoots her body back until she's able to swing her legs over the side of the table, as far away from Vicky as possible. She tries to regain her composure, still nervous yet noticeably more in control. Bridge places her hands flat on the table; now it is her face that seems baffled, as if she were trying to figure out some terrible mystery. Bridge shakes a tense finger at Vicky then back at herself, in what seems to be an attempt to explain her actions. "I'm a singular," she says, looking at the rest. "Singulars are very rare. But you!" She points her condemning finger back toward Vicky. "You, you're an Omni!"

Captain Reynolds, as impatient as usual, says, "What! What is the meaning of all this? We're about to allow you permission to see the prisoners, but if you continue this babble!"

Wei tries to regain control of the situation before anyone makes any rash decisions. "Mrs. Bridge, excuse me." He corrects himself. "Bridge, what are you trying to say? We would like to try and understand."

Again, Bridge attempts to regain her composure. Straightening herself up, she starts walking back around the table toward Vicky, her eyes meeting each participant in the room. Like a bitter old woman harshly correcting a small child, she waves her finger at each of them. "You don't get it. All of you were carefully chosen."

Captain Reynolds blurts out, "Chosen by whom?"

Bridge pays no attention to the captain's question. She continues. "Yes, all of you, except for you!" Her finger points directly at Vicky. "Everyone was chosen for a reason."

She waves her finger wildly around, indicating that she is referring to everyone in the room, perhaps even to everyone aboard the ship. In a condemning tone, her finger shakes at Vicky. "You! You were chosen just because you were good at your job! Good at … your … job. But you, you're an Omni."

Bridge continues her walk around the table. Moses very compassionately asks, "Tell us, Bridge, what is an Omni?"

Bridge glances at him and giggles nervous giggle. "I only know three Omnis: my father, the most powerful being in the universe, and two others."

An awkward silence fills the room; still tense, the crew glance back and forth at one another, hoping that one of them can make some sense of what Bridge is saying. The silence is finally broken when the grip of fear loosens from off Bridge's body, and she lets out a high-pitched giggle. Suddenly her demeanor transforms, and her appearance becomes carefree and light once again. Her expression toward Vicky also changes to one of amusement. "But you didn't even know that! Did you? You're not dangerous, are you?"

Vicky, very serious, says, "I can be."

Moses tries to regain order and to make sense of everything. He responds to Bridge, "I am sure no one understands what you're talking about. Perhaps you can explain it to us."

At this point, Bridge checks herself and reverts to her original script. "Oh, I have said waaay too much."

Now giddy and light on her feet, Bridge skips toward Vicky. "Let's go see those prisoners. I have a lot on my plate to do."

Vicky, with her hand up, stops Bridge in her tracks. Bridge, startled, jerks back. Sternly, Vicky finishes the instructions she had started earlier. "Before we go, I'm just to remind you, you are to remain at all times between myself and Private Rikes. You will be escorted everywhere, and you cannot divert or go anywhere unescorted. Is this understood?"

Bridge nods. "Sure, of course."

The door slides open as they start to walk out. Rikes, Bridge, and Vicky are the last three to exit. As Bridge passes Vicky, she pauses and looks up at Vicky. "You and I are gonna be good friends, I can tell."

The captain ponders what the crew will think when they see this person walking around under armed guard. Still, they have made their commitment; now they have to see it through. Lieutenant Minor nervously follows off to the side as if he were not with the rest of them. Vicky pauses. "Hold on one second."

Vicky motions with her hand for Wei to come close. He does. Rikes positions himself within earshot of Lieutenant Young but out in front just enough to keep his sidearm pointed directly at Bridge. Captain Reynolds and Moses stay patiently in front, one on either side. Vicky whispers, "According to Rikes's scans, this person, wherever she is, is not human. She seems to be almost pure energy."

Wei nods. Vicky continues, "Perhaps you can do some cognizance and see what you can find out about this energy signature. The more information we have, the better for us." Wei glances over at Bridge and nods. "I'll get right on it."

He hastens off past the group and grabs Captain Reynolds by his shoulder. He quickly whispers to the captain. The captain nods, and Wei rushes off.

Moses instinctively takes the lead, making sure that their passage is safe and goes as seamlessly as possible. Their first stop is the sick bay. Dr. Shome is tending to Dr. Long. Dr. Long is still unconscious; he is bandaged and badly bruised. His cuts, of which he had many, were carefully mended by the skillful hands of Dr. Shome. He is connected to monitors. As Moses enters, Shome looks up and acknowledges him. She quickly taps her wrist communicator and calls for Dr. Davis. "They're here."

Rikes had forwarded their findings to both Dr. Shome and Dr. Davis. Dr. Shome then glances over toward Bridge, who is just a few steps behind. Dr. Shome moves aside; hiding her curiosity about Bridge, she realizes this is not the time and remains quiet. Bridge walks along the opposite side of the bed and quietly considers the doctor. Dr. Davis peers in; she stands next to Lieutenant Young and scans Bridge from her vantage point. Bridge hesitates for a moment and then looks up and flashes a large smile. "Okay, I'm done! Let's go."

Confused and speechless, the crew look at one another, then they move out. Captain Reynolds turns to address Dr. Shome before they leave. "Thank you."

"No problem."

The next stop is to see Poison. The room is too small to allow Bridge in. There would be no way to keep Bridge under guard in such tight quarters. They do not trust Bridge, and they have no idea what her connections to the prisoners are. They do not want to get her too close to Poison. Nor, for that matter, can they predict what Poison's reactions would be. Vicky takes the initiative and goes in first. The soldier on guard again moves aside. "Madam!"

Vicky enters. Poison, who is now Pam, smiles when she sees Vicky. Vicky addresses her. "Pam, there is someone here who wants to see you."

Pam humbly says, "Alright."

Vicky reaches her hand out, and Pam takes it. Vicky guides her out of the room. There she sees Bridge in front of her. Bridge looks her up and down. Confused, Pam asks, "Do I know you?" Bridge crunches up her lips. "No," she states plainly.

With that, Bridge abruptly turns around. "Okay," she says, "next."

Still confused, Pam looks to Vicky for consolation. Vicky smiles as best she can. "I'm sorry, I'll explain to you later."

Pam trusts Vicky; she smiles and nods. Vicky gently guides her back by her shoulder. As soon as the soldier closes the door, Vicky walks off.

The last stop is to the brig. Hearing the commotion approaching, the gray alien walks toward the bars. As they enter, there is enough room for them to spread out. Bridge takes center stage; the gray alien creature seems unappreciative of her peering eyes. He looks first over at Captain Reynolds and then to Vicky. "Who is this, and why is she staring at me?"

Then he addresses her directly. "Whoever you are, keep doing whatever you were doing, and leave me alone!"

Bridge crumples her face in disapproval. "How rude!" She then turns around. "Okay, we're done." Bridge heads for the exit. Vicky looks over at Rikes and then at Captain Reynolds. They all exit.

Back in the control room, Bridge enters first, very satisfied with herself. This time, instead of sitting in her usual seat, she heads toward the opposite end of the table and sits at the very head of the table. The rest file in against the wall, waiting for Bridge to complete her part. The door closes behind them. Impatiently, Captain Reynolds starts. "Okay, young lady, you've seen the prisoners. Now it's time for you to hold up your end of the bargain."

She smiles. "You are so very impatient—and after I gave you such a great gift."

She points her finger toward the far corner of the room. The crew instinctively look toward the corner, but there is nothing there but the wall. Captain Reynolds turns back. "What are you talking about, young lady? Enough of the—"

Before he can complete his sentence, they realize that the chair is empty.

Chapter 3

Captain Reynolds is fuming as he paces back and forth, occasionally slamming his fist into the table. Lieutenant Minor is paralyzed with fear. Vicky, however, sits quietly, trying to replay the events in her head. Captain Reynolds yells out to Rikes, "Check all the security cameras, see if you can find her anywhere aboard this ship!"

Rikes nods. "Already on it, sir. Look at this. I've tapped into the security cameras from this room. It recorded her the entire time she was here."

The wall turns into a screen. Rikes maneuvers his wrist communicator, and the image comes up, starting from when Vicky entered the conference room. The lights go on, Vicky is startled and starts talking, but there is no one in Bridge's seat, and no reply is heard. They stare, astonished, for a moment. Captain Reynolds slams the back of his open hand against the image. "How is this possible?"

Before they can say another word, they are interrupted by Wei's voice over the intercom. "Captain Reynolds, sir! You all must come to the bridge right now!"

There is something different in Wei's voice, a certain tension. Captain Reynolds notices the urgency and replies, "Grant, what is it?"

The communication goes off. They look nervously at each other, then they hasten out. In seconds, they are on the bridge. Captain Reynolds rushes to the front, to his old friend. "Wei, what could it possibly be now?"

Wei glances up and fixes his eyes on the captain. "Sir, we have a distress call."

The captain stammers, "Wh-what?"

Wei places his finger on the switch and instructs the bridge, "Listen."

The cabin fills with a haunting voice. "Mayday, mayday, mayday. This is the warship *Liberty Crane*, *Liberty Crane*. Repeat, mayday, mayday,

mayday. This is the warship *Liberty Crane*, *Liberty Crane*. We have a crew of almost six thousand. We are stranded. Repeat, we are stranded. The ship lost all flight capabilities. Please respond! Mayday, mayday, mayday."

Wei switches it off. "It's on a loop, Captain."

"Warship?" asks Captain Reynolds in a whisper, almost as if he were asking himself.

Captain Reynolds looks up, confused and concerned. He looks toward Lieutenant Minor, who hasn't moved from his spot. He then looks toward Vicky. "Warship *Liberty Crane*, have you ever heard of any such thing?"

Vicky shakes her head. The captain turns again to Lieutenant Minor, who looks toward the captain but does not reply. The captain turns to Wei, placing his hand on his shoulder. "Where is it coming from?" he asks.

"The instruments show it is approximately 151 degrees from our current position, ascension zero."

"Ascension zero?" questions Captain Reynolds, his voice drifting off.

Captain Reynolds turns again toward Wei. "How far?"

Wei replies, "About 250 kilometers from our current position."

The captain straightens up. His eyes gaze off into the distance for a moment then back toward Wei. "How long would it take us to get there?"

Wei looks up and, in a very matter-of-fact tone, replies, "Just under three days, sir."

Self-preservation kicks in disguised as leadership. Lieutenant Minor steps forward and, in a rough tone, especially for addressing the captain, argues, "You are not seriously considering replying to that mayday, are you?"

Captain Reynolds turns to defend himself, but Moses, who is always ready to protect his captain, replies instead, "It is our duty to offer help to any vessel in need!"

Minor, frustrated by his response, counters, "We are barely able to move ourselves. Our first priority should be to get home. We can send someone to respond to them after we are safe!"

The captain's face hardens. He does not mind constructive arguments from time to time, but what is coming out of Lieutenant Minor's mouth is nonsense. The captain rebuts, "Sir, let me remind you that this is my ship. If we are or are not going to come to the aid of this *Liberty Crane*, it will be my decision, not yours! And as Moses stated, it is our duty to aid any ship in distress!"

Captain Reynolds turns toward Wei. "Wei, your assessment?"

Wei turns his chair to address both Captain Reynolds and Lieutenant Minor. "We're heading towards the sun right now. Our repairs are almost complete. We should be able to start our course back to Earth in about a day, two days, to be safe. We can easily change our trajectory and still gather all the solar energy we need if we respond to the distress signal. I don't think an extra day out would matter one way or the other. I believe we can sacrifice one day to save six thousand lives. At least that's my say, sir."

Captain Reynolds nods. Lieutenant Minor simmers. Captain Reynolds turns toward Lieutenant Young. "Lieutenant Young, your assessment?"

Lieutenant Young has been uncharacteristically quiet as she is in a precarious situation. She cannot overstep her commanding officer, yet her passion to save lives burns deeply within her. There was no way she will allow Minor to make a decision that will cost the lives of six thousand people. She hesitates for just a second before replying, "Sir, I'm sure that you are aware of the long-standing tradition for the military to help those in need. I doubt that you would want to do something unbecoming of our great heritage. Surely, if you reconsider, you will see that we are not only compelled, but we have an obligation to save them. Am I correct in thinking so, sir?"

Vicky realizes that the one thing greater than his fear is his pride; he would never want to admit that Lieutenant Young knows more about military procedures than he does. Minor has been feeling the heat of envy against Vicky from the moment they met Captain Reynolds. Reluctantly, Lieutenant Minor sucks in hard and replies, "Captain Reynolds, it is your ship, your call. The Chinese Military Alliance will back up your decision."

Respectfully Captain Reynolds nods. "Very well. Wei, set a course."

The rest of the conversation becomes babbled whispers in Lieutenant Minor's head. *He has to exit!* Just then, he notices Private Rikes hastening off, probably to check on some coordinates or to run an errand for Lieutenant Young. This is his chance to leave. Before the door can slide shut, he exits. Rikes is a few meters ahead. He calls out to him, "Just a minute, Private!"

Rikes stops and turns to him. "Sir, yes, sir!"

"Wei mentioned something on the bridge about zero ascent. Is that important? The captain seemed to think so."

Rikes replies, "Sir, yes, sir. Ascension zero is how we navigate up or down in space. There is no north or south. Ascension zero means basically that, when we turn towards the lateral angle of the distressed ship, it is lined up almost exactly with us."

Minor stares blankly. Rikes takes the initiative to continue. "It is a very odd coincidence, sir. It is a one-in-a-million chance that a ship would line up so directly. In space, it could have been anywhere, sir."

Lieutenant Minor nods. "Very well, Private. Dismissed."

Minor walks off toward his quarters, Rikes toward the conference room. Minutes later, Private Rikes rushes back onto the bridge. Vicky, Captain Reynolds, Moses, and Wei have been planning out their strategies. Rikes interrupts, "Lieutenant Young, Madam, Captain Reynolds, there's something I have to show you."

"Come forward," calls Captain Reynolds. His voice is comforting, like a father calling a small child to him. Vicky encourages him. "Speak up, tell us what you found."

With a clenched fist, Rikes takes a breath. "I had a hunch. I went back to the conference room and the best I could coordinate from when Bridge said she's giving us a 'gift,' then she pointed, and … well, look."

Rikes manipulates his wrist communicator, and an image of the conference room appears. A line shoots from where Bridge had sat to the spot where she had pointed. Then the line exits the ship. The ship shrinks as the line stretches across space to a bright spot in the hologram. Rikes continues, "It would seem that the spot that Bridge pointed to directly lines up to the distress signal!"

Captain Reynolds examines Rikes then turns to his old friend Wei. "Are you trying to say that she pointed us to that ship?"

"It's more than that," Rikes continues. "I looked at the time stamp from when she pointed and the signal first came in. The exact moment she pointed, the signal started to loop on our monitors."

Vicky, now with mouth half-open, her brain in pain, asks, "Are you saying that she somehow is leading us to this distress signal?"

Captain Reynolds straightens up and places his large hand on his temple, rubbing it. Wei speaks out. "It sounds impossible, yet with all the things that we've been through—"

Vicky interjects, "What's her game plan? What is she leading us to?"

Vicky turns to the captain. "Captain, we are not sure if it's safe."

Captain Reynolds nods. "I'm not sure I want to be manipulated by this Bridge person either! Could it be coincidence?"

He looks toward Vicky. In her heart, Vicky knows it is not a coincidence, and she knows that they also know it. Captain Reynolds takes a deep sigh. "Still, if there are lives at stake—"

Vicky finishes the statement. "We have to take the chance!"

Now Moses jumps in. "Sir, there are also the lives of every man and woman aboard the *Tiqu-Qi* that we are responsible for."

Captain Reynolds agrees. "We just have to be very cautious."

Lieutenant Young straightens up. "Now that we know what we're getting into, we can prepare at least as much as we can. We will not bring our ship directly to whatever's out there. If we find anything, we will go by shuttles, keeping our ship safe. That way, if anything happens, we'll have a minimum number of people on the shuttles, and the ship would be spared."

There is an air of somber consensus. The captain reads the room. He lets them know his heart. "We will not go through with this if it's not unanimous among those in the room here. Private Rikes, you get a vote also."

A silent nod from the four of them confirms what the captain already knows. Captain Reynolds nods. "Then it's settled. Wei, run the diagnostics, work with Private Rikes, try to find anything that will help in our advantage. We will not run from a fight, but we are no fools either!"

The next three days are quite uneventful in comparison to the ordeal that they have already been through. The crew nervously goes about its business, unsure of what it will find when it reaches the coordinates set by Wei. Overall, there is a quiet hope as the crew looks forward to returning home. Vicky spends much of her time in the makeshift sick bay, checking on her recovering comrades.

Lieutenant Minor spends most of the days either on the bridge or in his quarters, sulking. Although he spends a good portion of time on the bridge, he speaks fewer than ten words to Lieutenant Young, Captain Reynolds, and Wei. On the eve of the second day, the door buzzer rings, alerting Lieutenant Minor that someone is at his door, requesting an audience with him. Minor walks toward the door and presses the release; the door slides open. Expecting to see anyone but the one who is now standing in the door, the ship's social worker. More curious than annoyed, Minor queries, "You are the social worker, aren't you?"

Lieutenant Minor walks away before allowing him the chance to reply; he replies anyway, "Yes."

Lieutenant Minor mumbles, "Making house calls now?"

"Well, only to the patients who don't come to me."

Still facing away from him, Lieutenant Minor smirks, then he turns to him. "I did not go on either of the field missions, so therefore, I do not need a counselor. But thank you for your concern."

Now is the social worker's chance to smile. "With everything that happened, Lieutenant Minor, you are still the commanding officer here, aren't you? You share the responsibility of what happens to the crew. Your crew. You too need to feel a part of this. Maybe you feel disconnected. How did your interviews with the prisoners go so far?"

Lieutenant Minor frowns like that of a child caught in a lie. "You know, Doctor, it's getting kind of late; I have many things to attend to. If you don't mind?"

"Oh yes," states the doctor very apologetically, "I'm so sorry. I'll let you return to your work."

He exits, and the door slides closed. Lieutenant Minor's frown turns into contempt. Moments later, Lieutenant Minor is making his rounds in the sick bay. After about twenty minutes of bored observation, he finds himself walking into the brig. Minor walks over to the cell containing the gray alien, who has not slept or even sat down since his imprisonment aboard the *Tiqu-Qi*. The creature takes notice of him much the same as a cat notices a leaf blowing in the wind. He walks toward the bars to inspect him. Lieutenant Minor keeps a safe distance of about a meter from the bars. Minor initiates the conversation. "You are the unnamed alien, the slave of some great and powerful conqueror of galaxies."

The alien squints his eyes for a moment. "And who are you?"

Minor straightens up, chin up, and replies, "I am Lieutenant Minor, the military commander aboard this ship."

The gray alien cocks his head ever so slightly, as if questioning his authority. He asks, "You are the military leader?"

Angered by his questioning, Minor says, "Yes, I am the military commander of this ship, of this voyage! Is there a problem? Something you do not understand?"

With this, the gray alien creature walks off and drifts away, back into the depth of his cell. "I just assumed that the leader would have been on one of the missions with the crew. My mistake. I'll be sure not to do it in the future."

The creature turns and faces Lieutenant Minor, almost shaming him. "Did you have a question for me … Commander?"

Lieutenant Minor has not thought this far ahead. He has no questions. Now his frustration is fueled, his burning jealousy against Lieutenant Young grows out of control. He exits as fast as his feet can carry him. The gray alien creature quietly watches his departure.

Lieutenant Young spends much of her time in the sick bay, monitoring her crew and visiting the prisoners, especially Pam, with whom she has made a strong connection. Although Pam is hundreds of years old, she looks toward Vicky as a mother figure, and this gives Pam great comfort. Vicky is especially concerned with the progress of one of the patients in particular, Private Duncan. She goes to his bed, Private Brown at his side. As she enters their space, Brown quickly stands to his feet. "Ma'am, yes, ma'am!"

She waves her hand downward. "At ease, Brown. You may sit."

"Thank you, ma'am." He sits back down. "Don't worry, ma'am." He stands back up. "Don't worry, ma'am. I've completed all my duties. This is my break time."

Vicky smiles a small yet sincere smile. "He's your friend?"

Private Brown nods. "He's one of ours, ma'am."

"It's quite alright, you could spend your time by his side. I've read all you've been through. Without you, I doubt that he would have made it."

Brown looks down, shaking his head. "Ma'am, we all did what we could."

Dr. Shome walks in. "Lieutenant Young, good to see you again."

"So how's our patient?"

Dr. Shome gently grabs hold of Vicky's arm, leading her out toward her lab. "It seems that, other than the bite, he was not infected with the microorganisms. His quick action seems to have saved his life. Due to our low blood supply, we were not able to give him a transfusion, but Davis and I were able to siphon his blood from his arm and circulate it back into his arm. Keeping his arm alive yet its blood separate from the rest of his body. We strained and scanned his blood hundreds of times, with no signs of the microorganisms. It appears that we have removed all of them. However, we're keeping him sedated due to the vigorous treatments that we're giving him. Soon, we'll be able to allow the blood to flow back into his main bloodstream. Then we will continue to monitor him for a few more days."

Vicky is cautious. "Are you certain that you were able to remove all of the microorganisms?"

Dr. Shome looks Lieutenant Young in the eyes. "Yes, we are positive. Although the microorganisms are small to our eyes, they are not small to our scans. At this point, I can state with 100 percent certainty that he is free from all parasites. His friend spends all his free time by his side, and Private Jones and Wei have visited him quite often also. Even though we keep him sedated for his treatments, between treatments he is conscious and enjoys the company of his comrades. I think that encourages him, and that might be the best medicine for right now."

Again, Lieutenant Young smiles, and with a gentle nod, she walks off back to her duties.

While Lieutenant Young is walking down the corridor, her wrist communicator buzzes. It is Captain Reynolds. She looks at him on the monitor. "We are near."

Vicky places a hand back on her side and rushes to the bridge.

Chapter 4

Wei is at Private Craig's bedside. Wei states, "So I spoke to Dr. Davis. It seems like soon you'll be back on your feet."

Although even the slightest movement gives him pain, Craig manages to find a legitimate smile. His voice is gravelly and low, yet his spirit is strong. "All thanks to you, you and the crew."

Wei nods a gesture of thanks, when his wrist communicator buzzes. He answers the call. Captain Reynolds states, "Wei, it's time."

Wei looks back at Private Craig. "Excuse me, duty calls. I'll see you up and about soon."

Again, Craig smiles as Wei rushes off. Moments earlier, at a nearby guarded cot, Dr. Long is lying down next to his visitor, Lieutenant Minor. Long opens tired eyes on Lieutenant Minor. His voice is forced. "Lieutenant Minor, what brings you here?"

Lieutenant Minor scoffs. "So you're conscious?"

Long painfully waves his head back and forth. "I've been conscious on and off for a couple of hours. I see I'm in prison."

He lifts his cuffed hand to its limit; it clanks as it hits the bedpost it is attached to. Minor condescendingly and condemningly states, "Yes, for the crimes you committed on the planet, abandoning your post and costing the lives of your crew! You deserve to be in the brig if it was not for your injuries."

Long nods in condescending agreement. He turns to focus his eyes as best he can into Minor's eyes. He queries, "I hear of a distress signal. We're approaching another ship?"

Minor responds, cold and short, "We are."

Long coughs and continues, his voice concerned and anxious. "If there are any forms of life, I need samples."

Minor smirks. "I'll be sure to tell Davis and Shome your … request."

"No!" Dr. Long shakes his head. "They have to stay here. They'll probably send that hack Chang. And Young, she won't do it!" He coughs again. "No, not Young. I need a higher authority."

He quickly reaches out with his chained hand and grabs hold of Lieutenant Minor's wrist as hard as he can. Minor jerks away, but Long holds tight. He looks into Minor. "You are the higher authority! I need you. You would do it! You see the potential, don't you? You are over her, aren't you?"

Lieutenant Minor pulls away and straightens up, fixing his attire. "I am."

Long lets out a long, painful cough. "I know you are. Any life-form, bring me a sample. We need to analyze it."

He coughs and rolls his head back to the center of his pillow. Just then, Lieutenant Minor's wrist communicator buzzes. Minor looks at it. Captain Reynolds states, "Lieutenant Minor, we are soon approaching the vessel."

Minor nods. "Yes, sir, I'll be right over."

He attempts to leave but pauses to look back at Dr. Long. Long looks up toward him and nods. Minor unwittingly nods back, takes a deep breath, and then rushes to the bridge.

As Wei enters, Vicky, Moses, and the captain are discussing their findings. When Wei approaches the captain, Captain Reynolds takes notice of him. He rises from the seat, allowing Wei to move in. Captain Reynolds returns to the captain's chair. The door opens, and Lieutenant Minor enters. Wei instantly looks over the controls. Minor walks up to the front and gazes out the main viewing window. In the distance is a small yellow planet. Minor looks toward Captain Reynolds. "Is the signal coming from that planet?"

Wei shakes his head. "No, it's much closer. We're under four hundred thousand kilometers from the signal. We have slowed the engines. We should have visual in about two minutes."

The group fixes their eyes on the open space before them. Vicky points. "What's that? Is that it?"

They all focus their eyes to see what Vicky is seeing. Wei states, "I don't see anything yet. Screen magnification!"

The viewing windows digitalize and magnify; about 150,000 kilometers out is a rectangular gray object. Wei first squints to see it, then he looks toward Vicky. "Great eyes, Lieutenant Young! That's it!"

He points out ominously toward the object. With the screen digitized, Wei is able to control the screen from his seat by just pointing. Even though the large oblong viewing window is about five meters in front of them, it follows the motions of Wei's finger as if he were touching the screen. Wei points, highlighting the rectangular object; jerking his finger forward magnifies the image. It is a large rectangular metal ship. Captain Reynolds looks over at Wei. "How big is that thing?"

Wei's eyes widen as he tries to quickly absorb the data before him as best he can. He replies to Captain Reynolds. "It is huge. From our initial scans, it is at least twice the size of our ship and more than four times the mass."

Concerned, Captain Reynolds narrows his eyes. Glancing over at Wei yet never totally losing his focus on the image, he commands, "Let's take a closer look."

"Aye, aye, Captain!" Wei commands. "Magnify."

After two magnifications, the ship fills the entire viewing window. Details of the ship are pretty clear. Vicky points out, "There is the name of the ship."

Liberty Crane is clearly etched on the side of the ship. Directly underneath the words appear to be two flags, one red and yellow and another red, white, and blue. The captain stammers, "En-enlarge that image."

Wei replies, "Aye, aye, Captain."

The mood on the bridge changes from caution to concern and bewilderment; they hesitate. Wei points and magnifies the image. It is as they expected; now there is no question as to the identity of the two flags. Lieutenant Minor speaks out through the confusion. "That is the Chinese flag … Is that an American flag next to it?"

Wei shakes his head then looks up at the confused party before him. Lieutenant Minor steps back and stares directly out at the image. "Exactly how old is this ship?"

This is a question all of them are wondering, being that America has not been in existence for over two hundred years. Captain Reynolds fires back, "Wei, stop all engines!"

Wei replies firmly, "Aye, aye, Captain."

Wei hails the engineer room. "Full stop, all engines."

Miller responds, "Aye, aye!"

The ship's engines cut off, and the reverse rockets fire. The ship vibrates slightly as it comes to a jerking stop. Captain Reynolds cautions, "Let's discuss our options before we get any closer."

Wei commands, "Magnification off!"

The main viewing port returns to normal; they are much closer now, and although it is a little more than a rectangular speck in the distance, the ship can be seen with their naked eye. Captain Reynolds stands in front of them. "What are we going to do now? We are about one hundred thousand kilometers out from a ship that's not supposed to exist, sending out a distress signal, donning a flag of our country and a country which no longer exists. Suggestions? Are we still sticking to our plan? I want our decision to be unanimous."

Now it is Lieutenant Minor's turn for his eyes to widen. He stares deeply at the image before them. Greed takes its place in the line of his emotions, pushing fear behind, making way for a new concept: enterprise. Actually, this is an old friend of his. He was raised on enterprise; his family is renowned for it. They have a long history of high-ranking officials and politicians; he is an offspring of old money and influence.

He cannot, he will not, let his family down. None of them have great expectations of him, but all of them demand them of him. This is his chance to prove himself, not only to them but also to the world. Perhaps, after this, he won't need their approval anymore; he would be his own man, and that he can put in their faces. This ship is a possible endless resource; no one else knows of its existence. He would be the first one to plunder it, to strip it of all information and goods. Yes, it is not adventure or the desire to save the lives of those on board—he couldn't care less. It is his desire for profit that builds a perverted confidence within him. Lieutenant Minor is the first one to speak up, confidently saying, "Yes, we should proceed as planned."

The rest of the crew are hesitantly taken aback by his sudden display of courage.

They all nod. Vicky turns to look at Moses then Wei, Rikes, and finally, Captain Reynolds. "I agree," she confirms. "This changes nothing. If there are people who need help, we need to see if we can help them."

Just then, the doors to the bridge slide open. Dr. Shome and Dr. Davis ask permission to enter the bridge. "Captain, permission to board the bridge."

Captain Reynolds nods to Moses, and Moses waves the doctors in. "Come in, doctors."

Captain Reynolds and the crew turn to give the doctors their attention. The captain asks, "What can we do for you?"

Dr. Shome looks at Davis, and Davis speaks up. "Captain Reynolds, we were thinking that one of us should go along on the mission. Although we still have many injured here, most of them are on the mend. One of us should stay here, but if there are sick people aboard that ship, you need a doctor, and with Dr. Long incapacitated, you are shorthanded."

Captain Reynolds nods and looks over at Vicky and Moses. "I was thinking the same thing. What say you, Lieutenant Young?"

Again, Lieutenant Minor sneers in contempt and jealousy, hiding his emotions, which are boiling over, on the verge of contempt. How can he shine as a leader when he is constantly in Lieutenant Young's shadow? He asks himself, *Aren't I the commanding officer aboard this ship?*

Somehow, he has to show them, show her, who is in charge!

Vicky nods. "It is a good idea."

Captain Reynolds looks at the rest. "Gentlemen, are we in agreement?"

Everyone nods. "Yes, sir."

Wei adds, "Yes, I agree. We know what we have here; we have no idea what to expect aboard that ship."

Captain Reynolds addresses the two doctors. "Very well, which one wants to go?"

Shome smiles. "I think I'll stay here. Dr. Davis is the more adventurous one."

Captain Reynolds accepts their proposal. "Very well, prep yourself. Make sure that you take any supplies that we can spare."

They smile. "Yes, sir."

Together they turn to walk off. Dr. Shome pauses and turns her face toward Captain Reynolds. "And thank you."

Lieutenant Young looks over at Moses and Captain Reynolds. "Sir."

Captain Reynolds replies, "Yes, Lieutenant?"

Vicky's eyes scan the room. "I think that we should have as small a crew as possible, just in case we have to make a hasty retreat … sir. I would take along myself, Sergeant Yang to pilot, Private Rikes, and now Dr. Davis. Perhaps maybe one more soldier, sir."

Wei places one finger along his cheek, considering Lieutenant Young's request. "You don't think you would be extremely shorthanded. That ship is huge!"

Vicky nods. "That's why I am asking. I am not requesting. Lieutenant Minor, your analysis? What do you think?"

Lieutenant Minor adjusts his stance. "I have decided I am going on the mission with you, Lieutenant Young."

Vicky is taken aback. "Sir?"

Lieutenant Minor confirms his statement. "Yes, I'm going on the mission with you. I will go along on my own shuttle, and Dr. Davis can come along with me. I think it would be beneficial. As the military authority aboard this ship, I think that I should be present when we board this alien ship."

An awkward silence falls over the rest of the team. Trying not to make it obvious, they stare at each other. Wei, an ex–military man, understands that Lieutenant Young does not wish to challenge her superior officer. He speaks up. "Excuse me, Lieutenant Minor, I see why you would want to go on this mission, but using two shuttlecrafts is risky. In addition, who would pilot Lieutenant Young's shuttlecraft?"

Lieutenant Minor shifts his head slightly toward Wei's direction and very matter-of-factly replies, "Why, you could."

Captain Reynolds immediately interjects, "There's no way! That is impossible. Wei's presence aboard this ship at this point in time is paramount! There's no way I could allow him to go on another mission."

Moses, feeling the strife in the room and realizing that Vicky is paralyzed in conflict, steps up. "I'll go," he says.

Captain Reynolds begins to rebut, but Moses turns toward him. "I'll go, sir. If it's okay with you. I can pilot the ship. I'm sure Lieutenant Young could use a hand. You need Wei here … I can go," he emphasizes.

Captain Reynolds's eyes narrow as he considers the proposal. He looks toward Wei and Vicky and nods. "Very well." He turns toward Lieutenant Minor. "Is this acceptable for you?"

Lieutenant Minor also concedes. "Yes, quite acceptable."

Captain Reynolds turns toward Wei. "Wei, make ready the preparations."

"Sir." Vicky humbly interrupts. Vicky is a true leader; her voice is usually pronounced and strong, but for this occasion, a sincere humbleness is evident in her voice. For she knows what she is about to request is a stretch, at best. Although in her heart she believes that what she is asking is for the greater good of everyone, she still respects protocol. Lieutenant Young realizes the weight of what she is about to ask from both Captain Reynolds and her superior officer, Lieutenant Minor. Captain Reynolds pauses and addresses Vicky. "Yes, Lieutenant Young?"

Wei and Minor also give her their full attention, as well. Vicky continues. "Sir, I know this may seem unconventional, but I think I should bring Pam along with us on this mission."

Wei, surprised by her request, jerks back, not offended, more curious than anything. Captain Reynolds, always the captain of the ship, stares at her unmoving, pondering what is best for the ship. Lieutenant Minor discreetly turns toward Wei. "Pam?"

Wei looks up in a very matter-of-fact manner and replies, "The girl we found aboard the ship."

The pupils in Lieutenant Minor's eyes shrivel. He reacts as he usually does, straight from his emotions. "Poison? Are you talking about Poison? Are you mad, Lieutenant? She is a prisoner! Why would we take her off this ship? The only reason she is not in the brig is because the other prisoner is terrified to death of her, and you want to take her on the mission? Explain yourself, Lieutenant!"

Captain Reynolds cringes at both Lieutenant Minor's behavior and the fact that he agrees. He agrees that he, too, needs an explanation. Captain Reynolds, with the tone of a father more than that of a captain, questions Vicky. "Lieutenant, please explain, why would you consider taking her along with you on a mission? I know that you are seeing something that I don't. Please elaborate and enlighten us."

Vicky quickly absorbs the positivity generated from the trust emanating from Captain Reynolds. She responds, "Sir, it would seem that this ship, this *Liberty Crane*, is out of our wheelhouse. It is something we do not know anything about. I feel that, for some reason … Pam knows more about this than anyone. Perhaps her coming along might ignite a memory in her."

Lieutenant Minor jumps at the chance to exploit her words. "Ignite? What if she was to ignite aboard our ship? Her acid could blow a hole in our ship!"

Unexpectedly, Wei sides with Lieutenant Minor. "I agree, Lieutenant Young, it is risky. If an incident happened aboard our ship, we most likely could fix it without any loss of life. But on the shuttle, one small hole would put all of you in danger—you, Moses, Private Rikes, and Pam, as well."

Lieutenant Minor's eyes shrink back into his head; he steps out of the room and into his own mind. "This is the chance I've been waiting for. If she removes Poison onto the shuttle with her and an incident happens, it's her fault! Her reputation with Captain Reynolds shrinks to nothing. And if perchance they all die, all the better still! Yes, this is the opportunity I've been waiting for!"

Captain Reynolds defends Vicky. "Lieutenant, you have proven yourself many times over. I respect your decision. However, Pam is officially a military prisoner, and as such, the decision would be up to Lieutenant Minor."

All eyes turn toward Minor. Again, Lieutenant Minor surprises everyone. He first glances over at Captain Reynolds and then focuses his attention on Vicky. "Lieutenant, I will allow this. The prisoner P-Pam, is under your command. Do with her as you see fit."

Surprised, Captain Reynolds replies, "Very well then. Wei … make the preparations."

The entire crew remains baffled as to why Lieutenant Minor decided to go on the mission, let alone take one of the valuable shuttlecrafts. However, the work to make ready continues unhindered. In the meantime, Wei and Private Rikes have tried to hail the stranded ship to no avail, only to receive the same haunting message: "Mayday, mayday, mayday—this is the warship *Liberty Crane, Liberty Crane.*"

Lieutenant Minor insists on departing first. Sergeant Yang looks up at Lieutenant Minor for direction. Unemotionally, he commands, "Proceed."

Yang easily maneuvers the ship out of the docking bay, followed closely behind by Moses, Lieutenant Young, Rikes, and Pam. (With Moses along on the mission, Vicky felt confident that she did not need any more crew members, with the exception of Private Rikes. Also, in the event of trouble, she did not want to place any more of her people in danger—they had already gone through enough.) Soon they are engulfed by the dark void of space, heading boldly forward to a new, uncertain venture.

Although only seven are going, the fate of the entire ship may lie upon them, and the weight of it creates an emotional thickness in the air throughout the entire ship.

As soon as the hatch closes, the crew go back to their assignments, and Dr. Shome hastens to her lab. She casually walks by her experiments when suddenly the icy grip of fear grabs hold of her spine. She looks toward the jar of the microorganisms that they have collected from Private Duncan. She runs to the vial to examine it. She lifts her hand, grabs the handle of the image enhancer, and guides it down. She desperately views the jar through the lens. She commands the computer, her voice panicked and shaky. "Computer, scan for organisms!"

The computer takes over the image enhancer's functions and quickly runs scans up and down the vial. A moment later, the computer calmly responds, "No organisms found."

Dr. Shome's face changes colors. She mumbles to herself, "That's impossible."

She raises her wrist communicator. Although bold, her humility usually would not allow her to directly address the captain, but in this moment, she knows no one else that could help. Lieutenant Young is on the mission, so is Dr. Davis—she has no alternative. She adjusts the communicator for a direct line to Captain Reynolds. "Captain Reynolds."

The captain views his communicator and pauses. Instinctively, he knows that Dr. Shome realizes the importance of the mission before them and that she would not reach out to him if it were not of the utmost importance. His stomach knots in anticipation; he takes a moment to breathe before responding. "Yes, doctor?"

With urgency in her voice, she replies, "Can you come to my lab? I'm not sure ... It seems that there is a problem."

Captain Reynolds frowns, concerned. "I'll be there momentarily."

He clicks off and looks at Wei. Wei knows his old friend, and he can read the concern on his face. He asks, "Sir?"

Captain Reynolds shakes his head in frustration. "Dr. Shome says there's a problem."

Wei queries, "Should I be concerned?"

The captain grinds his teeth. "I'll let you know as soon as I find out."

Captain Reynolds takes one last glance at the screen. Both Lieutenant Young and Lieutenant Minor's shuttle's images are now displayed on their main port window. Before he exits the bridge, Captain Reynolds calls out to Wei. "Keep me posted."

"Aye, aye, Captain," responds Wei.

Chapter 5

In space, Lieutenant Minor suddenly realizes the immense vastness of the vessel before him. A chill freezes the blood in his veins, hardening his arteries and muscles, making it difficult to breathe or move. He now doubts whether he should have gone on this mission. Still maintaining his facade of bravery, he commands, "Sergeant Yang, proceed. Look for an opening."

Vicky's voice comes over the open channel of Minor's shuttle, echoing throughout the almost-empty chamber. "Sergeant Yang, look down to the right. There seems to be some sort of port." Yang responds, "I see it, ma'am."

Moses maintains a safe distance behind as Yang dips downward. Sure enough, on the lower side of the ship, there appears to be a landing bay. Yang looks at Lieutenant Minor for direction. Minor commands, "Sergeant, proceed."

Yang pushes forward. Vicky raises her eyebrows and looks toward Moses. "Proceed," she says, mimicking Lieutenant Minor.

They move in slowly, both cautiously and curiously. As they enter the docking bay, they have a closer visual of the design of the *Liberty Crane*. It appears to be a very old design, pre-twenty-second century, with steel beams and metal plating. This ship was not concerned with weight distribution but more with stability and strength. Either way, the ship seems solid. They hover over two open spaces. Yang and Moses maneuver back-to-back. They turn on their high beams and slowly rotate, searching the landing bay. As the light peers deep into the crevices of the landing bay, both Moses and Sergeant Yang pause, unable to move, amazed at what they see. Vicky and Private Rikes move in for a closer look. Even Dr. Davis unconsciously hangs uncomfortably over Lieutenant Minor's shoulder, staring out in awe. Anchored in place are vessels, flying vessels, the construction of which none of them have ever seen before. They are most similar to a twenty-first-century jet, although thicker, with large tubular engines on either side where the wings come out. Moses looks toward Vicky. "They seem like an early version of the original hybrid spacecraft developed in the Solar Wars."

Vicky nods. "They seem very similar, but perhaps a bit more … clumsy."

Sergeant Yang, in a whisper just loud enough to be heard, asks, "Sir, what are they?"

Lieutenant Minor, not wanting to look foolish, has to admit, "I do not know."

Aboard the *Tiqu-Qi*, Captain Reynolds enters Dr. Shome's lab. She addresses him anxiously, "Captain."

Bracing himself for the worst, he inquires, "Okay, Doctor, what is it?"

Dr. Shome pauses. "I don't know how to say this, but it appears that the microorganisms have disappeared."

This is not what Captain Reynolds expected. Sure, he did not know what Dr. Shome was going to tell him. He was preparing for some medical problem in one or more of the patients; that would be bad enough! This, however, is totally unexpected. Lost for words, Captain Reynolds asks, "What exactly do you mean? How are they gone?"

Dr. Shome shakes her head. "I'm not sure if they disintegrated, but they're no longer in this jar. I have just run a series of scans. If they did disintegrate, there should be trace elements left."

No sooner does Dr. Shome finish her sentence than the computer announces, "Scan complete."

Taking a deep breath, sure that this must be the explanation and the need to worry has passed, Captain Reynolds turns to Dr. Shome. "Continue, Doctor."

Dr. Shome commands the computer, "Computer, what did you find?"

The computer calmly explains, "The microorganisms are still alive and active in their container." Both Dr. Shome and Captain Reynolds's faces distort in confusion. The computer continues, "It would seem, Dr. Shome, that the microorganisms have shrunk to less than a tenth of their original size, thereby making them undetectable to our original scans."

Dr. Shome's jaw drops nervously. She looks toward the sick bay. Captain Reynolds shakes his head. "Dr. Shome, I don't understand. If they're still there, is that a bad thing?"

Dr. Shome, unable to speak, shakes her head almost hysterically. Finally, the words pour out. "If they were able to shrink in the jar, they would be able to shrink in their victims, as well, allowing them to pass undetected into—"

Captain Reynolds completes her sentence. "Into their bloodstreams."

They look at each other, and then the two of them quickly sprint into the sick bay.

As Captain Reynolds and Dr. Shome enter the sick bay, at first glance it is unusually calm, nothing out of the ordinary. Private Brown is standing over Private Duncan's bed, a usual place for him to be. However, as Captain Reynolds and Dr. Shome approach Private Brown, they notice that Private Duncan's bed is empty. Private Brown quickly notices the two and turns toward them. Concerned for his friend, he asks, "Doctor, where is Private Duncan? Did you move him?"

Dr. Shome anxiously responds in a hoarse whisper, "No, I definitely did not."

Shome looks up toward the captain with fear in her eyes. The captain looks down toward her, and the three of them scan the room. In addition to the missing Private Duncan, there are still three patients who are not well enough to be released to their quarters. At the far end is the guard, guarding Dr. Long. Captain Reynolds leads the charge as the three walk toward the guard. Captain Reynolds initiates, "Private, do you know the whereabouts of Private Duncan?"

The private responds, "No, sir … not really. As soon as the area cleared, when everyone went to see the shuttles depart, he just sat up and pulled out his wires. Then he left … He must have gone to his locker, because a few minutes later, I saw him passing by fully dressed."

Private Brown, irritated, says, "Li, you didn't think that was odd? Why didn't you report it?"

Private Li says defensively, "What was I supposed to report, that one of the sick people felt better and got up and left?"

Brown, still annoyed, responds, "Yes!"

Captain Reynolds defends Brown. "Yes! As guard on duty, you are to report anything unusual."

Private Li, the youngest soldier on this mission, is barely eighteen, straight out of boot camp. This is his first mission. Li, who hails from a long line of military men and women, was chosen for this mission mostly because his father is one of the few independent shippers in the solar system. In his civilian life, Li had his pilot license by the age of sixteen. Not wanting to seem inexperienced, he nervously stammers, trying to explain his actions or lack thereof. "I figured when … that the doctors must have known about it."

Dr. Shome speaks up. "I definitely did not know about it, nor did I authorize it! And I would never ask a patient to remove their own intravenous, especially Private Duncan, who's under monitoring and whose blood was recently just siphoned back into his"—she pauses and looks at Captain Reynolds before completing her sentence—"system."

Captain Reynolds cuts to the chase. "Private, which way did Duncan go?"

Private Li glances in the direction. "He went towards the elevator, sir."

Captain Reynolds breathes in deep, like a person would just before lifting a heavy package; the three of them rush toward the elevator. Private Li looks down in thought, realizing he had forgotten to mention something. Unsure what to do, yet not wanting to leave out anything, especially after his poor performance a moment ago, he cries out, "Wait. I do remember one more thing."

Quickly, the three stop in their tracks and proceed back to Private Li. The captain encourages him, "Speak up, son."

Private Li nods. "Hmph, sir. Before he left to get his clothes, he went to each of the other patients and whispered something to them, close. I found it odd, but I didn't say anything. Then he looked up at me, and that's when he left, sir."

Captain Reynolds considers the situation. He looks toward Dr. Shome. "Shome, Brown and I will search for Duncan. You remain here and check on these patients."

She nods and, without a word, proceeds to the first patient.

As soon as Captain Reynolds and Private Brown reach the elevator, the elevator door opens. Private Jones runs out, almost colliding with them. Brown is taken aback. He asks, "Jones, what are you doing here?"

Confused, she looks at Private Brown. "I was told to come here."

Captain Reynolds quickly asks, "Told? By whom?"

Private Jones looks at the two. "By Private Duncan. I just visited him earlier. When was he discharged from the sick bay?"

Private Brown responds, "He wasn't."

Captain Reynolds and Private Brown stare at each other. Before they can say another word, they are engulfed by red emergency lights and a piercing siren. A voice from over the intercom announces, "All military personnel, this is a code red, code red! All military personnel report to the hangar immediately! Repeat, this is not a drill. All military personnel report to the hangar—this is a code red!"

Captain Reynolds opens his mouth in disbelief. Private Brown turns toward Private Jones. "What? Wasn't that—"

Private Jones finishes his statement. "Private Duncan? Yeah!"

The captain cries out in frustration, "What in the world is going on?"

They proceed to enter the elevator, when Wei hails Captain Reynolds. Reynolds responds, "Wei, what in the world—"

Before Captain Reynolds can complete his question, Wei unknowingly cuts him off, "Captain, sir! What's going on? We lost all communication capabilities with the shuttlecrafts! It's as if someone has cut the link!"

Captain Reynolds commands, "Wei, lock down the bridge! Do not let anyone in!"

Wei responds, "Aye, aye, Captain!"

Anxiously, the captain asks, "Wei, do you have access to the ship's intercom?"

Wei responds, "Negative. I have been cut off!"

Captain Reynolds nods. "I figured as much."

He turns to Brown and Jones. "I have to get to engineering, now! Brown, you come with me. Jones, intercept the rest of your people, and keep them from that hangar!"

Brown and Jones answer in unison, "Sir, yes, sir!"

Jones rushes off to the hangar, while Captain Reynolds and Brown enter the elevator. The elevator door opens in engineering. There is an eerie, unnatural calmness. Only the quiet hum of the engines vibrates throughout. The normal hustle of the crew is mysteriously missing from the scene. Jones has his sidearm in hand. Captain Reynolds notices someone lying on the floor ahead of him. He rushes to his side; it is his old friend, the chief engineer Jacob Miller. Reynolds touches his two fingers to Jacob's neck, checking for a pulse. Miller mumbles. Captain Reynolds calls out to him, "Jacob, Jacob!"

He opens his eyes. As he turns his head, Captain Reynolds notices blood on the side of his scalp. Captain Reynolds exclaims, "Jacob, my god, are you alright?"

Bracing himself with his elbow, Miller props himself up. With his other hand, he waves to Captain Reynolds, indicating that he is okay. Jacob forces the words out. "I'm okay, Ed."

Captain Reynolds queries, "Jacob, what happened?"

Noticing the bitter pain in his head that runs down to his dislocated shoulder, Miller grunts before responding, "Aggh! That soldier, the one that was injured ... I think his name was Duncan, came off the elevator and threw me aside like a rag doll! Before I blacked out, I heard him take three of my men into the main control room. I heard the door clank shut."

Captain Reynolds tells his friend, "Stay here."

He pulls out his revolver as he rises from Jacob's side.

Miller reaches out toward Captain Reynolds, trying as best he can to grab him. "No, help me up. I'm okay. I can help you."

Reluctantly, Captain Reynolds and Brown help Miller to his feet. One of Miller's arms is hanging limp. With his good arm, he braces himself against the wall as best he can. Walking forward, soon they are at the steel door that separates them from the main controls. Captain Reynolds looks at Miller. "Can you open it from out here?"

"No." He shakes his head. "All controls are inside."

Carefully holding his pistol, the captain slams the grip of the gun against the door. He calls out, "Duncan, Private Duncan, are you in there? Open up and release those men."

Miller groans in pain once more. "Arrr, Ed." He calls out to Captain Reynolds, "Joe is in there!"

The emotional pain deepens, knowing that his friend is being held hostage or worse. Captain Reynolds grinds his teeth together, slamming the door even harder. He cries out, "Duncan, this is Captain Reynolds. Open up now!"

Captain Reynolds hails Wei on his communicator. He sums up the situation thus far. "It seems that Duncan has captured three of our engineers and trapped them inside this room. From there, he shut off communications to the shuttle and has called all of our men to the hangar."

Brown shakes his head in disbelief. "Why?"

Captain Reynolds turns toward him and honestly answers, "I have no idea. Dr. Shome and I fear that Duncan might have been infected, but even so, what would his agenda be? Why these men, and why stop communication with the shuttles? Wei, your situation?"

Wei responds, "Same, Captain."

Miller again groans in agony. Brown reaches and pulls him back up. "What's wrong, Mr. Miller, sir?" Brown asks.

Miller painfully turns toward him. "My arm … I think my shoulder's dislocated."

Brown looks at the limp arm. Suddenly, without warning, Brown braces Jacob with one arm, and with his other hand, he uses his massive strength to pull down on Miller's arm. The shoulder snaps into place. Miller's screams echo throughout the entire lower chamber. Captain Reynolds stares in disbelief at Brown. Brown apologetically shrugs his shoulders. Miller, recovering, defends Brown's actions. "It's okay, Ed. I actually think it's back in place."

Miller moves his arm painfully, slowly up and down, then straightening it out. Captain Reynolds raises his pistol once more in an attempt to bang on the control-room door. Private Brown humbly raises his hand, stopping the captain. Brown nods. "Let me try."

With his large fist, he hammers the door and calls out, "Duncan—"

But before he can call Duncan's name once more, the door slides open. Not knowing what to expect, Captain Reynolds rears his weapon, and the three of them take a step back in preparation. Duncan calmly steps out, followed by the three engineers. Their eyes are fixed on the floor; their motions are mechanical, almost as if they have to think about how to move each muscle. Surprised that his approach worked, Brown tries to reason with Duncan. "Duncan, what's going on?"

Duncan looks up at Brown with a vacant stare. "Where is Private Jones?"

Meanwhile, by the hangar entrance, Jones has convinced her fellow military brothers and sisters to leave the hangar. As best she can, she displaces them throughout the ship. Some she places on guard outside the hangar and some on guard outside the bridge, with instructions not to let anyone in or out. She sends some to search the ship from top to bottom and to report to her anything suspicious. The rest she sends to engineering to assist the captain. She herself goes to check on Dr. Shome. As Jones enters the sick bay, she spies Dr. Shome quietly tinkering over an instrument on a small metal table next to one of the patients. Jones calls out to her, "Dr. Shome."

So intense is her focus that she is startled but relieved when she sees Private Jones. Jones asks, "Have you found anything?"

Somberly she shakes her head. "Not quite. They seem fine." She points to the three soldiers lying on the gurneys; however, her expression indicates that she is not convinced of that assessment. Dr. Shome's face confirms a concern in Private Jones that Jones had hoped wasn't true.

Shome raises her finger. Her words are hopeful. "However, I'm in the process of adjusting this cancer scanner to isolate the microorganisms' unique cellular signature." She taps the device on the table. The device is flashing a pulsating small red light. Shome continues, "Also, studying the mice"—Shome points toward her lab—"I am developing a type of antimicroorganism injection."

Jones tilts her face and squints, trying to understand. "Do you mean like a vaccine?"

Shome nervously shakes her hand. "No, not quite. It doesn't prevent infection. It actually should kill the microorganisms directly. The mice have a very low pH balance in their blood, probably due to their lung functions as a result of the thin toxic air on their planet. I'm not sure of the exact principle of it, but they are immune to the microorganisms. In fact, I believe that they can absorb nutrients and energies by consuming them, making them addictive to the microorganisms much like a drug."

Jones, confused, asks, "You figured all this out in the past five minutes?"

Dr. Shome, embarrassed, grinds her teeth together. "Well, not exactly. The injection we've been working on since we found the anomalies in the mice's blood. The scanner I have just finished—" (The scanner beeps; the red light turns to a solid blue.) "Now!" She holds it up. "This should do it."

Suddenly one of the patients opens his eyes and grabs hold of Shome's arm. Rising, he pulls her back and throws her to the floor. Her head slams hard into the floor, rendering her momentarily unconscious. The other two patients jump up, and the three of them surround Private Jones. Jones moves into a defensive position. She cries out to Dr. Shome, "Dr. Shome, are you okay?"

Shome regains her consciousness, although extremely groggy. She shakes her head in an attempt to revive herself and rises to her knees. Placing one hand on her forehead, she feels blood. Realizing the desperateness of the situation, she ignores the pain, and as quickly as she can, Shome jumps to her feet. She looks toward Private Jones. Jones motions to her with her hand. "Run, get out!"

Running between the gurneys, Shome clumsily runs out of the room. The patients take a quick glance as she exits, but their interest is set on Private Jones. Jones looks at her comrades. "Guys, what's wrong? What do you want?"

Not wanting to hurt her fellow soldiers, she does not draw her sidearm. Jones attempts to raise her wrist communicator to request assistance. One of the patients seizes the opportunity to grasp her sidearm and pull it free from her belt. She quickly snatches it back from his hand. Using it as a blade, Jones slices him along his forehead. Blood gushes everywhere as he stumbles. He balances himself on one of the gurneys; however, it slips away, causing him to fall. The other two attempt to grab Jones. She responds, "I don't want to hurt you guys!"

As the second one grabs hold of her, she flips him over her shoulder onto the gurney. The impact causes him to bounce off the gurney and fall onto his comrade who was already on the floor. He was in the process of getting back up, when his partner landed on him, causing them to collapse to the floor. The third one puts his hand out as if he were trying to catch a small animal. Still not wanting to hurt her comrades, she knows nothing else to do but run. The third one pursues her. The two fallen patients get back on their feet. The soldier with the lacerated forehead wipes the blood away, looks at his comrade, and smiles. Then they also join in the pursuit.

Jones pivots to the left in an attempt to escape them, but one of the patients jumps in her way, blocking her. She quickly recalculates her momentum and moves to the right. Directly in front of her is the cargo bay; she makes a dash for it. She can't help but feel as if she were being corralled, as if they purposely were chasing her toward the cargo bay! But why? For what purpose? For the moment, she has no time to figure out their motives. Fleeing is her only option. The guard on duty by the cargo bay sees Private Jones racing toward him. Instinctively he moves into action, releasing his sidearm from his belt. Sweat rolls down his face as he nervously asks, "Jones, what's going on?"

Jones almost slams into the door. She stops long enough to take a breath. The guard crouches down next to her, with his sidearm pointing straight at her pursuers. The three patients slow their pace and cautiously walk toward them. Jones shakes her head. "That's our people, don't shoot!"

"What?" stammers the guard, not knowing what to do. "What do they want?"

Jones fearfully stares back at them. "Me," she responds. The guard studies the three then recognizes that one of them is his friend, Private Lin. Lin and he grew up in nearby towns and found that they had much in common. He cries out to him, "Hey, you, Lin, *ni zai zuo shenme? Zenme liao?*"

Not answering, they edge closer menacingly. Suddenly the middle one wipes the blood from his eyes and jumps forward, grasping the guard's arm. He slams the guard's arm into the wall. In the same motion, he disarms him and slaps him in the face with his own sidearm, a lesson he had learned well moments ago from Private Jones. Jones quickly pushes the button for the cargo door; it slides open. She kicks her booted foot into the face of the guard's attacker, throwing him back into the arms of his comrades. Jones grabs hold of the guard and pulls him in. She quickly pushes the button, causing the door to slam shut just as the three attackers slam into the door.

Chapter 6

Lieutenant Vicky Young walks through the metal doorway, followed by Moses, Private Rikes, Sergeant Yang, Lieutenant Minor, and finally, Dr. Davis. Vicky is surprised by how easily they are able to get in. The ship still seems to have enough power for the doors. What is even more surprising is that there are no alarms, and the doors are not locked. Vicky has decided that although she wants Pam to come along on the trip, she does not want to lead her into danger; there is no telling how she will react if her life is threatened. She asks Pam to wait in the shuttle until they know it is safe; afterward, Vicky will come back for her. For the time being, keeping Pam away from Lieutenant Minor is a bonus. However, Vicky's hope remains that something aboard the ship will look familiar and jolt Pam's memory back to her.

As they enter the interior of the ship, there is an eerie silence. Thick white gas rises to their knees; even with their space suits, they can feel the cold chill. Dim lights cast long dark shadows in the ship. The space is open and wide although the ceilings are low, low enough that the average person can reach up and touch them. Moses uncomfortably ducks his head to be sure not to scrape it on any of the protruding pipes lining the ceilings. In front of them and to their right are wide-open doorways, which appear to open into other wide rooms, similar to the one they are entering now. Vicky tries to remain optimistic but can't help the feeling that this place feels like a morgue. She looks toward her crew. "Lieutenant Minor, with your permission, I suggest that we split up. I'll go with Rikes and head forward. You go with Sergeant Yang, Dr. Davis, and Moses. Take the door to the right. We stay in constant radio contact."

Minor straightens up. "Yes, I agree. Let's move out."

Although Vicky would have preferred to have Moses along with her, she thinks that Sergeant Yang will need him more than she will. Vicky turns toward Rikes. "Still no communication with the *Tiqu-Qi*?"

He shakes his head. "No."

Vicky pouts and looks down. "I didn't think so, and now, inside the ship, it is less likely for us to have any reception at all. Let's go."

They march forward toward the open doorway. The entire ship seems to be covered with this white gas that hovers about half a meter from the floor. The ship seems like a maze, but they are not concerned; their communicators track them and monitor their movements, mapping out where they have been. Again, Vicky turns to Rikes. "Anything?"

Rikes searches his equipment. At first, he finds nothing, then a glimpse of hope shines in his eyes. "I seem to be getting some sort of power source up ahead. Maybe it is a control room."

Vicky nods. "Lead the way."

Rikes hastens forward. Vicky follows then pauses. Through her helmet, something catches her eye. Down the side corridor, it seems like the smoke is rising, almost completely to the ceiling. The lights down the corridor start to spark, then they pulsate from dim to bright. Vicky edges toward the corridor, her eyes wide with curiosity. Suddenly the lights stop pulsing, and although the white fog at the end of the corridor is still to the ceiling, everything else seems normal. Vicky doubts her instincts; she looks down. She looks forward to find Private Rikes. He is a good distance ahead. She starts to move forward to catch up with him, when she takes one last look down the corridor. Startling her, there is an image standing at the end of the corridor. Almost ghostlike, she seems as if she were being formed by the smoke itself. Vicky is certain: it is Bridge! Vicky whispers to herself, "Bridge?"

Surprisingly Bridge responds. Her voice echoes down the corridor like a whisper in the wind. Somehow, Vicky is able to hear her voice inside her helmet. "Lieutenant Young, do not take anything from here back to your ship!"

It is a warning. There was something in it that Vicky knows; she knows that is true! She cannot explain it, but she knows that nothing can be taken from this ship and brought back to the *Tiqu-Qi*. She cannot explain how she knows that this is true or why it is true at all. All she knows is that she must heed this warning; there is a dire mischief forming, something brewing that not only threatens her crew but much, much more! Even more than what Vicky can ever imagine. "What?" stammers Vicky.

She calls to Rikes, "Rikes."

Vicky does not lose eye contact with the image. Although the figure begins to deteriorate back into the smoke, like watching a cloud form an image in the sky, and as the wind blows, the image distorts and breaks apart. Although distorted, it is still clear to see that it is Bridge. Vicky calls again for Rikes. "Rikes!"

"Yes, ma'am—"

Rikes is standing right in front of her. Startled, Vicky jerks back. Rikes continues, "I didn't see you behind me. I came back to check." He looks down the corridor, as does Vicky. "Are you alright? Did you see something?" he questions.

Vicky stares long down the corridor; it is empty. Even the gas is back at the normal level as Vicky knows it will be, much like a person knows what is about to happen in a dream the moment before it happens. She looks again toward Rikes, her eyes shaking. "Yes, I saw something."

Moses taps his wrist communicator and then the side of his helmet. "Lieutenant Young? Lieutenant Young?"

Only static comes back. He looks toward Lieutenant Minor and shakes his head. "Still nothing." Minor nods. Sergeant Yang's instruments are not as sophisticated as Rikes's, nor is she able to read the findings as intuitively as Private Rikes does. However, she is still able to pinpoint energy readings and guide them successively through the ship. Finally, the three come to a sealed door. The door is narrower with a wheel handle in the center; the top of the door is rounded, resembling the door on a submarine or an old-time battleship. Yang tries to open it, but it seems to be locked. Both Sergeant Yang and Lieutenant Minor look back toward Moses. Moses moves forward and grabs the wheel in his large hands, proceeding to try to unlock the door.

For a moment, there is silence; the only movement is the slight shake in Moses's arms. Then slowly the wheel gives, moaning like a forgotten large animal echoing to its death. The wheel turns. A clank is heard followed by the popping sound as the chamber is opened. Feeling that the wheel has moved its full course, Moses places his palm on the door and pushes. The hinges squeak; the door opens. The room inside is dark; they turn on the wrist lights. The gas is slightly higher here than the rest of the ship and flows out against them.

They look toward Minor in respect. He takes a deep breath and walks through the open door. As best they can tell, the room is even larger than the others. At the far end is another door. A light shines from around it, indicating that the room is lit inside. They are drawn toward it like the proverbial moth to the light.

Unable to see far ahead of them, they proceed cautiously. Minor is followed by Yang, then Davis, and finally by Moses. Minor takes a few more steps when he trips; a muffled thud is heard as his foot collides against something on the floor. A moment later, Moses also trips. Minor turns his light toward the floor. In front of Minor on the floor is a man, a soldier, lying in a fetal position. Minor jumps back, his breath leaving him. The others also turn their lights to the floor. In front of Moses is another soldier. As the lights pierce through the fog, it appears that the entire floor is covered with bodies in different positions, some looking as if they were busy working, not knowing what happened to them.

Dr. Davis is the first to recover. As if waking from a dream, she shakes it off and rushes to the closest soldier lying on the floor. Davis runs her gloved hand over his body. She finds on his chest a black electronic device. The device seems to cover most of his chest; in fact, it wraps around to his back, and tubes extend from the main chest plate and travel his entire body, connecting to similar devices around his wrists, ankles, and feet. She continues to examine him with her gloved hands as best she can. Finally, she removes her equipment from her bag and begins to scan him. While Davis is examining the soldier on the ground, Yang and Moses reposition themselves; Yang tries her best to map out a course through the room.

Moses, however, is the first one to speak. Almost in a whisper of disbelief, he asks, "What is this?"

Then both Moses and Sergeant Yang notice Lieutenant Minor. He has moved himself back against a wall and is panting hard. Yang does not want to overstep her authority and steps up to a senior officer to ask him if he was having a panic attack. Moses realizes her predicament and takes the initiative; he walks up to Minor. Just as Minor's knees buckle and he starts descending, Moses grabs hold of his arm. Moses calls to him in an attempt to revive him, "Sir …Lieutenant Minor, are you alright?"

Minor turns to him; his body is shaking so much that it is visible through his spacesuit.

He stammers, "What … what, what could this be?"

Moses nods, accepting his condition. "Yes, sir, I understand." Again, he reconfirms. Moses strengthens his voice in an attempt to remind Minor who he is. "Lieutenant Minor!"

Minor snaps out of it, regaining his senses, and quickly stands to his feet. Upon standing, he pulls his arm away from Moses. Exerting himself, Minor puffs out his chest and, with great disdain, commands Yang, "Sergeant, analysis!"

Yang, not knowing what to say, responds, "Sir, I don't know."

Dr. Davis, hearing the conversation, speaks up. "It appears that he is in some sort of state of suspended animation."

Moses ponders the idea of suspended animation. Growing up with his medical condition, he has acquired a great deal of knowledge in science and medicine. He queries, "I don't understand."

Looking around, he spreads his hands out. "These people seem ... well, they don't seem advanced enough to have successful cryogenics."

Davis nods and looks up from her patient. "Agreed. However, it seems like they tried to work around it. Before we learned how to make space jumps, we wished to travel deeper in space. We utilized cryoprotectants, but it doesn't appear that they had this technology available. Look at their faces."

Moses bends down, as does Yang. Davis shines her light onto his face. Yang, physically and emotionally disturbed by the image before her, blurts out, "It's shriveled up! He looks like a prune!"

Davis nods. "It seems like they were rendered unconscious, most likely gassed. Then one by one, most of their body fluids were removed before the body was frozen, trying to minimize cell damage."

Yang, concerned, asks, "Do you think they can be revived?"

Very matter-of-factly, Dr. Davis shakes her head. "I doubt it. I admit that I do not understand the extent of their technology, but from all my research and historical data, this method does not work."

She looks back down at her patient then stands and moves to the next. Moses turns to Sergeant Yang. "Can you plot us a course around the bodies?"

"Yes, sir," she says, "it's already done."

As Yang is pressing her wrist controls, a green laser grid lights over the floor, highlighting the corpses. Moses takes a deep breath. "Let's go."

Moses, annoyed, turns to Lieutenant Minor. "Do you want to lead?"

Minor huffs and moves forward, brushing against Moses's shoulder as he passes.

Rikes is frustrated, trying to figure out the scientific method that Bridge used to communicate with Lieutenant Young. Vicky, on the other hand, just accepts it for what it was and keeps moving; her mind is ever focused on the task before them. They arrive at a steel door, which Rikes's instruments have indicated has a strong power signature inside. Vicky looks for a button to open the door. She finds one to the right and presses it, but the door does not open. As best she can, she places her gloved hand against the door and pulls. The door gives, and the light from within oozes out. Soon, she is able to edge it open enough to wrap her fingers around it. Rikes adds his hands, and soon the door is open.

Vicky and Rikes walk inside. It seems to be the control center of the ship. There are computers and machines all around the room. Although the lights are dim, they seem active, probably in some sort of sleep mode. There is no noise in the room, not the usual chatter heard from machines in a power grid. On the walls, they spy relays and what look to be the communications for the ship. Above the communication panels are computer screens. Vicky looks at Rikes, perplexed. What should she do? Rarely does Vicky find herself in a moral dilemma that she cannot overcome with logic or good sense. She asks Rikes, almost as if she were thinking aloud, trying to hear the choices in her head, "Should we turn the power on? If we do, there's no telling what the consequences would be?"

Although Vicky stops talking, her mind continues to race with the questions: *What will we unleash on this ship? Why is the power off? Is there enough power to turn this enormous ship back on?* Rikes shakes his head dramatically. "Ma'am, I don't know."

Then Vicky decides something. "The communicators, see if you can contact Sergeant Yang."

Excited, Rikes rushes to the equipment. Although the equipment seems old, it does not look terribly unfamiliar. It is not alien in appearance, and the instruments are labeled in English.

Lieutenant Minor reaches the door. He musters his courage and pushes the handle down. The door creaks open. Inside, the room is full of lights and electronics beeping. Even though it is a large room, it is small in comparison to the other rooms they passed, especially the one they just walked through. About a meter in, there is a step up, and the floor is slightly more elevated than the previous rooms. The ceiling is also higher, and there are no protruding pipes or wires on the ceilings. Instead, the ceiling is a neat grid of steel beams with well-placed circular lamps positioned across the room.

Above the beams is a round glass dome, which gives a view of the star system above them. On three of the walls are large viewing windows displaying the scenery outside. Stars to the left and to the right and directly in front of them a large reddish-brown planet. On the backside is one last window. Although narrower than the others, it still gives a view of the stars behind them. In the far distance is the *Tiqu-Qi*. Around the room, facing the windows, are multiple command chairs. This is definitely the bridge.

At first, it appears that the room is empty. Then, all at once, they notice that in the center chair, the captain's chair, there is a body. Curiosity drags them forward; they have to inspect this seat and find answers. Slumped forward as if he were asleep is a soldier in blue fatigues. Similar to their own design, although bulkier, overlaid his fatigue is what appears to be black body armor. The design is similar to the other soldiers; however, there are no tubes running out of the chest plate. Instead, the device on his chest seems to be tight against his body, almost as if it were attached directly to him. His suit is also thicker than the soldiers on the floor, and this one has a helmet on. Dr. Davis examines him as the rest gather around. Moses asks, "Do you think this is the captain?"

Yang studies the body. She carefully lifts his arm. Four stripes are around the cuff. Yang turns to Lieutenant Minor. "Sir, this was the captain."

Dr. Davis shines her light into his visor as she narrates, "The subject is the same as the others. His fluids were drained from his body, and then he was frozen."

Davis feels along his body and blurts out, "Curious, ..."

Moses asks, "What is it, Doctor? Did you find something?"

She looks up at Moses. Her eyes have more questions than answers. Determined to discover the answers to her questions, she asks Moses, "Moses, can you give me a hand?"

The two of them carefully grab him and gently push him back. The chair clicks into position away from the console. There is a long, thin tube from the chest of his body armor running into the instruments. Davis stares intensely. "Sergeant Yang, what do you make of this?"

Yang squints, examining the cable and the instruments, and replies, "It seems like he's attached. These instruments seem to have the ability to possibly—" She looks at Dr. Davis.

Lieutenant Minor impatiently cries out, "Looks like they can do what? What?"

Dr. Davis and Sergeant Yang both look at Lieutenant Minor and respond, "Revive him."

Lieutenant Minor, confused yet impatient, without considering the consequences, blurts out, "Very well, then ... revive him."

Moses wants to yell out caution, but everything is happening so fast he cannot form his words. Dr. Davis, impatient with curiosity, does not hesitate to try to revive him. Sergeant Yang, a soldier from head to toe, responds to the command without questioning, and Lieutenant Minor simmers in his accomplishments. On the control panel, among other buttons, are three main buttons. One is a button labeled "Power." Directly under it is a switch labeled "Reanimate Subject A1." Next to it is a dial labeled "RHU," with increments from 0 to 1500. Davis points to the panel and looks toward Yang. Davis shakes her head. "This must be it." Yang agrees, "Yes, ma'am."

They are about to attempt to reanimate the body, when from the speaker before them comes a familiar voice. Private Rikes hails Sergeant Yang, "Sergeant Yang, are you there? Are you there? Over."

The equipment is familiar enough that Yang knows instinctively what to do. Pressing the button, she responds, "Roger, we are here on what appears to be the bridge. Over."

Vicky and Rikes are relieved. Vicky cries into the speaker, "It's good to hear your voice." Sergeant Yang replies, "Yes, ma'am, it's good to hear yours also."

Lieutenant Young continues, "We have some important information for you, but first, what have you found?"

Yang replies, "Yes, ma'am, we, too—"

Before Yang can complete her sentence, Lieutenant Minor brutishly pushes her out of the way. Coldly and arrogantly unconcerned with what Lieutenant Young and Private Rikes have found, Lieutenant Minor states, "Lieutenant Young, it appears that we have found bodies in suspended animation. Many of them. We found them in one room, and there are probably many more across the whole ship. We're uncertain what happened, but we're aboard the bridge and we found a person. It seems like he is attached to this ship by some sort of cord. We are in the process of trying to revive him."

Lieutenant Young looks toward Rikes, concerned. She replies, "Sir, is that wise? We, too, are in what appears to be the main power room, and there are breakers on the wall. We might possibly be able to regain power aboard the ship, but, sir, is that our wisest action?"

Lieutenant Minor has not thought that far in advance. He does not like to be challenged, and this feels like a challenge to him. Defiantly he commands, "Yes, we need information, and we shall revive him and then report back to you as to whether to put the power back on the ship."

Vicky concedes, "Yes, sir."

Although she is unsure, this plan does seem sound, and her options are limited.

Aboard the *Tiqu-Qi*, Private Li, the guard guarding Dr. Long, is one of the few soldiers who has not been reassigned in the past half hour. Hearing the commotion, he witnesses Dr. Shome being thrown to the floor. He is conflicted about whether or not he should leave the side of his prisoner. He knows he can be severely penalized for leaving a prisoner unattended, but still, he cannot remain uninvolved. His first priority is his prisoner's safety. Pushing him away, he finds an empty storage room. Turning on the lights, he quickly moves him in and locks the door. Dr. Long cautiously opens his eyes. Seeing that he is truly alone, he scans the room. On the shelves are medical supplies, gauze, medicine, and the like. However, this room was originally utilized to hold electronic equipment and communication devices; on some of the back shelves, most of the equipment remains.

Upon his return, the soldier moves forward cautiously. Unsure how to proceed, he moves toward the gurneys. There he finds blood splattered on the floor. He removes his sidearm and decides to find Private Jones. He messed up once, not taking action; he will not mess up again. He races down the corridor, looking for them. He arrives just in time to see Private Jones's heroic attempt to save the guard. He moves into action. With his sidearm out, he calls to them, "You guys! What are you doing? Get down on the floor!"

Without giving him time to respond, the one bleeding from his head, Lin, uses the stolen sidearm to fire at the guard. The blast shreds part of his upper right chest and shoulder, throwing him hard to the floor. Luckily, the bullets entered at an angle and did not go in too deeply. Although he is losing a great deal of blood, he is able to regain the strength to return fire. He cries for help into his wrist communicator, "Man down! I'm under fire outside the cargo bay!"

Inside the cargo bay, Private Jones tries to help her fallen comrade who is lying on the floor. His arm is broken, and he is hemorrhaging from his head. He is in shock; his eyes are swollen and crying. Private Jones attempts to calm him, but he is inconsolable. He grabs hold of Jones and pulls her toward him. He screams in her face, "What is going on? That was Lin! That's my friend. He's a good man. Why is he attacking me? Why is he attacking you?"

Jones responds calmly, "Breathe, breathe."

Finally, the guard takes a deep breath and breathes in. He calms himself. "What's going on with Lin?"

Jones shakes her head. "I don't know what's going on, but that's not Lin! I'm sorry, not anymore!"

Suddenly they hear the shots outside the door. Private Jones gets on the wrist communicator. "This is Private Jones. We're under attack in the cargo bay!"

There is no response. They suddenly notice that they are not alone; there is movement in the darkness, a clank of metal against the floor. They quickly turn; it is Private Diamond emerging from the shadows.

In engineering, there is a standoff. Duncan and the three engineers have entrenched themselves in the main controls. Captain Reynolds, Miller, and Private Brown, along with five other soldiers, have taken cover behind various pipes and machinery in engineering. Occasional bullets fly from either side; however, neither side has a clean shot of their opponents. The elevator opens behind Brown. Captain Reynolds looks; it is Dr. Shome. Shome's face and head injuries are very visible, as she did little more to clean up than wipe the blood off her face and tape a gauze over the wound. She has a black strap over her shoulder. Brown, with a side glance, motions to her to get down. She complies and crawls up between Brown and Reynolds. They simultaneously notice her injuries; her hair still has blood in it. The side of her face is badly bruised, and the right eye is severely bloodshot. Captain Reynolds cries out in an attempt to whisper, "My god, Doctor! Are you okay?"

Brown, with deep concern, states, "Yes, ma'am, you don't look too good."

She shakes her head; she pauses and places two fingers against her forehead as the action aggravated her fragile condition. Still, she persists. "I'm okay for now."

Brown has an instinctive understanding of her situation. She would not be there if she didn't need to be there. At this point, in order to survive, they must all work as one unit. Brown respects her decisions and pursues no further.

Dr. Shome carefully looks around at their surroundings. She reaches back and pulls a black leather bag from off her shoulder to the front. Shome's voice grips their attention. "I have a theory, an idea."

Brown and Captain Reynolds fix their attention on her. She moves forward a bit, allowing herself to be unprotected. Shome points, directing their attention to various places around the engineering. "Do you notice everything is intact?" she asks.

Brown squints; he does not understand, nor does Captain Reynolds at first. Then something clicks in Captain Reynolds. His eyes widen. He feels her flow and starts to follow her path of thought, intrigued as to where she is leading them. Enthusiastically, he shakes his head. "Yes, yes. You're right!"

Brown takes inventory more carefully. Dr. Shome continues, "I believe that these viruses have a hive mentality. On the planet, they no longer had a mission. Their drive was primal. Here they have some unseen goal, it's almost as if they're being controlled. They need this ship." She points with her fingers to the three of them. "They need us." Then she circles her fingers above her head. "All of us. We're valuable to them, … for now!"

Brown contorts his face, trying to comprehend, or perhaps he does comprehend but cannot believe. He gasps, "What, why? What could possibly be their mission?"

She shakes her head then takes a long, painful blink. "I have no idea. There is not enough information."

Her voice now shines with a slight glimmer of hope. She continues, "But we can use what we know to our advantage. They don't want to damage this ship, and they definitely would not want to damage someone that is infected."

Captain Reynolds has been following her train of thought thus far, and at this point, he does not like where it's going. "What are you saying?" he demands.

Shome opens her bag and takes out a black handheld pistol. Captain Reynolds stares at it, pondering its use. "Madam, what is this?"

"I have an antidote, I think. It is highly volatile and dangerous, but I believe it will kill the organisms in the host, releasing their control over them. This"—she holds the pistol up in her hand—"is a dart gun. It already has four doses of the antidote in it."

Brown grabs hold of the gun carefully, as if he were caressing a small animal. He asks, "How will you get close enough? We don't have a clear shot."

Captain Reynolds knows the answer and stares intently at Shome, waiting for her to reveal what he already fears. Shome takes out two syringes, "This one"—she holds up one of the syringes—"has a single organism of the virus in it. I'm going to infect myself—"

Captain Reynolds interjects, "I will not allow that!"

Shome gently, yet firmly, pushes her palm against Captain Reynolds's shoulder. She continues, "If they can sense the organism in me, they will not kill me. I believe I have a small window before the organism takes over totally. I'll just walk right up to them, and I'll be able to use the dart gun and—"

Both Captain Reynolds and Private Brown shake their heads. "And then what?" asks Brown.

Dr. Shome looks into Brown's eyes. "As soon as I'm done, you run up to me with this second syringe and inject me with the antidote."

Brown looks down, shaking his head. "I'm not sure."

Captain Reynolds tries hard to always put the needs of the many over the needs of the few or one, but this is hard. The risk to this young lady, this young doctor, this person is high! He understands sacrifice, but he does not want to sacrifice needlessly. Captain Reynolds attempts to rebut, "Madam—"

Shome again cuts him off. "Captain, with all due respect. We have little time and no other options. I think this might work."

Brown considers it. "This antidote thing, does it have side effects?"

Shome remains quiet for a second. Captain Reynolds interjects, "Doctor, what are the side effects?"

Shome breathes in deeply. "The antidote is derived from certain acid balances I determined in the mice from the planet. They may very well kill the host, as well."

Captain Reynolds stands, disregarding the risk he's taking of getting shot. "No, madam! In that case, I refuse to—"

Before he can continue, Dr. Shome takes the syringe with the virus to inject herself. Brown instinctively grabs hold of her arm, trying to prevent her from infecting herself. He pulls her arm to the floor. Captain Reynolds scoops down to retrieve the other arm, but it's too late; the needle is stuck in her left bicep. Captain Reynolds quickly reaches to remove the needle, but the syringe has an electronic sensor. The syringe beeps three high-pitched shrills and then releases the liquid into her system. Reynolds's face turns pale as he stares at Brown. They now have no other option; they have to proceed with her plan, or she will die. Even if her plan succeeds, she still might die. They help her to her feet. Now they are on the clock; they have to move quickly for the plan to succeed, or all is lost! Shome then places the syringe in Private Brown's hand and closes his fingers around it. She looks at him through her watery eyes. "My life is now in your hand, Private Brown."

Shome tucks the pistol in her waistband behind her back. She grinds her teeth. "Sorry," she whispers to them.

She walks straight toward the enemy. Brown shoots cover fire, being very careful not to hit Shome. Duncan and his men return fire, but there is a moment just before they shoot when they notice Dr. Shome approaching. Instinctively, when they return fire, they also make sure that they do not hit the doctor. Within moments, she is at their doorstep, and they usher her in, quickly firing fiercely at Private Brown, Captain Reynolds, and the rest. As Dr. Shome had predicted, they are cautious not to hit any vital instruments in the engineering chamber. Without hesitation, while they are still returning fire, she removes the gun from her waist. To her surprise, she moves quickly. She did not expect that the virus would have infected her so quickly, causing her to have increased speed and strength; even the pain in her head has disappeared. Duncan's three companions grab hold of the dart, which she carefully shoots into the backs of their necks. They pull them out, but it is too late. They cry out in agony as the serum invades the microorganisms. Their necks swell and pulsate in a vibrating fashion. Soon it spreads to the head. The sides of their heads become so swollen it seems as if they will explode. Their bodies buckle under them, and they fall, twisting and turning uncontrollably.

Duncan is the only one of the four left standing. He turns toward her; there is a confused look in his eyes. He does not yet understand; still, he moves to remove the gun from her hand. Shome tries to raise her weapon, but her motions are now slowed as the microorganism is causing her to resist; there is a fight for control. Noticing this, Brown jumps into action. He rushes toward them. Not wanting to kill Duncan if he doesn't have to, he shoots him in the leg, giving Dr. Shome the second she needs. Her arm shakes as she points the pistol toward Duncan. The snap of the pistol and the dart is in his neck. Duncan rears back, his leg squirting blood as he bangs into the doorpost. He lets out a screech that echoes throughout the chamber. Duncan's neck convulses. He jerks forward in one final attempt to grab Dr. Shome. His body gives in to the antidote, and like a marionette with the strings cut, he collapses to the floor. On the floor, his body shakes violently.

Suddenly a blank stare takes over Dr. Shome. Her reflexes have returned. With catlike speed, she quickly removes Duncan's sidearm from his hand. Private Brown dives forward; he is barely able to stop his forward motion, almost crashing into Dr. Shome. Shome shoves the sidearm in his face. She tilts her head just before pulling the trigger. Brown moves out of the way just in time as the bullets fly past his face. His footing is awkward, and dodging the bullets causes him to fall to the ground.

By the time he reaches the ground, Shome has already repositioned the sidearm, pointing it directly at his head. Again, Shome tilts her head, but before she pulls the trigger, she notices that oddly, Brown is not staring at the sidearm but, rather, at her shoulder. Curious, she glances over at her shoulder; Brown had managed, as he fell, to shove the syringe into her left shoulder. Quickly dropping the sidearm, she attempts to pull the syringe out. However, three piercing beeps, and the liquid is administered into her system!

Her shoulder quickly swells, and then the swelling proceeds rapidly to her neck then upward to her head. Her head swells from ear to ear. Shaking violently, with her right hand, she grips Private Brown's arm. So strong is the grip it causes him to bleed. Shome musters a rusty "Thank you" before hitting the ground.

Chapter 7

Moses is narrating a play-by-play over the intercom to Lieutenant Young, describing the events as they happen. Dr. Davis prepares to revive the captain. Cautiously, Dr. Davis presses the Power button. The grid lights up, and suddenly, things are a bit more visible as all the grids around the room turn on. A small dark screen brightens, and a solid white line appears across the center. On the right side of the screen is a row indicating various body-function levels; however, every level is at 0. Sergeant Yang points and looks over at Davis, "Heart monitor?" she questions.

Davis nods. "Yes."

The captain, however, still seems unchanged. Dr. Davis then looks over toward Yang as if for approval. She switches on the dial labeled "RHU." For a second, nothing happens. Then, after being dormant for two hundred years, the machine kicks in, and the engine buzzes a rhythmic hum. The console vibrates, and the tube attaching the captain to the instruments starts to shake in small spasms. Dr. Davis, Yang, Lieutenant Minor, and Moses step back, not knowing what to expect yet expecting something. For long moments, nothing happens. Moses calmly narrates to Vicky, "Still nothing…" Suddenly Moses hesitates. "Wait, something is happening!"

The captain's veins become visible on his face and hands. They begin to swell; Davis moves in to get a closer look. Apparently, the tube is connected to thousands, perhaps millions, of microtubes throughout his body. Then, like a giant balloon, his body inflates, and the deep, sunken crevices in his face start to fill.

All the levels on the monitor remain at 0. Davis takes a deep breath and carefully grabs hold of the dial. Slowly, she turns it: 100, 200, 300. Davis pauses; there is no change in the captain's condition. She looks at them and takes another deep breath. Moses continues to narrate to Vicky. Vicky and Rikes hold their breath in anticipation. Dr. Davis continues: 400, 500. A low, crackling electronic hum becomes noticeable. The monitors, however, remain uneventful. Davis continues: 600, 700. The line on the monitor flutters just slightly; the numbers also flinch just ever so slightly, as if, perhaps, a glitch. Davis continues: 800, 900. Then she reaches 1,000. The line on the monitor beeps rhythmically, and the numbers change from zero to various increments. The beeping sound gives them hope; even Moses has to smile.

Dr. Davis, however, notices that the numbers are low. Again, she takes another breath and turns up the dial: 1,100, 1,200. The heartbeat becomes stronger, more regular. Although the instruments have increased, they still indicate low levels. Davis waits a few seconds; the heartbeat slows, and his vitals are declining. Nervously, Davis grabs hold of the dial and increases the output: 1,300, 1,400. The numbers return to normal. She reaches 1,500; the dial can go no more. Suddenly the monitor flatlines; a long, solid beep cuts through the center of the screen! All the vitals are down to zero! Vicky cries out over the intercom, "Moses! What's happening?"

Moses sadly shakes his head. "I think we lost him."

Dr. Davis jumps into action, yelling to Moses, "We have to try to revive him! Help me!"

Moses quickly grabs hold of the captain and pulls him back. Davis commands Sergeant Yang, "Yang, quickly go to the shuttle, and bring back oxygen and a blanket!"

Immediately, Yang responds, "Yes, ma'am!"

She switches on her wrist communicator to view the path back to the shuttle and runs off. Davis cries out to Moses, "Moses, we have to try to get this helmet off his head!"

The two of them fumble around, looking for the helmet's release. Suddenly the dormant captain grabs hold of Dr. Davis's arm. Startled, she lets out a gasp and quickly flashes her wrist light inside his helmet. His eyes are open, and he is gasping for air. An electronic voice calls out over the intercoms, "Caution, caution. Restart life support. Caution, caution. Restart life support."

The captain desperately reaches up, trying to grab hold of Moses, who is looming over him from behind. His fingers only tap into Moses' helmet.

Moses looks intently at him, trying to figure out what he wants. The captain repeatedly points toward the console. Finally, Moses understands and pushes him forward. The chair moves forward, bringing the captain within reach of the console. The captain reaches out toward the controls, his arm shaking as he manipulates a series of dials and switches. The three of them anxiously watch on, not knowing what else to do. The electronic voice announces, "Life support reengaged."

The captain's suit comes alive with lights, as do his helmet lights. His face is clearly seen as he takes his first real breaths in over 200 years.

The captain stares blankly into space for a brief second then turns and looks at Dr. Davis, Lieutenant Minor, and Moses standing around him. He moves forward, looking at the dials and instruments as if they were not there. The three of them look at one another, speechless. Vicky calls to Moses, "Moses, what is going on?"

Moses answers hesitantly, still uncertain what to make of everything happening. "The captain has been revived."

The captain's eyes dart over the instruments. He turns toward Lieutenant Minor. "The power … the main power is not on!"

Lieutenant Minor clears his throat. "Sir, I am Lieutenant Minor of the UPA—"

The captain waves his hand at Minor, preventing him from continuing. His face is detailed with concern. "My men … I don't know how long they can stay in this state! We need to revive them, but I have no power! There is a main power relay. I need to get there and restart the power."

The captain moves to get up, but his body is still numb, and he falls forward. Moses and Dr. Davis quickly move into action to steady him. They set him back in his seat. Again, Lieutenant Minor tries to address him. "Sir, we are aware. One of our personnel is in the control room already."

Lieutenant Minor looks toward Moses. "Moses."

Moses explains the situation to Vicky, "Lieutenant Young, we revived the captain, but he states that we need to restart the power in order to save his crew."

Vicky nods, "Yes, we have been following along over the intercom."

She then turns her attention to her superior officer. "Lieutenant Minor, orders?"

Lieutenant Minor again tries to engage the captain. "Sir, before we continue, we need to know who you are and what your mission is."

The captain humbly shakes his head, "Of course, of course, but before we deal with those pleasantries, I beg of you ... we need to help my crew!" He musters enough strength to place his shaky hand on Lieutenant Minor's shoulder.

Again, Vicky calls out to Lieutenant Minor, "Sir?"

Minor shakes his head. "Very well, Lieutenant Young, proceed."

Vicky looks at Rikes, takes a deep breath, places her hand on the lever, and pulls it down.

Silence engulfs the ship; no one can speak. Then the lights in the ship flash on. It takes a second for their eyes to adjust. Two hundred years of dormancy come alive aboard the ship as gears and mechanical equipment move once again. The captain shakes his head. "Thank you."

He pushes himself back in his seat and switches on a series of relays. The electronic voice states, "Ship's life support engaged."

The vents are reengaged, and the fog is slowly channeled out of the compartments. Even through their suits, the crew notices that the temperature is beginning to rise. The captain is noticeably relieved. He switches on a few more switches. The electronic voice announces, "Reanimation engaged."

The breastplates on all the soldiers lying on the floor light up and pulse with movement. The captain turns toward Lieutenant Minor. "It will take a while before they revive. Let's get acquainted."

Vicky hastens back to the coordinates with Rikes. As they enter the chamber, the soldiers are still on the floor, being revived electronically. Cautiously, Vicky and Rikes maneuver around them. They enter the bridge as the captain has already begun telling his tale. The captain has removed his helmet. He is sturdy-built, with a strong face, yet pleasant. Steel blue eyes peer out from under his thick wavy black hair and thick eyebrows. He has a thick yet well-trimmed black beard and mustache.

Moses notices Vicky standing there and tries to catch her up. His voice, although polite, is booming and firm, and interrupts the captain. The captain gives his full attention to Vicky as Moses addresses him, "Sir, let me introduce you. This is Lieutenant Young and Private Rikes."

The captain nods his head in appreciation. "You are the ones who turned on the power, saving my people! Much thanks."

Moses continues, "This is Captain…"

The captain interrupts, "My name is Captain Barr. Let me start from the beginning, if that's okay?"

Yang had returned from the shuttle only moments before Vicky, and she, too, was eager to hear what he had already said. Captain Barr asks, "Are there any more coming?"

Moses responds, "This is it for now."

He purposely does not mention Pam. He thought that, for now, it would be best not to mention her at all, not until they find out what is going on. Captain Barr continues, "Very well. A few months ago, we were visited by an alien from the far reaches of this galaxy. He came to Earth, to us, for help. Apparently, there is a political leader, a dictator, who not only enslaved multiple planets but had his eyes set on Earth next! Weel, we started to construct spaceships capable of traveling into this galaxy to bring the fight to him, so to speak. We were the first ones. When we came through the wormhole, things went from bad to worse."

Captain Barr's mind wanders. The images play before him as if it had happened just yesterday.

Electrical sparks and fires plague the bridge, filling it with smoke. Nervous soldiers run to and fro with canisters of coolant, trying to control the fires. Captain Barr turns toward his navigational officer, Lieutenant Lin, "Lin, where are we?"

Lin looks at the instruments, fanning the smoke away. He nervously shakes his head. "Sir, all instruments are down! We barely have any power!"

Captain Barr shifts his eyes sideways and then turns to the lieutenant. "Do you have a handheld?"

Lin responds, "Sir, yes, sir!"

Captain Barr continues, "Then take it out, take pictures of all these stars, and search the maps. Find out where we are!"

Lin responds, "Sir, yes, sir!"

Captain Barr calls down to engineering, "Engineering, this is Captain Barr. What's our status?"

The voice replies, "Sir, we have lost most power ... momentarily. But I think we'll be able to get it back on soon! Sir!"

The captain shakes his head; the words seem hopeful. Barr replies, "Report back to me immediately if anything changes!"

The voice replies, "Sir, yes, sir!"

Captain Barr looks at Lieutenant Minor. "Soon we were able to get our power back on, and not too long after, our instruments were up and running. We realized that we were off course in this unfamiliar solar system. Then, our instruments picked up a power signal ... stronger than any power signal that ever registered! It took us a day's travel to get to 'at planet..."

Captain Barr rises from his seat and walks toward the bow window. He points a condemning finger at the reddish-brown planet before them. Barr turns back and takes a moment to scan his audience. "We were approaching the planet when, suddenly, our power was drained."

Moses, Yang, Minor, Rikes, and Vicky all look at one another. The similarities between Captain Barr's story and theirs can't be dismissed. Barr notices their glances but decides to continue. "It takes a while for our solar panels to kick in. I only had a few minutes before life support would crash. I had no choice but to cryofreeze the crew. I left myself for last, with my space suit connected to the ship, hoping 'at, when it was safe, the ship would reanimate me. 'At's the last thing 'at I remember."

Yang speaks up. "Sir, the crew did not need space suits?"

A raspy voice from behind him speaks up. "The crew does not need their suits. Their breastplates have all their DNA in it. It holds their liquids, as well."

Lieutenant Lin, the ship's navigational officer, has regained consciousness and managed to stand himself up. Lin is thin but not bony. He is of average height with jet-black hair and a well-trimmed thin beard. His face is stern, and although he is about the same age as Captain Barr, he appears to be older. He looks capable. He is the person on this or any mission that will get things done and make sure that others do their part, as well. Vicky notices that both Captain Barr and Lieutenant Lin have very distinct features; Lin is undoubtedly of Chinese descent, while Barr seems European and, by his accent, definitely Scottish.

They turn toward Lin. The captain's face lights up. "Lieutenant, glad to see 'at ye're okay."

Lin replies, "Yes, sir."

Lin's legs buckle under him; quickly Moses moves to help him. Lin motions with his hands. "No, I'm okay."

He braces himself against a chair. Lin stands straight and scans the room. "Captain, sir, so these are the people who came to answer our SOS?"

The captain shakes his head. "Yes. This is Lieutenant Lin, my first navigational officer. And this is—"

Captain Barr pauses for a moment. "I'm sorry, I don't know who you are."

Lieutenant Minor clears his throat and once again states, "Sir, I am Lieutenant Minor of the UPA."

Grunts and moans interrupt Lieutenant Minor as the crew of six thousand begins to revive. Captain Barr looks around then looks over to Lieutenant Lin and then back at Lieutenant Minor. "Lieutenant, I think we need to table this conversation for now and tend to our people."

Minor nods. "Sir, yes, sir."

Davis steps forward. "Sir, I am Dr. Davis. I can help."

Appreciatively, Captain Barr nods. "Very well." Barr turns to Lin. "Lieutenant Lin, show her what to do."

Captain Barr walks over to Lieutenant Minor. "As soon as we get settled, we will continue this conversation."

Lieutenant Minor nods and calls out to Moses, "Moses?"

Moses nods. "Yes, I'm on it."

Moses and Sergeant Yang go off to help wherever they can, grabbing hold of soldiers and standing them on their feet. Some are amazed, seeing the size of Moses lifting them as Moses pulls them to their feet effortlessly.

Lieutenant Minor walks over to Lieutenant Young. "Lieutenant, any word from the *Tiqu-Qi*?"

Vicky glances over at Rikes. Rikes speaks up. "Sir, not yet, but I keep trying."

Minor nods. "Very good soldier, let me know as soon as you contact them."

Private Rikes responds, "Sir, yes, sir."

Lieutenant Lin walks alongside Vicky as he explains some of the equipment and procedures to Dr. Davis. Lieutenant Young turns toward Lin and politely places a hand on his shoulder. "Lin?" she asks. "We have a Lin aboard our ship. He's a good man."

Lin turns to her and smiles. "I'm sure. With the name Lin, he has to be good."

They walk off.

Back on the *Tiqu-Qi*, in the cargo bay, Private Jones and the guard are startled as the metal door behind them begins to slowly slide open. Jones, in a panic, turns to the guard, "They must have gained control. They're coming in!"

Instincts and training kick in as Jones grabs the guard and ushers him behind some of the crates. Before the door fully opens, Lin and the others rush in! Lin turns and presses the control to close the door behind them. The piercing sounds of bullets hit hard against the metal door; the other soldiers have arrived. Jones is relieved to hear her comrades outside, but she fears that it is too late for her and the guard, as they are boxed in. Private Diamond moves into action, stepping between Lin and Jones, with his guns manifested, spinning and ready to fire. Jones read Lieutenant Young's reports on how Private Diamond could produce these weapons. She also read that the weapons he duplicates are augmented and far more powerful than the original product. Jones cries out to Private Diamond, "Diamond, don't discharge your weapons! If you do, you could blast a hole through the ship! The air will suck out everything, and if the other soldiers get the door open, they will be sucked out as well!"

Feeling that he has the upper hand, Lin stares down the huge robot as his two comrades disable the door, preventing Jones's fellow soldiers from entering. Lin hisses at Private Diamond, "Stay back, you unnatural freak. We just want Jones. We won't kill her … not yet."

Diamond pauses. He realizes that Jones's words are true. He has no control over the devastating power of his weapons, and if he shoots, he probably will shoot not only Lin but also straight through the door, killing the soldiers on the other side, as well. Lin takes advantage of his hesitation as they move to position themselves to get Jones. Lin takes a glance over to his man on his left. With his finger, he motions for him to go to the left and around, behind Jones and the guard. Quickly the soldier rushes off, jumping and bouncing on the walls like a giant insect. Jones does not like the odds.

Although they each have a weapon, Jones realizes that Lin and his two possessed men are quick. She is unsure if she can keep her eye on all three of them before one of them manages to get to her. She's not fearful for her own life; the guard's life hangs in the balance. He needs medical attention, and she is quite sure in her heart that if one of them got to him first, he is as good as dead! Something needs to be done quickly, but what? Can she wait for her comrades to cut through the door? It would be too late! What do they want with her? Why her? These thoughts plague her mind as she tries desperately to think of a solution when suddenly her wrist communicator chimes. She looks down at it; there is a message on it that reads, "Hold on to something!"

She pauses and then looks curiously at Private Diamond. Diamond replies by turning his head toward her. Is Private Diamond actually reaching out to her? She is unsure, but she will take whatever advantage she can. Jones quickly moves into action, takes a handful of the netting around the cargo, and shoves the guard's arm into it. The guard whispers, "What?"

Jones brings her finger to her lips and whispers, "Just hold on, as if your life depends on it."

He complies, gripping his arms and locking them around the netting. Then Jones wraps her arms around the netting, as well. Suddenly Lin jumps out, crawling on the ceiling above them, sidearm in hand. The guard gasps for breath, assuming it will be his last. A loud clank is heard as Private Diamond clamps his feet firmly into the cargo bay floor. Jones notices the noise, but Lin is focused on his ambush. Behind them, the other soldier appears. They are trapped! She knows, in a moment, the third one will appear either to her left or her right.

Before another move can be made, Private Diamond's eyes glow. A hiss of air pierces the chamber, followed by the opening of the cargo door. Immediately, precious air is pushed out into the void of space. Jones and the guard are lifted off the ground and pulled; they hold tight to the netting. The guard screams in agony, his voice lost in the commotion of rushing wind. The possessed soldier right behind them is the first one sucked out. Then, banging over the crates, the second guard, who was waiting in ambush, flies violently out into space, leaving Lin desperately trying to hold on to the netting, as well. He cannot get a good grip before he is pulled uncontrollably toward the door.

In desperation, he grabs on to Private Diamond; Lin bares his weapon in defiance against the suction of space. He aims his weapon straight at the guard. Jones cannot move her sidearms as she fights to hold on. Despair momentarily conquers her spirit, for although the plan may have been good, it seems like it will still end the same way; the guard will die. Private Diamond again does something unexpected. With an echoing clank, he releases his own clamps. Then the merciless suction of space pulls him and Lin toward the door and into oblivion. Moments before he exits, the same bright glow in his eyes appears once again as Private Diamond causes the cargo doors to close, reassuring that, when he exits, Jones and the guard will be safe! Diamond's leg and foot scrape against the closing doors as he exits. The threat is gone, but so is Private Diamond. Private Jones gets on her feet, breathing heavily yet considering the great sacrifice that Private Diamond made to save their lives.

Chapter 8

Aboard the *Liberty Crane*, Vicky has visited Pam to reassure her that everything is alright and to make sure she is settled. After confirming that she is at ease, Vicky returned for their meeting. She hopes that the many questions she has, that they have, will be answered. She fears they may run into even more questions, both for them and for the crew aboard the *Liberty Crane*. However, even Vicky's fears could not imagine the depth of what she was about to uncover.

In the conference room sit Captain Barr, Lieutenant Lin, Lieutenant Minor, Lieutenant Young, Sergeant Yang, Moses, Dr. Davis, and Private Rikes. Lieutenant Minor starts off. "Sir, I am Lieutenant Minor of the UPA. Our ship, the *Tiqu-Qi*, was thrown off course like yours, and we received damage. After repairing our ship, we soon received a distress call, an SOS, from your ship. We came to your aid."

Captain Barr curiously looks at Lieutenant Lin. Lin frowns ever so slightly in confusion. Captain Barr turned toward Lieutenant Minor. "Am sorry, whit is the UPA? We've neva heard of it."

Lin shakes his head in agreement. Minor straightens himself. "We are from the United Planetary Alliance. We departed from Earth."

Reluctantly, Captain Barr accepts the information. He shakes his head. "Very weel, an the nature of your ship?"

Lieutenant Minor nods, carefully choosing his words. "We are an exploration ship, out mainly for mining minerals to bring back to the alliance."

Again, Lin and Captain Barr glance at each other, trying to make sense of the information they are given from Lieutenant Minor. Captain Barr leans forward, concerned. "An how goes the war?"

Minor is taken aback; he looks toward Lieutenant Young. Young speaks up. "Captain Barr, Lieutenant Minor, if I may, sir?"

Minor gives her the floor. Young picks up the conversation from there. "Sir, we are not at war."

Barr stares at her, confused, "Whit? Whit do ye mean, did we win?"

Vicky nervously looks at Moses and Lieutenant Minor. Vicky straightens up and continues, "Sir, there's no easy way to put this. From all historical data, there has never been a ship sent this far out into space. There's never been any mention of some galactic dictator nor war. Not even a mention of your ship, the *Liberty Crane*."

Captain Barr stands to his feet in frustration. "Whit? whit do ye mean, no mention?"

He looks at his lieutenant. Lieutenant Lin yells out, "Please explain yourself!"

Then the captain pauses for a moment. He turns cryptically toward Lieutenant Young. "Historical data?" He asks, "Exactly whit year is this?"

Young again looks toward Lieutenant Minor; she turns back to Captain Barr. "Sir, what year do you think it is?"

Barr's eyes narrow as he asks a question he never thought he would be uncertain of, "2034?"

Vicky looks down but only for an instant, not wanting to hide the truth from him any longer. "Sir, Captain Barr, I'm sorry to inform you. It is the year 2312!"

Captain Barr nervously places his hands behind him to grab his seat, slowly lowering himself into it. Fear and disbelief color his complexion to a pale white.

Lin scans their eyes. "I don't understand."

Captain Barr replies, "At is impossible, we were in cryosleep for almost three hundred years?"

Dr. Davis clears her throat and speaks up. "Sir, I'm afraid so."

Moses chimes in, "From the best Rikes and I could figure out, your solar panels are very slow at converting energy. After the initial strain, it took a long time to reboot your systems. For whatever reason, it never revived you. I'm sorry, we're not sure why."

Barr puts his head in his hands. Suddenly the conference room door slides open. The head of engineering, Lieutenant Chin, is standing by the door. "Sir," he said, "Captain Barr, sir, there's something you need to see."

With that, Captain Barr looks at the room. "Let's go."

Everyone rises and follows Chin to the bridge. Chin walks up to the main console. The captain follows and sits in his chair, the rest forming around and behind him. Chin points first to the main portal, still facing the ominous reddish-brown planet sitting in the depths of space in front of them. Then he points down to the monitor, which is analyzing the structure of the planet. Chin explains, "Sir, as you know, when we originally attempted to scan the planet, it was very difficult. Over 90 percent of the planet is solid iron ore. However, when we did our advanced scans, we found that in the center is a cavern."

Rikes, intrigued and full of questions, asks, "A cavern? Not a core?"

"No," replies Chin as he looks into Rikes's eyes. Then he shifts his attention to the rest. "Whatever it is, it is not a traditional planet."

Chin adjusts the screen, and it overlays the entire portal. Chin points at a small elongated gray dot in the center of the planet. "The cavern is small," explains Chin, "only about a third the size of our ship. But on recent scans."

Chin presses a button, and the image changes. Now behind the cavern appears a labyrinth of tangled gray lines. Captain Barr, confused, studies the knot of lines. "What is that?"

"Tunnels, sir," replies Chin. "It seems that something has been tunneling miles and miles of tunnels from behind the cavern. Some travel out to almost a mile of the surface before circling back to the center."

Chin looks back at his audience. "Something is there."

Captain Barr shakes his head. "Very good, Lieutenant. Thank ye."

Chin nods, saying "sir," and he walks off.

Captain Barr looks angrily at the image. He points his finger. "Ats the cause of o' problems! We need ti go there!"

Lieutenant Young moves in closer. "I'll go," says Young. "Sirs, with your approval, I will take a small crew, just myself and Private Rikes. We'll go and survey the planet, see if there's any entry points. If we could get to that chamber, we could find out what is happening, once and for all."

Lieutenant Young looks to Lieutenant Minor. Minor nods then turns to Captain Barr. Barr agrees, "Sounds good."

Minor returns to Young. "Sounds good. Being that we're still in communication blackout between us and the *Tiqu-Qi*, I think it'd be good for us to take what information we have here and get back over there and report to Captain Reynolds. We'll meet you there, Lieutenant."

Young nods. Moses, concerned for Lieutenant Young's welfare, cautions her, "Lieutenant Young, are you sure?"

Vicky understands where Moses is coming from, a genuine feeling of concern, but she is determined. She looks at Moses and does nothing more than a slight nod. Moses understands. Deep inside is a compelling force that even Vicky has not yet identified, but this is something she must see through to the end. Vicky looks toward Private Rikes. "Rikes, are you up to piloting?"

Rikes looks toward the red planet. He takes a deep breath. "Yes, ma'am."

Captain Barr stands to his feet and, in a very lively tone, speaks up. "Well, I guess we have a plan, let's get to it!"

Suddenly Captain Barr's eyes roll to the back of his head, and he falls limp to the ground! Lieutenant Lin rushes to his side, as does Dr. Davis. Dr. Davis commands, "Quick, bring him to the chair." They lift him and place him back into his chair. Lin quickly connects Barr back to the computer. He pushes a few buttons as they wait nervously. Lin pauses for a moment, as if he lost his breath. Dr. Davis looks over at him, but before she can comment, Lin gets right back to work. Lin then loses his footing; he tries to brace himself with the chair but misses. Moses catches him before he hits the ground and rests him in the chair next to the captain. Then, without warning, one of the other crewmen tumbles and falls.

Not long after that, a third of the crewmen has either fallen unconscious or cannot stand on their own. Captain Barr has regained consciousness, but he is very groggy. Dr. Davis explains her findings, "It would seem that, in their cryogenic sleep, their liquids and nutrients were sucked from their bodies to prevent cell damage. However, when they were reanimated, some of the vital enzymes and minerals did not survive, so their bodies are starting to shut down. I spoke with Lin. Unfortunately, their doctor is still unconscious. But I believe that, back on the *Tiqu-Qi*, with Dr. Shome's help, we could make a supplement to help boost their bodies back to health. I would just need to take some blood samples back with me."

Then Vicky, remembering the warning that Bridge told her, interrupts Dr. Davis. "Dr. Davis." Vicky's voice is shaky, almost nervous, at first. A rare tone for her, but she quickly recomposes herself. After a breath, she continues, "You're planning to bring some of their blood back to our ship?"

Dr. Davis nods. "Yes, I would like to analyze their blood before we make the serum. Is there a problem?"

Then Lieutenant Minor, quick to contradict Lieutenant Young, especially if he thinks she might be wrong, says, "Yes, it's to save their lives. Is there a problem, Lieutenant? We have to return to the *Tiqu-Qi* anyway!"

Young looks to the side for a second then replies, "Sir, I don't believe it would be in our best interest to bring anything back aboard our ship from here, at least not until we have tested and cleared everything."

Lieutenant Young looks at Dr. Davis. Davis nods. "She has some merit, we have not tested their blood. We could be running a risk. They have been in cryostasis, in this alien galaxy, for three hundred years. Sir, there's no precedent."

Private Rikes speaks up, first to Lieutenant Minor. "Sir, if I may?"

Then he speaks to Dr. Davis. "Dr. Davis, couldn't you test the blood from here and download the information?"

Dr. Davis excitedly cuts in. "Yes, yes! That will work. I could download the information here and bring it back with me. That would work just as well, without taking any risks."

Satisfied with the answer but not the outcome, Lieutenant Minor feels slighted by Lieutenant Young, again! For now, with no other choice, he concedes, "Very well. Download it into your computer and take it back."

Lieutenant Minor's eyes grow dark, as he falls down a deep, perilous pit. Like a fire that starts in the brush, if not halted in the beginning, it will burn and burn until it consumes all. Lieutenant Minor's thoughts are consumed by envy. Lieutenant Minor looks at Lieutenant Young. His voice is anxious as he addresses her, "This does not change our plans! You proceed to the red planet, and as soon as Davis runs her tests, we'll proceed back to the *Tiqu-Qi*. We will meet you there."

Vicky nods and hastens off to make the preparations. Before she leaves the bridge, she firmly grabs Moses's wrist. The two turn, and Moses crouches down to hear Lieutenant Young. Vicky whispers just loud enough for Moses and Private Rikes to hear, "Moses, do not let anything from this ship aboard the *Tiqu-Qi* until we meet up. I'll explain later."

Sensing that something is not right himself, he agrees, "I got that."

Within minutes, Vicky is aboard her shuttle and launches toward the ominous red planet. No sooner has she departed than when Lieutenant

Minor enters the lab where Dr. Davis is working. He interrupts her work. "Dr. Davis."

She looks up. "Yes, Lieutenant?"

Minor continues, "No need to waste precious time. Take what you need in test tubes, and bring it back to the shuttle."

Dr. Davis is confused. "Sir?"

Minor continues, "Isn't the blood in test tubes? Isn't it safe? Can anything, any parasite, anything escape from the test tubes?"

Dr. Davis looks down. "I suppose not, but, sir, still, to err on the side of caution,"

Lieutenant Minor cuts her off. "No! I've made up my mind. I see no immediate threat, and time's wasting! Take the blood, we launch in ten minutes! That is an order!"

Reluctantly yet obediently, she replies, "Yes, sir."

Lieutenant Minor marches off to prepare the shuttle for departure.

Chapter 9

As Vicky peers out the shuttle portal, the red planet grows larger and larger. Pam looks curiously at the planet. Vicky turns to her. "Are you sure this planet doesn't mean anything to you?"

Pam shakes her head. "I'm sorry. I don't remember anything about red planets or any of the things that you told me the captain said."

Vicky nods. "Very well." She looks forward with hope in her voice. "We'll find out together."

As the shuttle lands, great clouds of dust push to the sides. When the dust settles, Vicky scans the terrain with her eyes. She asks Rikes, "Doesn't this planet look odd to you?"

Rikes nods. Vicky continues, "I have been on many planets to mine minerals, even satellites, and they'll have craters and mountains."

Rikes shakes his head. "This one is virtually flat … almost as if it was … just made."

Vicky nods. She looks back toward Pam then back at Rikes. Vicky asks Rikes, "Did you find anything?"

Rikes reports, "There is no measurable atmosphere, and the surface is a mixture of sand and iron oxide."

Vicky squints her eyes. "Iron oxide? Is oxygen needed to corrode iron?"

Rikes replies, "Not necessarily oxygen, but moisture."

Vicky shrugs her shoulders. "Does this planet have any water?"

Rikes stares out at the dusty red planet. "The scans do not indicate any, but somehow, it's there."

Vicky hesitates for a minute as she ponders the situation. "Look at the original scans that the *Liberty Crane* took of the cavern, then compare them to the latest scans. Are there any discrepancies?"

Rikes compares the data. He pauses, tilting his head slightly, fascinated by the findings. Rikes points to his screen, "Yes, ma'am." He looks up at Vicky. "It seems that the cavern is slightly larger now than before. It is not much, just under thirty cubic meters, which is probably why Lin did not detect it. But it's definitely larger."

Vicky looks at Rikes. "Suit up. Pam, stay here, we're going to check out the surface."

Pam is noticeably frustrated, like a child who was left behind. Respectfully, Pam pleads to come along, "Ma'am, please take me along. You brought me along so that I can help you."

Vicky hears the longing in her voice, the longing to be needed, the longing to be more. Vicky understands it; she replies, "Let's make sure it's safe first. I tell you what." She turns toward Rikes. "Rikes, can you leave the communications open with her while we are on the surface?"

Rikes shakes his head happily. "Yes, ma'am, not a problem."

There's always something calming in Vicky's voice; perhaps it is that Pam can sense truth and honesty. So like a child who trusts in her mother, Pam is able to trust Vicky, and it gives her confidence.

Moments later, the side shuttle door opens, and Vicky steps out onto the planet. The planet's gravitational pull seems close to Earth's. The door closes behind her, and a moment later, it reopens with Rikes in the doorway; he steps down to join Vicky. Vicky turns toward Rikes. "So this is the closest distance to the cavern?"

Rikes explains, "This planet is virtually perfectly round. The cavern seems to be directly in the center. However, this is the point directly above the cavern. I figure, if there was an entry point, it should be in this vicinity."

Vicky smiles, accepting Rikes's judgment. After twenty minutes of unproductive searching and inconclusive advance scans from the shuttle, Vicky and Rikes are frustrated. Vicky and Rikes are scanning two separate locations. Vicky decide it is wise not to venture so far that they cannot keep the shuttlecraft in view. Vicky looks up toward the shuttle; she hails Rikes. "Rikes."

"Yes, ma'am?"

"Anything?"

"No, ma'am."

Vicky puckers her lips; suddenly Pam cries out to them from the shuttle. There is a slight tone of panic in her voice. "Ma'am, something's happening! There are red lights flashing—I think it's a warning!"

Quickly Vicky calls to Rikes, "Rikes!"

Before she completes his name, he replies, "I'm checking now! Private Rikes, it seems like something is approaching the planet, a ship!"

Vicky commands, "Head back to the shuttle now!"

One by one, they run back into the decontamination chamber and back into the shuttle. Rikes removes his helmet and jumps on the controls. Vicky comes right behind him. Pam is to the side, nervous; a stream of steam begins to rise from her hands. Vicky has just placed her helmet on a chair, when Rikes looks back to report. "Something is approaching! It's … it's small and slowing up as it approaches."

Vicky notices Pam's state and chooses to frame her words calmly. "Can we identify it? Have you tried communicating with them?"

Rikes replies, "I cannot identify. It is approximately half the size of the shuttle."

Rikes opens communication. "Unidentified vessel, this is Private Rikes of the UPA. You are approaching shuttle number one, tree, fife, niner, please identify!"

Suddenly the red warning lights stop flashing. Vicky searches the control with her eyes. Vicky looks to Rikes. "What just happened?"

Rikes pushes himself back in his seat then taps his instruments with his finger.

He replies, "Ma'am, it disappeared!"

"What?" queries Vicky.

Rikes continues to adjust the controls in an attempt to relocate the vessel. With his eyes peeled to his controls, he replies, "Ma'am, I don't understand, the ship just disappeared."

Vicky looks at the controls for herself. Speaking out loud to herself, she says, "That's impossible."

Then she kneels to adjust her line of view upward toward the sky. Vicky points upward. "Look up, three o'clock!"

Rikes looks up; Pam edges toward the windows to look out. A bright light burns bright in the sky, growing rapidly as it approaches. Vicky turns to Rikes and grips his shoulder. "Engage engines," she commands. "Get us off the ground! Prepare weapons."

Rikes hollers back, "Yes, ma'am!"

In seconds, the shuttle engines shoot, and the dust flies high in the air. Soon, the shuttle is off the ground as the unidentified vessel simultaneously approaches the surface. The engines from the unidentified vessel push dust off the ground. Vicky commands Rikes to pivot the ship, facing their weapons toward the incoming vessel. The vessel lands, but until the dust settles, it is a waiting game. The planetary protocols placed into effect since the end of the solar war have not changed in all these years. Although ships are allowed to protect themselves with extreme prejudice if necessary, they are recommended not to fire unless they feel that they are under an immediate threat. Rikes knows these laws as well as Lieutenant Young does; his finger stands ready on the trigger. Vicky does not sense an immediate threat, at least not yet. Rikes's voice echoes through the shuttle, "Unidentified vessel, this is Private Rikes of the UPA. Please identify! Identify! This is Private Rikes of the—"

Vicky places her open palm out, indicating for Rikes to pause. The three wait in silence for what seems like eternity. Once the dust begins to clear, Vicky and Rikes cannot believe their eyes. Pam moves closer to see the image for herself. Suddenly the control panel bleeps. Vicky and Rikes look down to read the message. Vicky stares out the portal. Whether she is staring into space in deep thought or gazing at the thing that just landed is hard to tell. Then she methodically turns toward Rikes and calmly commands, "Disengage weapons. Land the shuttle."

Rikes cannot say a word as he follows instructions. Soon, the shuttle is back on the ground.

The decontamination chamber opens; out jumps Rikes, followed by Vicky. Vicky takes the lead and walks out before Rikes does. She lifts her gloved hand and places it on the giant robot's chest. Vicky asks, "Private Diamond, what are you doing here?"

Inside the shuttle, Pam, still bewildered, looks down at the text that she cannot read, the one word that reads, "friend."

Vicky and Rikes have many questions. Vicky starts off. "Private Diamond, the *Tiqu-Qi*, is it okay? Why did you leave? What happened?"

Then their wrist communicators, as well as the control panel on board the shuttle, explode with beeping and electronic chirps and chatter. Vicky and Rikes look at their communicators, but there is only gibberish, an onslaught of many characters with no distinguishing words. Vicky turns to Rikes in hopes of gaining some understanding. "Rikes, what do you make of this?"

Rikes ponders the situation for a moment or two before presenting his assessment. "Perhaps Private Diamond is trying to communicate with us, but he has not yet mastered this specific ability."

Vicky frowns, considering Rikes's statement. She looks up, placing both hands up toward Private Diamond, "Wait, wait," she says. "Take your time, slowly tell us one thing at a time." Private Diamond pauses for a few moments, then the communicators bleep just one word at a time. 'The *Tiqu-Qi* is safe. Private Jones was in danger. The virus attacked some crewmen. To save Jones, I opened the cargo bay hatch to remove the perpetrators. I also was removed. I saw your shuttlecraft leave. I pursued.'

Vicky and Rikes look toward each other. Concerned, Vicky turns back to Private Diamond. "The *Tiqu-Qi*, is it safe?"

They turn toward their communicator for Diamond's response. A moment later, he responds, 'Yes. I believe the incident was isolated. It seems that the perpetrators just wanted Private Jones.'

Now Vicky really has to think; she frowns heavily. Vicky looks toward Rikes, shaking her head. "Jones? What does Jones have to do with all this? And I didn't think the virus was able to make intelligent decisions other than to eat."

Rikes shakes his head, both in agreement and accepting comprehensive defeat. Rikes asks, "Ma'am, should we go back?"

Vicky looks down, shaking her head. "Try once again to contact the *Tiqu-Qi*, also contact *Liberty Crane*, see if we can reach Lieutenant Minor."

Rikes tries to hail the *Tiqu-Qi* first. "This is Private Rikes to the *Tiqu-Qi*, do you read? Captain Reynolds, Wei, are you there? Please respond, please respond."

The only response they receive is static. Then Rikes tries to reach the *Liberty Crane*, and to both their surprise, the response from the *Liberty Crane* is also static.

Rikes looks up toward Vicky. "That is odd."

Again, Vicky stares off into space considering her options. She looks toward the *Liberty Crane* sitting motionless before them in space and asks herself, "What is going on?"

Vicky turns back toward Rikes; she has made a decision. "If Diamond says that it was isolated, I believe that Captain Reynolds and Wei can handle it. No, there are answers here. We are too close to give up now. We have to complete our mission. Others are depending on us! We have to have confidence that our crew will accomplish their objectives, as well."

Vicky looks back toward the surface, the very ground beneath their feet. Her eyes accuse it of holding back information from them; she condemns the planet itself for not revealing its secrets. Almost thinking out loud, she states, "If only we could find a way to get to the chamber, I feel that the answer is in front of me. I—"

Vicky takes a long pause, then with bright eyes, she looks up at Private Diamond. "There is a cavern in the center of this planet … Your weapons are enhanced, are they not? Do you think you could drill a hole to the cavern?"

Vicky and Rikes look to their wrists, waiting for his response. Moments later, he responds, 'Yes. I scan the cavern. It is many kilometers below the surface. I can try to drill.'

Vicky smiles. "Good enough, Private, let's get to it!"

Moments later, Vicky and Rikes are back aboard the shuttle. Private Diamond launches a few meters off the surface; his massive array of weaponry protrudes out both arms. Private Diamond unleashes a full assault against the surface. Approximately four minutes later and about one-fourth of a kilometer into the depth of the planet, Private Diamond has to stop. He flies out of the trench he made and lands back on the surface; the communicator bleeps. Rikes reads aloud the message, his voice dropping toward the end. "Sorry, ma'am. I cannot proceed further. Arsenal is out. It will take time to replenish."

Vicky and Rikes both look down; the heavy weight of defeat gnaws at their inner beings. Pam senses their emotions, and it saddens her. She walks up behind Vicky. "Ma'am, perhaps I can help."

Vicky forces a smile. "No, Pam. There is nothing you can do right now."

Pam interjects, "But, ma'am, I can go out there—"

Again, Vicky shuts her down, shaking her head. "No, Pam. If you put on a suit, you will not be able to use your abilities, and even so, that is many kilometers down. Thank you, I see your heart, and we"—Vicky points with her fingers to herself and Rikes—"appreciate it."

Pam wants to speak, to cry out, but she humbly holds back and walks toward the back of the shuttle. Vicky looks at Rikes. "I think it is time we should head back to the *Tiqu-Qi*."

Rikes accepts her decision and nods. "Yes, ma'am."

Suddenly the decontamination chamber opens. Vicky and Rikes turn just in time to see the door shut behind Pam. Vicky cries out, "Pam, no! You'll be killed without a suit!"

Vicky runs toward the decontamination door and presses the button to open it, but it's too late. When the door reopens, Pam is not there. Vicky yells to Rikes, "Quickly, suit up! We need to go save her!"

Vicky puts on her helmet, but before she seals it, she notices that Rikes has not moved. Vicky, frustrated, calls to him, "Rikes, did you not hear me?"

Rikes, with a blank stare, responds, "Ma'am, yes, ma'am, I did, but look, you have to see this." Vicky pauses, placing her helmet down, and walks toward the portal to look down.

Pam is standing on the surface without a suit. The lack of oxygen seems to have no effect on her. Pam walks over to the hole that Private Diamond bore into the ground. Private Diamond acknowledges her. Pam kneels, looking into the hole; she rises, looks toward the shuttle, and waves at them. Then she fans herself as if she were calling them to follow her. Vicky looks toward Rikes, confused. Suddenly Pam jumps down the hole. Vicky screams out, "Oh my god! She's going to kill herself!"

Quickly Rikes adjusts his instruments. "I have her. She is at the bottom of the hole. Pam's vitals seem to be fine."

Vicky shakes her head. "That is impossible."

Rikes states, "I agree, but she is there. Wait, something is happening."

Unexpectedly, a stream of smoke shoots up from the hole, rising over one hundred meters into the dark sky. Vicky again looks toward Rikes. Rikes responds, not even sure he believes his own words, "Ma'am, she is digging a hole!"

Vicky shakes her head in confusion. "Any success?"

Rikes shakes his head. "I can't believe it, she is evaporating the ore ... She's actually going down faster than if she was falling! I'm not sure how that works, but at this rate, she'll be to the center in less than an hour."

Forty-three minutes later, Rikes and Vicky have been monitoring Pam's progress anxiously. Rikes reports to Lieutenant Young, "Ma'am, she reached a large opening which seems to connect to the cavern. She's waiting for us."

Vicky straightens up, takes in a deep breath, and commands, "Then let's follow. Tell Private Diamond to follow us."

"Yes, ma'am," responds Rikes.

In moments, the engines are ignited, and they proceed down the long dark tunnel, followed shortly after by Private Diamond. The first quarter kilometer down, the walls are ragged and sharp. In contrast, where Pam bore into the planet, it is smooth and glasslike. In a few minutes, they can see Pam as the shuttle settles on the floor of what appears to be the entrance to yet another tunnel, a horizontal tunnel. Although this tunnel is not as smooth as the one Pam made, it is not as torn and uneven as the one that Private Diamond made either. The tunnel is evenly cut, and although the walls and ceiling are circular, the floor is straight as if it were made to be walked on. The walls have crevices in them, like you would find in a naturally made cave, but this cave is not natural! The iron ore seems to have almost disappeared from existence to form this tunnel; it definitely is not natural. It was made by someone, but who? They ponder its origin and what they will find at the end of it as Private Diamond lands a few meters from the shuttle. Without saying a word, Rikes and Vicky helmet up. Soon, they exit the shuttle, and the four of them venture forward down the corridor.

In a few meters, the team makes the first turn. Vicky quickly puts her fist up, causing them to pause. This portion of the tunnel is straight; it goes on for approximately three hundred meters or so. At the end is a light, not like the light of a fire; no, this light is cool, calm, white, and constant. Vicky removes her sidearm, as does Rikes. Private Diamond forms his weapons out from his wrist; his weapons automatically regenerate after a period, and they are now ready and deadly. The four of them walk cautiously down the corridor. The tunnel seems to open into a large area, the cavern they presume. Finally, they have made it! The cavern is a few steps ahead; hopefully, they are steps to success and answers, answers that can save them and the entire crew aboard the *Liberty Crane*.

As they approach the threshold, Rikes's instruments go dark. He reports to Vicky, "Ma'am, my instruments shut off!"

Vicky turns toward him; they approach even more cautiously now than before. As Vicky crosses the threshold, it opens up to a large room. The vastness of the room is the least of things in Vicky's mind as the chamber is like nothing Vicky had ever seen or she would ever have imagined! Her mind wanders as she walks deeper and deeper inside. *This place is amazing! The floors are marble, magnificent! There are two people at the end of the room. Is this real? How is it possible? The walls have Roman-style columns and arches, beautiful satin drapes. The ceilings are high and arched, and that is the most beautiful crystal chandelier I have ever seen. At the end, the two people, they are not wearing space suits; how is that possible? One is a woman; is that a bar she is sitting on? Yes, a great mahogany bar, with mirror* walls and shelves behind it. On every shelf is a glass or a bottle, bottles of all sizes and colors. Behind the bar, there are doors. I wonder if one of them leads to the tunnels that we saw on our scans.

This woman … she is gorgeous! She is wearing a gown, a beautiful, flowing gown. I cannot make out the material; is it metal or some sort of white sparkly stone? Whatever it is, it catches the light from the chandelier and shimmers its reflection onto the floor and the walls, causing the light to dance all around her. She is tall, at least two meters. Her long leg slips out the slit in her dress as she crosses it over the other. She is light-skinned, but not mixed. No, her features are from a time past. She's not European either, no more Middle Eastern, perhaps Jewish. I have never seen such red lips, and even from here, her eye makeup displays her stunning green eyes. And that man behind the bar, he is equally as impressive! He's also tall and well-built. He is wearing a suit, a white suit, white shirt, black tie, and black pants; he fills out the suit well! He is also light-skinned, but definitely European. His jaw is square, and in contrast to the woman, his eyes are dark, but his face is soothing; there is a transparency about him, a reliability.

Vicky's thoughts are cut off by the woman's voice. Her voice is both sweet and hard; she is a woman who takes control. "You can take off your helmet. You do not need them here."

Vicky, Rikes, and Pam have made it about halfway across the floor; Private Diamond lumbers a few paces behind them. They pause; the man behind the bar, with a champagne glass in hand, speaks up next, "She's right, you know." He lifts his glass. "You can be here without a suit."

Again, Vicky pauses, this time mentally. She slowly complies and removes the locks on her helmet. Rikes nervously tries to caution her, "Ma'am, we do not know the air quality here! I can't agree that we should."

Before he can finish his sentence, Vicky removes her helmet and places it under her arm. Rikes takes in a deep breath and complies. It is not obedience, although he is obedient, but rather he complies with the trust he has gained in Lieutenant Vicky Young and her decisions. Rikes removes his helmet, as well. The lady places her glass on the bar and points out her hand softly, barely pointing her finger. She asks, "Is that a robot? He has to leave."

Lieutenant Young interjects, "He is with us!"

The woman blankly stares into Vicky. "A ten-ton metal robot? No, he has to go to the surface." The man agrees with her, "No, she is right, a robot would not be good down here."

The woman continues, looking at their sidearms. "And those weapons," she states, "really not a good thing here."

Again, the man shakes his head in agreement. "I'm afraid not."

Vicky glances at Rikes then back at the couple before them. This is their place; Vicky wants answers, and an olive branch or two might build some trust between them. She motions for Rikes to dismount his sidearm. Vicky dismounts her sidearm, as well, then turns toward Private Diamond. She places her hand upon his chest and nods ever so slightly. "It is alright, go to the surface," she says. "If we need you, we will call for you."

Diamond is also obedient; he turns and clanks toward the tunnel. Once around the corner, they see the flash of his rockets as he returns toward the surface. The man cheerfully speaks up, "Very well, time for introductions! I am Devin, and this lovely lady"—he points with the glass in hand toward the lady sitting next to him on the bar—"is Me-g—"

Her glare catches him, and his words freeze in midsentence. He tries to fix his mistake. "This is M? Perhaps D?"

The lady turns toward them and answers for herself. "You can call me Defender."

Vicky squints her eyes, uncertain if she wants to accept this information as accurate. "Is that a title?" she asks.

The woman responds emotionlessly, "It is."

Vicky notices that Devin's accent is almost familiar, but she can't quite place it. Rikes leans over toward Vicky and whispers, "Ma'am, it's like a nightclub in an old-time movie from the early twentieth century."

"That's it!" she replies excitedly. As a child, she was not allowed to study ancient entertainment, but she was somehow familiar with it.

Vicky stares back at the two and replies, "I am Lieutenant Young of the UPA."

Defender cuts Vicky off. "We know who you are."

Vicky knows that she should be surprised, but she is rarely moved off track, and so she continues with barely a pause. "Very well, if you know who we are, then you know why we are here. We are here for answers."

Devin cheerfully speaks up as he walks from around the back of the bar to stand next to Defender. "And we shall try our best to answer your questions or at least as best we can."

Vicky scans the two; her stare is as equally intimidating as Defender's. Vicky continues, "The *Liberty Crane* has been stranded here for almost three hundred years. What do you know about that?"

Defender looks over at Devin; Devin shrugs his shoulders, giving her the green light. Defender casually waves her hand outward. "We do not know the specifics of that … ship. Have you heard about the Dictator?"

Vicky responds, "Yes, both Captain Barr of the *Liberty Crane* had mentioned him, as well as a prisoner we liberated from an alien craft a few days past when we were trapped. The prisoner claims that he was a servant for the Dictator."

Defender replies, "Let me tell you what I can. Many years ago, there was a warlord. This warlord experimented on his own people to form an unstoppable army. His greatest success rebelled against him, killed him, and took his throne! Eventually, he killed all his own men. You see, he trusted no one. He replaced them with an army of robots. He used his old master's idea and expanded on it, this time experimenting on other planets. The slaughter was great! He used lesser planets to make monsters that became his captains. Captains he used to conquer more advanced planets. Over twenty planets he enslaved, every intelligent planet in this galaxy. But he was not satisfied, he wanted more! His real name is not remembered, as each planet calls him by their own language, but the interpretation was always the same: 'dictator.'"

Vicky steps forward. Although she tries not to show it, her concern is entangled within her words. "And Pam?" Vicky points toward Pam. "Is she also one of his experiments?"

Defender squints her eyes. "Pam?" she asks.

Defender turns toward Pam. Pam's eyes shyly search the ground, but curiosity and the need to know who she is forces them back upward, toward Defender. Their eyes meet. Defender continues, "Is that what you call her? Yes, I am sorry. Yes."

Pam again looks down, lost and hopeless. Vicky also looks downward, saddened for her friend. Her heart searches frantically to try to find a solution to help ease Pam's pain, but she finds none.

Defender continues, "But her name is not Pam."

Pam looks up, hopeful, afraid to hope yet hopeful nonetheless! Vicky responds, "Do you mean you know her?"

Defender nods, "I know of her, yes."

She turns toward Pam. "Her true name is Cherut, which means 'freedom'!"

Slowly Pam raises her head; a whirlwind of memories floods Pam's mind. She remembers her planet.

The landscape is on fire; giant robots are everywhere as people are herded aboard ships like cattle! Pam is a little girl; she remembers an overwhelming fear and sadness. She sees her mom and dad forced from her, toward an alien ship. They march toward the ship. Like the masses, they have no will of their own; still, her mom fights enough to turn one last time to see her beautiful daughter. Pam is pulling, futilely trying to join them! Her mother cries out to her, "Al tirah, al tirah, Ruthie!" (Fear not, little Ruth!) Pam cries out, "Ima, Ima!"

The memory fades, and tears roll slowly down Pam's cheeks, emitting a quiet white steam before being reabsorbed into her skin. Rikes grabs her shoulder to comfort her. Vicky queries, "So what happened?"

Defender continues, "Cherut was never deployed … The Dictator became too greedy and reached too far! He was defeated by the most unlikely of planets … Earth!"

Rikes, confused, calls out, "But that was three hundred years ago, how is it that it is affecting us now?"

Vicky agrees with Rikes and adds, "How is it that it is not part of our history? Not at all!"

Devin replies, "Sorry, for that we have no explanation."

Defender scans the two of them; she fears losing her audience. She must convey to them the severity of the events yet to come. "You have to understand, the Dictator is not human! It has been feared all these years, in whispers across the universe, that he was still alive … somewhere. For all these years, plotting and planning. It would seem that now, after all this time, things are in motion again, that what is happening now had always been his backup plan. He is somewhere regaining his power, his armies, and using his nightmarish experiments to forge new captains!"

Vicky asks, "So what is his end goal, revenge?"

Defender very seriously responds, "Oh no, do not be fooled! His goals are not simply to regain his power or revenge … No, it is a reckoning!"

Vicky turns again toward Defender. "And what does this Dictator look like?"

Very seriously, Defender answers, "That's just it—"

Devin completes her sentence. "We can't remember! And that concerns us. It is as if some power erased his image from all our minds!"

Rikes's eyes open wide. "Madam," he calls out, "the *Liberty Crane*'s logs."

Vicky instantly catches on. "That's right," she exclaims. She turns to them. "There is also no computer image of the Dictator in the *Liberty Crane*'s memory, not even a description."

While they ponder whom they are dealing with who has the ability to erase history from everyone and everything, Rikes takes a moment to look around at the splendor and awe of the room. He turns toward Devin and asks, "What is this place? How can we have air and heat?"

Rikes turns toward the back and points across the great marble floor to the entrance where they came in from. Flustered by the illogicality of the entire matter, he asks, "And there is a tunnel that leads to the surface! How is it that the air is not sucked right out?"

Devin smiles as if Private Rikes's logic had no validity here. Devin points to Defender, "That's all her!"

He explains as if that were enough of an explanation for Rikes. However, it is perhaps as much of an explanation as Devin can give; science, after all, is not his strong suit.

Vicky seizes this opportunity to ask a more personal question, "This place … what is it?"

Again, Devin smiles. He raises his glass. "It is my sanctuary, for the time being."

Defender matter-of-factly corrects him, "It is his prison."

Vicky does not know how to respond, her eyes darting between the two. Vicky decides to focus her eyes on Devin. Thinking, as Vicky usually does, that the straightforward approach would be the best, she plainly asks, "Who imprisoned you here?"

Devin looks down, circling his finger around the rim of his glass. He ponders how to answer. Again, Defender, who usually does not fumble for words but speaks her truth, answers for him. "He imprisoned himself."

Vicky, curiously and cautiously trying to find information, looks up at Defender and asks her, "And you, who imprisoned you here?"

Devin snickers then responds, "M … Defender is nobody's prisoner! She is my guest, and she comes and goes as she pleases. We enjoy each other's company."

Devin smiles and moves back behind the bar to refill his glass. Vicky looks toward Rikes. Rikes frowns ever so slightly; they both feel as if

Devin and Defender were holding back information. Vicky looks toward Pam. Pam is still quiet, overtaken by the grandeur of the place, Defender's elegance and beauty, Devin's command and mystery, and the bittersweet effect of returning memories.

Vicky decides to try a different strategy; with her eyebrow raised, she asks, "Do you know a lady named—"

Vicky is interrupted by Devin, who happened to grasp Defender's hand on the bar just as Vicky started talking. "Pardon me." He apologizes to Vicky.

Then, looking back at Defender, he raises the champagne bottle and asks her, "Would you like me to top you off?"

Defender does not say a word. With her face only slightly turned toward Devin, she raises her open palm toward him, indicating that she does not want more. Devin nods to Vicky again apologetically and tells her, "Sorry, go on."

Devin walks to return back around to the front of the bar as Vicky picks up from where she left off. "Do you know a girl named Bridge?"

Devin, still not fully around the corner of the bar, almost chokes on his drink at the mention of her name. Defender's body language changes for the first time, from confident and strong to cautious. She grasps the bar pole with both hands and slips off the bar. As Vicky thought, Defender is tall, at least two meters, and with her high heels, she is even that much taller. Defender's heels and earrings match both her sparkling gown and the chandelier above. Defender responds, "Yes, we know her."

Devin completes his journey around the bar and casually braces his back up against it. He places his glass down and comments, "Slippery one, that one."

Defender grasps the sleeve of Devin's jacket. "That explains a lot."

Defender looks at the three. Her expression has changed; it is something one cannot fully describe or pinpoint. It is as if something shifted in their relationship; she understands now more clearly that they, all five of them, are connected. She realizes that she not only needs to trust them more but also rely more on them. Now it is she who needs to find information. "What exactly did she tell you?" she demands.

Sensing that she should be honest, Vicky tells them all that she knows about Bridge. "She appeared on the *Tiqu-Qi* shortly after we completed our mission. She wanted to see the prisoners. Then she told us she was going to give us a gift. Somehow, it seems that she pointed us towards the *Liberty Crane*—"

Rikes, not able to contain himself, calls out, "What exactly is she?"

Defender stares her bright-green eyes into Rikes. "She is powerful!"

Vicky, admittedly confused, says, "She told me something I did not quite understand."

She pauses, hoping that not only could they reveal the mystery of what Bridge had told her, but that they also would. Vicky continues, "She said that she was a Singular and that they were very rare. She also said that I was an … Omni and that they are even rarer."

Defender and Devin take a moment to look at each other. Defender places her finger on her lower lip, "It's true," she says. "I'm a Singular, as well, and they are rare."

Then with the same finger, she points at Vicky. "And you, you're an Omni?" The pitch in her voice changes; it is evident that what Vicky had said has intrigued her and perhaps even confounded her to a certain degree.

Vicky nods. "Yes, and she said that there are only three that she knows of. I would be—"

Defender finishes her sentence. "Four, you would be the fourth."

Vicky moves in closer. "What does that mean?" she questions.

Defender recomposes herself. She explains; her tone is different, almost like a big sister explaining a family secret to her little sibling. "We," explains Defender, waving her hand loosely between herself and Devin, "we're not trying to be coy. There is just so much that we can tell you. The only reason we are telling you anything is that you got in here, a place meant not to be broken into! Still, there is only so much we can say without it being dangerous to you and to all your people."

Defender raises her hand toward the heavens and perhaps toward Bridge, as well. "However, if Bridge is involved, that makes things so much different. You see—"

Defender pauses, considering what she is about to say, knowing that, once said, she cannot remove it from existence. Defender continues, "You see, Bridge has been looking for acceptance her entire existence, and lately she has been teaming up with someone."

Vicky and Rikes nod. Vicky responds, "Yes, she did indicate that she was working for someone."

Devin steps forward. "That someone is trouble!"

Vicky looks at Devin. "More trouble than the Dictator?"

Defender answers for him. "Yes, more trouble than the two combined! And if Bridge's friend is involved, then he is working hand in hand with the Dictator."

Devin turns toward Defender. Vicky continues, regaining their attention, "I saw her again, an image of her, when I was aboard the *Liberty Crane*. She warned me not to take anything from the *Liberty Crane* back aboard the *Tiqu-Qi*."

Devin turns toward Vicky. "Bridge appeared to you? Only you?"

Vicky, uncertain of what he was asking, hesitantly responds, "Yes, well, Rikes was nearby, but he did not really see her. Why? Is that important?"

Devin raises both eyebrows and smiles. Vicky is uncertain if this smile is one of amusement or caution. Perhaps it is the smile one gives when they have figured out something of value; after Devin's response, she assumes it is the latter. "Well, she must like you," he states, "if she is going off script to help you."

Vicky considers his assessment.

Defender leans in toward Vicky, almost as if she was about to grab hold of her. "Did you do it?" she asks Vicky. "Are you certain that they did not remove anything, anything! From the *Liberty Crane*?"

Vicky responds with a reassuring "Yes, I left strict orders, in good hands." As soon as Vicky completes her sentence, a strange sense of insecurity falls over her.

Aboard the *Tiqu-Qi*, Lieutenant Minor exits the shuttlecraft and is met by Captain Reynolds. Captain Reynolds greets Lieutenant Minor, "It's good to have you back. We had some serious scrapes here that I'm sure I need to catch you up on."

Lieutenant Minor nods. "Very good, sir. Are you alright?"

Captain Reynolds waves his head from side to side, weighing the experience with the question, "Yes, for now. I trust that you have quite the story to report, as well."

Minor replies, "Yes, we must debrief in the conference room, ASAP."

Captain Reynolds replies, "Agreed."

Reynolds looks around. "Where is Lieutenant Young's shuttle?"

Minor very matter-of-factly states, "She went to explore the red planet. It would seem that it is what caused the *Liberty Crane* to be stranded. I will explain in the debriefing."

Dr. Davis walks up behind him carrying two cases. Minor glances over at Davis then at the two cases she is holding. He turns back toward Captain Reynolds. "First we need Dr. Shome." Captain Reynolds nods. "Very well."

Bringing his wrist communicator to his face, he presses the button. "Dr. Shome, meet me at the landing bay immediately."

Shome's voice responds, "Yes, sir."

The three hastened toward the door. No sooner than they reach it, Shome meets them. Turning to the captain, she responds, "Sir?"

Dr. Davis answers, "Shome, these are containers with blood samples from the crew of the *Liberty Crane*. Take them to our lab. We have five more cases aboard the shuttle."

"Yes, Doctor," replies Shome as she relieves the cases from Davis's hand, allowing Davis to return to the shuttle to retrieve the rest.

Defender stares intently into emptiness. She turns toward them and states, "I will be right back."

With that, she turns and hastens off to a door behind the bar. Rikes jerks forward and restrains himself from running after her, an instinctive move. Instead, he asks, "Where is she going?" Devin smiles and turns toward him. "She'll be back, she has to check on something."

There is a moment of awkward silence among Vicky, Rikes, and Pam. Devin, however, is perfectly calm as he takes a sip of his drink and very comfortably rests against the bar. Moments later, the door swings open; Defender rushes back in and lunges toward Vicky and grabs hold of her arm. Rikes places his hand over his sidearm. Even Devin is concerned and startled by Defender's sudden actions, evident by his reactions. He straightens up, his features changing from relaxed and almost carefree to serious and concerned. Defender calls out to them, "Listen, the Dictator is forming an army to regain power and destroy the Earth! Last time ... last time he underestimated Earth, this time he is taking no chances! You must go and stop him from recruiting his army before he becomes too powerful!"

Vicky pulls away, although she can sense truth and sincere concern in Defender's voice, Vicky cannot deflect her duty or deny her crew. Vicky snaps, "Perhaps we can do that, but first, we have to return to our ship!"

In space, sitting in their respective positions, sit the *Liberty Crane* and the *Tiqu-Qi*. Suddenly the *Liberty Crane* begins waving in both time and space as if it were being viewed from underwater. Then it is pulled into a bright small ball of light before it disappears completely from its position in space. Seconds later, the *Tiqu-Qi* follows suit. In less than a minute, both ships have vanished.

Back in Devin's lair, Defender gently yet firmly grabs hold of Vicky's shoulder. She stares deeply into Vicky's eyes. Defender shakes her head violently and gasps, "It's too late!"

Vicky moves back. Defender releases her hold. Vicky is determined to get an answer, yet a thick foreboding air drapes over her; her very bones can feel the damp chill of imminent danger. Not the danger of harm or even death, but a distinct sinister ugliness. A threat that had been dormant for way too long and now rises its great ivory teeth against all who have ever wronged it. Vicky's voice is low and coarse. "What do you mean it is too late?"

Understanding her tone, Defender tries to deescalate the situation. As calmly as she can, she states, "Your ship is gone. Both ships are gone."

Vicky shakes her head in disbelief, while Rikes desperately tries once again to reestablish communications between them and the *Tiqu-Qi*. Vicky defiantly asks, "Did they leave? How do you know?"

Vicky turns to Rikes. "Rikes, we have to return to the surface immediately!"

The three turn to leave. Defender raises her hand to stop them. She calls out, "They didn't leave. They disappeared!"

There is a certain desperation Vicky can detect in her voice, but it's not a selfish desperation. It is, however, a passionate desperation, similar to someone crying out to a small child who has wandered out onto thin ice. A cry to save her life, although they cannot venture out on the ice to save her, fearing that they would crack the ice themselves. They cry out to the child to return, to save herself! For at this point, only she can save herself. Vicky stops in her tracks, turns, and marches back to Defender. Vicky stares into her eyes; she cannot tolerate any more. "Enough is enough!" she demands. "What does that mean? I am tired of games! Explain yourself!" Vicky waves her hand high in the air. "All of this, or we are leaving."

Defender's eyes dart back and forth between the three. With sincerity and desperation, she pleads, "You have to trust me, you do not have a lot of time!"

Vicky looks over toward her comrades to gauge their thoughts; they both quietly nod in reply. Vicky turns her eyes, first to Devin, then to Defender. "Go on."

Defender places one finger out, "Bridge … Bridge is very powerful, but she does have her limits."

Defender turns toward Devin for help. "Devin?"

Vicky and her two companions focus their attention on Devin. Devin takes a deep breath. "Very well, I'm not very good at this … science stuff. When you said that Bridge warned you, well, I believe that it was sincere. Bridge is not entirely bad, just very misguided, and she usually leaves herself a way out. She would have to make some sort of physical connection between your ships, your people, and those on the *Liberty Crane*. And it has to be significant, a person or a strong symbol! Once the connection is made, she can complete her task."

Vicky confidently states, "But that is impossible, I strictly left instructions not to transport anything."

Defender corrects her, the same tone of a mother correcting a child when they were mistaken or misled by some peers. "But someone did!"

Vicky thinks for a moment; she turns toward Rikes. Rikes's expression dims as he considers the possibilities. He asks, "Ma'am, do you think?"

Vicky opens her eyes wide. "Blood?" she asks Rikes.

She turns toward Defender. "What about blood?" Vicky asks. "What if they brought blood over from the *Liberty Crane*, would that be enough?"

Devin, having great experience with the occult and matters of the spirit, states, "Blood? Blood is not only a physical representation, it is also a powerful symbol as well. Yes, blood will do!"

Rikes, trying to make sense of everything, asks, "What exactly does Bridge do?"

Pam, as if waking up from a dream, responds, at first low and softly, "She is a bridge."

Devin smiles and points at her. Pam continues with more confidence, "She brings worlds together!"

Devin jerks his finger forward. "Exactly!"

Defender, seizing this opportunity, realizing that Pam's simplistic description is so easy yet so overlooked, is just the open door she needs. Defender explains, "You have no history of the Dictator, let alone his defeat. That is because it happened in our dimension."

Rikes, with a glimmer in his eyes, asks, "Are you talking about transdimensional planes?"

Devin sincerely nods. "Yes."

Vicky turns toward Rikes for clarity. "Explain."

Rikes tries to form the words in his mind. "It is the butterfly effect. If you change one minor event in history, it changes the entire course of events, creating a paradox." With that, he turns toward Devin. "It is a theory at best!"

Vicky, slowly gaining understanding, looks at Defender. "Is that what's happening?"

Defender nods. "Yes, when the Dictator lost in this timeline, he sought after another, one in which he could defeat Earth."

Vicky, putting the puzzle pieces together, asks, "But how would that help him? He already failed."

Devin agrees, "True, but now Bridge was able to link both of our worlds together."

Defender asks, "Let me ask you, when your ship came to our solar system, was the jump different than other times?"

Vicky again glances over at Rikes, both of them knowing it was different. With her mouth open in both surprise and trepidation, Vicky turns toward Defender. "Yes," she replies. "Yes, it was."

Rikes continues for her. "The jump was very hard, our ship was almost destroyed!"

Devin points his finger and waves it at him; he turns and reaches across the bar to grab a bottle. When he turns back, he uses the bottle as a model as he explains. "That is because you not only jumped through space but through doors"—Devin forms his hands in an arch over the bottle—"into our dimension."

Defender looks over at Devin then toward Vicky. "You were passing through as it was, our dimension, but now Bridge was able to link you to us."

"Link?" asks Vicky. "You said that before, what exactly do you mean?"

Defender responds, "Link … connecting the two dimensions so that one could affect the other or …" Her words fall off.

Defender is a force to be reckoned with; her humanity is strong within her, but it was something recently unwrapped. Hidden deep inside her, it slowly emerges, mostly thanks to her relationship with Devin. At times like this, sparks of her humanity pierce through; Vicky notices the sparks as Defender's words drift away. Vicky asks, "Or what?"

Defender sobers herself. "Or worse!"

Vicky, now sensing the truth about her enemy, desires to know the full measure of the peril they face. She asks, "How could it get worse?"

Rikes jerks his head up as if he saw a ghost! He trembles as he says the next few words. "They could … could merge."

Defender feels the time slipping away; she must reach Vicky and her team, and she must do it now! Again, she pleads to Vicky, "Listen, I, too, am military. I will try to help you find your crew, but I need your help also."

Vicky understands missions; each member plays a vital part to complete their goals. Vicky needs to save her crew; she needs to know what she must do to save them! She tells Defender, "Go on."

Defender continues, "We"—she waves her hand loosely between her and Devin—"have to be very cautious. We cannot interfere too much, but we will help as much as we can."

Vicky has exhausted her patience. "Why can't you 'interfere'? Isn't this your dimension?"

Defender stares at Vicky for a moment before answering. "It may be our dimension, but not our time."

Vicky tilts her head. "I do not understand."

Pam timidly asks, "Could you please explain?"

Devin puts his glass down, causing a clanking sound. When Devin has their attention, he explains, "Something is wrong. I feel like ever since the Dictator started putting things into motion, I have been imprisoned in here for a very long time, too long!"

Defender agrees, "I feel the same thing. We were knocked off our natural course. If we move too much in this time, we could affect the timeline, causing another rip."

Vicky comprehends as best she can. Still determined to find out her part, she asks, "Alright, then what do we have to do?"

Defender waves her hand out. "As I said before, the Dictator is trying to recruit an army. Currently, he is set on abducting a very powerful agent, a queen! I need you and your team to aid her and liberate her and her people. They cannot join his side!"

The moral dilemmas and repercussions clog Vicky's thoughts. How can Vicky, a soldier in the UPA, act on an alien planet, let alone with alien royalty in conflict with an opposing alien planet? Defender, a military person herself, understands Vicky's dilemma. Before Vicky can respond, Defender advises, "Understand this, the only way to save your crew is to defeat the Dictator. Earth is in peril! Either stop him now, or Earth will have to deal with him later, after he has gained full power. You are not prepared! Realize this, it will not take his army weeks nor days to defeat you. No, your planet will be annihilated within minutes!"

Vicky is a realist; she rebuts, "I am not sure what we can even do, but if it means saving our crew, we will find a way. What are you going to do on your end?"

Defender straightens up. "I will find your people, and when I do, I will bring you to them."

Vicky straightens her body to full stature. If she is going to do this, she is going into it with the consent of her team. She looks toward Rikes first. Rikes nods. "Yes, ma'am."

Vicky acknowledges his consent and then looks toward Pam. She asks, "Cherut, is it? What do you decide?"

Pam looks down shyly for a moment. She looks back up at Vicky. "My mother called me Ruthie. I was thinking that I would like it if you called me Ruth, if that's okay."

Vicky smiles. "Of course … Ruth, what is your decision?"

Ruth looks at Defender and then at Devin then back to Vicky. "Yes!" she says in a soft voice, but a firm response. "We have to stop him! I'm in agreement."

Vicky puts her head down and takes a moment to absorb her responsibility and her resolve. Vicky straightens up and turns toward Defender and Devin. She takes in a deep breath. "Very well, we're in this together. But the shuttle." Vicky's eyes wander upward. "If we are going to an alien planet, it's not capable of traveling that distance. And with the *Tiqu-Qi* gone…"

Defender interrupts her, and with a smile on her face, she announces, "Don't worry, I already arranged a ride."

Vicky, Rikes, and Ruth all look over at Defender, their faces puzzled. In unison, they ask, "What?"

Chapter 10

Aboard the *Tiqu-Qi*, a wave of energy passes through the crew, causing a strong sensation of nausea. When the energy wave finally subsides, the crew is left lightheaded. Captain Reynolds braces himself against the doorpost of the bridge, shaking his head to regain his senses. He straightens up before entering. The door slides open, and as soon as he walks in, Reynolds is taken aback for a moment; the bridge is not his bridge! The once bright and white walls are now dull and gray. The room is huge, and there is commotion everywhere. Directly in front of the viewing porthole, he spies his old friend Wei. Wei also appears disoriented. He stands up, looking at the strangers aboard his ship.

Wei firmly grabs the arm of one of the strangers directly in front of him, a thin man with a well-trimmed beard and a stern face. Reactively, the man circles his arm, knocking Wei's arm away and releasing his grip. In the same motion, with his other hand, he pushes Wei into the controls. Wei quickly counters, maneuvering his weight into the man and pushing him back. The two face each other, ready for conflict. Captain Reynolds's voice hollers from across the room, "Wei!"

Simultaneously, Captain Barr's voice stops his lieutenant. "Lieutenant Lin!"

The room pauses as the two commanding voices echo throughout the chamber. For a moment, in all the confusion, there is a sense of calm. How does a lion know a tiger? There is a sense of confidence that demands respect; the two acknowledge each other. Although they have never met, they each recognize a fellow leader, a fellow captain when they see one. Captain Reynolds straightens his uniform and walks toward Captain Barr. Barr stands to greet the oncoming captain. The two face each other. Captain Reynolds starts off. "Sir, I am Captain Reynolds, captain of the *Tiqu-Qi*."

Captain Barr stares blankly at Reynolds for a moment before replying, "Captain Reynolds, pleased to make your acquaintance. I am Captain Barr of the *Liberty Crane*."

A strange sensation falls over Captain Reynolds, as if a vacuum within him pulled in his emotions. Startled, he takes in what Captain Barr said. Reynolds glances around; somehow, it makes sense. Still, he must know more. What has happened to his ship? What happened to his people, and what has happened to the *Liberty Crane*? How is any of this possible? "*Liberty Crane*," repeats Captain Reynolds.

He looks over toward Wei and motions with his hand for Wei to come close. He calls out to him, "Wei!"

Within moments, Wei is standing in front of both Captain Reynolds and Captain Barr. "Sir, yes sir," Wei replies.

Politely, Captain Reynolds looks at Captain Barr. Reynolds states, "This is my first navigational officer, Wei. He is probably the smartest person I know. Between us, we should be able to figure out what is going on."

Captain Reynolds looks toward Wei, and in the best whisper Reynolds can muster, he asks, "Do you know Moses's location?"

Wei raises his wrist communicator, without giving a second thought to whether it still works or not. He calls to Moses, "Moses?"

Moses replies, "Yes, sir! I'll be on the bridge as soon as I can find it … You are on the bridge, right?"

His voice seems frazzled, an emotion that Moses had rarely displayed in the past. In all the years that Captain Reynolds has known him, he only remembers one other time when Moses seemed frazzled. Wei responds, "Yes, I am here, and so is Captain Reynolds. We are trying to figure out what is going on."

Moses responds, "I'll be there momentarily."

Moses rises above the commotion, trying to gain his bearings. On the bridge, Wei looks back toward Captain Barr. Captain Barr raises his eyebrows and smiles. "Weel, this looks quite impossible."

Captain Reynolds nods. "Yes, sir."

Captain Barr continues, "This is obviously not my ship. Is this your ship? Is this the *Tiqu-Qi*?"

Reynolds shakes his head. "No, sir, not the *Tiqu-Qi* either!"

Something catches Barr's eye, and he scans the room. His expression changes as he ponders what he is seeing. He turns toward Lieutenant Lin. "Lieutenant, aren't many of these our people?"

Lin shakes his head. "Sir, yes sir! I see a lot of our crew, but … the uniforms have changed somehow … but they haven't."

Out of the corner of his eye, Wei notices Moses walking in. He calls Moses over to join them. As Moses walks over, Captain Barr looks at Captain Reynolds and states, "Sir, ah do not totally understand whit 'as happened, but ah hev an idea. Does yer ship hev a conference room?"

Captain Reynolds puts his hand on his chin and nods. "I believe we should."

Captain Reynolds looks toward Wei. "Wei, you and"—Captain Reynolds turns toward Lieutenant Lin—"Lieutenant Lin, correct?"

"Sir, yes, sir!" replies Lin.

"Very good," continues Captain Reynolds, respectfully looking toward Captain Barr for his consent. "If it's alright with you, sir."

Captain Reynolds then points to both Wei and Lin. "Can the two of you go to the main control? See if you can get a map of this ship. We may not know everything on this ship, but I'm pretty sure the ship does, and we need to be up to speed for whatever happens! Someone is messing with us, and we need to be prepared!"

Both Wei and Lieutenant Lin reply, "Sir, yes, sir!"

They rush off just as Moses arrives, catching only the end part of the conversation. Moses lets Captain Reynolds know that he is there. "Sir!"

Without saying a word, Captain Reynolds looks toward Moses and acknowledges him. In the same unspoken gesture, he lets Moses know that his presence is greatly appreciated.

Lieutenant Minor, like everyone else aboard the vessel, is uncertain where exactly he is. However, unlike everyone else, Lieutenant Minor is totally disoriented. He stands in a corridor. Soldiers and crewmen rush back and forth past him, yet he is alone! His head is spinning, and he is panting terribly. His thoughts are not his own; he can no longer control them. An overwhelming sense of panic engulfs him! He thinks to himself, *I cannot let anyone see me in this condition!*

Minor edges toward the wall as if he were blind, feeling along the wall, trying to escape peering eyes and judgment. He spies a door. His sweaty palms reach for the handle; the door is locked. Placing his back against it, he pushes down on the handle with all his weight, and with the strength of desperation, he jerks back, forcing the door to open with a clank.

Carefully scanning to make sure no one sees him, with his back still against the door, Minor slips in. He pushes the door closed and places his forehead against the cold metal, grasping large gulps of air to breathe. The coolness of the metal and the dim lighting of seclusion begin to calm him, and he breathes much easier. He thought he was alone until a strained-yet-familiar voice cracks the silence. "Well, look who came to join me."

Vicky, Rikes, and Ruth are all back on the surface, standing alongside Private Diamond. The harsh, bitter cold of space seems to have no effect on him. Vicky and Rikes are suited up as they wait for their ride. Even after all they have already been through, this is a lot for Vicky to comprehend. There is something nagging at Vicky, deep into the crevice of her mind, perhaps even into her heart. There is a strange feeling. It is the feeling of familiarity, the feeling of normalness. This is something that Vicky cannot explain, so she rejects it. Logic dictates that none of this is normal! It is like a transcendent splinter in her emotions. When she is not thinking about it, she forgets that it is even there. However, Vicky is waiting, and the wait allows her mind to wander and venture into areas that she usually can dismiss. Still, Vicky strives forward. There is a task at hand. She has to save her crew, her people. She stands firm and sets her mind and her heart systematically on the task ahead.

Her ability to focus returns once again, for in the distance, a hazy green light appears. It quickly grows as it draws closer. When it is a few thousand meters out, it is recognizable as some sort of spacecraft. It slows and begins to descend beside Vicky and her comrades. As it gets closer, they can make out the details of the ship. The design is very unique; although the craft is not very large, about the length of a bus, perhaps thirteen or fourteen meters long. It is glowing green, and the engine emits a bright-green exhaust. The ship itself is triangular shaped, large in the back, coming to a point in the front. However, on a side view of the ship, it is noticeably separated into three tiers: back, middle, and front. Each tier is a little over a meter lower than the tier behind it, giving it a three-stair-staircase appearance. Along both sides of the ship is a single thin band of light, also green, but so bright it appears to be whiter than it is green. As the craft lands, very little, if any, dust is blown off the side, as the vehicle seems to have no downward thrusters. Rikes considers the overall design of the craft; it is very alien. Its very movement and design seem like nothing he could imagine. In other words, Rikes cannot figure out how this craft is flying, let alone how it is able to move across the depths of space.

The ship lands, the cockpit opens, and a person emerges. He definitely seems human, much like Defender and Devin are. He is wearing a green space suit matching his ship's design. His helmet is elongated; not only does it covers the head, but it also overlaps part of his chest. He jumps down to meet them. A green light emitted inside his helmet allows for his face to be visible. He appears to be Caucasian, in his midthirties; he is clean-shaven with curly hair. The man seems friendly, with a pleasant large smile. Curiously, the four of them look at this man, waiting for him to make the next move. He speaks to them. "My name is Angel. I'm here to transport you, old friend of mine, to the *War Queen*."

Angel's voice pierces into their intercom effortlessly. Vicky, Rikes, and Ruth are all unaware that even Private Diamond was privy to hearing his voice, as well. Vicky and Rikes look toward each other, a bit more confused than a moment ago but willing to accept what is before them. Angel continues, "I have the capabilities to tow your craft and your robot, as well, if you desire. We have to go a little slower, but we should still get there pretty quickly. I can, however, take one person aboard my ship with me, if one of you would like to join me."

Many questions plague their minds; however, Vicky can feel it deep within her that this is not the time for the answers. Vicky steps up. "Sir, I assume you know who we are?"

He shakes his head. "Not entirely, so if you would do the honors—"

Angel leaves the floor open for Vicky to respond. Vicky is puzzled; she wonders how he could not know who they were and still be willing to chauffeur them across space with such great urgency. Vicky responds with great professionalism, "I am Lieutenant Young of the UPA, and this is Private Rikes, my communication officer. Behind him is Ruth."

Angel interrupts, his voice notably calmer than before. "Ruth? Yes, you I know."

Ruth is taken aback, not liking her notoriety. This is the second stranger to say that they know her. *What does all this mean?* she wonders to herself. Why do so many people know her? Why? What makes her so important? Her concerns lie heavily upon her. Her fears rise again—the fear that she may be more of a danger to her friends than an asset, as Lieutenant

Young had told her she was. She shakes it off. There is something about Lieutenant Young's confidence that inspires hope within her.

Vicky notices the change in his voice and decides to continue. As she continues, Angel redirects his attention to her, and his appearance changes back to the friendly large smile he once had. Vicky calmly corrects Angel, "And this robot is actually Private Diamond. He is one of my men."

Angel bends forward from the waist up, almost in a bow. "Please, my apologies!"

He looks up at the stature of Private Diamond. "I meant no disrespect."

Angel pauses for a second. He looks up as if trying to see something in the distance. Then he turns toward Vicky. "You are from Earth?" he asks.

Vicky replies, "Yes, we are from the UPA."

Angel again cuts her off. "Sorry. So sorry. What year is it?"

Now the depth of their confusion falls further down to an even-deeper level of confusion. Rikes looks over at Vicky, dumbfounded, as Vicky very matter-of-factly states, "The year is 2312."

Angel straightens up. He blinks a few times before turning to Private Rikes and playfully slapping him on the arm. "So it has begun, hasn't it? The Dictator is finally making his move!"

Angel's voice sounds like a trumpet. "Time is of the essence. We best be on our way!"

His voice then returns to its normal excited pitch. "Who is joining me?"

Angel presents his craft by swinging his hands out, as a model would present a prize. Vicky knows that Private Rikes would love the opportunity to travel in this unique alien spacecraft and to converse with this equally unique alien being. She looks at Rikes. "You can go."

Rikes tries to control his excitement and appreciation. "Ma'am? Yes, ma'am!"

Before Rikes can move, she firmly reminds him, "Make sure to keep communications open the entire voyage."

Rikes replies, "Yes, ma'am!"

Then, without hesitation, he follows Angel up the stairs to the cockpit. Before entering the shuttle, Vicky walks over to Private Diamond. She places the palm of her hand just a few centimeters from the bottom of his chest plate. Vicky calls to him, "Private Diamond, do you understand that they are going to tow you? I am confident that you will be safe … all communications will remain open. If there is any problem, any discomfort, contact us."

Vicky's communication vibrates on her wrist. She presses the side of her helmet, and the text is displayed on her visor. The text says, "Yes, ma'am."

Vicky looks down for a second then back up at Private Diamond. She gives him a comforting smile then turns toward the shuttle and enters it with Ruth.

Minutes earlier

Aboard the shuttle, Rikes carefully maneuvers them up the shaft that was made by Ruth. Unable to sit, Vicky stands next to him, leaning over the controls. Directly behind Private Rikes, to Vicky's left, stands Ruth. Rikes, without moving his eyes from the controls, watches carefully the three-dimensional computer rendering of the shuttle as it ascends the treacherous, jagged terrain. Rikes asks Vicky, "Do you trust them? Do you trust Defender?"

Vicky stares out the portal, watching the wall of melted metal slip down as they rise. She nods. "I do. For some strange reason, I do. And I feel that we have to move quickly." She turns toward Rikes. "I also understand that knowing too much could be dangerous, so I am allowing for some leniency, for now. However, I do think the more we know, the more equipped we will be."

"Ma'am?" asks Rikes.

Vicky continues, "Any information we get from here on, we use. There's nothing off the table! If we ask and get an answer, we share the information."

Ruth nods. Vicky turns toward Ruth. "And you, what sense do you make out of all this?"

A strange expression comes over Ruth. She never thought she would be treated as a peer, as something more than just a weapon! Someone with values, with opinions, as a person. She appreciates how Vicky and Rikes see her; she knows that it is sincere. Ruth is also beginning to accept it as normal and, therefore, accepting herself as normal. Ruth responds, "It is like you said, Lieutenant Young. I feel a strange sense that we should trust them. I can't explain it. I did not feel this sense of trust aboard the *Tiqu-Qi* like I do now."

Vicky nods, turning back to Rikes. "Rikes, and you?"

Rikes continues to monitor their ascent. He responds, "Ma'am, with all due respect, I trust no one but you and Captain Reynolds."

He glances back at Ruth for a quick second. "And, Ruth, I trust you. I would give my life for you." Ruth blushes and tries to hide her smile. Rikes continues, "Therefore, if you trust them, I trust them."

Again, Vicky nods. "Very good."

Now

As the canopy closes over Private Rikes and Angel, Rikes checks his communications with Lieutenant Young. "Lieutenant Young, do you read?"

Vicky responds, "Yes, over!"

Angel turns to Rikes. "Get ready, here we go!"

Angel presses the ignition; there is a slight hum of engines, but again not the same fire and rumbling usually heard from a ship lifting off the ground. He raises the landing gear, and the ship rises with barely a bump. Rikes cannot control himself from looking over the sides as he views the shuttlecraft and Private Diamond getting smaller on the surface of the planet below. Angel again looks over toward Rikes. "Now we will engage the first tow. We will tow the shuttle."

Angel waves his finger over a screen, and a digital image of the two ships and Private Diamond appears. With the same finger, he draws a line down from his ship to the shuttle. The image on the screen matches his movement and places a circle around the shuttle. He double-taps his finger on the image of the shuttle. A green light shoots out from the bottom of his ship to the shuttle below. Soon, the shuttle is encased in a glowing surge of energy. Aboard the shuttle, both Vicky and Ruth look around as they notice that the outside of their shuttle is lit bright green! Although the outside of their shuttle is covered in this glowing green light, they are still able to see out past the light.

Soon, the shuttle is lifted off the ground. Angel carefully monitors the transaction. As soon as he sees that the shuttle is locked, he turns toward Rikes and confirms, "The shuttle is locked! Now let's get Private Diamond."

Angel turns back toward the controls. Rikes cannot help himself from staring out the side of the ship like a little boy looking through a toy-store window, amazed at everything he sees. Although in the twenty-fourth century they have attempted magnetic towing, ships are never towed from such a vast distance from each other; the shuttle is almost twenty meters away from Angel's ship. This technology is far beyond what Rikes can comprehend. Angel again looks toward Rikes. "Now for Private Diamond."

On his screen, Angel draws a line from the shuttle to Diamond. He taps it once, and a circle appears around the image of Diamond. With the second tap, the energy field surrounding the shuttlecraft extends itself and wraps around Private Diamond until he is also engulfed by its energy. When Vicky sees that Private Diamond is now attached, as well, she calls out to him, "Private Diamond, are you okay?"

Within a second, on her wrist communication, Diamond texts, "Yes, ma'am."

The red planet begins to shrink before Rikes's eyes as they lift higher into empty space.

Angel turns his head to Rikes and smiles. "Welcome aboard *Green Lightning*. Fasten your seat belts. We're about to go!"

Chapter 11

In the newly found conference room sits Captain Reynolds, Captain Barr, Wei, Moses, Jacob Miller, Lieutenant Lin, and Doctors Shome, Davis, and Lanthrop from the *Liberty Crane*. The room is large; in the center of the room is an elongated oval table with either end cut flat. In the very front of the table, on the wall, is a large screen. Both Captain Reynolds and Captain Barr decided not to sit at the very head so as not to indicate that one was in charge over the other. Rather, seeking equality, they decided to sit at the two front-most chairs across each other. On the right sits Captain Reynolds, with Wei immediately next to him. Wei has gathered a collection of charts. Next is Moses followed by Jacob Miller. On the left sits Captain Barr; next to him, Lieutenant Lin and Dr. Lanthrop. Lanthrop is a pudgy Caucasian man with a shaggy long gray mustache. He is balding, and his eyes seem tired and unapproachable. He has been an expert in his field for over thirty years. Captain Reynolds, as usual, starts off by looking toward Wei, "Wei, show us what you found."

Wei responds, "Sir." He stands up from his seat, placing the jumble of charts on the table before him, takes one large chart in hand, and proceeds toward the front. As he walks to the front, he points his finger toward Lieutenant Lin and explains, "Lieutenant Lin and I have researched as best we could. We are having some trouble utilizing all the technology aboard this ship, but I think we figured out what is going on." When Wei comes to the front, he spreads out a map of the ship. Moses rises from his seat, and as Wei tries to hold the map down as best he can, with both Barr and Reynolds trying to hold the ends of it down, Moses taps Wei on the shoulder. Wei gives him his attention as Moses places an adhesive disc on the front wall. He takes the map, and then he and Wei place it up on the wall. With great gratitude, Wei thanks him. "Thank you, Moses."

Moses humbly steps to the side and hovers behind Wei's chair, waiting to see if Wei needs any further assistance. Wei continues, pointing to the map. "As you see on this map, it would seem that everything that we had on the *Tiqu-Qi* and everything on the *Liberty Crane* is still intact. Some of it fused together, anything that did not overlap remained more or less the same." Captain Reynolds, ever impatient, speaks up, "So what does this all mean?"

Lin stands, trying to answer Captain Reynolds' query. He picks up from where Wei left off. "The two ships have come together into one. Even our uniforms are a mixture of both designs!" Wei continues, pointing back to the ship's schematics. "From our best calculations, the ship is approximately 20 percent larger than what the *Liberty Crane* was but almost half the weight it was. It seems that most of the steel was replaced with our plastic composites, allowing the ship to be considerably lighter overall."

Captain Barr's face frowns as he tries to make sense of everything. Finally, he looks up and slams his hand on the table. He questions, "Ur we able t' maneuver?"

Miller raises his hand. "Hi, I'm Jacob Miller, head engineer. Well, I have conferenced with your engineers, and well, from the engineering, we have some compromise. The engines have somehow become a form of nuclear fission." Miller looks toward Captain Barr. "Was your ship nuclear-powered?"

Barr stares blankly then adjusts his position in his seat before responding, "Aye, eh main source of power is nuclear…" Barr nervously looks around. Then trying to justify himself he replies, "Thir wis no way t' support eh power we needed t' move tis ship in-t' space."

Jacob looks toward Captain Reynolds and confesses, "It seems stable for now, but it is a highly dangerous source of energy. And there is more."

"Spit it out!" demands Captain Reynolds.

Miller continues, "Well,…also, it seems like our solar-power capabilities have been cut in half, but for the most part, even at half, it is enough to maintain life support and most functions aboard the entire ship."

Barr puts his head in his hand and shakes it woefully. "How is any of this possible?"

Captain Reynolds, never willing to give in to defeat, asks the question everyone is afraid to ask. "Wei, is this ship able to take us home?"

Wei shakes his head. "It will take us a while to figure out the mechanics. I'm not sure exactly how the *Liberty Crane* was able to get out here, nor are the engineers from the *Liberty Crane* able to understand our ski method."

Captain Reynolds slams his fist into the table. "And what about Lieutenant Young? Has anyone thought about how to rescue her? I have a policy of no crew member left behind, and by God, that includes Lieutenant Young!"

Moses quietly puts his head down. Wei shakes his head. Somberly he responds, "We are working on that."

Reynolds continues, pointing to Captain Barr. "As Captain Barr said, how is any of this possible? Any clue as to how all this impossibility is possible?"

Wei looks at Lieutenant Lin for a moment then back at Captain Barr and finally at Captain Reynolds. "No, sir. That part we have not figured out yet."

Captain Reynolds takes a deep breath and looks toward Dr. Shome. "Doctors, anything to report?"

Dr. Davis speaks up. "Well, oddly enough, all the mineral deficiencies of the crew aboard the *Liberty Crane* vanished as soon as our two ships became one. Everyone seems healthy."

Dr. Lanthrop chimes in. "Yes, I examined our people. They all seem fine."

Captain Reynolds looks down. "We need to get our minds together, figure this out!" He scans the room. Frustrated, he yells out, "And Minor? Where is Lieutenant Minor anyway?"

At first, the darkness gave Lieutenant Minor comfort, but now the fear of the unknown causes Minor to search for the light switch. Frantically, he runs his hands along the wall. Minor finds the switch; the electrical-supply room lights up. Lieutenant Minor discovers his roommate, still cuffed to his hospital gurney, Dr. Long. He is sitting up, patiently waiting for Lieutenant Minor. Long sees his opportunity; it is obvious that Minor did not enter here to find him. In fact, he is sure that Minor did not even know he was in there. Something has changed; the room has somehow grown larger. Long cannot explain it, but he is sure that not only the room expanded but also the electrical equipment even changed in appearance. This is his opportunity; he knows that Minor is on edge, grasping at mental straws. Minor's mental state is on the verge of collapse. Even Dr. Long did not realize how devious he could be in times of desperation. He discerns that he must handle this correctly, carefully. Although Minor is in a stressed mental state, he is no dummy. Long knows that Minor will see through his ploy, but hopefully, he can sell it enough that, regardless, he will still agree to help him. "It seems like fate has brought us together, good Lieutenant Minor," lures Dr. Long.

Minor's eyes squint in cynicism. Minor knows that he is being challenged, and it is a good diversion from his fears. It allows him to focus his thoughts once again. "What exactly do you want, Dr. Long?" Minor asks callously.

Long smiles. "Let's cut to the chase, Lieutenant Minor. This room has changed right before my eyes, as if by magic! I don't believe in magic, so this must be something more. I assume the rest of the ship has changed also? Am I correct? What is happening, Lieutenant Minor?"

Minor straightens himself up, as if getting ready for a fight. "Yes," he replies, "yes, the entire ship has changed. I'm not sure exactly what happened. It is different." He looks down for a moment then back up toward Long. Minor's face is not as stern as a moment ago; in fact, his expression is one of confusion, like a child looking for answers in a strange, scary world. He finishes his thought, his voice seeming to drift away. "Yet familiar at the same time."

Dr. Long's maniacal laugh cuts through the emptiness of Minor's words and bounces tauntingly off the walls. Minor, vexed by his reckless laughter in such a dire situation, asks him, "What is so funny?"

Again, Long smiles. "Good, Lieutenant, this is your opportunity."

Minor again squints his eyes in skeptical confusion. Long continues, "Your opportunity to shine, to lead, of course!"

Minor frowns. "What are you talking about?"

Long explains, "I've heard whispers from my bed. I've seen things in the sick bay. Whatever is happening here, does it have something to do with that distressed ship?"

Minor looks at him, blank-faced. Long continues, "I thought so. You know I have more expertise on alien life-forms than anyone in China, let alone aboard this ship. It has always been my desire to prove life on other planets. I have studied the theories and possibilities for many years. Imagine if you were to use me to help solve the mystery of what's going on here, and we did it together. You would be a hero! People would remember you as the person who saved everyone!"

Minor rebuttals, "I am sure that our other doctors are—"

Long interrupts, "Shome and Davis? Please, they were my assistants. In no way are either of them near as qualified as I!"

Lieutenant Minor displays a cold smile. "This has been fun, but as I told you before, I do not think working with a criminal—which you are—is wise. Having said that, I need to go find the bridge."

Minor turns and walks toward the door. Quietly, in almost a whisper, as if he were talking to himself, Long states, "I'm sure you are right. I'm so ashamed of the things that I've done, and I am sure that Lieutenant Young would have made the same decision."

Minor's brain curls in a cramp. He pauses for the slightest of moments. Without meaning to, he pauses just long enough that Dr. Long notices it. Long knows that he got under his skin. With a deep breath, Minor reaches out to grab hold of the handle that leads back to the corridor. Suddenly his wrist communicator buzzes. Lieutenant Minor responds, "Sir, yes, sir."

Captain Reynolds's voice bellows from the other end, "Minor, where in the world are you? We are all in the conference room. Please find your way here immediately!"

Lieutenant Minor attempts to reply "sir," but the communication is cut off.

His head boils; his emotions overflow. His thoughts race out in his head. *How dare they talk to me like that? Reynolds may be the captain of the ship, but I am the military leader aboard this ship! My position alone should demand respect!* He turns toward Dr. Long and walks abruptly toward him, stopping directly in front of his bed. Minor looks down at Long. "You know, what you said is correct. If I don't take matters into my own hands, I will never get the respect I deserve. I will take you up on your offer. I will free you, temporarily, under my custody. You will help me find out what is going on, and we will save these people."

Minor grabs hold of the gurney's railing poles to pull Dr. Long out of the supply room. Before Minor can move him, Long forewarns him, "Before we go, I would need some clothes. I cannot go around in a hospital gown."

Annoyed and impatient, Minor replies, "Yes, yes, of course, of course."

Minor pulls the gurney toward the door. He then steps out in front, opens the door, and pulls Long through into the corridor. Although there is still commotion in the corridor, the atmosphere is calmer. Like a boiling pot of water when the heat is lowered and the water settles to a simmer. Now that most of the combined crew has a job to do, the commotion of ten minutes earlier is replaced by intense busyness. They now have focus and purpose in their lives once again. Even if every answer is not yet answered, at least for now they know what to do.

One of the soldiers is quickly passing by. He is young, barely twenty if that, of large stock with army-cut blond hair and lake-blue eyes. His features are definitely from a time past, before the solar wars. Minor stops the soldier. "Soldier!"

Immediately recognizing an officer, the soldier stands at attention. "Sir, yes, sir!"

Lieutenant Minor orders him, "Stop what you're doing for the moment. Somebody took this soldier's uniform and handcuffed him to this bed. Take him to the sick bay, remove the handcuffs, and bring him a new uniform."

"Sir, yes, sir!" replies the soldier.

"Then escort him to the conference room!" commands Minor.

Minor looks around, still unfamiliar with his new surroundings. He asks, "Soldier, which way is the conference room?"

"Sir!" replies the soldier. "Would you like for me to escort you there first?"

Minor replies, "Negative, just point me in the right direction."

The soldier replies, "Sir, yes, sir!" He points forward. "Follow this corridor to the end, and then turn left. At the end, you will see the conference room."

Minor nods. "Thank you, soldier. Carry on."

The soldier quickly takes a firm grip around the gurney's railings and pulls Dr. Long toward the sick bay. Lieutenant Minor walks off to find the conference room.

The soldier leads Dr. Long down into the sick bay and looks around for the key. Confused, the soldier asks, "Sir, sorry, sir, do you know where I could find the key? Perhaps I could ask the captain or Lieutenant Lin?"

Tricking Lieutenant Minor was no easy task; however, Dr. Long did not want to take his chances to alert any of the other crew members, especially not Captain Reynolds or whoever this Lieutenant Lin was. Long responds quickly, "No, no, that's all right. Give me a second." Long looks around the room, then a sign over the door at the far end of the room catches his attention. Long points toward the door. "Take me to that room."

The soldier rushes him across the room to the door at the far end. The doorway label reads, "Operating Room." Long looks up at the soldier. "Bring me in there."

"Sir, this is the operating room," he replies.

Dr. Long impatiently responds, "Yes, yes, I know. Wheel me in."

As they enter, the lights automatically turn on. Long quickly surveys the room. He points with his finger, directing the soldier, "Bring me closer, over there."

The soldier obediently and carefully maneuvers the doctor over to a computer attached to a metal arm. The arm is connected to various electrical equipment, all of which is unfamiliar to the young soldier, yet Dr. Long has already identified it. Dr. Long throws his legs over the side of the bed and sits up. He examines the equipment. He grabs hold of the computer and states, "I think I can figure this out."

The doctor quickly flips some switches, turning the machinery on. The room lights up with an array of lights, mostly either red or yellow. However, Long cannot log into the computer. Embarrassed yet with no other option, he turns to the soldier. "Sir," he asks, "do you know how to access the computer?"

The soldier considers his question. "I'm not sure," he says. "I can try."

The soldier straightens up, clears his throat, and calls out to the computer, "Computer, this is Corporal Andreas Wilson of the *Liberty Crane*, requesting access."

The computer chimes for a second then responds, "Corporal Wilson, recognized. Access granted."

The computer screen opens, and Long's eyes widen. Within moments, he is able to access the surgical saw. He carefully runs his finger over the screen and maneuvers the machine into place. Then the computer initiates the test run. A white light shines down from the screen on the top to the platform below. As best he can, Dr. Long stretches his arm from the bed railing and places it under the ray. Another second later, the image of his arm appears on the computer screen. Using a surgical pen, he carefully draws a line on the image on the screen from the top of the cuff to the bottom. Confirming the action, a laser shoots from the top. A moment later, the cuff is cut open, and Long's hand is finally freed. Corporal Wilson is impressed. "Sir, are you okay?"

Long nods. "Yes, this surgical laser will only cut what I indicate on the screen. It cut through the cuff without damaging even one hair on my arm."

Wilson smiles and nods in appreciation of Dr. Long's knowledge of the equipment and the great technology they possess. While Dr. Long relishes his own achievements, Wilson remembers that he had one more assignment to complete. He turns toward Dr. Long. "Sir, I will go to retrieve a uniform for you now."

Wilson turns to complete his task, while Dr. Long looks at his arm and basks in his freedom. Suddenly an eerie voice invades Long's head. At first, he is not sure if it is his own thoughts or something else. The voice definitely does not seem like his own; it is raspy and determined. The voice in his head tells him—nay, it commands him, as if it were because of him—for Dr. Long to obey without question! The voice commands, "Ask for an airman's uniform."

Long involuntarily shakes his head, as if he were drugged and trying to recover from the sensation. Before he knows what he is doing, he calls out to Wilson, "Soldier!"

Wilson had just exited the operating room when Long calls to him; he pauses, turns around, and enters back in. Wilson faces Dr. Long, "Sir, yes, sir?" he asks, waiting for his next order.

Regaining his senses, Long looks around to see if someone were talking to him. Again, the voice is heard in his head, echoing through his emotions. His mind races. *Is there someone else in the room?* he asks himself. It is something possessive; it calls out to him even stronger than before. It is something he must do! Again, the voice commands, "Ask for an airman's uniform." Then, as if a light turned on in his head, Long turns toward Wilson, who is already standing at attention next to him. Long stares into Corporal Wilson. Long is focused, yet his eyes still seem far away, as if he were standing at the end of a long tunnel. He commands Wilson, "I need an airman's uniform."

Wilson is taken aback for a moment. He assumed that only the crew from the *Liberty Crane* had the title "airmen" and that the crew from the *Tiqu-Qi* had "pilots." (How and why he knew this, he did not know.) If the soldier before him was from the *Liberty Crane*, he is certain that he would have recognized him. However, Corporal Wilson understands to some extent that things have changed and that there are personnel aboard he does not recognize. His obedience kicks in, and he responds, "Sir, yes, sir! Sir, are you an airman?"

Dr. Long looks away and frowns, searching his thoughts, almost as if he were trying to remember if he was, indeed, an airman. He turns toward Wilson and, with a slight nod, responds, "Yes, yes, I am."

Wilson returns the nod and rushes off to retrieve the uniform for him.

Meanwhile, Lieutenant Minor enters the conference room. After a few minutes of debriefing, Minor is as informed as everyone else on the bridge. Captain Reynolds is concerned, and his face shows it. Consulting Lieutenant Minor, he states, "Our first order of business is to try to reunite with Lieutenant Young. We've tried everything. Miller even suggested sending out probes deep in space to increase our communication range. As of yet, we still have lost all communication with her. And on top of it all, we are not even in the same solar system we were in moments ago!"

Wei turns his chair to join the conversation. Wei elaborates, "It appears that we are in the same galaxy, however, even deeper in than we were before, next to yet another solar system." Captain Reynolds nods in acceptance. "Our engines are off to conserve power. We are basically drifting in space. Until we acquire our strategy and form a plan, there is no need to move from where we are. We might actually end up further from where we need to be. After finding Lieutenant Young, honestly, our next course of action will be to get us home. However, we are waiting on the doctors, Wei, Lieutenant Lin, Miller, and whoever else to try to decipher exactly what home is! As for now, all of us are still uncertain."

Wei picks up the conversation. "There are a few theories, but none of them can completely explain what is going on."

Agitated, Wei shakes his head and puts his fist in his hand. "There is something that we're missing! Some unexplained thing! And even now, our best theories are just that. This is beyond any known science. We have entered into the realm of the unknown."

For some strange reason, Lieutenant Minor has a calmness about him. Perhaps it is that the situation is so overwhelming that the depth of it evades him. Perhaps the lack of knowledge detours his very senses, forbidding him to even comprehend the extreme peril that they are all in. Or even still, it might be that the possibility of Lieutenant Young being lost forever gives him great comfort.

Suddenly the room turns red with flashing lights and a wailing alarm. Captain Reynolds stands up and calls to Barr, "Barr, what is this?"

Barr, Lin, and Wei check the monitors. Wei expands the screen, and the three nervously babble about the data. Wei turns to Captain Reynolds and ushers him to go closer. Captain Reynolds moves in, looking over Wei's shoulder. "What is it?" he asks.

Wei quickly transfers the image on the screen before them to the large main portal. With the computer image of the solar system displayed, Wei explains, "It would seem that we are directly in the path of this solar system's asteroid belt."

Captain Reynolds nods. "Do you mean something similar to the one between Mars and Jupiter?"

Wei responds, "Yes, sir, very similar."

Captain Reynolds asks, "Can we maneuver around it?"

Lin addresses Captain Reynolds, "Captain, it is difficult. It is over 150 million miles across! Our best bet is to fly forward, towards the planet ahead of us."

Captain Barr queries, "Dae we hev enough time?"

Wei responds, "I believe so."

Lin responds, "We actually have been drifting through its path. It is just that the asteroids are so far apart that we haven't encountered any yet. The alarms sounded because the long-range scans indicated that two of the bigger pieces are coming directly towards us. If we follow our plan, we should be fine."

Wei turns toward Captain Reynolds. "Sir, get Jacob online! We need the engines up and running!"

Captain Reynolds immediately hails Jacob Miller on the intercom. "Miller, fire up the engines. We're moving!"

Miller, from the engine room, responds, "Sir, I figured. We are already on standby."

Within moments, the engines are fired, and Lin and Wei help to maneuver the ship out of the path of the oncoming threat. They move forward at full power. The ship jerks and rumbles, shaken by the power of its engines. The ship is fast, much faster than either Lin or Wei expected. Soon, they are in the orbit of yet another unidentified planet. The planet is gray and ominous. Although it has an atmosphere, it does not seem to have any water or vegetation, just gray rock. The navigational rockets kick in, stabilizing them. Similar to the bridge aboard the *Liberty Crane*, there is also a back portal aboard this newly formed ship. The portal is an oblong convex glass about half the size of the main portal. No sooner do they stabilize the ship when the asteroid belt comes into view. They watch as the asteroids fly by; it is a magnificent sight. Wei and Lin, however, spend every moment reviewing the data and plotting the next move. Captain Barr also checks the data on his handheld device, occasionally looking over the shoulders of Lin and Wei, contributing to their discussion. At a leisurely glance, it would seem as if Captain Reynolds were enjoying the asteroid show. However, his mind is always on his ship and on the crew! He is trying his best to prepare them for whatever will come next, and he knows that something is coming! He and Jacob are in constant communication. Jacob Miller is on assignment from Captain Reynolds. Between helping Wei and Lin with the ship's navigation, he also has various crew members examining the designs and functions of this newly formed ship. This information allows Captain Reynolds to know what this ship is capable of and what it is not capable of. When they finally form a plan of action, he will know the best way for them to execute their plan. After a few minutes, the warning lights turn off. It would seem that they are safe. Reynolds glances over at Barr. "So back to business," he states.

Barr replies, "Aye."

Barr and Reynolds both move behind Wei and Lin, planning their next move. Just then, the red emergency lights flicker, like a light with a loose wire. Curiously, they look first up at the lights then at one another. They all turn cryptically and peer out the back portal. From behind the orbit of the gray planet emerge two of the asteroids. These must be two of the larger, if not the largest, ones in the belt. The first one takes a moment to come fully into view. It is about a fourth the size of the Earth's moon. The second one, just mere meters behind it, is about half the size of the first. It would seem that the gravitational pull between the two and between the gray planet has been affecting its course with each pass. The two large asteroids are pulled closer to the planet and to each other. Unfortunately for the crew of the *Tiqu-Qi* and the *Liberty Crane*, this is the impact event when the two asteroids collide. The smaller asteroid pulls toward the planet and collides. As it is deflected deeper into the belt, it scrapes alongside its larger brother. The larger asteroid seems to not move from its trajectory. However, although it continues its orbit within the belt, it does change positions, as the enormous asteroid begins to spin. Fragments shoot out toward the planet and toward their ship!

Wei stands to his feet and, aggressively into the intercom, announces, "Brace for impact!"

The red lights and the warning sirens cry out. Captain Barr commands Lin, "Lin, evasive maneuvers!"

Lin responds, "Sir, yes, sir!" Lin and Wei fire the rockets, trying to outrun the oncoming projectiles. Many of the asteroid fragments pierce into the atmosphere of the planet adjacent to them. As they burn through the atmosphere, the fiery streaks shoot down to the planet's surface. Soon, the crew hears ominous tapping as the asteroids rain past them. For the most part, Lin and Wei are successful in avoiding some of the larger fragments. After a tense few minutes, they manage to rest their ship on the far side of the planet. It would seem that the threat, once again, is over. Captain Reynolds commands, "Wei, get Jacob, assess any damage."

Wei responds, "Yes, sir!" Wei hails Miller on the intercom. "Miller, assessments!"

Miller responds, "We are checking. The preliminary assessments so far, we are not reading any major damage." Captain Reynolds motions for Moses to go near. Moses, who has patiently been waiting, is ever ready to help his captain and the crew. One of Moses's greatest strengths is to discern when to move and when to wait. Moses moves in closer. Captain Reynolds directs him, "Moses, gather a crew, and search the entire ship, starting from the interior hull and then working your way to each department." Captain Reynolds looks toward Lieutenant Lin. "Lin, see if you can link his camera to your computer so that, if there's any damage, he can send us the imagery. Also, connect him to the other people on his crew so they can send him images of any damage they find."

Lin responds, "Sir, yes, sir!" Lin turns toward Moses. "Moses, use code 23. I will make that an open link."

Moses responds, "Got it!" Moses hastens out of the door. As the door closes, Moses's voice echoes as he gathers soldiers and crewmen alike. Wei accesses the exterior cameras, flashing quickly, scanning the surface of their ship for any visible damage. Optimistically, the images seem well; the exterior of the ship has surprisingly little damage with just a few visible scrapes made by the asteroids.

Miller's voice comes back over the intercom. "Wei, so far no damage." He pauses. "Wait a minute."

Wei cries out, "What is it?" Reynolds, Barr, and Lin listen intently. After what seems like a long period of background chatter between

Miller and the other engineers, Jacob responds, "Wei, do me a favor. Do you have access to the ship's surface diagnostic cameras?"

Wei nods. "Yes, I do."

Miller states, "Check sections S5 through S12!"

Wei looks toward Lin; Lin nods and punches up the image of the cameras onto the main screen. As Lin works, Wei asks Miller, "Miller, what's going on?"

Miller, still consulting with the other engineers, responds, "For some reason, we're starting to show an energy deficiency in some of our systems. It is almost as if there were a leak in the energy supply. Nothing major, but still, if it continues like this, we could be in some trouble. I want to check the solar panels to make sure they are intact."

The entire bridge scrutinizes the images as they appear on the screen. As Lin searches the different angles, two large solar panels seem to be obstructed. The panels are designed to angle themselves and rotate toward the strongest energy source. The two center panels, the main panels, are pointed upward at an 80 percent angle. Not only is their ability to absorb energy in this position almost nil, but they are also obstructing the view from the surrounding panels. Wei asks Lin, "Can we get around—" Before Wei can finish speaking, Lin, anticipating his question, nods and responds, "Yes, yes."

On-screen, the next camera angle reveals a large fragment wedged in the hydraulics between the two main panels. One of the four main cylinders is severely damaged. The column is bent and ripped open by the force of the asteroid. It is bleeding thick gel as the hydraulic fluid freezes from the bitter cold of space. Large cables are severed, shooting sparks. Some sparks are powerful enough to scorch the surrounding metal. Wei shakes his head and looks toward both Captain Reynolds and Captain Barr; the room is silent. Wei calls out to Miller, "Miller, Miller, are you seeing this?"

Miller views the image Wei transferred to him on his wrist communicator. Miller, without a sound, glances at the other engineers. He then adjusts the feed to a 3D image so that they all can view it. Simultaneously, they breathe in heavily. Over the intercom, Wei repeats himself, "Miller, Miller, can you see it?"

Assistant Engineers Lui and Johnson walk closer to the image to examine the problem. Miller clears his voice before answering Wei and the others on the bridge who are anxiously waiting for his response.

Miller feared the problem before he saw it; the visual was just the confirmation. Captain Reynolds's voice interjects, "Jacob, how bad is it? Can we function without them?"

Miller responds calmly, trying not to worry them, yet he is direct, like a doctor giving a family bad news. "Captain," he replies, "if this problem is for a day or two, we should be good. However, longer than that, I'm not sure. We do not know the inner workings of this ship nor how the power inputs and outputs work. On top of that, as you know, the *Liberty Crane*'s main power source is nuclear, while ours is an energy conversion system. I cannot tell how the two are now working together. I'm concerned that if we lose our solar power completely, which for right now is supplying over 50 percent of the ship's main functions, and we have to resort to the mixture of the nuclear and our energy conversion system, it could be disastrous."

The crew aboard the bridge all look at one another in despair. At this moment, Captain Reynolds longs for Lieutenant Young's leadership. She has the innate ability to see the problem yet to see past it, to see the need for a solution before the need for worry. He wonders to himself, *Where is Lieutenant Young now?*

Chapter 12

Vicky stands aboard the shuttle, amazed as she peers out the portal. Similarly to when driving down the road on a long trip, the trees seem to zip by, but the images in the distance seem almost to stand still; this is called a motion parallax. However, as Vicky is flying through space, towed by Angel's *Green Lightning* ship, the stars are moving! Some stars disappear, and other stars appear. Vicky, mesmerized by the spectacle before them, turns toward Ruth. Vicky gently taps her on the shoulder to get her attention. "Do you see this?"

Ruth nods. She does not understand the phenomenon before her, but like Vicky, she is captivated by its awe and beauty. Vicky points out toward the stars. Her finger adjusts as a cluster of stars just vanishes and others appear. "Do you see when these stars," she explains, "some disappear and others appear?"

Again, Ruth nods. "Yes, what is that?"

Vicky continues, "It is the Abner effect. We are moving faster than the speed of light, much faster! That is why we can actually see the stars move as we pass them. The reason they disappear is because we are going so fast. Light travels in straight beams, and when we pass the beam, it seems to disappear. We would have to wait for the light to reach us again. If we were to suddenly stop, eventually they would reappear."

Ruth walks to the portal and places her hand on the glass, her eyes shimmering. "Amazing" is all she can say.

"Amazing, isn't it?" asks Angel to Rikes.

Rikes turns his head, remembering his assignment, and engages Angel. "It is … amazing, that is. You are not plotting wormholes?"

"Be careful with wormholes," Angel cautions. "They can appear anywhere! In fact, the planet we are going to has a wormhole in it, making it very valuable." Angel smiles. "No, this ship is capable of traveling many times the speed of light. We don't have to plot one junction and then another and another. We can travel a straight line to our destination."

Rikes questions, "How? How is it possible that this ship can travel at such speeds?"

Again, Angel smiles. He turns toward Rikes and states, "I'm actually going slow because I'm towing your comrades."

Astounded, Rikes's jaw drops. He straightens up and asks, "Are there other ships that can travel this fast?"

Angel shakes his head. "No, there are only two: the *Green Lightning* and the Spaceman's ship."

Rikes glances downward and asks himself in a mumbled whisper, "The Spaceman's ship?"

He looks back up toward Angel. Angel continues, "Well, actually now, since I died, there's only one ship left."

Angel's eyes remain forward. Again, Rikes looks down; something doesn't quite sound right. Suddenly he catches it! Rikes looks up; his skin pales. He asks, "Since you died?"

Angel looks up again, turning his head toward Rikes and smiles. Then his eyes wander, and his expression changes to that of content confusion. Angel then looks forward again, focused on their destination. Rikes, not willing to accept that as a response, states, "You have to explain that!"

Angel solemnly nods his head. "Very well," he replies, "I guess that does require some explanation."

His eyes widen as his thoughts expand. Angel's mind dives back, his memory rises, and the vivid imagery of his past fills his head. Angel continues, his voice taking on the highs and lows as if he were reading a story. "Well, many years ago, I was the police of the galaxies. Those who relied on me for safety and justice loved me and called me the Green Angel. Those who opposed justice and caused pain and harm to others knew me as the Green Demon. After many years of fighting for the helpless, I gave my technology over to a man to take my mantle and continue my fight. He was called the Spaceman. We did not know at the time the reach of the Dictator's hand nor the extent of his greed! War had started, and the Dictator's desire was to control or destroy. The only options for those who opposed him were to be enslaved or annihilated! The more the war turned to our side, the more the Dictator simply killed.

He did not have the patience or resources to enslave. He wanted to wipe out entire planets before they could choose to side against him.

"*Green Lightning* was still functional and deadly, although its speed was now limited. I was not ready to let him cause any more suffering. I found the Dictator's mechanical army en route to an unsuspecting peaceful galaxy. My ship was no longer capable of flying for help. I had to do something, or they would have invaded and murdered innocent planets, innocent lives ... So I drove my ship into their ship!"

Angel looks at Rikes and smiles a mischievous smile. He continues, "The ship was huge, larger than Earth's moon!"

Angel faces forward once again. His words are calmer, soft, and painful, "I had one chance to stop them. I flew *Green Lightning* to the ship's core. I engaged her weapons, but I did not fire ... Instead, I allowed them to overheat ... I blew us up. I blew up my ship, their ship. I sacrificed the ship and myself to save countless billions."

Angel's voice slowly revises to its former cheerfulness, and he smiles again. Rikes remains overwhelmed. He cannot move; he cannot blink. All he can do is listen. He listens to an unbelievable story that somehow he knows is true! Angel continues. Rikes hangs on to his every word. "Although most of my ship was blown into smithereens, there was one piece left floating out among the wreckage of the destroyed enemy ship. Somehow, the emerald energy that ran through me and my ship cannot be so easily destroyed. My mission to help those in need is still not over yet. Somehow, the spirit or the energy remains! Whoever possesses that piece of my ship and calls my name can retrieve us to protect those in need."

In his very pupils, Angel can see Defender guiding her ship through the wreckage of the Dictator's robot army to find the last remaining fragment of Angel's ship. Back in Devin's lair, in the inner room, she lifts the artifact from its pedestal and calls out, "Green Angel, I summon you! We need your help!"

Her voice echoes in the chamber and somehow escapes into the void of space. Angel concludes, "And here we are! And there is our destination. The planet Malak-Beth."

Vicky notices that their ship has slowed down considerably; they are going slower than the speed of light at this point. Once again, the stars appear stationary. In the distance is a planet. This must be Malak-Beth. As they grow closer to it, they can tell that it seems very similar to Earth, with a thick white atmosphere and a mixture of blues and greens. It also appears to have an abundance of water. Vicky and Ruth, who have been privy to the conversation between Angel and Rikes, remain as awestruck as Private Rikes. Vicky calls out to Angel, "Angel, who exactly are we meeting on this planet?"

Angel states, "Gebhirah Shaghal, the Ravisher. But you can call her the Army Queen."

Back aboard the *Liberty Crane/Tiqu-Qi*, Jacob Miller enters the bridge followed by his two assistant engineers, Lui and Johnson. Both Captain Barr and Captain Reynolds stand with their backs toward Miller. They are hunched over in deep conversation with Wei and Lieutenant Lin. While Lui fidgets with his handheld, Johnson observes the inner workings of the bridge; having not been aboard this new bridge yet, he is intrigued by it. Both he and Lui have searched over 70 percent of the ship, looking at the designs and functions and trying to figure out their capabilities. Miller walks up to Captain Reynolds. "Sir."

Captain Reynolds immediately stops his conversation and gives his attention to Miller. Barr, noticing Reynolds's reaction, also turns to hear what Miller has to say. Anxiously, Captain Reynolds asks, "What do you have, Jacob?"

Miller replies, "Lui and Johnson have a plan, and, sir, I think it just might work!"

Captain Reynolds and Captain Barr give them their full attention as Wei also turns in his chair to face them. Lieutenant Lin continues to monitor the data retrieved from Moses as he and his crew search the ship for damage.

Johnson walks up. "Sir, I think I have an idea. Aboard the *Liberty Crane* are fighter ships. They each have LEP cannons, laser-enhanced projectile cannons. Each cannon can discharge an explosive charge. Now here is the good part …"

Johnson pauses to scan his audience. Excitedly, he continues, "The charges' outputs are adjustable. The pilot controls the size of each explosion. Now if we shoot a calculated charge at certain points—"

Lui rushes up to the front. "Small charges," Lui clarifies as he accesses the controls.

Lui maneuvers the controls as if he had been working them for years. His knowledge of the technology is amazing; it comes naturally to him. Knowing this, Wei sits on the side, allowing Lui full rein. From his chair, Lin side glances at the commotion, but he diligently continues his work.

On the main portal screen, Lui brings up the computer schematics of the obstructed solar panels with the asteroid wedged under it. With his finger on his handheld, he highlights two points that simultaneously appear above on the large screen. Lui explains, "With the right blast, at these two points …"

He points up toward the screen. "It should break up the asteroid with only minor damage to the shields. Also, it will knock out this piece of broken hydraulics, which we need to get rid of anyway!"

Johnson turns toward Captain Reynolds and Wei. "We need to shut the power off the solar panels."

Johnson walks toward the screen. He places his hand on Lui's shoulder and instructs him, "Put the live feed of the panels back, please."

Lui immediately complies, and the live image of the solar panels is back on the main portal. Johnson points, directing their attention to the severed sparking cables. The sparks have already burned small holes into the hull of the ship. "These broken cables," he explains, "need to be capped off from inside the ship. That is what's draining our power! We are currently draining more power than we are able to absorb."

Captain Reynolds straightens and considers their proposal. He knows the mettle of these men; they know what they are talking about! Even in this alien situation, Captain Reynolds knows he can rely on their judgment. He looks at Jacob. Jacob nods. He then looks toward Wei. Wei interjects, "Sir, it's the best we have right now. I think it can work."

Finally, he turns to Captain Barr. Barr responds, "Iv' you trust these min, thir logic seems sound ta' me."

Moments later, Wei makes a shipwide announcement, "All airmen report to the hangar, ready for departure. Briefing in five minutes."

Captain Barr instructs Lieutenant Lin, "Ye know the min, brief them and then pick … two?"

Barr looks over toward Johnson. "Two."

Johnson confirms, "That is all we need."

Captain Reynolds speaks up. "Our engineers, Lui and Johnson, will send the coordinates for the exact angle and increment for the explosions directly to their onboard computer."

Lin stands at attention. "Sir, yes, sir!"

Lin exits the bridge and heads for the hangar. Lieutenant Minor has been all but forgotten in all the commotion. From the onset of the threat from the asteroid belt, Lieutenant Minor has moved himself to the side of the bridge, where he stays unable to move. Crewmen go back and forth, passing right by him; eventually, he becomes more of the background scenery than an actual person. Finally, as reality slowly begins to resurface, Minor remembers Dr. Long. Minor thinks to himself, *Where is Dr. Long? Why hasn't Wilson brought him to me?*

Stepping off the bridge, he turns to find the sick bay. Minor wanders until he eventually finds the sick bay; it is empty. The entire medical staff is positioned in a separate isolation ward on the lower level, tending to the casualties from the earlier insurrection. Unsure what to do next, Minor decides to walk back toward the bridge. Confused and deep in thought, he actually walks right into Private Wilson. Minor, dazed, looks up at the wall of a man he just walked into. Wilson humbly responds, "Sir, sorry, sir! I didn't—I was not looking where I was going, sir!"

Lieutenant Minor straightens up, taking full advantage of his authority, and shouts at Wilson, "Where is Dr. Long? I asked you to bring him to me, Private!"

Wilson responds, "Sir, yes, sir! I brought him his airman uniform and when—"

Minor shakes his head, like a cat splashed in the face with water. He cuts off Wilson midsentence. "Airman uniform? You brought Long an airman uniform?"

Private Wilson, not realizing the additional condescension in Minor's voice, continues. "Sir, yes, sir! He requested his airman uniform. I brought it to him. I left momentarily while he changed to continue my other duties! A few minutes later, when I came back to escort him to the bridge, he was not in the sick bay, sir! I assumed he came to you himself, sir! Sir, sorry, I should have reported to you, but … with the asteroid and all. We all have been working multiple assignments, sir!"

Now panic is layered on top of his last panic! Minor's thoughts are flooded with worry. Where did Long go? Will his plan to use Long to showcase his leadership backfire and make him look even more incompetent than before? Then he realizes he could be court-martialed for letting a prisoner escape! He pushes the private out of his way and, in a panic, runs back toward the bridge. Like an intoxicated man, he stumbles over his own feet and bumps into people along the way. He rushes onto the bridge. Out of breath, he pauses for a moment to catch his breath. He slowly walks toward the front, not sure what he is going to say. He pauses once more as he realizes there is some sort of commotion brewing up ahead.

The two captains, Captain Reynolds and Captain Barr; Wei; and Lin are viewing the surface cameras as the fighter ships are being deployed. Captain Barr turns to Lieutenant Lin. "Lieutenant Lin, how min'ny ships did we deploy?"

Lin looks up at the three ships on the screen exiting the hangar. He turns toward Captain Reynolds and then toward Captain Barr. Noticeably bewildered as to why he sees three ships instead of two, he responds, "Two, sir. I only gave clearance for two airmen to suit up."

Two of the three ships are on course toward the solar panels; the third one, however, is flying away from the ship. In addition to this, the third ship's path is not straight; it is veering to the left and to the right, up and down. Even the ship's speed is sporadic, slowing up then launching forward. Captain Barr points at the craft, turns to Lin, and asks, "Can ye access the oanboard cameras oan 'at craft?"

Both Lin and Wei reply, "Yes, sir!"

The image pulls up inside the fighter craft; despite the helmet and the glasses, the long, thin features are immediately recognized by both Captain Reynolds and Wei. In unison, they exclaim, "Is that Dr. Long?"

Minor's eyes expand, and any color left in his face leaves at the mention of Long's name. Wei abruptly grabs hold of the controls; Lin moves back. Wei calls out to Dr. Long, "Dr. Long, do you read me? Dr. Long, whatever you are doing, cease! Immediately bring that craft back to the hangar!"

Long, who obviously seems overwhelmed by the controls, fumbles with them, trying desperately to guide the ship. Captain Reynolds, as impatient as always, bends forward into the intercom and calls out to Dr. Long, "Long! This is Captain Reynolds. I command you to bring this ship back to dock now! We will not repeat!"

Long does not respond. Instead, he flies his ship on course, moving farther away from the mothership. Moses enters the room. Instantly he notices the commotion in the front and lumbers forward to investigate. Midway, he almost walks into Lieutenant Minor, who has only made it thus far. Placing his large hand on Minor's shoulder, he asks, "What's going on?"

Minor glances up at Moses for the slightest of seconds. He realizes that he must say something. He marches forward with authority and blurts out, "Dr. Long has escaped and has commandeered a fighter ship! He is heading away from our ship!"

Moses responds, "What?"

Minor walks up between Captain Reynolds and Captain Barr. Wei turns to him and responds, "How could he have escaped?"

Lieutenant Minor replies, "I was wondering the same thing myself! I shall launch a full investigation and get to the bottom of this!"

Lin interrupts, "Sir, sir!"

Both Captain Reynolds and Captain Barr, as well as the rest, give Lieutenant Lin their attention. Lin continues, "Sir, it seems like he's moving towards that planet."

Captain Reynolds looks toward Captain Barr. "Barr," he asks, "do you know anything at all about this solar system? Specifically, that planet?"

Barr shakes his head. "This solar system is uncharted t' us also!"

Captain Reynolds asks Wei, "Wei?"

He circles the data with his finger, looking up occasionally while he states his findings. "Best we can tell, it seems to have an atmosphere that can sustain life. But I don't know, most of it seems to be made out of solid rock."

Lin then announces, "It seems like his trajectory will lead him to this point, right here!"

Lin blows up the image on the screen. Lin continues, "It is interesting that he would pick this point. Right there is the only point on the entire planet that has some sort of crevice. In fact, it has an underground cavern! It is huge! Kilometers long in every direction!"

Barr stares at Lin. He frowns his eyes in suspicion. "'At canny be a coincidence! 'At eh only place on eh planet that he kin hide, he would go directly thir! How cuid he possibly know?"

Lieutenant Minor, also baffled, asks, "How?"

Meanwhile, aboard the stolen fighter craft, Long feels as if he were losing his mind or, more precisely, losing control of it. The voice in his head becomes stronger and more dominant. Long yells out for his sanity, "I can't do this! I'm a doctor. I did not think that this ship would be so hard to fly!"

Then the voice in his head crackles. "You have already done it! You are doing it. You are flying exactly where you need to. Below is a friend of mine. My friend can save you! You will be safe, freed from your prison!"

Long cries back, "But what? Why? I don't understand!"

The voice, now seemingly coming from all around him, demands, "Silence! Do as I say!"

Long stays silent for the rest of the trip. However, his body answers in uncontrolled trembling and cold sweats running down his face from under his helmet. As his ship enters the atmosphere, it burns red hot.

Lin looks up at Captain Barr. "Sir, there's more."

Lin turns back toward the data and continues, "There is an energy source."

He places the image on the screen. It is a thermographic image of the planet below. Lin enlarges the image; the center is pure white surrounded by a thick yellow ring. The white light pulsates; at times, it expands and covers the entire screen. Lin continues, "There is an energy signature here like I've never seen before! It fluctuates from high to low. However, when it's low, it is powerful enough to run an entire city. When it's high."

Lin looks up at Barr. "It's off the charts!"

Barr has rarely seen Lin express any emotions other than frustration. However, there was something in Lin's eyes—a concern, perhaps even a deeper emotion than concern, or maybe a more primal one: fear! Not a fear for himself, but a dread, like the dread that looms over a child when woken from a terrible nightmare. Barr and Reynolds look at each other; a growing chill covers them, like morning frost on a window. All of a sudden, they all have to accept that what is happening is far more than what any of them had thought. This is definitely not coincidental; it is planned! What they do not know is how Dr. Long could have known about this, nor do they know what his objectives are. Captain Reynolds shakes his head and states, "We need answers."

Although his words are few, the statement is loaded; they are in a desperate situation. Lieutenant Minor sees his opportunity, or to be more exact, he feels it. There is something within him prompting him to speak, guiding his words. The anxiety welling in him allows it to speak for him. Perhaps he does not even notice that his words and thoughts are not his own. He speaks, "We should ask the alien."

Barr, confused, turns to Reynolds. Captain Reynolds returns the look. He takes a breath and explains, "We have an alien prisoner that we saved on our mission. We do not know much about him."

Minor interjects, "But he knows about this galaxy! He may possibly know about this solar system, maybe even about this planet."

Captain Reynolds tilts his head upward, considering Minor's words. He glances at Minor and calls to Wei, "Wei?"

Wei replies, "He is from this galaxy. There's no telling what he knows. He might just know something about that planet. Maybe he can shed some light on it for us."

Captain Reynolds presses his lips tightly together and shakes his head. He turns toward Captain Barr and asks him, "So do you want to meet an alien?"

Minutes later, almost the entire ensemble from the bridge is in the brig: Captain Reynolds, Captain Barr, Lieutenant Lin, Moses, Wei, and Lieutenant Minor. They decided to leave Jacob Miller in charge of the bridge in their absence. The alien is as silent, as usual. The gray alien creature has changed since they first found him; his body is no longer bony. His arms are muscular to the point where the shackles are clamped into his skin. If he is in pain or uncomfortable, he does not show it. He stares at them, seemingly emotionless; it is not certain whether he was expecting them or whether he was surprised by the intrusion. Wei holds up a handheld and walks toward the bars. He addresses the alien. "Excuse us, as you know we are in your galaxy. We have some questions. Maybe you can help."

The alien glances at Wei and steps forward to comply. Wei holds up the image of the planet. Wei attempts to inquire, "This is where we are."

For the first time, the alien expresses emotion. At first, it appears to be fear on the alien's face, but upon more careful analysis, it is an expression more resembling remorse than fear. The alien steps back momentarily. He regains his composure and stares deeply at the company before him. He asks, his voice hoarse and gravelly, "Why have you traveled to this planet?"

Captain Reynolds controls himself and allows Wei to ask the question for them. Wei asks, "What is it? What is this place?"

The alien responds plainly, "This is Efazinok."

"What?" asks Minor.

The alien glances at Lieutenant Minor and states, "Ef-u-zin-OK."

Wei wraps his hand gently around the bar and asks, "What is Efazinok?"

The alien takes a minute to pause. He steps back before he replies, "Its literal name means 'dark pit.' It was once inhabited by millions. They were not technologically advanced, nor did they know the origin of how they came to that planet or who they were. Underneath the rocky surface run streams of water; they were able to siphon water and minerals straight from the ground, sustaining themselves. Some trees and bushes actually grew as the roots were launched deep into the ground. They used the trees to make simple clothing; the storms on the planet were fierce! Their bodies were strong, but even they could not survive the harsh weather. Their nails, however, were composed of an almost-unbreakable substance. Using the sheer strength of their fingers, they were able to dig into the rock, forging caves. Soon, one cave became many, and as the families grew, each cave expanded. All the caves connected; there was no fear, and there was no reason to live isolated. As they multiplied, they dug further into the ground. Something was drawing them toward the center. Finally, when they reached the center, they discovered a large pit. This was the source of all the water on the planet. There was something mysterious about the pit—life-giving yet, at the same time, threatening. The pit had properties, energies to strengthen the people. When the pit was uncovered, the invaders soon followed.

"Our bodies are different from yours…"

He pauses and looks up at the crew standing before him. He continues, "We live for hundreds of years. At the time when the invaders came, I was barely twenty years old. For our civilization, I was still a young boy. They exterminated us … like pests!

"They kept only one hundred alive and enslaved them. I was fortunate to be a slave for the master. Within his household, there was abundance, and I was treated well. I soon became the head over all the other slaves—slaves, all of different cultures, raked from their home planets." The alien looks up, a deep sorrow welling in his eyes.

Wei points to the fluctuating light on his handheld. His voice is slow and sympathetic, yet there is an urgency lying close to the surface. He asks, "What is this energy source? Is this what you uncovered at the center?"

Now the face of remorse on the alien turns to one of fear. He steps closer and explains, "That is what drew the invaders to our planet … Unlike your technology, some of the weapons developed were devised from living organisms. Therefore, they needed time to develop, to grow, to power up before they could be used. They placed a dimensional door inside the center of the cavern. Within the dimensional door, he placed one such weapon. This weapon was the ultimate weapon! When he realized that the battle could be lost, he placed it there to keep it safe while it fully charged … If he had the chance to retrieve it, he would have destroyed everything!"

Captain Reynolds queries, "Everything?"

Very plainly, the alien states, "The entire universe."

A hush falls in the brig.

The alien warns, "I did not expect it to still be there after all these years, but if it is there … you need to get to it before anyone else does!"

The group immediately moves themselves a few meters away from the bars. They huddle to discuss their findings. Lieutenant Minor begins the conversation, but Wei quickly interjects with an upward hand indicating to stop. Wei glances over at the alien prisoner and states, "Let us meet back up on the bridge."

Moments later, back on the bridge, they gather around Miller, quickly filling him in almost verbatim on what the alien had said. Captain Reynolds speaks up first. "We do not know what connection Dr. Long has with that energy source, but we cannot let him get to it, that is for certain! Somehow he is working with this Dictator person, and we cannot let either him or the Dictator get that device!"

Captain Barr agrees, "If 'is is true, we must go!"

Captain Barr turns toward Lieutenant Minor and asks, "Lieutenant Minor, I believe ye ur in charge o' yer military operation aboard th' *Tiqu-Qi*. Whit is yer assessment?"

Again, rising inside Lieutenant Minor, a controlling, overpowering wave drives his words. "I believe we should make a military presence down on that planet! If Long has gone into those caverns, proceed after him! Find him, bring him back! Locate that device, and bring it aboard this ship and then get us home!"

Minor's voice is so authoritative that instinctively the entire group nods. Captain Reynolds leads the charge. "Yes, that sounds good!"

Captain Barr queries, "But how minny soldiers shuild we deploy?"

Lieutenant Minor straightens up and walks toward Barr. He looks up into Barr's eyes and states, "All!"

Barr's face squinches as he tries to understand exactly what Minor is trying to say. Minor repeats himself, "All! I say we bring every soldier available into those caverns. The caverns are huge, kilometers wide. There is no telling what is in there! We need to show a great military presence on that planet!" Then, as if he remembered, he finishes with "Sir!"

Barr looks down and turns away. He walks through the crowd, considering what Minor had said. The rest remain quiet, in thought. Although Lieutenant Minor may be in charge of his troops, Captain Barr has almost six thousand soldiers under his command. Barr turns around and walks back to the front. Reynolds queries, "Captain Barr, what say you?"

Barr slowly nods, as if he were fighting against himself. He looks at Lieutenant Lin. "Lin … th' planet … whit ur th' conditions?"

Wei answers, "The planet has oxygen."

Wei glances toward Lin and queries, "But do we also have—"

Lieutenant Lin, already knowing what Wei is asking, answers Wei before he can complete his question. "Yes," he answers. "We have protective gear and oxygen masks for all our soldiers, even lightweight space suits if needed."

Wei turns, facing Barr and Minor. "Then there seems to be nothing prohibiting them, no immediate hazard."

Lieutenant Lin speaks. "Sir, if I may? If a threat arises, our ship will be right there! We can retreat within minutes."

Captain Reynolds also agrees. "It would seem sound. However, as the alien stated, there are many caverns. Can we scan a direct route to the center?"

Wei shakes his head. Lin responds, "Sir, no, sir. Those energy surges are not allowing us to map out a direct route. We couldn't even scan the underground water channels that the alien described."

Wei, considering all foreseeable scenarios, is concerned. He states, "This could be a problem. Our men could be in there for hours and still never find the center!"

Minor, glowing, speaks up. "Let's take the alien with us!"

Captain Reynolds interjects, "What?"

Lieutenant Minor counters, "He is the only one that knows his way around there. He lived there for twenty years! He could guide our troop to the center without casualties."

Captain Reynolds puts his chin hard into his hand and shakes his head. "This doesn't sound good," he states.

Captain Barr chimes in, "I agree wi' Captain Reynolds, 'is is very risky sending our soldiers doon thir. But sending an alien, 'at we know little 'til nothing aboot."

Lieutenant Minor again argues his case. "Think about it, who would know the way better than he would?"

Wei interjects, "He was there, yes. But that was three hundred years ago! How could he possibly remember?"

Minor shrugs his shoulders. "I am not sure. Do you remember your childhood home if you were to go back there? Obviously, all his people died. There were no changes made to it after he left. I say it's the best chance we have, and we should take it! He will be under constant guard, surrounded by six thousand soldiers."

They bow their heads, unsure of what to do. Moses, not wanting to speak out of turn, has been quiet this whole time. He speaks up. "I don't think it is a great idea." He looks up toward Captain Reynolds. "But if it could save lives, it might be our best choice."

Captain Reynolds gives ear and heart to Moses's statement. He looks toward Barr and states, "It is your decision."

Barr looks up as if he were looking out to the sky, perhaps to heaven for answers. He turns toward Lieutenant Minor. Slowly he shakes his head. "Okay, let's do it."

Barr looks at Lieutenant Lin and commands, "We do it by the book!"

Chapter 13

Aboard the stolen fighter, Dr. Long fights with the voice in his head. The voice is so strong now that the words burn into his brain, causing pain.

"Let the ship land!" commands the voice. "It is on autopilot!"

Long wraps his arms around his head and screams in pain. He surveys the rocky terrain and cries out in fear, "No, we're going to crash!"

He disables the autopilot. With his sweat-soaked hands, Long grabs hold of the controls. Despite not knowing what he is doing, he flips switches, trying to engage the landing rockets. Instead, he fires the downward port rockets, causing the ship to tilt downward sideways. The landing gear is shoved hard into the rocky terrain. Soon, the treads of the tire are stripped away, leaving the metal unprotected. As the metal scrapes the surface, sparks fly out. Long pulls back on the controls, but his efforts are futile as the ship continues to tilt. The friction causes the ship to shake violently. The gear continues to scrape against the rocks, and soon the whole left side of the landing gear is ripped off. The ship falls to its side, bounces, and rolls sideways. Amazingly, when it finally stops, it is upright. Small streams of smoke rise from under the ship, and the lights flicker. Dr. Long remains unconscious in darkness.

Minutes later, the hatch opens. Donned in a space suit, Dr. Long emerges, his legs unstable from the crash. His head finally seems clear and free from the voice that consumed him all this time. He looks forward and sees a deep, dark cavern in front of him. The entrance is wide, and he can only assume that the interior is even larger, much larger. As he approaches, he is dwarfed by the immense size and darkness of the entrance, kilometers long in either direction. He continues forward toward the entrance. The cave and its darkness have their own foreboding terror, yet at the same time, something is drawing him closer. The lure of its mystery weaves into the essence of his emotions, pulling him forward into the embrace of her darkness. As he moves closer, Long realizes what draws him is not a sensual feeling, but a primal one. It is a hunger. As he steps toward the entrance, a voice—or what he thinks is a voice—calls to him from within the void. The voice is soft and haunting, begging, "Help me."

Back aboard the *Green Lightning*, Angel is landing. He has already settled down both Private Diamond and the shuttlecraft and disconnects them from his toe. His ship gently lands at the foot of what appears to be a village. Angel opens the canopy, and Private Rikes steps out. Lieutenant Young has already exited and is waiting for Ruth. When Ruth comes out, the two of them walk over to join Rikes. Angel remains in the cockpit. Vicky looks up toward him and calls to him, "Angel, you're not staying to say hi to the queen?"

Angel looks over at Vicky, smiles, and shakes his head. "No." His voice has a soft, sincere sense of sorrow about it. Angel looks up toward the sky and then back toward the three of them. He continues, "I have one more errand I have to do."

He looks at the three of them. His eyes speak what his heart is thinking, *These three are the hope for the universe!* He forces a smile—not an insincere one, but forced because he knows that, for them, the road ahead is going to be very difficult, perhaps impossible. Facing the likes of the Dictator is a forfeit at best for even the most formidable of challengers. But he has confidence that they will overcome, they will succeed. He states his confidence in them as he cries out, "Best of luck to you!"

Vicky returns the sentiment. "And to you!"

Both Ruth and Rikes wave and call out, "Goodbye."

Rikes adds, "I hope we will get to see you once again!"

Angel looks down for a moment then back toward Rikes. "That would be nice," he states. "But I hope you understand when I say I hope we don't have to!"

With that, Angel closes the canopy. The three of them step back as the *Green Lightning* rises off the ground and then toward the sky, soon out of sight.

Now, with Angel out of sight, Vicky, Ruth, and Rikes get a chance to survey their surroundings. They are standing on plush, thick grass. Although some bald spots are visible, the dirt looks to be thick and rich.

The sky is a clear blue, and the clouds are puffy and light. Before them is a village, very similar to something you would see in a nineteenth- or early-twentieth-century European village. Overall, Malak-Beth is a very beautiful planet. The town sits upon a large plateau resting on an even-larger hill. The hill is steep and rocky, a hard terrain to climb up or down. Around the village is a stony wall, which appears to be made by hand of gray rocks of various sizes. There is no gate, simply a worn wide path to the entrance of the town where the wall winds down and then starts up again.

Vicky looks ahead and notices that there is a person in the distance staring at them, or at least what appears to be a person. When they catch eyes, the person bows and walks toward them. At first, Rikes tenses up, placing his hand alongside his sidearm. Vicky calmly places her hand down, palm facing Rikes. She fans her fingers, as if to say "Calm down!"

Once the person is closer, they can see her more clearly. She is a beautiful, brown-skinned young lady. Her skin is as deep and rich as the land. She stands tall, slender, and eloquent. She has a long neck and a bald oval-shaped head, slightly enlarged. Her eyes are wide and large, and her pupils are dark, almost black. Her long lashes flutter in the cool breeze. Her face is welcoming. She has on a dress of sorts, which falls just above her ankles. The dress is closed with a row of latches in the front. The dress is silky, and the colors are a reflection of the colors of nature, varying greens and different shades of brown. Her feet are bare. She quietly walks up with her head bowed and hands pressed together in a praying position. When she reaches about three meters from them, she stops. Vicky waits patiently; Rikes, however, is a little anxious and fidgets. Ruth admires her beauty and stays quiet, in awe of both the lady and this beautiful planet. The lady looks up and addresses the three of them with her eyes. She introduces herself, "My name is Eliana. I am a representative"—she waves her hand back toward the town—"of the town. We saw when you landed, you were accompanied by the Great One."

She curtsies and spreads her arms out wide. "We welcome you to our humble homes!" She then again places her hands together. "How might we be of assistance to you?"

Vicky notices a slight accent; however, she cannot place it. She realizes that English was not her native tongue; it was something she must have learned later, although she has mastered it beautifully. Vicky steps forward and nods peaceably. "I am Lieutenant Young of the UPA. These are my companions, Private Rikes and Ruth, and behind me"—Vicky waves her hand toward Private Diamond—"is Private Diamond."

Eliana nods in acknowledgment, looks up, and states, "It is a pleasure to meet you." She looks at each one as she responds, "Lieutenant Young, Private Rikes, Ruth, Private Diamond. How can we be of assistance to you?"

Lieutenant Young states, "We are here to see the ... Army Queen."

Eliana smiles and nods. "Yes, she would be very glad to receive you. Anyone brought to us by the Great One is accepted and welcomed here. I shall get someone to escort you to her." She turns her head and calls out, "Boy!"

Soon, a young boy, about twelve or thirteen years of age, runs up to meet Eliana. He is different from the lady; although he is also dark-skinned, he seems to be human, from Earth. He is wearing a robe tied at the center. Although it also has shades of brown, it is not as elegant as Eliana's outfit. It is dirty and ripped, and he, too, seems soiled. The boy bows his head. "Yes, ma'am."

Eliana looks the child over. She asks him, "Please escort our friends to the Army Queen."

The boy looks up at her and takes a moment to soak in what she requested; he stares at her, confused. She nods, indicating to him that what she said was correct. He then looks at the three, smiles, and nods. "Yes, ma'am." He tells them, "Follow me."

Vicky's wrist communicator vibrates. She looks at the message from Private Diamond: "Ma'am, I will stay here and guard the shuttle. I can monitor the situation from here and collect data." Vicky turns toward Private Diamond and nods her acceptance. Vicky then turns toward Rikes and, in a low tone, commands, "Keep an open communication between us and Diamond. He is staying here to guard the ship."

Rikes nods and says "Yes, ma'am" and adjusts his communicator.

Vicky looks up and steps forward, followed by Rikes, and lastly, by Ruth. Ruth can no longer hold her enthusiasm. As she is passing by Eliana, she stops, turns toward her, and bows her head. Ruth addresses her, "Ms. Eliana, your dress is so beautiful!"

Very humbly, Eliana bows her head and replies, "Thank you. Our clothes imitate and honor the nature around us. After the Great Separation, when people left their mother home, each tried to seek independence differently. Some endeavored in science, others decided to reconnect to nature, animals, plants, or the world around them. Our people tried to connect to the land." Both Vicky and Rikes have stopped to listen to Eliana, intrigued. Vicky looks toward Rikes, her face plagued by a question. She looks up at Eliana and asks, "You stated the Great Separation. What was your home planet?"

Eliana smiles and states, almost as if Vicky should have known, "Erets."

Eliana places her hands together and walks forward to follow the boy. Ruth follows; however, Vicky is taken aback and does not move. Rikes notices Vicky's hesitation and circles back to check on her. Vicky's face seems almost comatose as she stares out deeply into thought. Concerned, Rikes whispers, "Ma'am, what is it?"

"Erets," she explains. "That is an ancient name for Earth!"

Rikes, stunned, eventually slumbers forward, trying to comprehend all the thoughts swirling around in his head. Vicky, gaining control of her thoughts, once again presses forward. She barely takes a step when a familiar voice calls to her from behind, "Wow! Look how far you've come."

The voice seems almost to be mocking her, but in a teasing sort of way. Vicky pauses and turns around. There, behind her, standing up against the shuttle, legs crossed and arms folded, is Bridge. She stands there staring at Vicky with an expression of disappointment. Rikes also turns and is about to accompany Vicky when, once again, Vicky fans her open hand, stopping Rikes in his tracks. Vicky turns her head ever so slightly toward Rikes without ever losing eye contact with Bridge. Vicky commands (loud enough to be heard by both Eliana and the boy as well), "Go ahead into the village with Eliana, and wait for me. I will catch up with you."

Rikes hesitates, but he is obedient. He responds, "Ma'am, yes, ma'am!" He turns to follow the boy. Both the boy and Eliana glance at Bridge, Eliana sure not to make eye contact. Eliana bows her head, turns, and walks off to follow their guide. The boy leads them into town. Vicky shuts her open communication and walks toward Bridge. Bridge pushes herself off the shuttle and straightens up. Vicky is all business; thousands of lives, perhaps millions, perhaps billions, or even more, are at stake. She asks, "What are you doing here?"

Bridge smiles a large smile from ear to ear! She replies in a giddy, childlike voice, "Why, just look at you!" Bridge looks around at the sky and the trees. She points her hand out, palm up, toward Vicky. She states, "You've come quite a way, young lady!" Then, pointing her own two fingers toward her eyes then toward Vicky, she states, "I've got my eyes on you!"

Vicky, unsure how to respond, just pauses and waits for Bridge to actually answer her question. Bridge pouts. "I see you're not in a playful mood."

Vicky remains glaring at her. Bridge leans forward and nudges Vicky's shoulder with her fist. She confesses, "Weell, like I said, there's something about you." Bridge steps back, and a laugh shoots out from her as if she has no control over it. She continues, "I just like you."

Vicky shakes her head; she does not like games. She demands, "Bridge, why are you here? What is going on?"

Bridge straightens up, her expression changes, and she sternly and dramatically points her finger at Vicky. Bridge scolds, "I warned you, but you didn't listen to me!"

Vicky barely gets a "What?" out when Bridge continues.

"I told you not to take anything from off the *Liberty Crane* and bring it onto your ship! But nooo." Bridge brings her finger almost directly between Vicky's eyes. Bridge continues her rebuke. "You just had to go and not listen!"

Vicky searches her mind for a second before responding. "No! It is not true. I commanded them not to take anything from off the *Liberty Crane* and ..."

Vicky pauses, wondering. "Minor?" she states out loud to herself.

Bridge interrupts, "Well, whoever...they did it, did! And now"—she places her hands out as if she were giving herself up—"my hands are tied!"

Vicky looks down, concerned. She timidly looks back up at Bridge, an expression she rarely remembers ever having before. Expecting the worst, she asks, "So what does this mean?"

Bridge raises an eyebrow. She turns to one side and then starts to pace back and forth while she talks, as if she were lecturing. "You see," she starts. "I have powers ... I set some limits for them ... for this project! There were certain ..." Bridge places her finger against her head, searching for the correct word. She points her finger straight up and excitedly yells out, "Criteria! Yes, criteria!" She points her finger up, as if she were counting. "One of them was that somehow the two universes would have to blend somehow. But now"—she squats down and points dramatically at Vicky—"once again, you or they did it!" Bridge stands up; she turns, walking in the other direction, tapping her finger against her lips. She stops and turns toward Vicky. Her voice is serious. "Now there will be a merging."

Vicky's eyes squint as she tries to comprehend. "Merging?" she asks.

Bridge's voice is absent of its usual stain of insanity as she warns Vicky, trying her best to explain the critical situation they have now found themselves in. "Yes, now the two universes will merge into one." Bridge grinds her teeth together. "It's not good," she states.

Vicky again looks down, her heart racing as she looks back up at Bridge and grabs hold of her shoulders. This action startles her, as Bridge is not used to anyone daring enough to touch her. Vicky commands, "Explain what exactly this means!"

Again, Bridge raises an eyebrow, but this time, she is more serious than before. She steps back out of Vicky's grasp. "Weeellll," she replies, "the two universes become one. The 'Universe' then tries to make sense of everything! Some things combine, but other things which cannot fit will simply disappear! Finally, when it is all said and done, there is a link between the two which cannot be broken!"

Vicky gets closer to Bridge and stares into her eyes. Vicky asks, "What does that mean?"

Bridge tilts her head. She then puts one finger down, as if placing it on a table. As she explains, "Well, that means whatever happens in this universe"—Bridge moves her finger to the other side, placing it down on another imaginary table—"will also happen in that universe." Vicky places her hand over her forehead, trying her best to not only comprehend what is happening but also to understand what the consequences will be. Finally frustrated, Vicky blurts out, "Why? Why would anyone want to do this? Why would you want this to happen?"

Bridge nervously giggles. "Oh no no no!" she responds. "Don't put the blame on me! First of all, I warned you not to do it! Second of all, I have no desire for this to happen! I was asked to do it by Doc. He and the Dictator, they want the universes to merge!"

Vicky commands, "Explain!"

Bridge responds, "You know why … don't you?"

Vicky considers what Bridge said. She wonders, does she know why? Unsure yet at the same time confident, she explains her thoughts to Bridge to confirm her suspicions. Her words are slow as she hesitates to see if Bridge will indeed validate her thoughts. She speaks, "If he, the Dictator, had already lost in one universe, he needed to find a similar universe so that he could achieve the goals that he could not achieve three hundred years ago. Is that correct?"

Bridge smiles. "Ooh, you are smart!"

Bridge squats and then immediately stands back up, like a life-size jack-in-the-box. "It's more than just that," she states. "You see, if anything happens in the *Liberty Crane*'s dimension, it can affect you and your timeline because now they have become part of your past."

Vicky is forever focused on the solution; she never gives up hope. Although she does not take stock in hope, she also does not take stock in failure. Failure, she feels, is something that people allow when they give up. Vicky takes a breath and takes control of the situation both emotionally and mentally, and she is about to do so physically and literally, as well! She questions Bridge, "There must be a way to stop this!"

Bridge shakes her head. "No, sorry, Lieutenant Young. Once this has now been set into motion, there is no stopping it."

Vicky concentrates and stares back into Bridge. There is something! Vicky can feel it. There is a way to stop this! Again, Vicky asks Bridge, "There must be a way. You said that you felt a connection between us, and it was not your idea for us to be destroyed. If so, then tell me how we can stop this."

Bridge squints half her face into what might be described as a smile. "Well," she replies. "Being that this merge is composed of the precepts of the Dictator's plans, if you can stop the Dictator, if you can defeat him, the merge should not only break but separate, and each dimension will return back on its own path, unscathed. However, defeating the Dictator will not be easy! He's probably almost as powerful now as he was three hundred years ago. And you"—she points and waves her finger at Vicky—"do not have the power they had back then!"

Vicky elevates her chin; a challenge was set before her, and she will meet it! Bridge, understanding Vicky's action, smiles and laughs. She yells out, "Ooo, he has a fight on his hands!" Bridge smashes her fist into her hand. "You go, girl!" she charges.

Vicky almost smiles but controls herself.

Bridge then points one finger up in the air. Her expression changes, an expression of cautioned curiosity falls over her. Bridge asks, "By the way, how exactly did you get here?"

Vicky at this point is very confused as to what Bridge is privy to and what she is not. It seems to Vicky that, at times, Bridge knows things that no one else knows, yet at other times, the things that Vicky assumes she knows, she does not. Vicky responds out of this confused place in her emotions. She replies, "I was sent here by the Defender. She told me that I needed to meet the Army Queen in order to stop the Dictator from regaining his power."

Bridge's expression changes to one of shock and amusement. Her eyes open wide. She jerks back just ever so slightly; even her complexion seems to change one tone lighter. A giggle rises from deep within her throat and comes out as a low growl, like from a small dog. Then, like a storm, it explodes on the scene as a full laugh. She asks, "So … you met Defender? Where?"

Vicky slowly responds, "In the center of the—"

Bridge cuts her off. "So who was there?"

Vicky is still cautious; she is not sure how much information she should divulge to Bridge. Vicky responds slow and low, "I met Defender and Devin."

Bridge looks up at Vicky as if she were examining her for the first time. She questions, "Uh-huh, it was only those two?"

Vicky, unsure of her questioning, nods. "Yes."

Bridge responds by lifting her head and clenching her lips. "Hmm!"

Vicky, extremely curious, asks, "You know them?"

Bridge smiles. "Oh yes, yes, yes, yes, yes! Of course! We are not the best of friends, but we are not enemies either. We kind of have a mutual understanding, and we stay clear of each other. As for Devin, no one, and I mean no one, in their right mind would mess with Devin. Defender, she's okay, I guess."

Vicky glances away. There is a question eating at her; perhaps Bridge could answer it. She looks back at Bridge and asks, "Our scans indicated that there are tunnels through the metal. Do you know anything about them?"

Bridge's face turns blank. She responds, "Did you ask Defender about it? What did she say?"

Shamefully, Vicky nods and replies, "Yes, she didn't say much. She said we were barking up the wrong tree."

Bridge stares at Vicky, uncomfortably quiet for a moment or two. Then she falls back so hard that she bangs into the shuttle. She lets out a loud laugh that bellows into the sky. Vicky, uncertain of Bridge's response, shakes her head and questions, "What? What is it?"

Bridge, regaining her composure, shakes her head, still snickering. She replies, "No, no ... I didn't realize that Defender had a sense of humor! That's all." Bridge looks up as if she were sarcastically laughing at Defender. "Ha, ha!"

Vicky ponders their relationship. She knows that Bridge is not telling her everything she knows. However, she feels that the tide is turning in their favor. Sincerely, Vicky discerns to ask something of Bridge. "Bridge, can you do me a favor?"

Again, Vicky talks to Bridge differently from how anyone has ever talked to her before. All her life, she has been either mocked or people tried to use her. For someone to ask her for a favor, as if she were a normal person, or perhaps even a friend, is very alien to her. She is not sure if she likes the feeling, not willing to compromise herself. Living in hurt and pain has been her known life for a long, long time. Accepting anything else, any sort of change is difficult, even if the change is good. Still uncertain about how to react to her emotions, she can sense the sincerity of Vicky's words. Cautiously, she replies, "What?"

Vicky nods. "Stay here with Private Diamond and guard the shuttle until I get back. Also, if anyone else comes, guard the village."

Vicky turns to walk off. Bridge jerks her head as if she just returned to consciousness. "What? What do you mean? I didn't say I would do it!"

Vicky turns back and directs her, "Just stay here until I get back. Thank you."

Vicky walks off. Pouting, Bridge leans back up against the shuttle and crosses her arms.

Back aboard the *Tiqu-Qi/Liberty Crane*, the vessel has entered into the planet's atmosphere and makes ready for its final approach. The entire deployment anxiously waits in the hangar, making ready for departure into the mysterious caverns where they presume Dr. Long has entered. The ship's steward, Bo Sun, is going from soldier to soldier, checking their equipment and making sure that the oxygen and helmets are secure. He walks up to one of the soldiers and hands him his helmet. The soldier reaches to grab it, but Bo does not let it go. The soldier pulls it and then jerks it from his hands. Bo acts as if he did not even realize that the soldier had removed the helmet from his hands. He stares long at the soldier's face. The soldier, frustrated, asks, "What is wrong with you?"

Bo snaps out of the trance-like state and humbly bows his head. He replies, "I am sorry, but are you Boqin Sun?"

Second Lieutenant Sun looks around, uncertain how the steward knew his full name. He responds, "Yes, I am, but how?"

Again, Bo bows his head, this time three times in a row. He smiles, almost giddy. Bo replies, "You… you are Boqin Sun! You are my great-great-great-great-great-grandfather!"

Unsure how to respond or if he even heard him correctly, Second Lieutenant Sun looks at him strangely. "What? What did you say?" he asks.

Bo responds, his voice cracking, "I cannot explain it, but I recognized you from old pictures. You are Boqin Sun, my great-great-great-grandfather. The first in our family to join the military, you began a legacy, a long line of military leaders! You are one of the reasons why I joined exploration ships. You inspired our entire family. You were a great war hero!"

Second Lieutenant Sun takes a moment, then he smiles. He points first to himself and then back at Bo. To clarify that he understood what Bo said, Second Lieutenant Sun asks, "I am your great-great …"

Bo finishes his sentence for him. "Grandfather. Yes, not sure how many *great*s, but yes!"

Second Lieutenant Sun reaches out and embraces him. He moves him back for a moment to look at him. "Wow!" he replies. "I can't believe it!"

Quickly they realize that they are in a military setting, about to deploy on what could be a dangerous and very important mission! The two of them straighten up. Bo again bows. "Sir, let me help you with your helmet!"

Back aboard the bridge, Lieutenant Lin rushes in for one final check with Wei. Lieutenant Lin hangs over Wei's shoulder. The port window before them gives them a great view of the landscape. *Great* is a relative word, for all that is visible is gray rock, with the exception of the large cavern about one thousand meters out. Lin checks, "How are we?"

Wei confirms, "Everything is a go!"

Then something odd catches Lieutenant Lin's eye. As he looks out the port window, no more than five or ten meters from the entrance of the caverns is a young girl, perhaps no more than fifteen or sixteen years of age. She lies on the cold stone. Her attire is some type of toga, badly ripped and dirty. She herself looks very tattered and dirty. Her long hair is covered in mud yet somehow still long and draped over most of her body. She props herself off the ground by one arm. Around her wrist are cuffs with chains extending back behind her all the way into the caverns.

Apart from the obvious stress she is under, she also seems emotionally drained, and she appears to be sobbing. Lin straightens up in shock and horror at the image before him. Before he can utter a single word, the girl is suddenly jerked backward by the chains. As she is pulled into the caverns, her weakened body is scraped along the ground. Although it is impossible, Lin can hear her cries, "Help me! Help me!" The chains pull her arms over her head and drag her back into the cavern to be consumed by the darkness.

Lin's face is hollow, as if he saw a ghost. He points his finger out, grabbing ahold of Wei's shoulder. He calls out to Captain Reynolds next to him. "Did you guys ... did you see that?"

Captain Barr, concerned by the rare tone in Lin's voice, rises from his seat. He walks over and asks, "What is it? What did ye see?"

Not knowing any other way to say it, he just blurts it out, "You did not see it? There was ... a girl, a young girl! In her early teens, wearing a dirty gray robe, torn up!"

"Where?" asks Barr, both astonished and confused.

Lin points out the port window. He replies, "There, just outside the cavern entrance. She looked beaten and in bad shape."

Moses overhears Lin. Concerned for people's welfare, he moves in closer. Moses asks, "Was she conscious?"

Lin turns to him. The recent sting of shock is still engraved into Lin's face. He answers Moses, his voice trembling, "Yes, but I believe she was crying. Screaming for help! She was handcuffed and chained! And then pulled into the caverns!"

Captain Reynolds questions, "Pulled in by who? Who pulled her in?"

Lin shakes his head, his voice far away, lost in the image he saw, which repeats in an endless, horrifying loop in his head. He replies, "No one! The chains were so long, she was pulled from within!"

Wei looks up at Captain Reynolds, his face heavy with worry. He turns back to his instruments and scans the caverns. Glancing up at Captain Reynolds, he confirms, "Sir, there is a life-form deep within the cavern. It could be her!"

Captain Barr chimes in, "Or it could be Long."

Wei shakes his head. "It is so far into the cavern it could be both of them and reading them as one. I am unsure."

Captain Reynolds interjects, "Anyhow, we are going in now, full force! We will find who or what is in that cavern. And when we find this young lady, we will set her free from whoever is enslaving her!"

Captain Barr agrees, "Aye!"

On the planet's surface, the troops are moving out. The hatch opens, hitting the ground with a thud. The dust is pushing away in every direction. Captain Reynolds and Wei had a separate meeting with Captain Barr and Lieutenant Lin. They suggested that Private Jones should be in charge of the aircraft and that Private Brown should be in charge of the ground forces. They are the only two aboard the combined vessels who have already battled with aliens on the previous mission. Although battered and tired, the two seemed like the best option, and both Wei and Captain Reynolds put a lot of stock in their character and their abilities to lead. Captain Barr, who appreciates Captain Reynolds's judgments, quickly agreed, as did Lieutenant Lin. Although it is highly unorthodox and without precedence, Captain Barr does not have the military power to appoint privates to lead a campaign. However, the condition is extreme, and the necessity to save as many lives as possible far outweighs the legality of military protocol. They also take advantage of the fact that the majority of the *Liberty Crane*'s crew does not know Jones or Brown or their ranks, for that matter. Therefore, they will not question if they were put in charge by Captain Barr. This is also why they did not include Lieutenant Minor in the meeting, knowing that he would not consent. Most likely, he would not notice if no one brings it to his attention.

As they suspect, the entire platoon and all the airmen accept them as their leader and address Brown as "sir" and Jones as "ma'am."

As they exit onto the surface, Brown is perched upon a double-width A-TIV. He nervously calls out to Private Jones on his communicator. "Jones, are you ready?"

Jones responds, "Are you kidding me?"

Brown smiles to himself. *How can they be ready for anything, yet at the same time, they were ready for anything!*

Brown gives the charge. "Move out!"

The troop moves out, approximately five thousand foot soldiers and an array of hover tanks. Jones, who has quickly mastered the controls on the airships, commands, "Move out!"

They follow her as she carefully maneuvers the ships out of the hangar. It feels weird to Private Jones; the other pilots are second lieutenants and far outrank her. Still, she understands the necessity of this mission to succeed, and she also puts stock in Captain Reynolds's decision to put her in charge. Jones pensively presses the communicator. She commands, "Bring out the prisoner!"

A double-width shuttlecraft rises from the hangar floor and flies out between the array of warships to the front, alongside Private Jones's fighter ship. Inside the shuttle, the gray alien prisoner sits in the copilot's seat. Lieutenant Taylor is the pilot. He is young but experienced and has flown numerous successful missions on Earth, of which he led the last three. Positioned directly behind the prisoner are two armed soldiers, one on either side. Behind them are twenty guards, and on a scaffolding above them sits a gunner.

Chapter 14

On the outer rim of the Milky Way sits a most impressive creature. It appears to be a lady approximately seven meters tall, her body burning with bright-yellow fire. She illuminates light like a living sun, sitting on an invisible throne. Quietly she waits in the emptiness of space for the next scene in the theater of eternity to unfold before her. In the distance, a green light appears, slowing as it gets closer. It is the *Green Lightning*, and soon Angel stops mere meters away from this amazing creature. Her eyes open, her pupils ablaze with red fire in the center of blue. The flames dance out and surround her head like hair. She looks casually toward Angel; amazingly, the power of her fire does not affect the *Green Lightning* or Angel, as she can control the amount of heat she emits. Equally amazing, Angel can open the canopy in deep space without losing oxygen or being pulled into the deep void of space. He looks toward his old friend and warns, "Be careful!"

Remarkably, his voice is heard in her head, an ability that few creatures possess. A handful of creatures in space can project their voices into space, most as a form of telepathy, casting their thoughts into another's brain. Others have a very unique ability to send actual sound waves through space. Those with these abilities can usually also hear transmissions from spacecraft and even speak to others aboard the ship through the ship's communication devices. Lastly, some have a darker power enabling them to transfer thoughts and communicate across the span of airless space. Angel warns again, "Be careful, he is coming! He would seek to destroy you!"

Almost as if she did not hear him, she closes her eyes; she seems tired, exhausted even. She slowly turns her head away and opens her eyes, staring out toward the center of the galaxy. She speaks, "I have lived quite a long time. If it is my time to finally die, then so be it! I gladly accept it, and if not …" She pauses, turns her gaze toward Angel. It is the heat of her conviction that grips him, the nails of the cold sincerity of her words cutting deep into Angel's heart. He will not, he cannot, forget her words. She continues, "If not, he will have quite the fight on his hands!"

With that, she closes her eyes and turns her head, facing *Green Lightning*. Angel closes the canopy, and *Green Lightning* turns to pure green energy, slowly shrinking and then disappearing.

As they walk through the village, Vicky, Ruth, and Private Rikes admire the people they see. Similar to Eliana in appearance, most of them are farming or tending to their houses in one way or another. The apparel of those farming is made from a coarser material than that of Eliana's dress, although they have similar colors and patterns. The villagers glance up at the visitors, yet they try not to look directly at them. Although curious, they have great respect for visitors and even greater esteem for the Army Queen. So if anyone is allowed to have an audience with her, they are perceived as royalty.

Vicky, however, cannot fully enjoy the great people she sees, for her concern is for the child. No longer able to take it, she calls out to him. "Young man!" He turns his head. Although his pace decreases, he continues walking forward. Vicky carefully asks, "Why do they call you boy? Do you not have a name?" The boy turns away. "I cannot say my name!"

Vicky pauses for just a second then continues so as not to lose step or conversation between her and him. She asks, "What do you mean? Who are you? Are you here of your own free will?"

The boy turns toward Vicky; he understands her concerns. He nods. "Don't worry, I want to be in no other place! I am not forced to do anything!"

Vicky's face droops. Eliana also understands Vicky's concerns. She humbly states, "Madam, please be assured the boy is well taken care of. And he is here of his own will. Please, madam, allow us to go to the Army Queen. She will explain all."

Again, Vicky looks down, but she can sense the sincerity in Eliana's voice, and her fears are calmed. When they get to the end of the town, the landscape changes; no longer are there patches of thick green grass in rich soil. The ground is replaced by flat gray stone. As they walk, they step up to a higher plateau, then another and another. Finally, at the top again is grass and soil, although it is drier and coarser than the plush soil below. They stand at the base of a steep hill. The young boy leads them to stone steps rising upward to the queen's castle. When Vicky reaches the top, she pauses on the top step. She turns and looks out at the village below. From this vantage point, she can see the entire village and far beyond that, to the meadow that lies in front of it. Surrounding the castle is a tall stone wall; the young boy leads them to the entrance. Rather than a door or gate, the wall just simply ends, with a wide gap before it begins again. The boy stands on one side, and Eliana stands on the other side of the entrance. The boy bows and announces, "Go in, the queen is expecting you."

Rikes, Ruth, and Vicky pause; they look at both the boy and Eliana. Vicky asks, "You are not going in with us?"

Eliana responds, "If the queen needs us, she will call us. Proceed straight, she is waiting for you."

Vicky gives a curious look toward Rikes. Rikes returns the look, for he also has no response; he is as confused as she is. Vicky bows her head toward Eliana and thanks her, "Thank you." She turns forward, and they timidly walk in. The courtyard is large but empty. As they walk, they are amazed that there are no guards; in fact, there are no people in the courtyard at all. They walk to the castle. The castle has a large wooden door. The door is not like those in old pictures of castles, with arched tops, metal bars, and metal bolts protruding from it. No, this door is rectangular, and although it is large, it looks relatively plain. They pause for a second in front of the door, expecting someone to open it for them. Vicky wonders to herself, should she knock? She places her hand on the door, and the door pushes open quite easily. She looks at Rikes and Ruth, bewildered. Vicky raises an eyebrow, as if to say, "Should we just walk in?"

Rikes's expression is blank; he states, "I guess we should go in." His words seem more like a question than a definitive answer. Vicky enters first, followed by Rikes, then Ruth. Rikes scans the castle but finds little more than what they can see with their own eyes. The interior of the castle is quite interesting. The place has more of an appearance of an eighteenth-century mansion. The floors are polished wood, and the walls are plastered and painted white. Some lovely solid wood furniture is placed against the walls around the room. They leave a short, wide hallway and enter a large room. Still, there are no people.

At the end of the room is another door. This door has an arched top and very impressive designs engraved into it. The door is wide and separated into two sides that open inward toward them. Each door houses lovely metal handles; they appear to be brass with silver trimmings. Each handle points from the center outward, away from the other. Vicky grabs hold of the handles, one in each hand, and pulls them in toward herself. The doors glide open. They walk into a well-lit room. There are similar pieces of furniture like the ones they found at the entrance. However, the floor here is carpeted with a red rug, trimmed with an intricate design at the edges. The rug extends perfectly from wall to wall. Overlaid on the rug is a narrow carpet, flowing down the center from the door leading to a throne.

On the throne is a beautiful woman. Her attire is very different from those in the village; she seems to be wearing a silken white robe with a sash, very similar to Eliana's dress, with the colors of nature—rich browns and greens swirled with sky blue, imitating the movement of wind. Her hair is dark, as are her eyes. Her skin is light, although she does have a warm tan from the sun. Her lips are bright red. Behind her is a red velvet curtain draped from one end of the wall to the other. Displayed in front of the curtain but behind the throne are spears and swords of various types. Alongside her on either side are beautifully designed iron baskets holding weapons. Some are ancient, like bows and arrows, others are modern, some even Vicky and Rikes cannot make out, just that they appear to be extremely menacing.

The throne sits on three tiers of marble slabs, each approximately twenty centimeters thick. Each slab is perfectly round. The top tier that houses the throne is about two and a half meters wide, the middle about three meters, and the bottom is almost four meters. The tiers function as stairs 360 degrees around the throne, with the narrow carpet up the center to the throne.

Directly in front of them and to her left is a large wood table and chairs. The chairs are upholstered with cushions that match the carpet. The three of them lose their breath at the splendor of what is before them. The queen summons them with her hand. She calls to them, "Come, my friends, join me."

Her voice is soft, yet like Defender's voice, it demands respect. Slowly they walk forward. Vicky and Private Rikes bow down to the

Army Queen. Ruth follows suit, and she also bows. Vicky states, "Your Majesty. I am—"

However, the Army Queen stops Vicky. "No," she states as she rises from her throne, "I am not that type of queen. Come this way." With a hand, she motions toward the table. She walks down the steps of the throne toward the table. She sits, putting her two hands out, pointing to the chairs, inviting them to sit. Vicky nods and pulls out a chair and sits, as do Rikes and Ruth. Vicky continues, "I am Lieutenant Young of the UPA and this is Private Rikes—"

Again, the Army Queen cuts her off. "I know who you are, and I know why you came. What I do not know is if I can help you."

Vicky impatiently grinds her teeth and grabs hold of the edge of the table; she knows what is at stake, and she refuses to believe she came all this way for nothing. She challenges the Army Queen. Vicky pauses; it just does not sound correct. She asks, "Is that your name? Army Queen? Is that what you wish to be called, Your Majesty?"

The Army Queen looks out a window on the far wall. She watches the fluffy clouds in the distance. She turns toward Vicky and explains, "I've had many names. I do not even remember my original name anymore, and the names that were given to me afterwards I wish to forget! Please call me Army Queen, it is the best I can offer you for now."

Vicky nods in acceptance and continues. "Very well," she states. "We were sent here by the Defender. She told us that the Dictator is regaining power … to destroy us!"

Rikes interjects, "There was a war that we know nothing about—"

The Army Queen extends her hand, stopping them. She looks at each of them in their eyes. She states, "You three were sent by the Defender. You come to me, and you do not even know who I am nor how I could help you. Well, let me enlighten you. Let me tell you a tale of who I am, and then you shall understand that the best way I can help you is by doing nothing at all!"

Vicky, Rikes, and Ruth look at one another. Information has been kept from them since the very beginning of this mission! The three of them greatly desire to know more about what is going on and how all this came to be. If the Army Queen is willing to tell them some vital piece, then they are intrigued; the three of them look at her with eyes wide open. As she speaks, her mind wanders, remembering a time long ago. She states, "When man first became violent, it was not a slow succession, it was quick and brutal. The men from my city went to war against a band of evil, ruthless men. They plagued our civilization, going from town to town, city to city, raiding, destroying, killing everyone and everything! They were wanderers, and there was no defense against them! Our men fought to save the lives of their wives and children, but they were no match for them. There was no way they could have been prepared for the brutality these wanderers possessed! They were destroyed before they started …"

She pauses. Even though this happened many, many years ago, the vivid images remain fresh. She takes a moment to pause before speaking again. She stares deep into their eyes. Her expression overwhelms the three of them. They can feel her loss. Suddenly, her expression changes, from victim to warrior. She rises in her seat, the muscles in her arm flaring as she pushes herself up. She roars, "I fought back! I raised an army of the women and children. Soon, for my heroism, I was given power. My army of women fought back … After endless battles, war was finally put to a stop, but not without its casualties! The children—"

The Army Queen looks out the window, her eyes welling with tears. She holds them back. She continues, "The children were taken to a safe place, they had gone through more than any child should have to! The rest of us joined the Great Separation."

This is the second time that Vicky has heard this term, *the Great Separation*. She is intrigued, perhaps even more now, if that is possible. The Army Queen continues. Once again, her continence changes. Now, as she speaks, her thoughts seem far away. Similar to a scarred person talking about a past life of pain and regret. "Well," she continues, "people settled, civilizations grew, there was peace. I was a warrior with no war. I traveled from planet to planet without a cause, lost. When the Dictator came into power, he approached me. He gave me purpose once again. We made a covenant together. He needed warriors, and I could make them. I never thought to ask what he needed them for. To be honest, I deeply regret the fact that I was so consumed by my desire for purpose. I didn't care about anything else, I was blinded."

She turns to them and painfully states, "Weapons are not evil. It is what you do with them. I was given power to protect. Little did I know I was helping him to destroy. When I found out the true nature of his goals and the horror of how many civilizations he enslaved and killed! The mass genocide! I left him. The problem with leaving a covenant like this is that you can't! You either stay or die. Still, war had broken out, and he was preoccupied, unable to focus his attention on me. If he had realized that I had abandoned his cause, he would have surely sought to kill me. Also, I posed too much of a threat for him to engage while fighting a war at the same time."

Her eyes glare. "It would not be easy to kill me."

She continues, her eyes looking out as if she were watching herself relive what transpired all those long years ago. "I ran," she states. "In my wanderings, I discovered firsthand what he was doing, how he was searching out planets ... searching out certain individuals who had special innate abilities. He inflicted them and changed them to become generals in his army."

She turns toward Ruth, sadness overwhelming her. She calls out to Ruth, "Cherut, your planet ... I know what happened ... I am so sorry for you and your family ... and that I could not stop it! I was too late."

Heavyhearted, Ruth looks down, confused. She did not expect someone else to know of her or the tragedy that befell her and her people.

The Army Queen continues, "I had found Malak-Beth in my travels. They were good people, warm and loving! They were people lacking a protector. It is as if we were made for each other. They were willing to allow me to stay but with only one condition: I would be their queen, their protector."

She takes a moment to adjust herself in her chair before she continues. "Once the Dictator discovers that someone is special, he sends out drones. They search the galaxies, planet by planet. They orbit, secretly."

She looks up and points her finger upward, gently waving it as if she were following their movements with her finger. She continues, "Listening in on any transmission, any mention of that person. Once they find them, that is the end, for that planet and for that person!"

Ruth's eyes light up. She straightens up as if she were looking at something in the distance. Ruth looks at Rikes, then Vicky, and finally, at the queen. "The little boy?" Ruth asks.

A moment later, Vicky also catches the revelation. She looks at Ruth and nods. Vicky turns toward the Army Queen and states, "The little boy, that is why you cannot say his name!"

The Army Queen calls for the child. "Boy, come!"

A moment later, the door opens, and the boy walks in humbly, yet at the same time, there is a sense of belonging in his step. He walks up to the queen and responds, "Madam?"

She lifts her fingers and gently wraps them around his shoulder. She smiles at him then looks out at the three to tell his tale. She states, "This young man is special. One of the Dictator's many drones spied him using his amazing abilities. Not long after that, his planet was attacked. They destroyed everyone on his planet. The boy cried out for help, and I found him. He was hiding. I rescued him and took him away from there. That is why we can never say his name. We believe that drones are still out there, searching!"

Again, the Army Queen glances out the window; the clouds have shifted, and a storm is coming. The sky is turning gray.

At the edge of town where Vicky had asked Bridge to wait for her, Bridge paces back and forth, talking to herself. "Why should I wait here?" Bridge argues with herself. "Who does she think she is to ask me to wait?" Bridge points up as if she had an amazing idea. "Well, she did ask me—" Then she points her finger out as if she were accusing someone. "That's probably the reason why you're staying! Only because she asked!"

Suddenly two bright lights appear in the sky. Bridge notices them, squints her eyes, and cups her hands around her eyes to get a better look. The lights turn into two Sheol ships. Sheol ships are so terrifyingly designed that even nightmares could not have fashioned them! Although their frames are metal, the outer skin is formed from a double layer of a canvaslike substance. Dark gray, almost black, the material is stronger than steel yet as flexible as a thick cloth. Shredded and ragged from battle, the torn outer skin waves in the wind as it descends. The ships look more like a pair of evil ravens burnt in a fire, seeking revenge, rather than a ship! Fire from the engines presses against the ground as the two ships land less than twenty meters from the entrance of the town.

Bridge, quite unimpressed, looks at her satchel and says to it, "Let's go and investigate." She stomps over like an old lady dispatching ruffians from her front yard. Sheol ships' canopies are cut in half, with two blackened oval doors made out of shiny, smooth glass, one on either side, giving the appearance of eyes. One "eye" on each ship opens upward. Out step Ze'ev Warriors, mercenaries from numerous planets under the Ze'ev control.[1] These are not the original pilots of the Sheol ships. The Dictator despises and distrusts all intelligent organic forms of life; therefore, his original army was mechanical. However, with the need for expansion, he had to rely on other life-forms, so rather than destroying the barbaric Ze'ev people, he enslaved them to fight in his army. The Ze'ev are vile creatures; although their roots and structures stem from humanity, they are vicious, with sharp teeth. Their senses are heightened. They are fast but not much stronger than your average human. Their uniform is made out of a similar material as the ship's exterior. Their helmets have a sharp downward point above their foreheads. The visors are made from the same black glass as that of the ship's canopy.

They exit the ship, remove their helmets, and walk toward the town. They are intercepted by Bridge. She calls out to them, "So where do you think you are going?" The two quickly turn toward Bridge, hands over their weapons, a large pistol holstered to their belts. Looking her up and down, they scoff at her. The first one, Tuku Ripclaw (Commander Ripclaw), is taller and heavier than his comrade. His beard is rough, very rough, as if he tried to shave it off with a dull knife. Clenching his teeth, he responds, thick white saliva and small pieces of food flying out between his pointed teeth as he growls his words. "Move out of our way, little girl, or we shall kill you where you stand!"

Bridge, highly offended to be spoken to in such a manner, rears for the attack. She screams out at them; her fierceness catches them off guard. "How dare you scream at me! Do you know who I am? I am the daughter of the most powerful being in the universes! Y'all have to respect! Don't make me call Impulse, she's my friend. She'll just destroy you and your entire army!"

The two mercenaries look at each other and remove their weapons from the holsters. This upsets Bridge even more! She increases the intensity of her rant. "Oh no! You did not just take your guns out on me! Now I'm gonna' have to get Dead Cat!" Bridge reaches into her satchel and pulls out Dead Cat. She starts swinging him by the tail over her head. She warns them, "Don't make me use Dead Cat!"

---

1 The Ze'ev are warrior people from the planet Zev who predate the Dictator's reign by hundreds of years. They were the original raiders of the planets in this galaxy. Once the Dictator gained control, they became his servants, forcing them to join his army and helping him fight his wars. Since the Dictator's defeat and disappearance, for the past three hundred years, the Ze'ev have regained much control, and although not a dominant presence in their galaxy, they have managed to gain control and enslave a handful of planets.

Even the two hardened villains take a moment to try to absorb the image before them. However, having little regard for life or emotions, they proceed to raise their weapons. Suddenly they stop. Not many things bring fear to the Ze'ev mercenaries, but the sight of Private Diamond's huge body walking up behind Bridge is enough to make their hearts skip a few beats. The second mercenary turns to the first and stammers, "Tubu, ki khan meka-spirit gen gen meka-spirit? Ki terror etta han ka'dool?" (Commander, do you see it? It is not like any robot I've ever seen! It's twice the size, and are those horns on top of his head?) Commander Ripclaw nods. He adds, "And look at his skin, it is metal! That is impenetrable metal!"

Fear and panic overtake them, for in their hearts, they are bullies and cowards! They quickly muzzle their weapons back into their holsters. Bridge, as confident as always, mocks them, "Oh, that's right! That's right! You best put those toys away before I unleash some Dead Cat on you! You better get back in your ships and get out of here!" She flares her hand as one might to dust crumbs off a table. The two walk toward their ship, but not without a warning. Commander Ripclaw cries out, "We will leave now, but be warned, we will return soon! In full force, one hundred thousand strong! and this"—he points outward toward the town—"shall all be destroyed! And your 'queen' shall be ours!"

Bridge continues to swing Dead Cat above her head. Accidentally, Dead Cat collides with Private Diamond standing behind her, releasing a hard, metallic thump. Bridge, unaware that Private Diamond is now standing behind her, looks up over her shoulder at Private Diamond. She questions him, "Oh, you here to help?" She yells out at the ships, "Well, I don't need him! You come get some from me! Threaten me, I'll show you! You best go!" Bridge continues to taunt as the ships fire up and exit into the gray clouds. Bridge strokes Dead Cat, squishing his face and pulling his ears back. She puckers her lips and, in a squeaky voice, compliments him, "Oh, you were so good! You scared away the bad guys! Yes, you did. Yes, you did."

Bridge, content that Dead Cat is properly complimented and loved for his bravery, places him back into her satchel. Suddenly a blue light appears in the sky, shining down on her. Unlike *Green Lightning*'s green glow, this light is ominous and threatening, swerving and whipping in and out. Private Diamond scans the odd phenomenon, but he cannot get a reading or an originating point. Bridge looks up toward the light and, with a mischievous smile, says, "Hey, Doc, what's up?"

A voice responds from within the light. The methodical voice is both deep and tormenting. "You interfered!" he bellows. "You sent away two of the Dictator's warriors! Let me remind you, your job is not to interfere but to serve!" Bridge does not like this tone, and her face shows it! She jerks her head back, stands up straight, and points defiantly toward the light. She hollers back, "Oh, first, you've been all one type of a way, and now you're another type of a way! I serve no one!" She points to herself and repeats, "I serve no one! I was doing you a favor because I thought we were friends!" The voice interrupts, "There is no relationship between you and I! You do what we tell you to do! You have a job to do now! Do it, or there will be consequences!" Bridge looks at the light as if it has spoken to her in a language that she does not understand. Suddenly she bursts into maniacal laughter. The mysterious voice tries to continue, tries to intimidate her, but it cannot get a word around the deafening laughter. Finally, it has no choice but to give in, and it ceases its rant. Bridge, on the other hand, is not finished. Her words are stained with attitude and defiance. "Oh," she states, "I'll do my … job! Not because you told me but only because I already agreed on it, and I always keep my word! You best remember who I am! And don't ever threaten me again!" With that, the blue light sputters and disappears. Bridge frowns in anger and turns away. At the last moment, her face turns into a terrifying grin.

In the queen's castle high above the turmoil, Vicky turns toward the queen and asks, "Question, you said that they could not find him, but you found him. How was it that they could not find him and yet you could?"

The queen smiles; she looks graciously at the boy and then back at her audience. She speaks as a mother would speak proudly of her child, "You see, he has special abilities, and certain people, like myself, can see through those abilities. They do not affect me." The queen releases her hand from around the boy's shoulder, allowing him to move forward ever so slightly. She looks at him and tells him, "Show them." The boy bows his head toward her and replies, "Yes, madam." He then turns and looks at Vicky, Rikes, and Ruth as if he were preparing to perform. Then suddenly he disappears!

Rikes and Ruth search frantically around the room for the boy. Rikes yells out to Vicky, "He's disappeared! Where did he go?" Vicky, confused, calmly calls out to Rikes, "Rikes, check your scans. See if you can find him." Rikes complies, as Ruth quietly searches around the room to see if she can see him. Rikes responds, "Ma'am, I cannot find him! He's disappeared! He must have teleported somewhere." The Army Queen smiles and lets out a little giggle. "No, no," she responds, "he's right here." The boy reappears. Again, the queen places her hand gently over his shoulder. She looks at the boy and smiles proudly at his accomplishments. She looks up at her audience and elaborates, "He can also project his thoughts to other people, even across space. That is how I knew that you were here before you came in. He told me."

Ruth, Rikes, and Vicky look at one another, bewildered. Before they can ask another question, the door bursts open, and Eliana runs in. She stops before the queen and bows low. She quickly rises and states, "Your Majesty, two Sheol ships have entered the front courtyard, just before the entrance of the town!" She waves her hands toward Vicky and states, "It would seem that your comrades have chased them away!" Eliana directs her attention to the queen again. She continues, "However, I fear they shall return! I am sure of it!"

The queen grabs hold of the boy ever more tightly. Eliana humbly continues, as if she were afraid to speak it, in fear that, if she says it, it will be true. She states, "Madam, there is more." The queen urges, "Speak." Eliana continues, "I fear they're not after the boy." She looks into the queen's eyes. "I think they were here for you!"

Chapter 15

Private Jones leads the troop into the caverns; evidently, Captain Reynold's choice to put her in charge was not made in error, for she has already forgotten her sense of inferiority. Not arrogantly, she has focused her attention on the mission ahead. Although the cavern's opening is huge, it is considerably smaller inside. It is still quite large; however, only a little over half a kilometer is safe for her aircraft and the foot soldiers to traverse. They continue to scan for life within. The scans all indicate some form of life ahead, but they cannot pinpoint the distance, nor, for that matter, can they be certain how many life-forms there are. The reading is obviously too small to indicate a large group; however, it could be more than one or even a small group huddled close. Only time will tell. A few hundred meters in, the main cavern branches off into three large tunnels. The center one is the largest and the only one safe enough to fly her aircraft. Private Jones calls out to her comrade, Private Brown. "Brown, do you see this?"

Brown responds, "Yes, ma'am, I see it. How should we proceed?"

She thinks for a second, but the choice seems obvious. The center is the larger and highest of the three caverns; this is where the majority of her aircraft should proceed. She hails the alien prisoner, "Guide 1, how should we proceed?"

He ponders the situation for a moment. Finally, he responds, "It has been some time. All three ways used to lead to the center, but it has been a while. I could not tell you if they all remain intact. I do remember that the tunnel to our left is the quickest way to the center. The other two tunnels lead to various storage areas and housing. The tunnel to the left was made to be the quickest way to the center. However, it is also divided into a maze, designed to keep intruders from the center. There are our greatest possessions: energy and water."

The alien's report confirms Jones's strategy. Jones hails Brown, "Brown, I believe that straightforward is the quickest and safest path for our airships. Brown, divide your men into two companies. Company One, proceed left flank; you lead. Let guide 1's shuttle lead you through the maze. Sergeant Yang, proceed right flank. You are in charge. They might be living establishments and storage, but they also might be clues!"

Brown and Yang respond, "Ma'am, yes, ma'am!"

Jones continues, "Brown, I will send a shuttlecraft at your rear for additional air support, as well as for you, Sergeant Yang—"

She reminds them, emphasizing the urgency of the mission, "It goes without saying, any findings, report to me immediately!"

Again, the two respond, "Ma'am, yes, ma'am!"

Jones hails Rivera and Carter, two young fighter pilot lieutenants. "Rivera and Carter, you remain here for additional support for either Yang, Brown, or myself!"

Rivera and Carter both enthusiastically respond, "Ma'am, yes, ma'am!"

Finally, Jones concludes, "Shuttle 9, shuttle 10, set camp here. You will be a gofer between the three troops, bringing whatever aid is needed."

The shuttle pilots respond, "Ma'am, yes, ma'am!"

Jones looks forward with fire and determination in her eyes. She gives the charge. "Proceed!"

In an instant, like lightning hitting a dry forest and the flames bursting out, her words ignite movement, and the three troops move out.

In the palace, the Army Queen rushes off her throne. "We must get to the courtyard!" she states. She turns to Eliana. "Eliana, place the boy in the isolation room."

The boy screams out, "What? No! I am a prince. I need to go with you! I need to help!"

The queen grabs the boy by the shoulders. She looks him in his defiant eyes and tells him, "No, you must stay protected! You are my valuable little boy. Stay here! The room is the safest room on the planet."

She turns to Eliana and commands, "Bring him, and set two servants outside the room to guard him."

Eliana curtsies and responds, "Yes, ma'am."

She grabs hold of the boy's hand to lead him to the isolation room. The boy leaves reluctantly, pleading his case every step of the way. The four hasten off to the courtyard.

The sun is starting to set, and the storm clouds make the sky even darker, almost as if the planet itself were reacting to the ominous threat that was approaching. The Army Queen, Vicky, Ruth, and Rikes all hasten through the town toward the courtyard. The townspeople stand at their doorposts in awe of their queen. They bow and with their voices pay great homage to her. Still, there is a great concern rising up in their hearts. They all saw the Sheol ships, and they know that this is an evil sign. They wonder, 'What could this possibly mean?'

Vicky's communicator is chiming as Private Diamond updates her. She reads the message, then turns to Rikes and the others. Vicky relays his message to them, "Private Diamond says that there are ships about to enter the planet's atmosphere! They are large!"

She looks at Rikes and states, "Larger than the *Liberty Crane*!"

Whereas Vicky moves up ahead of everyone, Rikes has to pause. This information is numbing, and he needs a moment to process it. The troop almost totally passes him by, but he quickly catches up. Vicky enters the courtyard. No sooner does she enter than when Bridge rushes over to her. Bridge, in no uncertain terms, states, "Listen, Lieutenant Young, I have to go! I have something I have to do, and I can't—"

Her words are cut off as Vicky moves aside and the Army Queen comes into Bridge's view. Bridge is stunned! Her jaw drops, and for the first time since Vicky met her, Bridge's expression changes from confident to innocent. Bridge's eyes open and well up like a child's. She calls out to the Army Queen, "Em! Gebhirah Shaghal, Em!"

The queen pauses; their eyes meet. The queen's eyes also grow large; her face is nurturing. She lifts her hand toward Bridge and gently strokes her cheek. She calls to her, "Bridge, my young one. How good it is to see you."

Bridge steps back and cries out, "You? You are the queen they are after?"

Bridge turns away in anger, frustrated that she did not realize whom they were after. She feels used! She chastises herself, "Of course, what did you expect? Who else would be the 'queen' they wanted?"

Bridge continues mumbling to herself. The queen calls out to her, "Bridge, my young one, it's alright."

Again, Bridge steps back. She wipes her eyes before facing the queen again. Bridge apologizes, "Em, Em, sorry … I have to go. I have a job to do … but now I know exactly what I must do!"

Vicky, Rikes, and Ruth are all confused. Vicky turns toward the queen and asks, "Your Majesty, you two know each other?"

The queen turns and responds, her words soft and reminiscing, "I've known Bridge for a long time, way before she was ever Bridge."

Before the queen can continue, a cry of despair rises out from the townspeople. They turn toward the townspeople. With fear in their eyes, the townspeople stand there trembling, pointing upward toward the sky. Vicky and her team look up. The warships are breaking through the clouds! Although the clouds conceal most of their form, the ships' lights give them away. In fact, three large ships can clearly be made out. Two seem almost next to each other, and the third, larger than the first two, is positioned even farther up into the sky. Vicky turns to the Army Queen and assures her, "We will hold them off as best we can! Is there any way you can evacuate your people?"

The queen stands silent. She had feared that this time would come for a very long time now. Two years ago, when she found the boy, she knew it was coming that much sooner! Still, she is no more prepared now than she was when she first came to Malak-Beth. The people here are simple; they do not have advanced technology. They love their land and will refuse to leave. The Army Queen knows this. She has made up her mind; she will die protecting her people if needed! She turns to Vicky and directs her, "You defend the courtyard as best you can! Keep them from entering the town! I will stay here and protect the entrance to the town! Those large ships"—she points up—"they cannot land in the courtyard. There is not enough space for them. They will have to land in the clearing below. There is only one path in the rocky terrain wide enough for their tanks and soldiers to climb. That is good! It would mean that they can only come at you a few at a time."

Vicky nods. Her strategy is strong, but the odds are great. It is the only strategy they have: to fight the few against the many.

Vicky turns to prepare for the battle, but before she can move, the Army Queen reaches out and grabs a hold of her arm. Vicky turns and looks into the eyes of a mother. The queen speaks. "There is a small ship suitable for space flight. It is fast! It is behind the palace. If they reach the town, save the child!"

Vicky puts her hand over the queen's hand and softly rubs it. She nods; a pact has been made. Vicky will do her best to achieve her end of the bargain. The queen quickly turns and stands before the entrance of the town. She calls out to Eliana, "Eliana, my sword!" Anticipating her queen's needs, as soon as the child is secure, Eliana retrieves the sword. Moments later, Eliana appears with a long sword wrapped in a sheath of fleece. Vicky ponders her weapon choice. *Will she defend the town with a sword?*

Vicky looks around to find Bridge; however, Bridge is nowhere to be found. She calls out to Private Diamond, "Private Diamond, what is Bridge's location?"

Vicky's wrist chimes. The text reads, "I cannot scan her."

Vicky frowns, confused. "Where could she be?" She wonders "How does she get around?" She calls out to Rikes. "Rikes, unload the weapons on the shuttle!"

Rikes responds, "Yes, ma'am! Which ones?"

"All," replies Vicky.

Rikes responds, "Yes, yes, ma'am!"

They hasten to the shuttle's weapons storage hatch and open it. Vicky instructs Diamond and Rikes on how to spread the weapons. Vicky did not ask Ruth for help unloading the weapons for two reasons: for one, Ruth is not military and, therefore, not familiar with the weapons, nor does she even know their names. Secondly, Ruth has been nervous, ready for battle ever since the enemy warships showed themselves. Ruth's hands have been steaming since that time; Vicky was concerned that Ruth could accidentally damage the weapons and/or hurt herself.

Vicky has the weapons spread out strategically, some in trees and some on the ground. Others she placed along the side of the stone wall. One she even buried under a handful of grass. She also attached two additional sidearms to her belt and four cartridges for each. The ships have moved closer, but they have not yet started the attack. The most likely reason is that they are considering the best option to land and deploy their troops. Vicky knows that they can bomb them from above and wipe them out in minutes. She also knows that they want something, someone, either the Army Queen, the boy, or perhaps both. This will be to Vicky's advantage as the enemy is forced to engage in a land assault. This brings the battle to Vicky. Still, they have mere moments to prepare!

When they are finished, Rikes stands at attention, ready for action. Rikes asks, "Ma'am, what is our plan of action?"

Vicky commands, "Rikes, you take the shuttle. You are our best pilot. You meet them in the air. As soon as they descend, you rise, take out as many as you can! Private Diamond and I will stay down here to handle the ground forces!"

Rikes responds, "Ma'am, yes, ma'am!"

Rikes obediently runs toward the shuttle. He pauses. "Ma'am," he asks, "any idea how many are coming?"

Both Vicky's and Rikes's communicators chime. They look at Diamond's text: "100,000."

It does not matter to Vicky the amount; she has set her mind. Not only must they complete this mission, but they also have to save their people! Somehow, they will make it through regardless of the odds. She must find a way to succeed. Her determination is unwavering! She nods; it is not a normal nod. It states that she acknowledges the circumstances but the circumstances must also acknowledge her! Rikes receives her determination within his heart, and it empowers him.

They both run toward the shuttle. Ruth runs alongside them, ready for action. Vicky pauses for a moment. She cups her finger over her chin then looks at Ruth. Before Vicky can say a word, Ruth interjects, "I want to help! I have powers, let me help."

Vicky acknowledges her. She looks her straight in the eyes. Sincerely, Vicky tells her, "Yes, but you have not tested them yet. As powerful as you are, you do not know if you can be harmed ... Do as much damage as possible, but stay out of sight. Protect the perimeter as best you can so that we keep the fight in the one path up the hill."

Ruth looks toward the path and then back at Vicky. She responds, "Yes, ma'am."

Respecting Vicky's concerns, Ruth rushes toward the edge of the courtyard to get her bearings and form her strategy. Vicky would have preferred not to use either Ruth or the queen. Although capable, they are civilians. However, Vicky realizes that these are desperate times. Not only the fate of her people is at stake, but that of the entire village, as well! She has no choice but to use whoever is available. No sooner does Ruth rush off than when one of the warships moves aggressively toward the ground. Vicky yells out, "Positions, we are up!"

As they predicted, the enormous ship must rest in the open meadow, which lies in front of the hill that the town sits on. Engine fire and smoke burn into the grass. Before the smoke has a chance to clear, the hatch opens. The hatch is almost as wide as the entire ship.

Private Williams and Chen are the two shuttle pilots Jones commanded to set camp at the mount of the cavern. Williams is an energetic, enthusiastic Black woman. She is short and stout. Her desire was always to help others, a dream that she pursued for years as a nurse in Texas. However, becoming sick and tired of the politics at her job, she decided to follow her father's footsteps. She got her pilot's license and joined the Chinese military. Chen is about the same age, but he is a military man and enlisted the day after his eighteenth birthday.

Lieutenants Rivera and Carter have stepped out of their fighters to stretch their legs. As Williams connects the rest of the equipment aboard the mothership, Lieutenant Lin continues his communications with Chen. Chen replies, "Sir, yes, sir! The troops have moved out, and Williams has completed securing the perimeter. So far, all things are a go."

Lin replies, "Roger, very good! Proceed, keep us posted on any changes."

Chen replies, "Roger!"

Suddenly, out of nowhere, a thick red fog pushes through the cavern, as if a giant dragon exhaled his smoky breath! The fog is so forceful that even though they are wearing their space suits, they instinctively raise their arms to protect themselves; Rivera even crouches into a fetal position. The fog runs through. Aboard the *Liberty Crane/Tiqu-Qi*, Captain Reynolds, Captain Barr, Lieutenant Lin, and Wei witness the thick crimson smoke exiting out from the mouth of the cavern. Barr cries out, "Whit in th' world wis 'at?"

Captain Reynolds points down at the controls, indicating for Wei and Lin to identify the gas. Wei replies, "Analyzing, sir!"

Lin calls out to his men, "Chen, come in! Are you okay?"

The fog moved out as quickly as it came in. The team seemed unaffected by it. Chen replies, "Sir, I think that we are fine!"

Chen calls out, "Williams, Rivera, Carter, status!"

The three all look one another over. They check their instruments and shake their heads, confirming their wellness. Carter takes the initiative to answer for them. "We're fine, none the worse for wear."

Chen reports to Lin, "Sir, we're fine."

Rivera asks, "Lieutenant Lin, what was that?"

Lin looks over at Wei and replies, "We are analyzing it now."

Wei looks puzzled. He turns up at Captain Reynolds and Captain Barr. With notable concern in his voice, he announces, "Sir, the gas has some sort of organic crystallized acid!"

"Acid?" yells out Captain Reynolds. "Are they okay?"

Wei states, "Their suits should have protected them, it was mild, but there is something else."

Lin looks up, concerned. He announces, "There's also some sort of hallucinogenic substance within the gas itself!"

Lin calls out to Chen, "Chen, do you read me?"

Chen responds, "Sir, yes, sir!"

Lin commands, "Hail Private Jones. Send her this information we are transmitting to you! The gas had some sort of acid and also a hallucinogenic! We want you four to abort your post and return to base immediately for evaluation by our medical team!"

Chen replies, "Sir, yes, sir! The gas was nontoxic! Good news."

There is silence on the bridge. They stare at one another, confused. Assuming that Chen did not understand the communication, Lin repeats himself, "Chen, do you read me? The gas *is* toxic! You are ordered to send this data to Private Jones and then return to base!"

Again, Chen responds, "Sir, yes, sir, we read you! The gas is nontoxic, Roger that!"

Captain Reynolds takes hold of the controls. He shouts into it, "This is Captain Reynolds, we are ordering you to come back aboard the mothership this instance!"

However, this time, the only reply is static.

Five minutes earlier

At three hundred kilometers per hour, the slowest the fighters can fly without fear of stalling; they have traveled a little over thirty kilometers. Every twenty seconds or so, the cavern dips downward to a deeper level, bringing the crew further into the depths of the planet. Almost as soon as they enter, they lose radio contact with both home base and the mothership. Still, the mission is a go. They have their contingency plan in place; a shuttle will act as a liaison between the mission teams and home base. Jones leads seventy-five fighters down the cavern in twenty-five rows of three. She pilots the center fighter in the first row. The walls are fairly smooth; although bumpy, they are not jagged. They were definitely carved, just as the gray alien creature had told them. For the past couple of minutes, the walls have become wet and slimy. In fact, the further they travel down the cavern, the slimier the walls get. Jones tries once again to contact home base. "This is Private Jones, Lieutenant Rivera, Lieutenant Carter, come in, please."

Static comes over the channel. Unable to reach Rivera or Carter, she addresses her squadron, "It would seem that we are so far into the caverns, we lost communications with base camp, Brown, or the mothership. Shuttlecraft 7, do you read me?"

From the end of the long line of fighters, Sergeant Song replies, "Yes, ma'am, I read you loud and clear!"

Jones continues, "After another thousand meters, go back to base camp."

Suddenly the red fog blows through the tunnel, as if shot out from the very pores of the cavern walls itself! So thick is the fog that the instruments momentarily shut, and the ships go dark! The engines choke. Jones cries out to her pilots, "This is Jones, do you read? Do you read?" The lights in her fighter flicker on and off; she can see the other fighters to her left and right are experiencing the same difficulties. Miraculously, the ships do not stall completely. In fact, Jones believes that their speed did not decrease. However, without communications, she cannot slow up or land, in fear of causing a collision! Frantically, Jones cries out once more, "This is Jones, do you read? Do you read me?"

The advanced warships do have the ability to hover and to even patrol; however, this maneuver requires stabilizing rockets. In the empty void of space, this would not be a problem; however, in the closed interior of the caverns, the fire and smoke from the stabilizer rockets would not only endanger the mission but also limit visibility.

Horrifyingly long second later they respond, "Jones we read you! What was that?"

Jones replies, "Analyzing!"

Jones regains her composure. She commands, "Reduce speed to 130 knots. Starting with shuttle 7, roll call!"

Sergeant Song, shuttle 7's pilot, replies, "Yes, ma'am!"

The stabilizing rockets fire up as the ships reduce their speed. While she waits for the report on the welfare of her team, Jones analyzes the gas. The light blinks on Jones' computer screen, ANALYSIS COMPLETE. Jones takes a breath then presses the button. The computer announces, "Analysis complete. The gas structure seems organic in nature: 10% unidentifiable, 90% an unknown concentrated crystallized acid."

Jones looks out, her eyes dilated. Her words are quivering as she cries out, "What in the world?"

Sergeant Yang leads her troop down winding tunnels. Yang is convinced that these truly must have been dwellings for the gray alien's people, but now they are barren. The main tunnel branches out into hundreds or thousands of narrow tunnels just large enough for a person to easily crawl in and out of. They open into small circular rooms, barely big enough for three people to sit comfortably in. After about two kilometers of searching and analyzing, Yang has found little to nothing. Exiting yet another empty tunnel, Yang feels frustrated. She pauses and stares ahead, contemplating her next move. She notices that the tunnel ahead of her seems to change; she wonders if her eyes are playing tricks on her. She walks forward to investigate, her stride and speed increasing. Her team notices her enthusiasm and follows suit, following her with renewed energy. After a few meters, the walls of the cavern change to a pinkish hue. Yang reaches out and presses her hand against it. The wall gives; it seems soft, almost rubbery. Yang turns toward her tech specialist. She commands him, "Soldier, analyze!"

Obediently he responds, "Ma'am, yes, ma'am!"

He removes his handheld; a green light scans the surface walls. After a moment of silence, he turns his face toward Sergeant Yang. He is confused, and his confusion can be heard in his voice, "Ma'am, its readings are the same! It is composed of the same substance as the rest of the cavern!"

Yang usually relies on logic, but these readings do not match with what she sees. It does not make sense; something is wrong. She waves her hand forward. They move out in full force. After about two hundred meters in, one of the soldiers investigates an opening similar to the ones that they have found earlier. He slides down into the tunnel, into the small round opening. Hunched over in the confined opening, he reaches up, touching the ceiling above his head. He then examines his hand; it is covered in a gooey pink slime. He does not realize the opening is closing behind him until it is too late! He is trapped inside! He calls out on his communicator, "Sergeant Yang, Sergeant Yang, I'm trapped!"

The hole constricts around him. He pushes against the walls and desperately cries out again, "Sergeant Yang, Sergeant Yang, I'm trapped!"

Yang walks forward, unaware of what has happened. The sense of uneasiness hovers over her, weighing her down. In fact, it has since they ventured on this mission, but none more so than when they entered this new section of the cavern. It is a sense of not belonging, as if they should not be there! Something was off, something was wrong, and she could feel it, but the mission remains; lives are at stake! So she moves on. A soldier cries out over the open intercom, "Sergeant Yang!" She pauses and turns; she scans her team to see who hailed her. She calls out, "Who said that?"

Private Forde raises his hand and fearfully replies, "Ma'am, it's me, Private Forde."

Yang sees his hand through the crowd. The soldiers spread as she walks toward him. Yang comes face-to-face with him and asks, "Soldier, what happened?"

He scans the ground frantically. "Ma'am, I'm sorry!" he replies. "I thought I saw something move on the ground! Ma'am, I'm sorry, I must have been seeing things."

Yang walks over to her tech specialist. "Scan the ground," she commands.

He scans the cavern floor. He replies, "Ma'am, it states the same thing. It is weird, ma'am." Yang queries, "How so?"

He responds, "Well, ma'am, there should be some discrepancy, some changes in the rock structure every hundred meters or so, but nothing! It's exactly the same as it was a thousand meters back. It is not possible."

He looks up at Yang, his mind lost, his face pale and blank. Yang stares defiantly at the ground under her feet, challenging it to show its true self. She does not have to wait long before the ground replies. Bumps rise across the entire surface of the ground. Then bumps continue to rise, forming brown, pinkish wormlike creatures. Each creature is about half a meter in length and as thick as a human's wrist. The soldiers fumble, trying to move their feet to avoid the worms. However, their efforts are in vain, as the worms are everywhere, and new ones rise out from the ground! "What in the world?" cries Yang. "Scan them!"

The tech specialist fearfully analyzes the creatures. "Ma'am," he cries out, "it cannot scan them! It's as if they are not there! It scans only rock!"

One of the soldiers carefully picks up the worm in his hand. He states, "It's real. I can feel it!" Yang looks out. The worms are all around them, under their feet. They even start coming out of the walls. The floor fills with worms, higher and higher, until they are up to their ankles and rising. Yang commands, "Retreat! Move back!"

They quickly reverse and head back toward the rocky section of the cavern. Suddenly the worms on the floor begin to come together and harden around the soldier's feet. The places where they harden form a new floor, and new worms rise from the newly formed floor. Most of the soldiers' feet get stuck! Yang, however, quickly pulls her feet free before the worms can harden around them. She jumps on top of the newly formed floor! New worms begin to emerge from the floor. Cries of panic flood Yang's communicator, "Ma'am! Yang, ma'am! Our feet are stuck! Advise, advise!"

With no other forcible option, she commands, "Engage!"

Within seconds, the crew light the tunnel up with gunfire! The weapons give them some relief. Most of the crew are able to pull their feet free and stand on top of the newly formed floor. As the bullets rip through the creatures, some minor casualties occur. In their panic, a few soldiers shoot their own foot or leg. However, the more they destroy the worms, the more they reappear. Now they are forming from the walls and ceilings of the cavern, falling on them like rain. The team races toward the rocky portion of the cavern in an attempt to escape. In the chaos, one of the soldiers stumbles and falls. Within seconds, he is covered by worms! The worms almost instantly harden over him, turning into solid ground.

One of his comrades, Private Anne Marino, witnesses the incident and screams in horror! Thinking quickly, she removes a spade from the side compartment on her leg. Falling to her knees, she attempts to dig him free. The worms flood over her legs and wrap around her hands. She pulls free and stands up then, in a panic, aims her sidearm and, in desperation, fires into the ground, trying to free her fallen friend. Her fellow comrades run around her as they try to save themselves.

After a minute of fierce firing, her sidearm empties! The pit where her comrade lies is finally free. She again jumps down, tossing bits of worm and ground off him. She grabs hold of his uniform to pull him up; however, it rips to shreds. To her horror, she realizes that most of his body has already been disintegrated! She sobs hysterically and falls to the ground in anguish. One of her fellow soldiers grabs hold of her arm, pulling her free, almost dragging her toward the rocky section of the cavern.

For the first three kilometers or so, the tanks' threads picked up zero to nothing, perhaps some dust and a few pebbles. Further in, thick dirt got jammed into the threads as they pressed forward. Now, the dirt is replaced by mud: thick, heavy mud. Private Brown halts his troops as they come to a fork in the cavern; a smaller section falls to the left. Brown ponders what to do. He hails Guide 1, "Guide 1, this mud, why is the ground so wet and muddy?"

The gray alien replies, very matter-of-factly, as if Brown should have known the answer already. "I am not sure. There was no moisture except in the center when I was here." Brown eats his rudeness and decides to ask a different question, "Where does this other tunnel lead to?"

The gray alien replies, "I do not remember. However, I am certain that the best way to proceed is straight forward."

Brown bites down on his lip and mumbles to himself, "Thanks, for that wonderful insight."

Brown, not totally trusting the alien and at the same time sensing that the side tunnel needs to be searched, calls over one of his sergeants, "Sergeant!"

Sergeant Pierce steps forward. Sergeant Pierce is a career soldier. He is Caucasian, thickly built, similar to Brown but a good deal shorter. He has a deep, dark shadow on his face that no razor can tame. His front two molars on the left side of his mouth are crooked, causing his lip to protrude noticeably on that side and causing him to spit frequently when talking. Sergeant Pierce responds, "Sir, yes, sir!"

Brown commands, "Take tank A1 and A2, left flank, proceed two klicks, and then circle back. We will continue forward. When we reconvene, report. Scan and analyze every centimeter of that tunnel!"

Sergeant Pierce salutes, "Sir, yes, sir!"

The good sergeant hollers, "Fall out! A1 and A2, move out!"

Sergeant Pierce scans the ranks. He walks through the soldiers to one of the specialists. Pierce reads his tag, "Specialist Clay, you're with me!"

Clay responds, "Sir, yes, sir!"

Sergeant Pierce turns and points forward dramatically. "Move out!" he hollers once again.

Corporal Benjamin guides a double A-TIV over to Sergeant Pierce. Pierce mounts the vehicle and motions for Specialist Clay to ride with him. Pierce moves forward and proceeds to lead the tanks.

Brown commands, "Forward!"

Sergeant Brack, a tall younger man, commands the rest of the troops, "You heard the man, forward! Move out!"

After about five minutes in, the terrain deteriorates considerably; first, the mud becomes littered with puddles. A little further in, and they are tramping through about five centimeters of murky liquid. Brown raises his hand. Sergeant Brack commands, "Platoon, halt!"

The troops stop. The squeal of the tanks' brakes echoes throughout the cavern. Brown looks ahead. Before them is what appears to be a lake. It is as wide as the cavern and extends forward as far as the eye can see. Brown calls his technical specialist, "How deep does this go?"

After a quick scan, the technical specialist reports, "Sir, at the deepest point it is about half a meter."

This is good news for Brown; he knows that the tanks can cut through two meters like nothing. Half a meter will barely be noticeable. Brown gives the command, "Forward!"

The technical specialist had scanned correctly. After about two minutes, they are knee-deep in murky liquid that Brown assumes to be water, but it is not! Those riding A-TIVs are forced to fold them up and strap them to their backs. A few minutes in, one of the soldiers approaches Brown. "Sir, excuse me, sir."

Not wanting to stop their progress, Brown continues forward. He turns toward the soldier and asks, "What is it, soldier?" The soldier replies nervously, "Sir, it's just that my space suit seems to be losing oxygen."

Brown motions with his hand for the technical specialist to come over. Brown asks, "Santos? Yes?"

Technical Support Santos replies, "Sir, yes, sir."

Brown commands, "Santos, link with this soldier's suit, see if you can find what the problem is. He says that he is losing oxygen."

Santos replies, "Sir, yes, sir."

Quickly Santos attaches a wire from his handheld to the port on the wrist of the soldier's spacesuit, all this while they continue to push forward. The caverns fill with the sloshing sound of mud and liquid splashing against their thighs. Santos reads the data; he is both confused and concerned. He moves closer to Brown and reports, "Sir, seems like there is a leak in his suit."

Brown queries, "A leak? How is that possible? Can you pinpoint it, Santos?"

Santos responds, "Sir, yes, sir!"

Brown raises his hand to halt. Sergeant Brack commands, "Troop, halt!"

Within seconds, the deafening silence haunts the tunnels, and all that can be heard is the hum of the tanks' engines purring. Santos states, "Sir, it seems to be a leak in his boots."

The private instinctively lifts his boot. The entire bottom of his boot is partially disintegrated, as if it were eaten away. In fact, most of the boot is severely damaged. Brown, troubled, commands, "Show me your other foot!"

Quickly the soldier changes feet. The other boot is as bad. Brown slowly lifts his own boot out of the muck, and as he feared, his boot also is deteriorating. He commands Sergeant Brack, "Have all the troops check their footwear."

Brack replies, "Sir, yes, sir!"

Brack turns toward the troop and commands, "Soldiers, inspect all your footwear and report!" Soon, the whole troop frantically examines their boots, and to his great horror, Brown discovers that all their boots are in various degrees of distress. Santos stares blank-faced at Brown and nervously asks, "How is this possible?"

Brown replies, "I was going to ask you the same thing! Did you analyze this liquid we are all walking in?"

Santos, embarrassed, responds, "Sir, no, I … sir, I'll do it now!"

Santos removes a white test strip from the back compartment of his handheld and dips the tip into the liquid. They wait for a moment, then Santos stares at the results. He nervously reports, "Sir, the liquid is—"

Brown finishes his sentence, "An acid?"

Brown firmly places his finger in the air and rotates it. He commands, "Sergeant, give the orders, abort the mission! We are out of here! Then get on the horn and hail Sergeant Pierce, tell him to reconvene with us. If you cannot reach him, send the shuttle to retrieve him!"

Sergeant Brack replies, "Sir, yes—" but Sergeant Brack does not move.

Brown stares at Sergeant Brack, waiting for a response. Then he notices the soldiers, the entire troop, nervously looking around. Brown looks back at Brack, and in the reflection of his helmet, he, too, sees what the entire troop is nervously monitoring. All around the cavern, triangular black objects are protruding through the cavern's walls. Brown is unsure what they are. They are about seven to eight centimeters long and slowly increasing in size. Brown does not know what they are, nor does he want to stay around to find out. He steps in front of Sergeant Brack and grabs hold of his shoulder to regain his attention. The sergeant regains his composure and looks toward Brown. Brown firmly asks, "Sergeant, do you copy?"

Brack takes a moment then shakes his head and replies, "Sir, yes, sir!" Sergeant Brack hollers, "Abort! Abort! About-face!"

The foot soldiers turn around. The tanks, in harmony as they are trained to do, move forward and gradually turn around. At this point, Brown does not want to analyze. He does not want to investigate; he just wants to get out! They are not supposed to be here; he knows it in the core of his bones, which, at this moment, feel as if ice were forming in them. He is moving the troops out as fast as he can!

As they move out, Brown suspiciously eyes the triangular pieces protruding from the walls, which are now about ten centimeters long. There is something odd about them other than the obvious, and Brown can feel it! As he marches forward, Brown cannot help himself but to look at the odd phenomenon sticking out from the walls. Brown thinks to himself, *What are they? I could swear that they have eyes!*

Then, almost as if they read his mind, little black eyes open on the sides of the creatures. Brown is not even sure how he can see the little eyes from such a distance, being that the things themselves are so small and the walls so far from him; it is almost as if the image were in his mind. Brown momentarily loses all ability to breathe! Suddenly the triangular creatures fly off the wall toward the soldiers at amazing speeds. They cut through the air, making a terrifying whooshing noise, similar to the noise of a powerful waterfall. Brown is barely able to blurt out, "Watch out!" he warns. "Take defensive action!"

Before the soldiers can react, the creatures are upon them, flying past them, careful not to fly directly into them. The wings, like razors, slice into their space suits as they pass. Only their helmets they slam directly into, causing loud echoing taps against the special compressed glass. Even though the helmets protect the soldiers, the attack is similar to being hit in the head with a metal bat. The impact causes the soldier's head to jerk violently, either back or forward, depending on the direction of the attack. As hard as they hit, their own trajectory barely changes. The creatures speed forward to the wall on the opposite side. The walls receive them, opening up and swallowing the creatures almost as if the wall itself were alive. A second later, the creatures reappear and fly out once more! The second time around, they seem even faster than the first time.

Sergeant Pierce is kneeling next to Specialist Clay as he analyzes the ground, which has now turned an odd pinkish hue. Pierce turns toward Specialist Clay and inquires, "Anything?" Clay stares at the data blank-faced. He shakes his head. "No, sir. It's odd. It seems that the ground here is exactly the same as it has been."

Not understanding the problem with the findings, Sergeant Pierce stands up to take in his surroundings.

He suddenly hears a sound, a sound far away, almost as if he can hear it through his helmet. He hears the cry of a lady, a young lady, maybe even that of a little girl calling out, "Help me! Help me!"

Startled, Sergeant Pierce looks around. He calls out to Specialist Clay, "Clay, did you hear that?" Clay looks up at Pierce. "Hear what, sir?"

As if he does not hear Clay's response, he calls to the tank commanders, "Tank Commander A1, Commander A2, scan for life-forms!"

They reply in unison, "Sir, yes, sir!"

Then, as they have trained, they fan out, A2 toward the right flank and A1 toward the left flank, scanning the cavern. Specialist Clay takes it on himself also to scan for life-forms. A moment later, the two tank commanders reply, "Sergeant, sir! No life-forms found!"

Clay confirms, "Sir, I also analyzed and found—"

However, Sergeant Pierce pushes his hands out, preventing Clay from finishing. Pierce is still frantically looking around. Then, to Clay's great surprise, very uncharacteristically and illogically, Pierce lifts the shield on his helmet visor to hear more clearly. Almost in response to his action, the voice cries out again. This time, the voice is crystal clear. "Help me! Help me!"

He frantically looks in the direction of the voice. He sees a young girl, perhaps a teenager, in a tattered white robe running ahead of him, further and further into the darkness until it consumes her totally! Momentarily regaining clarity, he realizes that he has lifted his visor, and he quickly brings it back down and sealed it, as if it never happened. Pierce no longer cares whether Clay has heard the girl or whether the tank commanders scanned any life-forms. He has determined that they will go and save her! He jumps on to his A-TIV and almost pulls Clay up with him. Pierce turns to the tanks and commands, "A1, A2, move out! Forward!"

Pierce then hits the engine full throttle; the A-TIV shoots forward. Clay almost falls off; he wraps one arm around the bar of the A-TIV to stabilize himself. The commanders throw the tanks into gear and push forward, determined to keep up with Sergeant Pierce.

Chapter 16

At the entrance of the cavern, Chen stands in front of Rivera's fighter, fidgeting with the equipment. He is perplexed, as he has not been able to hail the mothership for the past few minutes. He had asked Lieutenant Rivera to try to reach them using the communicator aboard his fighter. Williams and Carter are at the back of Carter's fighter, checking the engine. Chen asks Rivera, "Still nothing … any luck on your end?"

Rivera is bent over, looking under his dash, trying to boost his signal. He looks up toward Chen and replies, "No, no luck."

His words trail off as he peers out his canopy at Chen. Behind Chen is a tall creature looming over him, almost two and a half meters tall! Its shape is humanoid, but it is definitely not human. Its skin is wrinkled and brown like the dark bark of a tree. Its face has no mouth, no nose, and no eyes, just two deep dark sunken pockets where the eyes should be! Lieutenant Rivera calls out in a panic, "Chen!"

Chen looks up, still baffled by their communication problems. Rivera yells out a second time, "Chen, Chen! Behind you!"

Quickly, Rivera jumps out of the cockpit and bravely jumps to the ground. Chen casually turns around, uncertain of what Rivera has seen. However, as Rivera's feet hit the floor, causing an echoing thump, he cannot believe what he sees—or, for that matter, what he does not see. The creature is not there! Chen, confused, turns toward Rivera. "What? What's behind me?"

Rivera runs over to Chen. His approach, however, is not straight. Rivera crouches, darts forward, and stops suddenly, similar to a cat stalking its prey. Finally, when he reaches Chen, he grabs hold of his shoulders. Chen is astonished, not sure what to do or how to react. Rivera pulls

Chen close to himself so that he can look over Chen's shoulder. Then Rivera pushes Chen aside; without meaning to, he almost pushes him to the floor. Rivera runs behind him and then behind his ship, searching frantically! Finally, when he finds nothing, he returns to Chen, with his head slumped downward as if he were ashamed, like a child losing a race. His mind races; his thoughts are incoherent. Did he really see something? He is uncertain. Chen, baffled, asks, "What? What is it?" His words are long and drawn out.

Rivera looks up and shakes his head. "I thought I saw something."

Hearing the commotion, Williams and Carter come over to see what the fuss is about. Williams asks, "What's going on?"

Chen responds, "Rivera saw something!"

Carter asks Rivera, "What did you see?"

Rivera is not one to doubt himself, and he refuses to doubt himself now. He blurts out, "I'm not sure ... maybe I'm hallucinating, maybe I'm going crazy! I saw a creature!"

The three of them are not expecting to hear that word from his mouth. Especially on an alien planet, it is a word they most definitely do not want to hear! The sound of Rivera's statement startles them. Carter asks, "What?"

The tone of disbelief is evident in Carter's voice; in fact, he seems downright irritated. He and Rivera are pilots. Pilots are calm, cool, and collected. They are not the ones to fall apart on a mission. This will reflect badly on him if one of his comrades, his friends, is losing it right there in the middle of this important mission! Carter cannot accept this, nor will he allow it. Rivera continues, "I don't know how to explain it. There was this tall creature behind Chen. Big and brown."

Williams asks, "He was black?"

Rivera shakes his head. "No, no!"

He knows how it will sound, but he says it anyway, "Brown like it was made out of wood or something! It had no eyes, just holes staring down over Chen! I don't know what it was, but it was not here for anything good!"

Williams walks over to Rivera and grabs his shoulder, in an attempt to both comfort him and calm him down. Rivera pulls away. "Look, maybe I need a minute, but I don't need that!"

Rivera forcefully points his finger at Carter; in this gesture without words, he is telling Carter, "You better back me up. I am one of us!"

Carter understands and changes his attitude from pessimism to one of confidence—confidence in his friend and the willingness to back him up at his word. Rivera, unwilling to believe that he was hallucinating, commands, "Just fan out and look around!"

Carter chimes in, "You heard the man, let's fan out! Chen, search for life-forms."

Chen nods. "Sir, yes, sir!"

Rivera reports, "I will go back to my ship and see if I can reach the mothership one more time." Williams asks, "Should I take some equipment and walk out to the front of the cavern? Once the mothership is in view, we should have no interference."

Rivera considers her request. He shakes his head. "Negative, I don't think we should separate at this point. If we don't find anything now, and I can't reach the mothership, then we will go outside together!"

Williams nods. "Sir, yes, sir."

She does not know if anything is out there, but she likes the idea of not being alone.

Rivera climbs aboard his ship and picks up the communicator, but it is not working. He sits in his seat and starts up the ship. The communicator lights up. He grabs hold of the speaker and speaks into it, "*Liberty Crane-Tiqu-Qi*, this is the away team, Lieutenant—"

However, before he can finish his sentence, he loses all color in his face as he stares through the canopy glass. He sees the creature once more! It is back behind Chen. Rivera jumps from his seat. As Rivera moves his head out from the canopy glass, the creature disappears; he can no longer see it. Rivera pauses, gripping the rim of the canopy. He slowly lowers himself back behind the canopy glass. Once again, he can see the creature as clear as day! The creature rears his four-fingered, clawed hand behind Chen. Rivera yells out in desperation, "Chen, watch out!"

However, it is too late; the creature jabs Chen in the back. Rivera again jumps out of his fighter, almost falling to the ground. Williams and Carter hear the commotion and run to Chen. Chen is standing up straight, shoulders arched backward, his eyes rolling back in his head. They cannot see the creature. Chen's mouth is open and bubbling. Williams grabs hold of Chen's helmet and peers in at Chen. Inside his helmet, water is gushing out of his mouth. Williams grabs hold of the helmet release and shouts, "Help me take this helmet off!"

The two pilots assist, then they grab Chen by his arms to hold him up as Williams pulls the helmet off his head. The helmet had already filled with water and splashes down on his suit onto the cavern floor. Water still pours out of Chen's mouth like a fountain. Williams screeches, "Oh, mother of pearl ... what in the world?"

Williams, Rivera, and Carter carefully lower him onto the floor. Chen's arms and legs are swinging wildly as he tries to gasp for breath. Rivera stands on one side and Carter on the other, staring down like two lost boys. Williams jumps on Chen's chest and starts compressions. Williams, in desperation, yells out to Carter, "Quick, go to the shuttle, and get the emergency first aid kit!"

Carter scurries away so quickly that he loses his footing, placing the fingers on his right hand onto the floor and pushing himself upward to regain his balance. He runs past his fighter and around the shuttle to retrieve the first aid kit. As he moves alongside the shuttle, his own speed and anxiety keep him off-balance, and he uses the side of the shuttle to brace himself. Suddenly he notices that it is getting darker. His hand slips off the shuttle; he jerks forward but is able to stop his momentum. Carter reaches out again to brace himself on the shuttle, but his hand waves aimlessly in the air. Carter turns to find the shuttle, but it is gone.

Williams desperately compresses Chen's chest, then sadly, Chen stops moving. With a few last compressions, the water finally comes out. Chen's head lies motionless on one side as the last of the water oozes out of his mouth. So much water was let out that the three of them are in a huge puddle about ten centimeters deep. Williams shakes her head, sobbing, "How, how?"

Rivera looks around as if he were trying to find something on the floor, then regaining his composure, he responds, "It was that thing, that creature!"

Williams, frustrated and worn out with remorse, looks up and cries, "What? What are you talking about? What creature?"

Rivera's eyes flare. "I saw him again! He was behind Chen, he took his fingers like knives and stabbed him in the back!"

Williams yells out in confusion, "What?"

Rivera, determined to prove that he saw what he saw, falls on his knees into the puddle. To Williams's surprise, he recklessly turns Chen over. Williams jumps up just in time, or she, too, would have been thrown to the floor by Rivera's recklessness. There are no puncture holes in the back of Chen's suit. Williams looks at him, palms open facing outward. Repulsed by Rivera's total disregard for the deceased and flabbergasted at his actions, she stands there shaking in disbelief! She cries out to him, "What are you talking about? There's nothing there!"

Rivera, unwilling to accept that he was seeing things, turns Chen back around. He removes the collar from the space suit and seemingly almost takes Chen's head off with it. He then proceeds to unzip the suit. As he attempts to remove the gloves, Williams grabs hold of Rivera's shoulder and pulls back hard, yelling, "Stop, stop!"

He pushes her away. Realizing his determination, Williams searches for a way to stop him. Not able to see anything around her, she remembers the spade strapped in a pocket on her leg. In her anxiety, she fumbles to remove it. Meanwhile, Rivera had already maneuvered the inner layer over Chen's head and unbuckled the primary layer. Within a minute, he has most of the suit down off Chen's torso. Rivera is about to turn Chen over and lift his shirt to examine his back when Williams attacks him. Spade in hand, she strikes Rivera's helmet! Once again, Rivera pushes her aside. She stumbles and drops the spade into the water. While she searches in the water to recover her weapon, Rivera finally removes Chen's shirt, revealing his bare back. Williams stops in her tracks as she stares in disbelief. Sure enough, in Chen's back are four distinct, deep puncture wounds, three alongside one another in a crescent shape and the fourth slightly below them. Still oozing out from them are thick water and blood. Williams points a trembling finger at the body, a horrifying chill clenching her bones! In almost a whisper, she utters, "What … what … what is that?"

Rivera drops Chen back into the water. He stands and points downward dramatically. "That's what I've been telling you! Something killed him!"

Williams loses it. She grabs hold of Lieutenant Rivera under his arms and shakes him. "What did you see?" she demands.

As gently as he can, he removes her hands from him to gain some distance between them. Rivera takes a deep breath, and with his hands outward on the sides as if he were sculpting the creature, he explains, "There was this creature, tall! It was not human. Its body was made out of wood or bark or something wrinkly. It had no face, just holes for eyes! It had four claws on its hand, long pointy claws!" He points dramatically again at Chen's lifeless body. "It stabbed Chen in the back, and then … well, you saw the rest."

Williams cannot comprehend what he is saying. She slaps her helmet repeatedly. Rivera, realizing that Williams is having a mental lapse of some sort, tries to calm her. He gently reaches over to grab her shoulder. He calls to her, "Williams, calm down."

Williams pushes him away. She pauses for a second as if she were shocked or forgot where she was. She looks around, realizing that Carter has still not returned. She asks, "Where is Carter?" Rivera also looks around, "I don't know. He went to get the first aid kit."

They both call out to him, "Carter, Carter, where are you?"

Meanwhile, Carter is still fumbling around in the dark. He is in a panic because being in the dark is his greatest fear! Then, up ahead, he sees a light. He moves toward it. The light is a tunnel. Carter enters the tunnel, calling out, "Hello, Rivera? Chen? Williams? Are you there?"

He walks through the narrow cavern, feeling his hands along the wall as if he still could not see. As he gets closer, he sees that ahead in the light is a person, a young lady in a tattered white robe, sobbing. She is saying something, but he cannot make it out. As Carter gets closer, he hears her voice. It is worn and raspy. "Help me, help me."

He hastens, his boots slamming into the wet floor below him. Carter rushes toward her. She is kneeling on the floor, back toward him. He quickly rushes and grabs her shoulder to help pull her to her feet. She turns to face him. He sees her face; it is ghostlike, almost as white as the clothes she is wearing. Her eyes are dark and deep as if they could draw even the very soul out of a person! Carter shakes her. "Are you okay? How can I help you?"

She opens her mouth. "Help me, follow me," she cries. Her teeth are brown and spikelike, like splinters of wood!

He should be frightened; he should run in the opposite direction. But for some reason, he has to follow her as she leads him down a dark tunnel. The only light somehow is from her.

Williams stares hard at Rivera. They cannot find Carter or any signs of him anywhere. Williams's expression has changed; she seems demented, her pupils dilated. She asks, "How is it that you saw that ... thing and I didn't? How did you see it, and I did not see anything?"

That is a good question, and Lieutenant Rivera knows it. He pauses for a second to consider it, then an idea comes to him. Rivera looks up at his fighter and states, "The two times I saw it, it was through the cockpit window of my fighter. Perhaps the protective coating on my window allowed me to see the creature!"

Williams stares him down. "All right then!" she responds, as if he asked her a question. "You go to your fighter and look through the cockpit window, and see if you can see any signs of this creature. I will go into Carter's cockpit—"

Rivera stops her. "Wait a minute, wait a minute! Only the pilot assigned to a fighter should enter his fighter. No unauthorized persons can enter another pilot's fighter!"

Williams shakes her hands in rebuttal. "There's no time for these procedures. I'm just going in to see if I can see the creature through the window!"

Again, Rivera disputes, "The cockpit is probably locked."

Williams cuts him off. "Why would it be locked? He was just out walking around. I'm sure that all systems are open. Besides, like I said, I'm just going in to look out the window. You go in yours! There's no time to argue. We must find Carter and the creature!"

Rivera, realizing the obvious, suggests, "We could just walk out to the front of the cavern and wave down the mothership. I'm sure that they will send someone—"

Williams, extremely annoyed, grasping her hand in the air as if she were killing an imaginary insect, exclaims, "There's no time! While we're going out there, that creature could attack us! We need to see where it is first and then … then decide what to do next!"

Rivera drops his head in uncomfortable submission. "Very well," he states, not wanting to argue anymore.

Rivera quickly jumps up into his fighter, as Williams runs and awkwardly climbs up into Carter's fighter cockpit. Rivera instantly reads the scans. Williams looks around, then she sees it. Up ahead to the left of the cavern, she sees Carter held by the creature. The creature is pulling him into the cavern. Williams screams out, "I see him! I see him! Look!"

Rivera looks through his cockpit window. "Where, where?"

Williams yells back, "Eleven o'clock!"

Rivera looks, but he does not see the creature, only the tunnel. Rivera turns the spotlight toward the tunnel. When the light hits the tunnel, Williams's eyes flare as she sees the creature clearly drag the lieutenant deeper into the cavern beyond the illumination of the light. She yells out, "Did you see it?"

"What?" replies Rivera, searching frantically with his eyes.

Again, Williams cries out, "Did you see it drag Carter down the corridor?"

Rivera, confused, moves the spotlight up and down the corridor. "No, I didn't see it!" he replies. "Are you sure?"

"Of course, I saw it!" retorts Williams. Her words are anxious, and the sense of sanity has seemingly vacated her mind. "We have to save him, we have to save him!"

Rivera, in agreement to save his comrade, responds, "Yes, immediately! We'll get down and go to the shuttle and retrieve some weapons, then we can track him!"

Williams stands up inside the cockpit, arms spread searching around, and cries out. Her voice is irate. "Are you insane? We have no time for that! We have to go quickly!"

Rivera, half out of the cockpit with one foot still on the telescopic ladder foothold, asks, "What do you suggest?" He is trying to make the most reasonable decision possible.

Rivera weighs their options. "We could perhaps follow in the shuttle."

Again, Williams shakes her head in anger. She screams, "The shuttle doesn't have weapons like that!"

Rivera blurts out, "Weapons? What are you talking about?"

Williams responds with venom in her voice. Her words no longer even sound human! She screeches, "We need to kill that creature!"

Leaving Rivera momentarily speechless, Williams sits herself down inside the cockpit and closes the canopy. Rivera now stands; he yells out, "What are you doing?"

Williams blurts out, "We have to kill that creature."

Her voice has changed once again. Now it is as casual as if she were talking to her husband on a Sunday afternoon about going shopping or some other mundane activity. And with that statement, she ignites the engines and maneuvers the plane to face the cavern—the cavern that she saw the creature drag Carter into!

Rivera is livid! Not only does Williams have no authorization to even be inside the fighter, which he had protested from the beginning, but also, for her to power up a military fighter is downright reckless! He is surprised that the systems were even operational, as she had stated Carter must have had them on when he exited. Even still, he is shocked that Williams is able to pilot this ship. A fighter is very different from a shuttle. In untrained hands, the fighter is extremely dangerous. Just one HQ Pulse, a hypersonic quasar pulse missile, has the potential capability of bringing down about half a kilometer of the cavern's rock. Rivera cannot allow this destructive power in unstable hands; she could kill the entire team, burying them in the caverns! Quickly he closes his canopy and powers up, setting course to intersect Williams. If he has to forcibly remove her from the cockpit, he will! Williams is moving quickly toward the cavern. Rivera moves in her path and commands, "Cease and desist! Power down your engines now, and remove yourself immediately! This is not a warning."

However, before he can finish, again to his surprise, she fires the thrusters up! Carter's fighter flies upward off the ground and clumsily runs over Rivera's fighter. With the wheels still out, Williams runs along the top of Rivera's fighter and then continues forward toward the cavern! The landing gear is not fully retracted until she is already almost a quarter of a kilometer into the cavern. Rivera clenches his teeth and slams his fist into his controls. This means that he has to make a U-turn, which will take time, and time is precious! The longer it takes for him to stop her, the closer she gets to Brown and his team. Greater is the potential for destruction the deeper she goes.

Quickly, Rivera maneuvers his plane around, and within seconds, he is on her tail. Williams is barely able to control the jet, and the cavern she has chosen is far smaller than the cavern that Yang flew her fighters down to. She sways from side to side, occasionally scraping the tip of her wing against the wall. However, for someone who has never flown a fighter, she is somehow doing extremely well, almost as if she were being controlled by some mysterious outside force.

Williams spies the creature ahead of her. Like the moon in the sky while driving down the road at night, it follows you. So the creature somehow maintains a distance in front of her. It appears to be running from her, staying just about one hundred meters or so in front. No matter how fast she goes, it is there! Rivera commands repeatedly, "Cease and desist! Land the craft! Cease and desist! This is not a warning. You are unauthorized."

Defending her actions, Williams cries out, "But I see it! It's ahead of me!" Her voice is possessed. "I have to get it!"

Rivera increases his scans; however, he sees no such creature. He then taps into the live feed from Williams's fighter. Now he can see what she sees. He searches desperately, wanting to see the creature, wanting to see Carter! He does not want to believe what he already knows: that Williams has gone insane. Rivera tries to reason with her, "Williams, I cut into your live feed. I can see what you see. There is no creature; you are hallucinating! Repeat, you must be hallucinating, there is—"

Williams, salivating like a famished predator, desperate for the kill, cries out, "I tell you." She looks back as if she can see Rivera behind her. The plane swerves to the right; the wing cuts into the cavern wall. The wing sparks, and the plane vibrates. It starts to dip. When Williams turns forward and regains control of the fighter, she cries out again, "I see him! I see him!"

Williams arms her guns. Rivera cries in terror, "What are you doing?"

Before he can say another word, she opens fire! Rivera loses it. He cannot take anymore. "Cease and desist!" he commands. "Now! Immediately! Williams, don't make me do something I would regret! You have to stop!"

She fires once again. The bullets fly recklessly, hitting into the walls and floor, sending debris and smoke into the air, making visibility difficult for both Williams and Rivera. As Rivera flies through the smoke, the sounds of thousands of rock fragments hitting his fighter echo throughout the tunnel. Finally, she shoots the creature, but instead of killing him, the creature doubles with every hit. First, there are two creatures, then four. By the time she is finished, there are thirty-two creatures, all running defiantly down the cavern.

Brown's men are in bad condition; their suits are badly shredded. The triangular creatures have made three passes already! Brown stops in his tracks for a moment or two. He raises his hand and yells out to the troop, "Freeze!"

Sergeant Brack repeats the order. "Troop halt!"

Brown looks to the left and then to the right. He commands, "Half of you form one line left flank, the other half right! Run forward facing the walls. The creatures are coming from one side to the other. When I give the order, fire, but continue advancing forward!"

The troops cry out, "Sir, yes, sir!"

Quickly the troops align themselves, facing the walls on either side, about ten meters from the walls. Brown and Sergeant Brack position themselves in the center of the two lines. In unison, they run forward while facing the walls, weapons drawn. They look like a great synchronized dance team. No sooner are they set when Brown spies the creatures emerging from the cavern walls. "Fire, fire!" he commands.

The cavern lights up, half shooting one side and half shooting the other! The creatures fly out. Some manage to maneuver around the array of projectiles; however, most cannot avoid the spray of bullets. The creatures are shot out of the air, tossed violently into the mucky acid. The strategy seems to have worked. The acid had traveled even farther into the tunnel. Still, they are nearly out of the pool, only a few hundred meters or so to go!

The troops advance when suddenly they stop. They sense something. There is a shift; they all feel it. They pause for a second and look into the acid lake below their feet. Brown's face turns colors. Then, without warning, the creatures erupt from beneath them out of the acid, shredding them with a vengeance! So hard is the force of the creatures flying upward that some of the soldiers are pushed off their feet. One soldier is even pushed all the way to the top of the cavern, crashing headfirst into the ceiling before falling back down into the acid. Brown instinctively rushes over to see if he can save him. However, when he pulls him from the acid, the image Brown sees, he will never forget. Inside the soldier's helmet is one of the triangular creatures. The creature is flying wildly, slamming back and forth around what was left of the face of the fallen soldier. Apparently, the force of the creature tore straight through the soldier all the way up to his head. Brown, momentarily paralyzed with disgust, tosses the soldier back into the acid and then runs toward the dry ground ahead.

Rivera's medium-range scans pick up movement ahead. The computer informs Rivera: "Multiple life-forms identified ahead, three kilometers and closing."

Rivera commands, "Render computer image and enlarge!"

The computer displays the image. It is as Rivera feared; it is Brown and his company!

Brown and his team have almost finally reached dry land. Brown hears something. He pauses. In all the chaos, he is frozen, as the soldiers seem to move in slow motion around him, running onto the rocky terrain and to what they believe to be their salvation. Brown squints his eyes to see down the tunnel; there is a light. He adjusts his visor, magnifying the image: two times magnification, four times magnification. Now he can clearly see Williams's fighter coming in hot! Brown's voice drops. "Why does it always happen to me?"

Brown grabs hold of Brack's arm and jerks him hard. Brown commands, "Run!"

Sergeant Brack, confused, responds, "Sir, what?"

Brown points and screams out, "Incoming, run! Run! About face, run!"

Brack looks back nervously. Seeing the incoming fighter, he gives the command, "About face, run!"

The tunnel vibrates violently from the force of the approaching fighters.

Williams grunts with frustration, the bullets obviously not having the effect she desired. Williams's facial expression has diminished, her eyes are enlarged, bloodshot, and her pupils have shrunk to the point that they're almost invisible. Her skin is pale, yellowish, with dark black and purple rings around her eyes. Her lips are also turning an odd purple hue! Her face has sunken inward. Williams looks as if she lost fifty pounds in the past two minutes. Something is happening within her, taking control over her! Determined to destroy the creature, Williams has decided to use more lethal force; she arms one of her HQ Pulse missiles! Back aboard Rivera's fighter, his computer alerts him that Williams's missiles are armed. Rivera cries out, pleads to her one last time, "Williams, what are you doing?"

Williams, like a spoiled child not wanting to answer, responds, "I have to get him!"

Rivera has to make a decision. He cries out to her, "Williams, cease and desist! This is your final warning!"

Williams's eyes focus intently on the creatures running ahead of her. She is obsessed; she sees and hears nothing else! She tries to lock her missile on the target. Rivera yells to himself in frustration, "Contra!"

Not wanting to kill her if he does not have to, he tries using his gun to shoot her right wing in an attempt to force her to land. Williams's wing shreds under Rivera's onslaught. Instead of attempting a crash landing to save herself, Williams makes a last attempt to fire her missile. The result is her ship hits the ground hard, causing it to explode! Rivera instinctively, as trained, deploys his speed brakes in an attempt to avoid collision. The resulting firestorm from the ship's explosion jets a firewall in both directions, both up and down the corridor toward Rivera and toward Brown and his company! However, as bad as that is, it is not the worst of it! The second before impact, Williams manages to launch the missile! Because of the angle of her descent, instead of firing downward, the missile misfires upward. It detonates about one thousand meters before

Brown's troop, hitting the cavern ceiling. The explosion is catastrophic. So powerful is the explosion that some of the tanks that are closest to the impact are flung more than fifty meters into the air, crashing down on soldiers and other tanks! But the pulse weapon effect does not end there; as designed, the nanosecond of impact, thousands of microbursts penetrate into the target, breaking apart molecular bonds within the cavern's wall! This effect then ripples across the cavern, hundreds of meters in every direction. This section of the cavern begins to collapse, starting from the point of impact and then flaring out. Brown and his troop desperately try to outrun the avalanche of rocks. The soldiers and remaining tanks splash through an even-deeper pool of acid. The acid floods into their torn suits and then becomes trapped inside, burning the soldiers' skin. Brown commands the soldiers to climb up on the tanks. The tanks are not only faster but will also keep them out of the acid. Within seconds, the tanks are so packed with soldiers that the tank itself is barely visible.

Back aboard the bridge of the *Tiqu-Qi/Liberty Crane*, the conversation is fired. Wei calls out to Captain Barr, Captain Reynolds, Lieutenant Lin, and Lieutenant Minor, "Drones report they scanned a major explosion in one of the tunnels."

Lin frantically bends down to examine the data for himself. Captain Reynolds, with great concern for his people, asks, "How bad was it?"

Wei shakes his head. "Pretty bad, sir. One of the tunnels has partially collapsed; it seems at least half a kilometer is gone!"

Captain Barr shakes his head. "How is 'at possible? An' how 'bout our men?"

Wei responds, "Our scans cannot pick up life-forms so far underground. We do not know."

Lin stands up. "We have to do something! We have to go in there and pull those people out, if I have to do it myself!"

Meanwhile, in the caverns, one of the lieutenants, Second Lieutenant Sun, has helped many fallen soldiers to get a foothold onto one of the tanks. Although they are still running for their lives, Brown notices the chivalry of many of the people, especially the leaders! Rather than having concern for themselves, their concern is for the soldiers they are leading. Brown turns to see if he needs help. He notices that the lieutenant is not in his line of view anymore. He wonders, "Where did he go?"

Concerned, he knows he should continue running from the rain of falling rocks, but still, he has to check! He runs back. As the tank passes by him, Sergeant Brack calls out, "Sir, we need to keep moving!"

Brown cannot even verbally respond. He holds up his pointer finger to indicate to Brack to give him a minute. Brack understands, but he himself continues forward. Brown realizes what happened to the lieutenant when his foot accidentally collides with the lieutenant's fallen body. The lieutenant had fallen face down in the acid. Brown instinctively bends over, grabs hold, and pulls him to his feet. He is still conscious, but he is in bad shape. Brown asks, "Are you all right?" The lieutenant's communicator has been damaged, and his voice is staticky, but Brown can still make it out: "Yes, I ... I tripped and fell."

Brown notices the tears in the bottom section of his suit are severe. He realizes that, as the lieutenant helped the soldiers, he must have allowed for the acid to burn his legs. He sacrificed his legs to help others! Brown imagines that the acid might be down to his bone at this point. The pain must be excruciating! The lieutenant did not trip; he just can no longer walk! Brown grabs him under the arms and props him up. He asks him, "You, Lieutenant, what is your name?"

"Sir, my name is Lieutenant Son, sir."

Brown puts his helmet against Lieutenant Son's helmet to look him in the eyes. He reassures him, "Lieutenant Son, you are not dying today!"

Although the top of Brown's suit is shredded, from the waist down, it is in fair condition, and the acid has not penetrated his legs or feet. He grabs hold of Son with his mighty arms and throws him over his shoulder. Lieutenant Son protests, "No, don't! Leave me, save yourself!"

Brown reminds him, "No, we are getting out of this together!"

Brown trudges forward as best he can with Lieutenant Son over his shoulders.

Sergeant Pierce and his small crew heard the explosion. In fact, their section of the cavern shook violently from the impact, but Sergeant Pierce decided to disregard it. Rather, he is focused on their pursuit. They are in pursuit to save a girl, although Specialist Clay and the two tank commanders do not know it. Tank commander A1's computer's intermediate scans read multiple life-forms ahead. He reads the report to Sergeant Pierce, "Sergeant Pierce, sir! My intermediate scans are picking up multiple life-forms up ahead."

Pierce assumes that he is referring to the girl. Pierce grunts, "We are in pursuit!"

Tank commander A1 magnifies the image on his screen. He throws his head back in fear! Up ahead is what must be an alien army! About one hundred men, green-skinned, with red uniforms. They have three triangular tanks. The tanks are hovering about one meter off the ground. Each tank has large cannons all pointing toward them. Without warning, the center tank opens fire! Commander A1 screams out, "Oh my god! Oh my god! They fired at us!"

The projectile passes by and explodes on the wall of the cavern about fifty meters away from them! Sergeant Pierce calls tank commander A1, "What in the world was that, soldier?"

Tank commander A1 responds, "Some sort of alien force up ahead, firing at us, sir! Their tank fired at us!" The tank commander's eyes are glued to the screen. The alien tank cannon is slowly starting to glow. The tank commander continues with urgency in his voice, "And I believe they're gearing up to fire again!"

Sergeant Pierce yells a command. "Then what are you waiting for? Return fire!"

Tank commander A1 straightens up. "Sir, yes, sir! With pleasure!"

Finally, the cave-in has stopped. Those who make it out are exhausted. Brown orders them to stop so that they can regroup. This section of the cavern is also out of the acid lake, and although the ground is still muddy, the soldiers are relieved to be standing on "dry" ground once again. The troops are in bad shape. Many of them are lying on the ground panting, barely alive. Most do their best to remain standing and to give a hand to their fellow soldiers who are in worse condition than they. For the moment, Brown knows that the cavern has caved in, and they do not know if there is another way out. But that problem will be visited fully momentarily. Right now, they need to assess the condition of their people and give any immediate medical attention they can provide. Brown attempts to lay Lieutenant Son on the ground, but Son refuses. "No, no. Please don't lie me on the ground. Just prop me up against one of the tanks."

Brown quickly ushers him over to the nearest tank and props him up against it. Brown calls out to Sergeant Brack, "Sergeant Brack, Sergeant Brack!"

Brack is about twenty meters ahead helping out three soldiers. Brack waves his hand high for Brown to see and calls out to him, "Sir, I'm over here!"

Brown sees him and walks toward him. As he is walking, he commands, "Brack, assess as best you can. See if there are any other sergeants able to walk. Let them help you assess the condition of our soldiers. See if there are any available medical personnel. And send me a specialist. We need to scan this area. We do not need any more unexpected surprises!"

Brown reaches Brack just as he finishes talking. Sergeant Brack helps one of the soldiers to his feet for the other two to walk him over to the side of the cavern to prop him up against the wall. Sergeant Brack stands at attention and faces Brown as he approaches. He replies, "Sir, yes, sir!"

Immediately on his open channel, Brack calls, "Any specialist come to my position."

Specialist Reed runs over. "Sir, yes, sir! I am scanning the area as we speak, sir!"

Brown reaches out and grabs Brack's shoulder. "I think that our best option is to continue towards the center. We should meet up with Sergeant Yang and the others. Hopefully, the main tunnel is still in one piece."

Brack nods. "Sir, yes, sir!"

Brack walks off to complete his mission, calling for medical personnel. Suddenly something catches Brown's eye. Up ahead, down the tunnel, there is movement. He immediately calls out, "Brack." He points. "What is that?"

Brown's visor scans are still intact. He magnifies the screen. A smile runs across his face. Brown states, "Sergeant Pierce is approaching with his two tanks."

Sergeant Brack smiles. "Good. I'm glad that they have survived!"

Brown hopefully states, "Finally, some good news!"

Just then, the light flares through the tunnel, and the roar of the incoming shell races toward them. Instinctively Brown and Brack and those who can jump to the ground, as the shell is flying fairly low. It zooms just about two meters over Brown's head. Brown has barely a moment to turn and witness the shell colliding with the tank behind him! Brown screams out in anguish, "Lieutenant Son!"

The sound of the blast is deafening. Anyone close to the tank dies immediately! The fire bursts out in every direction, scorching over Brown's suit!

Sergeant Pierce yells out, "What the hell was that, Commander 1?"

Tank commander A1 is confused. He nervously responds, "Sir … I was returning fire, sir! Returning fire at the aliens, sir!"

Now Sergeant Pierce's anger rages to a new height. His skin turns a purplish hue, as spittle fills the bottom half of his helmet. He screams out, barely able to control his words, "Are you insane? Those are our men! You fired on Brown and the rest of our troop! You just destroyed one of our tanks!"

Commander A1 is speechless. He, too, turns colors. Sergeant Pierce continues, "Stand down, soldier!"

Pierce turns to Specialist Clay. "Clay, get aboard and commandeer tank A1!"

Clay, surprised at his request, reminds Pierce, "Sir, sorry, sir! I do not have the training nor authorization to commandeer tank A1, sir!"

Pierce, knowing that he is correct, grunts a howl in his throat, like that of a bear. He snarls, "Very well." He points with anger up toward the tank, "Board the tank, and watch command A1 like a hawk! As we bring the tank in, if he does anything wrong! You stop him."

Clay swallows hard. "Sir, yes, sir!"

Clay hesitates. Pierce jerks back as if he were in pain. "Soldier, what are you waiting for?"

Clay was scared to ask. "Sir, if he does anything wrong?"

Pierce, frustrated at the amount of time being wasted, spews out his command, "Oh, I don't know … if he looks the wrong way, presses the wrong button, shoot, I don't care if he farts and it smells wrong! Oh, and especially, do not let him fire another shell at our own people!"

Clay responds, "Sir, yes, sir!"

He removes himself from the A-TIV and races toward the tank, climbing the side ladder and entering. Pierce yells the command, "Forward!"

They reply, "Sir, yes, sir!"

Aboard the *Tiqu-Qi/Liberty Crane*, the ship's steward, Bo Son, is helping Dr. Shome to move some equipment from one room to the other. Bo Son is helping her push a cabinet. Dr. Shome is in the front, pulling it, guiding it through the door. Dr. Shome, appreciative of his help, cheerfully thanks him, "Thank you so much, Bo Son. There are so many people aboard the ship, and I still could not find one person to help me until you came along."

Steward Bo Son smiles a healthy smile that lights up the room. "I am glad to help. It's one of the reasons I joined—"

Before he can finish his sentence, he disappears! As if a trick on an old television show, he simply vanishes! There is no smoke, no sound. He does not slowly, dramatically fade away. He just is there one minute and gone the next. Dr. Shome pauses for the briefest of moments. She climbs over the cabinet, out the door, and looks around. She calls out for him, "Bo Son, are you there?"

Her words drift off, as do her emotions and her fears! Shome calls on her wrist communicator for Dr. Davis, "Dr. Davis, come to the new lab immediately! This is of the utmost importance!"

Nine minutes later, Shome and Davis burst onto the bridge. They march all the way to the front, and Davis addresses Captain Reynolds, "Captain Reynolds, sir!"

Captain Reynolds gives them his attention. With all that is at stake, there are few people whom Reynolds will give an audience to at this moment. Only a handful of people are allowed this intrusion. Dr. Shome and Dr. Davis are two such people. They have proven their mettle time and time again! Captain Reynolds knows that Shome and Davis would not be on the bridge if it were not of the utmost importance. Something deep in his heart sings a song in anticipation of whatever they are about to tell him. It is not a happy song; it is sorrowful, like a funeral song. Although he does not hear actual words or melodies, his bones chill, and the hairs on his arms dance to its tragic rhythms.

Calmly he asks, "Dr. Davis, Dr. Shome, what is it?"

Shome walks up past Dr. Davis with a small computer file in her hand. She hands it intrusively over Wei's shoulder and into his hand. Shome tells him, "Put this footage on-screen. We need to show you something."

Wei gingerly holds the file and looks up for approval from Captain Reynolds. Captain Reynolds nods his approval, and Wei responds, "Sir," and places the file into the port.

Wei is about to put the image on the large screen when Davis taps the top of his hand and waves her pointer finger, indicating for him not to. She says, "Let's just keep this for our eyes only."

Now intrigued all the more, they look intently as Wei presents the image on the smaller screen. The screen opens up to the scene just minutes earlier. Bo Son is helping Dr. Shome to move the cabinet. Suddenly he disappears! Wei squints, wondering if he saw it correctly, assuming it to be a glitch. He attempts to rewind that part of the clip. Lieutenant Lin also reacts, thinking there is a problem with the data. He checks the system for any type of corruption from the file. Captain Barr responds, "Whit ... whit just happened? Where did he go?"

Captain Reynolds nods. He looks at Dr. Shome. "Good question."

Shome takes a deep breath and decides just to blurt it out, which seems to have been the best thing to do up to this point. She states, "Sir, Captain Reynolds, Captain Barr, Lieutenant Minor, it would seem that Bo Son just disappeared out of thin air. But when this happened, I had some suspicions. I quickly called Dr. Davis."

Davis nods. Shome continues, "And we worked quickly to pursue my theory."

Captain Reynolds, trying to hold back his impatience, asks, "Doctor, what exactly is it?"

Dr. Shome continues, "Well ... it turns out that Bo Son is directly related to one of the soldiers on the away mission, Lieutenant Son."

Lin nods. "Yes, Lieutenant Son. He's a very good man, and he's down there right now."

Shome continues, not sure how to say what she is about to say, "Well ... sorry ... we suspect that he is no longer with us."

Captain Barr shakes his head. "Whit ur ye trying t' say?"

Davis speaks up. "Sir, I am sorry. We believe he is dead."

Captain Barr, confused, asks, "Am no' understanding th' connection. An' how did ye come t' 'is conclusion?"

Davis speaks again, this time with more authority. "Sir, somehow our universes are connecting! What happens in your universe's present affects us in our past, therefore affecting our present as well!"

Wei, starting to understand and not liking what he is hearing, sits forward on the edge of his seat, like he is watching the climax of a good movie. Lin, Captain Reynolds, Captain Barr, Moses, and Minor all try to follow along. Shome continues, "It would seem that Lieutenant Son has died, and because he died, in our universe, Steward Bo Son never lived!"

Davis interjects, "It gets worse! It would seem that somehow whoever organized this handpicked the *Liberty Crane* to achieve maximum impact! To achieve the most damage possible on Earth!"

Captain Reynolds, confused, waves his hand in front of him. "What do you mean, 'damage'?"

Davis explains, "Almost the entire crew of the *Liberty Crane* has a direct descendant in our current military!"

Captain Barr speaks up. "So ur ye're saying if they die, it'll affect yer military present noo?"

Davis nods. "In theory, yes! In fact, we estimate that they would wipe out almost 80 percent of Earth's entire military!"

Shome clarifies, "Not only Earth, but the entire alliance!"

Captain Barr jumps up. "How is 'at possible? Thir's only five thousand soldiers oan eh *Liberty Crane*!"

Wei adds, "And over sixteen million in the alliance."

Shome slowly shakes her head. "Realize that, if you pick the right five thousand people, ten generations later, they could produce over half the population of Earth, easily! That is how we know that this crew was handpicked."

The room is quiet.

Chapter 17

The Ze'ev warships have four circular hatches on the top. They open, and one by one, Sheol fighters rise from each hatch. As commanded, Rikes takes off to intercept the fighters. Shuttles cannot match fighters in weaponry; most of their projectiles are made to flatten surfaces in rocky terrain. He uses what he has to cut into the Sheol fighters as they rise. Unfortunately, both he and Lieutenant Young have forgotten that most of the drilling apparatus was used up trying to cut through the iron ore back on the small red planet. Rikes frustratedly slams his fist down on the controls! He quickly searches his inventory to see what he still has available. He realizes that he has a full accompaniment of Split-Bit projectiles. Split-Bit are nanorockets designed to penetrate solid rock at supersonic speeds. They do not explode; instead, they expand quickly, cracking the rock. This allows the pilot to then use explosive projectiles to penetrate further into the holes already made. The Split-Bit would not have worked on solid iron ore, but they work just fine on the Sheol fighters.

Rikes takes the Sheol fighters by surprise, as they were informed that the Army Queen did not have air support. The projectiles rip into the side of one of the fighters and then the canopy of another. The canopy immediately shatters, causing the plane to go out of control, flying almost a kilometer away and crashing into the forest. Unfortunately, this is about as much success as Rikes will get. Although the shuttle is a tank in comparison to the fighters, the fighters' speed and weaponry far outmatch it. As soon as the Ze'ev pilots realize what is happening, they maneuver and open fire on the shuttle. Within seconds, their fighters mercilessly shred the shuttle's main rockets. The rockets explode, and the shuttle catches fire. The shuttle is going down, and it is going down hard! Rikes tries to engage the secondary rockets, but all systems are offline. He does not stop in his efforts to engage the secondary rockets. Moments before impact, the ship abruptly stops. Rikes is thrown to the floor. Private Diamond has caught the falling shuttle in midair and safely brings it down onto the grassy plain.

Vicky has the advantage; up on her perch, she is unseen. With rifle in hand, she takes shot after shot, hitting each target center chest. The soldiers return fire blindly. This strategy is too slow; the troops are advancing up the hill quicker than Vicky can take them out. She arms two of the sidearm disks for remote use. Vicky is not sure if this will work, but desperate times call for innovation! She flings the first disk over the hill, toward the advancing Ze'ev soldiers. Once the disk is just over their heads, she presses the fire button. The disk rains down bullets on top of the approaching forces. Any soldiers who look up to attempt to shoot down the disk, Vicky takes out with a headshot. When the sidearm's ammunition is finally spent, the disk loses its velocity and crashes, annoyingly, into the forehead of one of the Ze'ev soldiers.

Vicky is satisfied with the strategy; she decides to try the second sidearm. Vicky flings the disc, but this time she swings it higher up to let it soar farther. Her plan works well as it picks up the wind and flies all the way down the hill. The soldiers still exiting the ramp do not notice it as it flies mere meters over their heads. Just as it enters the mothership, now less than half a meter from the soldiers' heads, she opens fire.

The disk enters the ship! The soldiers inside do not know what hit them. In the darkness of the mothership, all they can see above them are fiery blasts and the echoing sounds of bullets raining death down on them! From Vicky's vantage point, she can hear the angry screams of the soldiers inside the ship. The strategy worked; for the briefest of moments, the flow of soldiers ceased from spilling out of the ship. However, there are so many soldiers who soon the swarm continues, a never-ending herd of violence!

Vicky is forced to change tactics as she now turns to her two main sidearms. She has to stand to use them correctly. She knows this makes her an easy target, but she is not afraid. Her lack of fear enhances her focus and gives her a great advantage. Not wanting to get shot, the Ze'ev soldiers fire at Vicky without aiming. The sidearm bullets are less effective against the Ze'ev armor than the rifle was, and Vicky knows it. Instead, Vicky aims for their legs. She disables their lead soldiers, causing them to fall down the hill in a domino effect, taking two or three and sometimes ten or more soldiers with them.

Vicky realizes that, despite her efforts, they will reach the plateau. By the time it takes her to reload her sidearms, the first three Ze'ev soldiers are up on the plateau. In rage, they fire at her. Bullets are flying, and Vicky has to dodge, but even her reflexes are not fast enough. She grinds her teeth, knowing that she will get hit. She hopes that it is not fatal; she has to protect the queen, the village, her people and help save her crew and the crew of the *Liberty Crane*. Suddenly, Private Diamond jumps between her and the increasing spray of bullets. The bullets bounce off his metal body.

Ruth is handling her corner. As predicted, only one or two of the soldiers at a time try to climb up that section. Ruth's heart is innocent; she does not want to kill them, even though they are dead set on killing everyone. She knows she has to help Lieutenant Young defend the village. Ruth tries her best to focus her acid on only their weapons. However, she has never trained, and she is unable to control such a small amount of acid in such a small area. For the first fifteen or so, she accidentally disintegrates both the Ze'ev weapons and their hands, as well. Each time she gets a little better, disintegrating only their fingers along with their weapons. However, when more than two or three come at her at the same time, she loses focus, disintegrating whole arms, and one of them she accidentally disintegrated his entire chest.

Ruth is occupied with her assignment and does not pay attention to the battle between Vicky and the troops coming up the hill or to Private Diamond using his body as a shield to protect Vicky. Before Private Diamond can retaliate, the remaining soldiers on top of the plateau fire wildly at him. One of the stray bullets flies across the field and strikes Ruth in the shoulder. Ruth screams out a scream never before heard by any living creature. So high-pitched and powerful is the scream that it cracks the helmets on the nearby Ze'ev soldiers.

Rikes falls to the ground, covering his ears in pain! Even electrical equipment is affected by the power of her screech. Private Diamond's systems falter, and he loses balance, stumbling around like a drunk. Two Sheol fighters lose control and crash into each other, falling just to the side of the plateau and bursting into flames on the trees below. Around Ruth's eyes, red liquid oozes out. Then moments later, her eyes erupt with what can only be described as lava pouring out.

Seemingly unaffected by gravity, the lava does not simply flow downward but spreads all over her body, including upward onto her face and over her head. The lava is then reabsorbed by her body. Ruth clenches her teeth and snarls like a beast so loud it can be heard even at the bottom of the hill. Ruth moves forward with amazing speed toward the edge of the hill. She lifts her hand in front of her, and in a fit of rage, an enormous acid hand forms. The hand is as wide as the entire hill passage. She pushes her hand forward, and the acid hand pushes down the hill, dissolving every soldier and tank along the way.

Finally reaching the bottom, the hand grows a partial arm from out of the ground. It lifts up and continues to grow in size until it is the same size as the Ze'ev warship. Ruth slams her hand downward, and the acid hand follows, smacking down on the warship like a giant wave, disintegrating almost the entire ship, leaving nothing but a deep hand-shaped trench in the ground.

Vicky is astonished; her mouth hangs open. Never before has she seen such raw power; Ruth's power is frightening! Rikes, still on the ground, looks up, and for the moment, he is more afraid of Ruth than he is of the Ze'ev army. Ruth is hunched over, breathing deeply, arms on the side, ready to pounce. Steam is rising off her body. Ruth tries to contemplate her next move, but her senses will not allow her to make a sound decision.

Vicky realizes that she has to calm her, and instinctively, she goes to her friend, not worrying about the potential danger. Vicky wraps her arm around Ruth's shoulder. At first, Ruth does not respond, as if she did not even notice. Vicky is so trusted in Ruth's eyes that she has no reason to react. Vicky quietly calls to her, "Ruth, calm down."

Suddenly, Ruth snaps out of it; her eyes turn back to normal. The remaining lava seeps back into her body. Amazingly, Ruth's outfit does not look bad; it is slightly scorched in some areas but basically intact, as well as Vicky's uniform. In some areas, it is scorched but not badly damaged. It is obvious that Ruth has a subconscious control of the acid's destructiveness. Vicky stands Ruth up straight and stares into her eyes. She tells her, "You need to calm down. You need to take a moment."

Ruth looks over the cliff at the destruction. Vicky gently guides her face away. She calmly tells her, "No, you need to relax. Do not worry about what happened. You need to gain control."

Vicky's words are soothing. She moves Ruth away from the cliff.

The second Ze'ev warship drops to three thousand meters. They do not land in fear that what happened to the first warship may happen to them as well. Instead, they deploy their fighters. The Sheol fighters rise in the sky like a swarm and begin their descent. Private Diamond has regained control; he blasts out to intercept them.

As Diamond rockets toward them, the head Sheol pilot sees him. He calls out to the warship commander, "Tubu Ar! Khan, ki ki Etta Ha Ka'dool Ar zee?" (Commander! Look, is that the Eater of Flesh off Bone that Ar reported?)

The commander replies, "Ki ki Ethan Han!" (Yes, that is the Bone Eater!)

The commander commands, "Moht Ethan Han!" (Kill the Bone Eater!)

The squadron begins to chant, "Moht Ethan Han!"

The commander sends the message, "Die, Bone Eater!"

Vicky and Rikes receive the message; their wrist communicators chime. They both glance at the message. Rikes, confused, mumbles to himself, "Bone Eater, what is a Bone Eater?"

The warship, after discharging the fighters, turns further out into the forest and begins its descent, hoping that the distance will protect it from Ruth. At about half a kilometer out, it lands in the forest, the trees splintering into little pieces and bursting into flames as the massive ship lands.

The Sheol fighters discharge their black bullets against Private Diamond. The bullets hit Diamond's shell. They give him something he never thought he would feel again: pain! He grunts a sound like a wounded animal, trying hard not to scream out in pain, not wanting the enemy to know that, somehow, they hurt him. Diamond realizes he cannot simply tolerate the bullets. He has to take defensive actions; he maneuvers to avoid the bullets.

Now it is time for Diamond to return fire. His weapons are even more effective against the Sheol fighters than theirs are against him. Diamond shoots holes into their ships. They explode and come crashing down in flames. Diamond is careful not to shoot the ships when they are directly over the village. The head Sheol pilot, frustrated, fires missiles at Diamond. Diamond now has to be even more on the defensive; he uses his weapons to destroy the missiles. Unable to use his weapons against the Sheol fighters, he changes tactics and uses his body as a weapon! He crashes into one of the ships, pushing it toward the forest, where it crashes and burns.

Meanwhile, two of the Sheol fighters fly out to attack Ruth, whom the Ze'ev identifies as their biggest threat! Ruth is still panting. Even though she is calming down, she is disoriented, almost unsure as to where she is. An array of bullets fired from the Sheol fighters blasts the ground just meters away from her, snapping her out of her coma-like trance. Ruth screams at them, however, with more control than before. She angrily flares her fingers, sending up tentacles of acid. However, the ships are too high, and Ruth cannot reach them. She tries and tries again and becomes frustrated.

They turn for another run; this time, their bullets hit even closer. One of the Sheol ships accidentally flies directly overhead. Ruth, in anger, throws up an open hand over her head. From out of the ground rises a seventy-meter-long arm, with an open hand. The palm of the hand is wide enough to hold twenty people. The hand grips the unsuspecting fighter. She wraps her acid fingers around it, dissolving it totally. When the acid disappears, it is as if it were never there, leaving only smoke and fire in the air. The lead Sheol pilot screams out over the intercom, "Khan yatan, lemahtah-lemahtah N'ki mohtnu!" (Focus on Poison. Fly high out of reach so that she cannot kill us!)

The Sheol fighters fly high; soon they are joined by others. The fighters line up and rain down a barrage of bullets against Ruth. Ruth, with no defense, falls to the ground in a ball as the bullets graze her. The Ze'ev pilots see that Ruth is helpless on the ground. This gives their dark hearts great amusement; they laugh out loud. They scream their laughter into the outward speakers to taunt her. As their ships pass, as if the relentless onslaught of bullets were not enough, they also mock her. Their horrifying cries echo into the air like the caw of a hideous bird!

Vicky, noticing the peril that Ruth is in, runs to her side, dragging a MAC-22 from the grass. (A long-range, rapid-fire, land-to-air, missile assault cannon.) This gun is designed to be mounted, but Vicky harnesses it on her shoulder as she would a sharpshooter's rifle. Vicky stands in front of Ruth, defiantly in the path of the oncoming fighters. She takes aim and fires; she takes out two fighters and grazes the third. The fighters scramble. Vicky reaches her hand out and wraps her fingers around Ruth's arm; she helps her to her feet. Ruth's eyes are wide; she hugs Vicky. Vicky acknowledges her and then gently moves her back. She looks at Ruth and calmly yet firmly tells her, "You are in danger out here. As long as they have fighters, they will continue attacking you until they get you! Go to the village, and find the boy and protect him. There is a ship."

"What?" asks Ruth.

"There is a small ship behind the castle. If they get past us, bring the boy and the Army Queen to the ship, and save yourselves."

Ruth feels that she has let Vicky down. Vicky knows this, but they cannot address it now. Vicky's words are strong; there is no condemnation in them. Something about her voice inspires confidence. Vicky tells her, "Come."

Vicky places Ruth's arm over her shoulder to balance her, and the two rush toward the village. Unfortunately, without Ruth guarding the hillside, a handful of soldiers have managed to climb up. Quickly they advance toward the village. Vicky sees the soldiers approaching the village, and panic grips her and Ruth. Vicky's mind races. "The Army Queen, I have to protect her!"

Vicky and Ruth dash toward the gate. However, before they can take another step, the soldiers, still a good distance away from the queen, unleash a barrage of bullets against her. Vicky's heart jumps into her throat. She gasps, unable to speak; a sense of hopelessness falls over her. Ruth is still unsteady, but Vicky raises her weapon. She attempts to fire, but she is out of ammunition. Vicky screams out a roar of frustration.

However, the Army Queen is not defenseless; quite the opposite. Her reflexes are so quick that Vicky can barely see her move. Before the soldiers know what is happening, the Army Queen is upon them and beheads the first one! She moves to the next two; with one slash, she cuts their backs, and they fall over. The last two soldiers do not even realize they are under attack until they pause for the briefest of moments. They notice that their three comrades have fallen violently. Then the queen slices the legs off the first one; before he reaches the ground, she takes off his head. She then catches the last one in his back. So powerful are the force and speed of her sword that she severs his torso from his hips. The queen then returns to her perch by the entrance of the village; she is not even breathing hard. Vicky stops; she looks up at the Army Queen in amazement.

A sudden crash gets Vicky's attention. She turns; from over the ledge, she can see the trees falling. The Ze'ev warship has unleashed its package of soldiers and what must be tanks. Vicky turns toward Ruth; Vicky's eyes say all that is needed. Ruth nods and rushes toward the village as Vicky races toward the edge. Rikes has perched himself at the edge, waiting patiently with his sidearm ready. The trees are not falling in a straight line; they are fanning out, surrounding the plateau from every direction. The Ze'evs do not want to give Ruth another chance to strike them so easily as she did when they were all grouped together. The roar of rockets fires over Vicky's and Rikes's heads as Private Diamond lands next to them. He sends them a message; Vicky and Rikes read, "Out of ammo, out of fuel."

Diamond is a combination of mechanical, organic, and something mystical; he will replenish, but it will take time. Vicky looks down; she knows that they will all soon run out of ammo. Vicky suddenly realizes that, out of all their weapons, it is the Army Queen's sword that will be the most efficient. At the end of the day, it will never run out.

Trees fall as the tanks advance. The situation is not good; soon they will be overrun. Vicky taps Rikes to get his attention. He looks up at her; she gestures with her hand that she will position herself on top of the tree. Rikes nods. Vicky climbs up a tree at the edge of the plateau; she aims the last weapon. Rikes and Diamond both know that they are pinned down and that the situation is grim, but they will fight; the fire that is within Vicky is inextinguishable, and it ignites them. She fuels their hope, not only to fight but also to win.

A second wave of Sheol fighters rises from the forest. This could be the end, as still one last Ze'ev warship resides high up in the clouds, looking down ominously on them. Vicky takes aim from her perch and fires a careful shot into the canopy eye of one of the Sheol fighters, cracking it. Immediately the pilot turns his efforts toward Vicky and fires relentlessly at her. The tree is shredded, and Vicky falls to the ground, rolling onto the grass. She quickly regains her footing, but she has no time to react.

Over the plateau come the tanks. Diamond quickly jumps on top of one of the tanks and rips the hatch off. He reaches in and grabs one of the Ze'ev soldiers by the head, smashing his helmet and throwing him out. Diamond snags the other soldier by his arm, yanking him out so hard that his head collides with the rim of the hatch, shattering his helmet into pieces. Diamond flings him into the air directly in the path of the fighter that had shot down Vicky. The nose of the fighter pierces the ejected tank soldier, and his body becomes entangled on the canopy. The pilot, unable to remove him, decides to make an emergency landing. Meanwhile, Diamond, just mere meters away, takes hold of the tank.

Slowly his hand opens up to a giant tunnel, and he begins swallowing the tank within his body.

Meanwhile, Vicky meets the foot soldiers and addresses them one by one in hand-to-hand combat. She has no weapons, and for some reason, she cannot operate their weapons. Rikes, following Diamond's lead, fearlessly climbs one of the tanks. He opens the hatch and opens fire within. The soldiers return fire. Rikes loses his footing and falls to the ground.

Diamond has completely integrated the tank with himself, and after a second of adjustment, he transforms his arm into a tank barrel. His back, just below his right shoulder, distorts and transforms into a turret, which immediately, independently locks onto Sheol fighters and fires. The turret gun is not extremely accurate and in fact misses as much as it hits, but with the augmented gun, when it does hit, it evaporates the fighters. Diamond proceeds to use his tank cannon arm to, one by one, take out the advancing tanks. His augmented cannon annihilates the tanks with one shot! After Diamond has downed three of the tanks, he turns his attention to the Sheol fighter next to him. The Ze'ev pilot had just finished removing the dead body of his fallen comrade when Diamond surprises him, swatting him away with his tank cannon arm. The pilot falls hard to the ground.

Diamond's hand opens again, slowly swallowing the Sheol fighter. This time, something is different; his body begins to vibrate. Diamond shakes it off and completely swallows the ship. Seconds later, he produces wings out of the side of his body. Rockets fire, but he only gets about two meters off the ground when he suddenly sputters and falls to his knees.

Something is wrong. The wings retract; his armor changes color to the grayish black of the Sheol fighter. His eyes flicker back and forth from his "star" eyes to black orbs. Diamond stumbles, unbalanced. The fallen Sheol pilot looks up at him and laughs a sinister laugh. Diamond tries once more to fully stand, but instead, he spins around and falls on his back. There is a vicious battle within him. The vibrations start up again, this time even worse than before; so quick are the vibrations that his body seems to be a blur to the naked eye. Diamond rolls over onto all fours. He tries to push himself up. He slams his fist into the ground in frustration, throwing up dirt.

After moments of what seemed like total anguish, Diamond opens the tunnel in his hand again and vomits up the Sheol ship. Like a giant hairball carcass, the ship is unrecognizable. Diamond then momentarily seems better; he regains his composure. He attempts to stand, only to fall to the ground, motionless. The Sheol pilot reports on an open channel, "Ethan Han moht!" (The Bone Eater is dead!)

Chapter 18

Jones has decided that the squadron should take a moment to land and assess their equipment before they proceeded. Kneeling down, curious, she pressed her two fingers into the rubbery ground. Jones lifts her fingers and inspects the slimy pink residue on them. She then stands up and looks around. Something catches her eye; she looks at the far wall and wonders, "Has that always been there?"

Jones walks toward the wall to examine it more closely. Protruding through the wall are triangular black objects. With her finger, she touches one, causing it to come further out. Startled, Jones jumps back. Two little eyes open on the object. The chill of the unknown runs down Jones's spine. On her communicator, she commands, "Board your fighters. We are moving out!"

The pilots responds, "Yes, ma'am!"

The pilots advances toward their fighters to board them. Suddenly, the triangular black creatures fly out of the walls, zooming at the pilots. Their attacks hit so hard that most of the pilots fall to the ground. Jones commands, "Get back in the fighters now!"

Quickly the pilots board their ships. As the canopy on Jones's plane is closing, one of the triangular black creatures gets stuck inside the canopy with her. Jones pulls her hands back, unsure of what to do. The creature maneuvers to attack Jones, but she punches it hard with the back of her fist. It slams into the console. With the creature momentarily stunned, Jones grabs it, opens her canopy, and flings it out. She closes the canopy. The creatures do not stop; they continue striking the fighters at great speed. The noise is disturbing, terrifying even. Each strike is worse than the one before. They are becoming faster and more powerful. When they hit the compressed glass of the canopy, it scratches it, and with each pass, the scratches are getting deeper. Jones realizes that these creatures, whatever they are, will soon damage or even destroy their ships. Jones commands, "Move out, take to the air!"

One by one in rows, with Jones leading, they fly off down the cavern!

Suddenly the cavern ceilings seem to melt. Thin ropelike strands fall from the roof of the cavern. The strands snag the fighters. At first, it is a minor inconvenience as they easily push through, snapping the cords. Soon, the vines seem to not only grow in number but to strengthen, as well. The fighters rattle like a car on a bumpy road.

One of the fighters' wings gets caught in the strands. The fighter is thrown off course and swung into the wall. The explosion is great. The fighter directly behind maneuvers out of the path of the explosion, not realizing that his comrade to his right is entangled in the webbing-like vine. He crashes into him, and the two fighters fall to the ground in a firebomb!

Jones clenches her teeth and calls out to her two lead pilots, "Lieutenant Lee, Lieutenant Chu, arm your weapons. Use only guns, let us pave a hole for our fighters!"

They respond, "Ma'am, yes, ma'am!"

The three of them, Jones, Lee, and Chu, light up the skies with bullets. They fly through, cutting holes into the cascade of vines. This helps the first few rows that pass, but after the first ten rows, the vines grew with a vengeance. Lieutenant Myers, from the seventeenth row of fighters, calls out, "Ma'am, we cannot s… clearly… we're…ing, flying blindly!"

The communications were starting to falter, the words getting chopped off. Jones commands, "Use your digital outputs to maneuver! Repeat, squadrons 15 to 25, use your digital outputs to maneuver!"

Myers responds, "Ma'am, yes, ma'am! All fighters, 15 to 25, engage digital output only!"

Squadron leader 15 responds, "Roger!"

The pilots engage their 3D digital outputs. Their portal screens change into a digital image, allowing them to better plot a course around the vines.

Miraculously, Rivera has survived the explosion from Williams's ship. With his superior piloting skills, he is able to maneuver his fighter and land it safely. However, he is caught in the avalanche of rocks from the missile Williams fired. Still, for the moment, he is safe. His ship, although badly damaged, is in a pocket between the falling rocks. Slowly he opens his canopy manually, hoping that he will not cause the rocks to fall into the cockpit. Successful, he climbs out of the ship to survey his surroundings. First, he checks his communicator and calls, "This is Rivera, to mothership. Anybody, this is Rivera!"

There is no response. Suddenly he gets the sense that he is not alone. It is not a feeling that one can explain; it is a chill that travels up his spine. He tries to turn on his wrist light to see what is out there. It flickers, and after a few seconds of tapping, he manages to get it to work. Then, in front of him, still hidden in shadows, he spies three humanoid figures. He cries out, "What?" His light goes out.

Meanwhile, Yang's troop barely makes it back to the rocky section of the cavern. Yang places her hands on her thighs, panting, trying to catch her breath. She calls out, "Did everyone make it out?"

Yang stands up straight to see her crew. Suddenly she is startled. Next to her is a creature, as if it has appeared out of nowhere. Its form is like a gorilla, but it seems to be made out of the very rock in the cavern. It has black orbs for eyes. It looks at Yang. Yang gasps and jumps back. She prepares to fire. The creature then turns its attention to a nearby soldier, startling him. Yang commands the soldier, "Move away, and open fire!"

However, before the soldier can react, the creature's mouth opens. Rows of jagged long teeth the size of children's fingers grip over the head of the soldier and pull him off the ground. The teeth push him further into the creature's mouth. Instantly a second row of fingerlike teeth shoots out in front of the first and pushes the soldier deeper, to be replaced in front by another set of teeth pushing him in, and then again and again, as the soldier gets swallowed.

Yang and four other soldiers shoot at the creature. The bullets make a muffled thud as they pierce its rocky body. The creature takes one last look at Yang before it falls. It crumbles, dissolving into the ground, feet, then legs, then the head last. When the head crashes, it bursts into powder. However, the soldier it was consuming remains in its mouth the entire time. The soldier's hips and legs re left protruding from what is now a hole in the ground.

Yang and the four soldiers rush over to pull their comrade free. Yang and a soldier grab hold of one leg, and the other soldiers grab his other leg. They pull, but as Yang fears, all that come out are his hips and legs. They turn away horrified. One of them vomits in his helmet at the sight of the guts that fall out when they freed the body from the hole. However,

Yang cannot get the image of the creature's eyes out of her mind. Her head bursts in pain as if her very brain were on fire. She screams and falls to her knees. One of the soldiers helps her back up to her feet. Then, as suddenly as the images and excruciating pain manifest, they stop. The soldier asks, "Ma'am, are you hurt?"

Yang waves her hand in reply. "No, no, I am fine."

Suddenly, all around the cabin floor, holes open up. The holes become the mouths of creatures that rise from the ground. One soldier is unfortunate enough to be standing right on top of where a hole opens and falls right in as the creature rises. It takes the soldier up with it, with only the arms, shoulders, and head remaining protruding from its mouth. The soldier lets out one final bone-chilling scream when he is swallowed whole.

Yang has to make a choice; the large stone creatures are all around them, and the worms are before them. Before she can decide what to do, the shuttle rises from out the back and lands on three of the creatures, crushing them. Instantly they turn to dust. The shuttle pilot yells out to Yang, "Yang, Yang! Move your troops forward!"

There is no escape. They cannot go back, and the pink worms are still before them. Yang feverishly ponders what to do. Yang bangs her fist into the shuttle portal. She commands, "Quickly, as many soldiers as can, get inside!"

The soldiers pile inside as Yang and the other soldiers open fire on the advancing rock creatures. The pilot calls to Yang, "Ma'am, come inside!"

Yang shakes her head. "No, we still have soldiers left out here! Go forward in front, and pave a way for us!"

The pilot takes a moment, then she understands what Yang is saying. Her eyes light up. "Yes, ma'am, yes, ma'am!"

She pushes the shuttle forward, just fast enough that the remaining soldiers can trot behind. She unleashes a barrage of her arsenal against the worms, digging a trench into the ground for the soldiers to follow. The broken ground makes the path difficult, but they press forward. When she runs out of one type of ammunition, she changes to another. Yang feels that this will work; it will work until the shuttle runs out of ammunition, but they will cross that road when they get to it.

Jones's squadron is having difficulty with the vines. Lieutenant Myers cries out, "Ma'am, the vines are too much! My sh… is descending … can't ke her up! I'm going to—"

All of a sudden, an explosion is heard as Myers's fighter crashes. The ship directly behind Lieutenant Myers manages to successfully avoid the explosion; however, the two ships behind him also crash, causing a domino effect. Horrifying moments later, ten rows of ships are down. More importantly, to Jones, thirty more lives are lost. Jones's tears run down her face. She grinds her teeth, and in frustration, she yells out, "Move up ahead, there is a clearing!"

The fighters zoom forward to what seems to be a clear area up ahead.

Ruth bows down to the Army Queen. The queen's eyes seem cold. They are not; she is focused on the battle. She waits for Ruth to speak. Ruth takes a breath and states, "My queen, I can no longer fight in this battle. I was—I will go and protect the boy."

The queen nods. "Fear not, Ruth. You cannot control your powers. Go and protect the boy." Just then, the village wise man walks up behind the queen. She pauses and turns to him. Behind him is their entire village, all the men and all the women who do not have small children to tend to. The village bows before the queen. The queen acknowledges them, and she, too, bows, perhaps even more humbled than they. Feeling that she has failed them, she declares, "My dear children, I love you so! I am so sorry—"

The wise man interjects, "Your Highness, our queen, I am sorry to interrupt you, but we"—he pauses and looks to his right and to his left at the accompaniment behind him—"we request that you allow us to help. We can fight."

The queen looks at them. She knows that they have determined this in their hearts. She asks, "Are you sure?"

One of the ladies in the crowd yells out, "Yes, my queen! We will fight for you!"

The people respond, "We will fight with you, my queen!"

The wise man waves his hand downward. "Calm down!" he cries over the crowd.

He turns toward the Army Queen once again. "Your Highness, you have protected us well! But this is our village, you"—he points with his finger—"and us. And we will fight for it!"

The queen bows, looking up at them with her eyes. She asks, "You do understand that this is something that, once done, cannot be undone."

The wise man responds, "We will fight with you!"

The villagers from behind, one by one whispering a confirming "We will fight with you!"

The queen lifts her head. "Very well! Women, quickly run to the village. All children move to the higher plateau, by my castle. Leave able women to care for them, then meet the men by the castle."

Some of the women run up to carry out the queen's order. The Army Queen turns to the rest and informs them, "You will go into the castle and retrieve all the weapons by my throne!"

She calls out for Eliana. Eliana goes forward. The queen instructs her, "Eliana, show them to the trophy room, let them pick whatever weapons they desire."

Before Eliana moves to lead them, the queen turns to the wise man. She places one hand on his shoulder and instructs, "Then bring all the ready men and women back here, we will have a fight!"

The queen turns her head to Eliana and glances at Ruth, who has nervously been watching the gate for the Ze'ev invasion. The queen commands, "Eliana, escort Ruth to the chamber. Ruth, make sure the boy is safe, stay with him. Eliana, when you are finished with everything, you stay with Ruth and the boy in the chamber, that place is protected."

As soon as the queen finishes speaking, Eliana hastens up toward the castle. "Follow!" she calls to her fellow villagers and to Ruth. The entire village follows her. Eliana leads them up to the castle, where they meet up with the rest of the women. Eliana then leads them to the queen's throne and, more specifically, to the baskets of weapons. She points, "Pick whatever you want."

The villagers rush in, excited. Eliana then calls for one of the servants. "Seabreath, come!"

Her voice echoes through the palace. Moments later, Seabreath runs in. They acknowledge each other. "Quickly," she commands. "Take Ruth to the boy, she will help you protect him!"

"Yes, ma'am!" Seabreath bows. He then tells Ruth, "Follow!"

The two of them race off. Eliana turns her attention toward the villagers. The villagers do not understand weaponry, but they do understand things that are pointy and can be used to stab. Consequently, most of the weapons they choose are the more primitive ones: bows, arrows, swords, staffs, slings, and spears.

Vicky has basically held the fort the entire time. With Private Diamond down, Ruth taken out of the equation, and Vicky unable to use the Ze'ev weapons, Vicky is forced to engage each invader head-on! She dodged bullets and fought relentlessly. There was no way that Vicky could have stopped the tanks; there are now at least ten tanks on top of the plateau. If they want to rush the gate, there is nothing stopping them. The only reason they have not raided the village is the fact that they want the Army Queen alive.

The Sheol squadrons circle overhead, looking for Ruth. Vicky is tattered; her suit is worn and torn. At the moment, she is facing twelve soldiers. The closest soldier, expecting an easy target, shoots at Vicky. She throws her body into him and pulls his arm, causing him to misfire, shooting his comrade in the face. While still holding the soldier, Vicky breaks his arm then his leg at the knee before letting him go.

Vicky is outnumbered; she knows there is no way she can defeat the other ten without getting shot, but she will not give up. She will never give up! Then, like an answer to prayers, the way prayers are usually answered, at the last minute, in a gust of wind enters the Army Queen. In seconds, the soldiers are dispatched, violently. Just then, over the hill comes the full troop led by Commander Ripclaw. Behind him are thousands of Ze'ev soldiers, littering the forest. Ripclaw punches his chest; his second turns toward the approaching troop. He also bangs his chest, a sigh for them to halt. The troop mimics him, and they stop. Ripclaw calls out to the Army Queen, "Army Queen, the Dictator calls you! Come or your village dies!"

Vicky actually thinks that she catches the Army Queen smiling. The queen turns to Vicky and casually requests, "Hold them off for a minute, I will be right back."

Vicky, with confusion painted over her face, responds, "Ma'am, I am not a politician."

Now she knows that the queen is smiling. "No, you're not." She snickers. "Speak to him, see if he will negotiate."

The queen hastens toward the village to meet her people. Ripclaw's eyes follow her. He is about to give the command to attack, when Vicky steps up. She firmly yells out, "I am Lieutenant Young of the UPA."

Ripclaw turns his attention toward Vicky in disdain. He sneers, "N'tubu, do not talk to me. I will only talk to the Army Queen! You, I kill!"

The queen meets the villagers back in the village as they return from the castle with Eliana. Firmly the queen turns toward Eliana and commands, "Quickly, run back to the castle, and stay with Ruth and the boy!"

Eliana nods and runs off. The queen tells the people, "Line up before me!"

They quickly move into place, holding the weapons awkwardly in their hands. Meanwhile, in the castle, Seabreath takes Ruth to the chamber. He then turns and stands outside the door with the other servant, an elderly lady. The two stand on guard. Ruth looks at them. Perplexed, she states, "Please, open the door. I want to check on the boy."

They are embarrassed; they do not realize that Ruth wants to go inside. Humbly they reply, "Forgive us!"

Quickly they turn and unlock the door. Ruth thanks them and walks into the bare large room. The room has white walls and sparse furniture; the floor has white tiles. There is only one window in the room. The window is different from the other windows in the rest of the palace. It is square and small, and it seems as if it were made out of a different material than the other palace windows are. In fact, the entire room seems out of place from the rest of the castle.

Ruth looks around; she does not see the boy. To her right, there is a door. Quickly she rushes over. She is about to knock, when she notices that the door is not locked; it is not even closed all the way. Ruth gently pushes it open. It is a restroom, like the rest of the chamber, white and simple, with only one window. However, the boy is nowhere to be found.

"Seabreath!" she calls out in panic. The two guards rush in. The lady stops for a second to look around, shocked that she does not see the boy. Seabreath runs straight to Ruth. Ruth walks over to the window; under close examination, she notices that the window seems to have been pushed open. Ruth exclaims, "The boy is missing!"

She rushes out past the bewildered guards, just as Eliana rushes to the door from outside. Ruth nervously grabs hold of Eliana's shoulders. "The boy"—Ruth glances back toward the room—"he is gone!"

In the courtyard, hiding behind one of the houses, just mere meters from the rest of the villagers, the boy peers out. He is invisible, but he is not hiding from the villagers. He is hiding from the queen. The Army Queen's voice deepens and becomes as if it were part of the wind and the air all around them. "Are you ready?" she asks.

The chill of her voice, although it does not frighten them, causes them to temporarily lose the ability to speak. They respond by standing straight and tall like the proud army they know they can be. The Army Queen dramatically raises her sword and slams it into the ground. However, the point barely pierces the surface.

The queen, on one knee, stays frozen for a second. Suddenly she glows, as does her sword. Her hand vibrates, the very ground vibrates, and lastly, so do the people! Then something comes over them. As a wild wind whirls around them, they begin to grow. Their bodies stretch; their muscles grow, still long and thin; but now they are solid. The men grow to approximately four meters tall; the women, almost three meters. Their eyes grow larger as their pupils adjust to see clearly in the night.

Their natural skills and characteristics are enhanced; those who are fast become faster. Those who are strong, stronger. Those who are wise, wiser. Their ability to understand mechanics and science grow in leaps and bounds. Even their senses grow: hearing, sight, even the ability to feel movements under them from hundreds of meters away. The slightest whisper they can hear, as they now have the ability to communicate with one another from great distances by just whispering. Their fingers become claws. The weapons in their hands also transform, growing larger and somehow becoming one with them. The holder has knowledge of how to use it, without any words or instructions. The villagers' blood races in their newfound bodies.

For a moment, they are bewildered, looking at one another. The Army Queen lifts her sword and points at them. She declares to them, "You are now a fierce army! Each of you is stronger than one hundred men, faster than a land predator. It will not take you long to become familiar with your abilities. Your body itself will assimilate you to understand what you can do, even how to control your weapons! Here is the strategy."

The queen addresses the women. "Women, go to the far edge of the town, there you will find a narrow exit hidden by vines."

One of the women speaks out. "Yes, Your Highness, the Fishing Gate, we know it. There is a small, narrow path down the side of the cliff, barely big enough for two people to walk."

The queen nods. "Yes, at your size, only one at a time can go. If you follow that path, it leads you towards the far edge of the forest. Run that course, and come behind the enemy troop. At your speed, it won't take you long."

She turns to the men. "Men, you will attack head-on! When you see the women approaching from the back, pull back. Let them think that they are winning. Then push forward! Women, when they rush forward, you attack from the back. Use your speed! They will be caught between the two of you!"

Just then, Ruth goes rushing toward the Army Queen, Eliana following close behind her. Ruth stops abruptly, throwing her hand out to gently brace herself against the queen. The queen is startled. She can sense that something is wrong. The queen searches the canvas, almost as if she knows what they are about to say before they say it. "What? What is wrong!" she asks.

Ruth straightens up. Just then, Eliana catches up. Ruth anxiously states, "The boy! The boy, Your Highness, the boy is gone!"

The queen looks around even more carefully. She squints and catches a glimpse of him staring out from behind a building. He sees her glance and quickly ducks behind the building. The queen snarls, "Come out!"

The boy turns visible and walks out from behind the house; he, too, was transformed! He walks toward her, with his head down in shame. He is not as tall as the others; in fact, he is about the size of a normal man. He looks like a grown adult. Aside from his skin being grayish and leathery, the boy has the same features. His fingers are long and clawlike. His body is muscular. His clothes have adapted to his body, forming a type of bodysuit. He bows before the queen. The queen stares down at him.

Ruth bewildered, bends her head downward to look up into his eyes. Surprised, she jerks back and grabs Eliana by the shoulder and exclaims in a hoarse whisper of disbelief, "It is the boy!" Eliana's mouth falls open. "Oh my," she murmurs as she turns to the queen.

"Madam"—she points toward the boy—"is this the boy?"

Now, for the first time, Ruth and Eliana take a moment to notice the giants who were once the villagers. Speechless, they look around in amazement. The queen commands the boy, "You stay here with Eliana and Ruth! I will deal with you."

The boy interjects, "Ma'am, I—"

The queen points her finger out to silence him. He knows better, and he remains quiet. The Army Queen regains her composure. She turns to the women and commands, "You go ahead and begin your journey to the edge of the forest!"

"Yes, ma'am!" they shout in a whisper.

As they hasten to depart, the queen calls out to one of the lead women in the community. Rainfall, the village leader of the women, often helps Eliana as a liaison between her and the village. "Rainfall."

All the women pause and turn to their queen. The queen calls out to them, "Be blessed!"

In reply, they bow, placing their palms together. In unison they reply, "Be blessed, my queen!" They turn back and run through the village toward the Fishing Gate. The Army Queen then turns her attention to the wise man. She commands, "Stay here and wait for my signal."

The wise man asks, "Ma'am?"

"We will fight," she tells him.

The queen announces, "Let me go and see how well Lieutenant Young is faring."

She runs toward the gate, pushing the boy into Ruth's arms.

Vicky has already exhausted all her diplomacy, as she has marched toward Commander Ripclaw. Vicky is human, unarmed, and a woman, three things that would cause Ripclaw to think she poses no threat. However, there is something in Lieutenant Young, her tenacity and her voice! Her very words state that she is defiant against them; this causes him to hesitate. His greatest concern is, first and foremost, for his own life. Still, Vicky refuses to surrender, she will not let him pass. If she has to rip apart the entire Ze'ev army with her bare hands, starting with Commander Ripclaw, she will! Ripclaw snarls, "Woman, move! This is your last chance before I rain my entire army on you!"

Vicky clenches her teeth. "Rain!"

However, before Vicky can take another step, the Army Queen calls out from the gate of the village, "Cease!"

A silence fills the air with its void. Ripclaw looks up. "Finally, you have come out of hiding, to give yourself up!"

The queen takes a few steps toward Vicky. Vicky turns and notices as the queen waves for her to go closer. Vicky reluctantly, taking one last defiant look at Ripclaw, turns and walks toward the Army Queen, meeting her halfway. The Army Queen addresses him. "I have never hidden from you, nor do I now come to surrender!"

Ripclaw taunts, "Then what have you come to do?"

The Army Queen discreetly grabs Vicky's wrist and pulls her alongside her. The Army Queen stares into Ripclaw and very matter-of-factly yells out, "We will fight!"

Chapter 19

The villagers jump over the wall, but they are no longer villagers—they are now warriors! The Army Queen's ability not only enhances the recipients physically but also gives them coherent knowledge of their new physique and abilities. Although it does not teach them fighting skills, they are very aware of how to use what they have. Vicky, who does not startle easily, ducks down defensively before she realizes what is happening. Her eyes open wide in amazement as she watches these warriors jump over her head. Likewise, the Ze'ev soldiers jump back. Commander Ripclaw wisely retreats behind his troops as he yells out, "Moht! Moht!" (Kill! Kill them!)

The Ze'ev soldiers open fire. One of the warriors grabs a soldier, lifts him, and slams him into the ground. Another warrior instinctively crouches, lifting his arm to protect himself. Out of his forearm grows a shield. The shield seems to be part of him, as if made from his own bone and skin. The Ze'ev's dark bullets barely scratch it. The warrior rushes forward. With his great speed combined with his strength, he plows through them. The soldiers are tossed to the ground. The warriors are so fast they can dodge bullets, causing the Ze'ev soldiers to fire wildly, often shooting one another.

One of the warriors lifts his bow, which is almost twice the size of the Ze'ev soldiers. The warrior uses his bow as a club. With wide swipes, he takes out two or three soldiers at a time, throwing them to either one side or the other. Suddenly a tank blast sends two warriors flying. The blast accidentally kills three of his own men, but Ze'ev soldiers have no regard for life, not even for their own people. The two warriors are thrown but not dead. As they start to rise, the tank prepares for a killing blow.

One warrior with a sling picks up a rock the size of a man's head. The rock transforms, bursting into flames. He places the rock into his sling and throws it at the tank. It explodes as it hits the tank cannon. The tank does not explode, but the cannon is on fire. A Ze'ev soldier opens fire at the warrior. He turns to avoid the shot; however, two bullets hit him in the back. But rather than penetrating, they burst into small blasts of fire, causing the warrior to shriek in pain. However, he is able to endure. He picks up another rock from the ground and quickly flings the fiery projectile at the soldier, sending him flying back into the tank, where it explodes.

Noticing that these warriors pose a threat, Ripclaw calls for air support. "Sheol, moht n'nu!" he commands.

The roar of the rockets vibrates the villagers' homes as the fighters circle back and begin targeting the warriors. Ripclaw taps his second-in-command hard in the chest. With his head, he motions for them to leave. The two walk off back down the hill.

Vicky moves forward to enter back into the fray. The Army Queen reaches out and grabs her by the arm. Vicky pulls away and turns to the queen. "Your Highness, I cannot stay here and not help your people fight!"

The queen extends her palm up. "You are unarmed ... Give them a chance, they are learning. Allow them to fight for their freedom!"

Vicky reluctantly bows her head; for the moment, she will obey.

Just then, Ruth, Eliana, and the boy go running to the queen. The queen turns, and with just her eyes, she addresses them. Ruth and Eliana freeze, unable to speak. The boy, however, speaks up. "Your Highness, ma'am, I want to help!"

The queen can sense the sincerity in his heart. She places her hand on his shoulder. "Yes," she tells him in a calming voice, "you have grown stronger, but you're not as strong as the adults nor as fast."

He pulls back, not defiantly but almost as if to center himself. The boy places his palm up and closes his eyes. He states, as if he were feeling the very words coming out of his mouth, "But I can feel it! I can feel that somehow ... your power has affected my powers! I can do things, I can help!"

The queen looks at him curiously. For a moment or two, she is silent, intently staring at him. Then she nods. "Yes, I can feel it. There is a strange power running within you now."

As the battle goes on around them, it is as if time has stood still for the five of them. Vicky, Ruth, Eliana, and the Army Queen stare at the boy. The queen instructs him, "Stand steady for a moment and concentrate. Use your powers, but before you use them, feel them. What can they do now?"

The boy's eyes open wide. He stays quiet, closes his eyes, and concentrates. Then suddenly he disappears. Ruth and Eliana would have assumed that he turned invisible if he had not instantly reappeared about three meters in front of them. The queen's and Vicky's heads jerk back in amazement. Then the boy closes his eyes and appears back in the spot he was a few seconds earlier. Vicky, almost as if she were talking to herself, states, "He can teleport from one place to another."

The queen looks at Vicky and smiles. "Yes … yes, he can!"

Just then, two Ze'ev soldiers run up, screaming, "Moht, moht!"

The soldiers manage to fire off two shots. Ruth, who has nervously been watching the perimeter from the corner of her eye, dodges one bullet and catches the other in the palm of her hand. She has swelled a ball of acid in her hand, and the bullet instantly disintegrates as it hits the acid.

Ruth, annoyed, turns the ball into a long cylinder. It extends from her hand through both soldiers' chests, leaving gaping holes. She then retrieves the acid into her hand, as if it were never there. The soldiers fall to the ground. Vicky, noticing what Ruth has done, walks over to her. She places her hand around Ruth's shoulder. Ruth is shaking. Vicky says nothing but guides her down to one knee. As the two of them kneel, Vicky, almost in a whisper, asks, "Can you form a pool in front of you?"

Ruth looks at Vicky curiously. She looks forward and concentrates. From out of her hand comes an oval pool of acid. She extends this paper-thin pool out from her hand about ten meters in front of her. Ruth proceeds to expand it to the size of a large puddle. Vicky nods in approval. "Very good."

Vicky then carefully places her hand over Ruth's hand and lowers it. Vicky instructs Ruth, "Now lower it just off the ground."

Vicky's words are comforting. Even in the midst of the battle and confusion, somehow they encourage and empower Ruth. Ruth smiles. She lowers her hand, causing the pool of acid to hover just off the ground. As she lowers it, any protruding blades of grass disintegrate instantly. Vicky calmly asks, "Can you keep this here?"

Ruth says nothing but nods as she focuses, extending the pool's width slightly to the right and to the left. Just then, as if out of nowhere, three of the Ze'ev soldiers rush in at them. Spying Ruth, one of them yells, "Yatan, Yatan! Moht, moht!"

Vicky stands defensively; however, confident in her strategy, she leaves one hand on Ruth's shoulder, encouraging her to hold her position. In their eagerness to kill Ruth, the Ze'ev soldiers do not see the pool of acid directly in their path. The first two run right into it, their feet instantly dissolving. They fall over, one to one side and the other to the other side. They scream in agony as they squirm on the ground. The third, unsure of what happened, rushes forward and steps right into the pool with one foot. With the loss of his foot, he clumsily falls forward directly into the pool and disappears. His hand, with his weapon still in it, the only part of his body that does not fall into the acid, falls to the ground.

While Ruth is dealing with the soldiers, the queen extends her hand to comfort the boy. He lifts his hand, preventing her from touching him. His hand is trembling. He places his other hand on the side of his head, as if in pain. He then turns toward the queen and states, "I can hear their thoughts, all of them. Even the bad people. I can't understand their words, but I can feel their emotions!"

He points out toward the battle. "Their commander ... Ripclaw? He is leaving. He is leaving his men to fight, and he is going somewhere else."

Vicky hears the boy. She gently squeezes Ruth's shoulder and encourages her, "Keep practicing."

Ruth manages a smile. Her trembling has ceased. Vicky quickly stands next to the queen. The boy looks at the queen and Vicky, frustrated. "It is important, but I don't understand ... Sorry, I don't understand!"

The warriors are faring well. In fact, they are doing better than just holding their own; they are outmatching the Ze'ev soldiers! However, avoiding the Sheol fighters is difficult. The fighters do not have concern for their own soldiers and will not give any thought to killing them along with the warriors.

One of the warriors is engaged in combat with a Ze'ev soldier. He slams the soldier into the ground and rips his gun from his hand. In the heat of the battle, he does not notice two other Ze'ev soldiers hiding in the shadows. They quickly take advantage and shoot him. Before he can react, a Sheol fighter rains down fire. The Ze'ev soldiers die instantly, and two of the bullets tear into the warrior's back! The warrior screams out in agony and falls to the ground! Even though the noise of the battle is fierce, the voice of the fallen warrior echoes through the plateau and down the side of the hill.

Knotwood, his fellow villager, hears his friend's cry. Knotwood's weapons are two glowing white blades attached to metal bands around his fists. As he slices two of the soldiers, their insides boil! They begin to burn internally until their eyes evaporate as they fall to the ground. Knotwood rushes back up the hill and crosses the courtyard, slicing into soldiers as he moves forward. His friend still has not recovered and is in the path of a tank! At great speed, Knotwood jumps and slices the tank tracks with his blade. The tracks spark violently but do not break. Not knowing what else to do, he races toward his comrade to move him out of the way. However, in his haste, he trips and accidentally falls on top of his friend!

Back by the queen, the boy suddenly looks up at the queen. His eyes glare, then without warning, he disappears. The boy appears between Knotwood and his comrade. He grabs their arms and teleports them from the tank's path. The boy and the two warriors reappear in front of the queen and Vicky.

The queen, concerned, looks down at the two warriors. She asks, "Are you two alright?"

Knotwood stands to his feet and helps his friend up. His friend's injuries have already begun to heal, and in fact, they are almost totally healed. They bow before the queen. "Yes, Your Highness … he saved us."

Knotwood thanks the boy, "Thank you."

Before the queen can say another word, they acknowledge the queen with a nod, "Your Majesty."

Embarrassed that they were injured, they turn and quickly run off back into the battle.

The queen looks down at the boy. Humbly, he bows his head. "I'm sorry, ma'am. I heard his cry, felt the danger!"

Just then, Vicky points. She cries out, "Look, Your Highness, the tanks!"

Ripclaw, frustrated at the outcome of the battle thus far, has decided to deploy a full-scale attack. If they cannot capture the Army Queen alive, they will destroy everything, including her! The tanks on the hill maneuver themselves, forming a line around the plateau, waiting for the entire platoon of tanks to go up the hill.

Then come the Chariots! The Ze'ev people are not at all tech-savvy, and the Chariots are one of their most advanced pieces of weaponry. Only the highest-trained officials are able to operate Sheol fighters or Chariots. The Chariots hover off the ground, powered by four to six rockets, depending on the design. They are one-man armored vehicles. The pilot controls them with one hand, placed inside an oval-shaped control panel. With the other hand, the pilot mans a large mounted gun. The gun's impressive ammunition belt is attached to the side of the gun and hangs inside the Chariot. Unlike the Sheol fighters, which are piloted by a special subgroup of Ze'ev people, the Chariots are pure technology, not magic.

Vicky yells out to the queen, "The tanks are forming a line! They are going to rush us and destroy the village!"

Before Vicky can finish her sentence, the first wave of Chariots opens fire on the warriors and the village. Vicky instinctively springs into action! For the moment, her enthusiasm outweighs her thoughts. Vicky dashes toward the edge of the plateau. With catlike grace and agility, she jumps onto the side of a tree. Using it as a springboard, Vicky bounces off it, landing inside one of the Chariots. Her momentum causes the vehicle to pitch sideways. Simultaneously, she kicks the Ze'ev soldier out. The Chariot spins wildly, but Vicky holds on, trying to gain control. The Chariot plows into the ground.

Vicky, unharmed, takes a moment to study the weapon. Although advanced, its design is familiar. She releases the clamp and grabs hold of the gun. Now this she understands. She pulls it free from its mount. Vicky grunts. The weapon is not made to be carried; it is like deadlifting a person. She lifts the barrel off the ground and begins firing at the incoming Chariots. Just as the tide of the battle is turning in favor of the invaders, the warriors hear a voice. It is their wives, their sisters—the women from the village have arrived. The men hear their whisper, "We are in position."

As commanded by the Army Queen, the men retreat. The Ze'ev soldiers, thinking they gained the advantage, holler a victory cry. Just as the men retreat, the women attack! Unlike the men, the women chose more modern weapons. Although at the time they have no idea how to use them, once they transform, the weapons transform with them. The weapons become part of them; they understand what they can do and how to use them. The women warriors do not climb the hill; no, they stay in the forest below. In the forest that they are all so familiar with, they climb trees and position themselves behind hills.

They shoot at the Chariots, the tanks, and the soldiers, allowing their fight to be from a distance. Their blasters are powerful enough to bore holes into the tanks and blast the Chariots right out of the sky. They are twice as fast as the men; they shoot and then move. The Ze'ev army cannot even see them. It is like fighting ghosts.

Vicky, out of ammunition, drops her weapon. She and the men momentarily pause by the Army Queen. Vicky glares, trying to figure her next move, when she hears a familiar voice behind her. "Wow, you really are something, aren't you!"

Meanwhile, Ripclaw and his second have just entered the second warship, about half a kilometer out from the plateau. There is commotion and chaos everywhere as the last of the troops and Chariots are being deployed. Ripclaw walks by unconcerned, as if they and the entire battle no longer matter; he is focused on something else. They enter the hangar, which is almost totally bare. He approaches a crescent-shaped ship; in fact, it is more similar in appearance to a backward letter *C*. The ship is more than four times the size of a Sheol fighter. Unlike the rest of the Ze'ev designs, which are either black or dark gray, this craft is light gray, almost white. This is Ripclaw's private transport. His second glances around at the commotion, confused, and asks, "Tubu Ripclaw, ir?" (Commander Ripclaw, where are we going?)

They walk up the ramp in silence, entering the ship. Ripclaw walks past the captain's chair and sits himself in the pilot's chair. He adjusts his equipment. He lifts the ramp, seals the door, and fires the engines. His second hastens to sit and prepare himself for liftoff. The ship's rockets scream inside the hangar as it ascends. Ripclaw presses the release for the hangar doors. One of the circular portals opens, and Ripclaw pilots the ship through it. As they leave the atmosphere, he turns toward his second and finally answers, "We are going to Planet Miedobeth, to welcome the return of our master!"

Vicky turns. Bridge is standing there with half a silly grin on her face, as if she were trying to hide her amusement by all the chaos. Bridge pretends to clap. "Bravo, bravo!"

Vicky is annoyed, but for some reason, she cannot remain angry at Bridge's antics; despite herself, they amuse her. Vicky glares. "What are you doing here, and where did you go?"

Bridge notices Vicky's seriousness and imitates her frown. Reverting to her carefree expression, she asks, as if she were correcting her, "What? No hello! How are you? We missed you."

Then, as if Vicky has asked her a second time, Bridge opens her eyes wide as she responds, "What? Where did I go?"

Bridge pauses, studies her fingernails, and then extends them. "I told you, I had something I had to do."

Bridge looks around. The scene is electric with battle. "I just came to see … So … how are you guys doing?"

Almost in response to Bridge's query, the Army Queen points her sword and gives the men their charge. "Attack!"

The male warriors shout their own battle cry and push forward. The invaders are now fighting two battles: the one in front and the women behind them. The queen catches Bridge's glance and walks toward them.

Suddenly the third and final warship, high above in the clouds, almost forgotten in the course of events, lights up and moans a disturbing grumble. Its booster rockets flare as it changes its direction, maneuvering directly over the battle. There is a chilling silence for the briefest of moments. Then, as if in response to the warship's actions, the Ze'ev soldiers burst out in fierce anger as the battle takes a turn for the worse. The Ze'ev soldiers fight with even more vigor to destroy the queen and her people! The noise on the battlefield becomes deafening, with bloodcurdling screams filling the air.

Momentarily forgetting about Bridge, Vicky scans her surroundings, strategizing the best way to enter back into the battle. Bridge, looking up, states, "Hmm, that's not good!"

Her words have a tint of caution in them. Vicky notices her tone and pauses. She looks at Bridge. Vicky asks, "What? What is 'not good'?"

At first, Bridge looks at Vicky almost as if she does not know her. Then, using only her eyes, she looks back up at the warship, with her nose pointing upward. "That!" she states. "That's not good."

Vicky moves in closer, tilting her head in concerned curiosity. She commands, "Explain!"

Bridge smiles, excited to have an opportunity to explain something to someone who does not know. She opens her hands wide. "Okay, okay! Look, listen, the Ze'ev people, they're like this. They … they do things in order. Okay, in order. For instance, here"—she points downward, referencing the battlefield—"they sent three warships" (She brings up three fingers.) "… right? The first warship is to get the Army Queen, *duh*! Obviously! Those are the warriors, sorry to say … that they don't care about.

"But they did not know that the queen was going to work her magic and produce warriors! Ta-da!" Bridge extends her arms and waves her hands as if she performed a magical feat herself.

She continues. "The second warship, it's the real warship! This is their army, a whole platoon, coming to either take or destroy! However"—she pauses dramatically, pointing her finger upward—"the third warship, the third warship! It is their fail-safe, in case the other two fail! Its purpose is to destroy everything! It will bomb not only the village but the entire planet! The Ze'ev soldiers," Bridge points out, as if she were pointing to individual people. "The soldiers know that if they don't win now"—Bridge clenches her teeth—"they're all dead!"

Vicky looks up at the warship and points, "So they are positioning themselves to bomb us!"

Bridge replies, "Yup, yup!"

Just then, a bright light appears before them. It is as if a star has fallen from the sky. The light erupts, and out of the light, like something emerging from a hole, appears Defender! Her garment has changed. Although similar to the gown she wore before, it is now armor, shiny, bright silver armor with a hint of gold. In her hands is a metal double-headed spear. It has a needlelike point on either end. The shaft is corrugated, like an ancient Roman column, with silver rings at either end just before the spikelike blades.

Vicky stares in awe! It is almost surprising that, with all that Vicky has seen in the past few days, anything would still surprise her, but the sight of Defender emerging from nothing leaves her stunned. Both the Army Queen and Bridge take it in stride, as if it were just another normal day in the midst of any other day. Although Bridge's expression does change from carefree to a more pensive one; similar to that of a cat when another cat enters the room. Defender looks around anxiously, and then her eyes catch Vicky. She calls to her, "Lieutenant Young!"

Immediately Vicky snaps out of her trancelike state. It is back to business. Her people, the village, the Army Queen, the universe are all in a desperate situation! Defender does not wait for Vicky to respond. She runs toward her and grabs her shoulder. She is focused; there is fire in her eyes. There is something burning within her that has to come out. She informs the lieutenant, "Lieutenant Young, I have found your people!"

Vicky shakes her head. "What?"

From behind Vicky, Bridge sarcastically replies, "Oohh, dramatic!"

Defender's eyes dart off of Vicky for a moment to look at Bridge then back at Vicky. However, Defender cannot help herself. She turns her attention back toward Bridge. She asks, "Bridge?"

Bridge smiles and moves out from behind Vicky and replies, "Mag? What are you doing here? Shouldn't you be—oh, I don't know—guarding something? Or perhaps tending bar?"

In general, Bridge does not like many people, especially women. In fact, the more powerful and/or attractive they are, the more Bridge's claws come out, and right now, her figurative "claws" are down to the ground. However, this is quite a defensive reaction on Bridge's part. In reality, neither Bridge nor Defender has any true animosity toward the other. Their relationship toward each other may be described as a lion and a leopard passing each other in the forest, cautious yet respectful of the other's abilities. In fact, for Bridge, this is a very friendly welcome.

The Army Queen senses the tension. She realizes that there are more important matters at hand. She steps forward to get Defender's attention. "Defender."

Defender turns her attention to the Army Queen and gives a slight bow of her head in respect and replies, "Queen."

Vicky, finally able to gather her thoughts, speaks up. "Defender, tell me, where are my people? What is going on?"

Defender regroups her thoughts and spears one tip of her weapon into the ground. She stands firmly in front of Lieutenant Young and states, "Lieutenant, your people are on a planet. They are being led by someone. They are looking for a power source."

Vicky, concerned, asks, "A planet? What planet?"

Defender replies, "It is a planet of caverns. It is called Efazinok. It literally means 'dark cave.'"

Bridge lets out a sharp laugh. "Ha!"

Defender and Vicky look over at Bridge. Defender asks, "What?"

Vicky chimes in, "Bridge, please, if it is important, tell us. What do you know?"

Bridge takes in a deep breath and then smiles. "All right, all right," she says as she steps forward. "This planet, Efazinok, does not mean 'dark cave.' It literally means 'dark dimension' or 'dimension of hell'!" She points at Vicky. "Let me tell you what that place really is."

Chapter 20

The battle rages on; the chariots have turned their attention toward the women, blindly blasting at the trees. However, when the women attack, it is not just one that responds, but six or seven at a time, all shooting at one chariot! The chariots burst into flames, diving into the forest. There are small fires all throughout the forest; if not for the lush richness of Malak-Beth, the entire forest would have been an inferno! The battle against the tanks has not been very successful. Even with all the women's firepower, the tanks are very durable. The women have only been able to eliminate one tank. One reason for this is that it takes many women multiple shots to take down just one tank, and for the most part, the women have been on the defensive. The tanks have not been targeting the women or the forest but have been gathering at the top of the hill, preparing to overrun the village!

The women are busy fighting the chariots and the Ze'ev soldiers, not to mention trying to avoid the Sheol fighters. Some of the women warriors' weapons have fared well against the Sheol fighters. One of the women in particular, Morningdrop, managed to become quite effective against them. Morningdrop's weapons are a bow and arrows. Honestly, at first, she has no luck at all against the Sheol fighters! The bow and arrows are quite amazing, as the arrows are actually able to shoot high enough to reach the fighters. Unfortunately, as they pass, every shot is a miss. The arrows themselves are devastating, traveling at blinding speeds. Morningdrop's aim is also not the problem, as the transformation gave her the ability to be extremely accurate. In fact, two soldiers that she fired upon, while balancing on a tree branch, had arrows go directly through their hearts! They were dead without even knowing they were hit.

Although she has understanding and accuracy, it does not compensate for her lack of experience. Frustrated, she eventually runs out of arrows. Resting her hand on a branch, she feels a strange sensation come over her. She looks at the branch and imagines an arrow. The branch breaks off; hundreds of tiny blue lights appear and transform the branch into an arrow with a glowing blue arrowhead. Morningdrop looks at it curiously. Suddenly she hears the roar of the Sheol fighters approaching. She aims; this time she fires before the fighter comes directly overhead. Success, the arrow sinks deep into the jet's cockpit, piercing the leg of the pilot! Now she knows what to do, and with new vigor, she gets to work.

Morningdrop breaks off branches and turns them into arrows. Soon many of the Sheol fighters are torn or riddled with arrows, one to the point that it can no longer fly; the pilot has to land the fighter in a nearby field. In addition to the pilot who is shot in the leg and soon also shot in the foot, she manages to shoot another pilot in his shoulder and another one through the back of his chair, cracking the back of his helmet. After every shot, she quickly gets better; Morningdrop is soon able to shoot straight through the canopy. She kills two Sheol pilots, causing their planes to crash. The pilots change position, flying just out of range, firing down blindly into the forest. However, they end up killing more of their own soldiers and chariots than she can.

The approaching tanks are mere minutes away from meeting with the tanks that are already in line at the top of the hill. In fact, more than half of the garrison has already positioned themselves at the bottom of the hill, waiting to advance. The warriors realize that, once this happens, there would be a never-ending wave of tanks toward the village, and at that point, nothing would be able to stop them!

Meanwhile, the young boy has been teleporting those injured from the battlefield to the palace courtyard, where untransformed villagers tend to them. The boy stands in the palace courtyard, searching. He can feel someone in need. Finally, he has pinpointed their position! He teleports just in front of the line of tanks, at the very tip of the plateau, where it hedges downward toward the oncoming garrison of tanks. Invisible, he looks around. He cries out a whisper, "Where are you?"

He can sense him, feel his pain, his fear. The boy pauses; he hears a muffled cry on the side of the hill, he rushes toward the sound. There, entangled in some roots, half covered in dirt, is a barely conscious Private Rikes. The boy removes the roots; Rikes begins to slide down the hill, but the boy firmly grabs hold of him. As gently as a young boy, as strong as a gorilla can, he lifts him in his arms. Rikes is bleeding from his head. The boy teleports Rikes to the palace courtyard and places him down on a blanket. One of the older women rushes to tend to him.

Suddenly a Sheol missile misfires near the sidewall of the palace. The explosion sends debris and some larger stones falling on the injured below. Without thinking, the boy pushes the nurse to safety and covers Rikes with his own body. The destruction to the palace wall is minor, but the debris is enough to injure the boy, as a stone gashes his back. The boy yells out in pain. Spotting the Sheol fighter, he teleports inside the Sheol fighter's cockpit. The pilot cannot see him, but he feels him as the boy unbuckles the pilot's harness and wraps his arms around the pilot The whole time, the Sheol pilot is screaming out in fear, "Yatan, yatan!"

The boy teleports them just outside the fighter. Once again, the boy teleports himself to the Army Queen. The pilot is left in midair to fall hopelessly to the ground. His fighter flies off into the night sky.

The Army Queen grabs the boy by the arm. With the concern that only a mother can have, she gasps, "Your back! You're injured!"

Vicky and Ruth rush over. The boy defiantly pulls away. He responds, "I'm—"

Just then a chariot fires into the village behind them, blasting holes into its buildings! Without thinking, the boy disappears and reappears inside the chariot. Forgetting to turn invisible, the driver attacks him. The boy does not notice when the driver removes a serrated blade from his boot. Quickly the boy overpowers him, slamming his arm into the side of the chariot. The driver retaliates by slashing the boy in the arm. The Army Queen yells out, "No!"

Her word is filled with deep agony and hangs bitterly in the night sky!

Aboard the chariot, a low growl, like that of an injured beast, rises from deep within the boy. Suddenly his appearance changes, his eyes turn yellow, and his body sprouts hair. His teeth grow long and sharp. The grip the boy has around the chariot driver's arm tightens to the point where the bones break. The driver, in panicked fear, lashes out at the boy with his blade. The boy retaliates with his now-clawlike hand, slashing his arm so deeply that it almost severs his hand from his arm. Then, with another slash, he slices into the chariot driver's stomach. Suddenly, as if being pulled by some unknown, unstoppable force, the boy vanishes.

The chariot and the driver crash into the ground. The boy appears before the Army Queen; he looks up at her and murmurs, "How, how?"

The boy transforms back; a tear runs down his face. The queen lifts him and hugs him. She brings his face back enough to look him in the eyes. She explains, "My son, this is why I did not wish you to be enhanced by my power. The way it works, the weaker, more innocent a person is, the more ravenous it makes them! That is how it compensates for their vulnerability."

Suddenly the boy's character changes; he pulls away from the queen. His eyes are once again yellow and glaring. The boy's voice is deeper and raspy as he declares, "But I am no longer vulnerable, am I?"

The Army Queen lifts her hand to calm him. He steps back and states, "No, and I no longer have to hide my name."

The queen pleads, "No, don't…"

The boy, eyes flaring, declares, "I am a prince! My people were massacred trying to protect me! No longer do I hide."

His teeth again grow long and sharp; he cries out to the universe, which stole his very innocence. "My name is Naama Razzev! I will be afraid no more!"

The queen cries a defeated whisper, her voice seeming to disappear with the passing breeze, "Naama, noo!…"

High above, aboard the bridge of the third and final warship, there is constant commotion. The bridge is a large rectangular area with porthole windows all around the front three walls. There is a round portal in the center of the floor, overlooking the scene below. The controls are littered with screens spying on the battle. The bridge itself is made out of a grayish-white material, walls, floors, even the control panels, obviously not a Ze'ev construction. The back wall closes the bridge off from the rest of the warship. It has a large doorway, leading to a short hallway, with retractable blast doors raised on either side.

On the bridge are many top Ze'ev officers, monitoring the situation below, yelling commands at one another. The situation is fire, as they prepare to annihilate the planet! In the center of the control panel is a robot. The robot is over two meters tall. Although it looks formidable, there is something old about him, almost ancient. A metallic black breastplate covers his torso. He has matching black boots and what can only be described as metallic long black gloves forming his hands. He has a metallic face mask, which looks like the upper part of a human skull.

The rest of the robot's movable parts are visible, silver and black gears, hydraulics, and wires.

The robot calls out, "Naama Razzev!"

He calls two of his inferiors to him, "Zahov-Arbim, Zahov-Eser Shimon, come to me!"

In run two other robots. Although very similar in design, their body armor is slightly wider and yellow, battered and stained, but still yellow. In unison, they reply, "Sir, yes, sir!"

The general commands, "Naama Razzev, the weapon is found! He is on the planet below. Go to the planet and capture him, he is valuable to our cause. I am sending you his voice confirmation and the data we retrieved."

Zahov-Arbim questions, "Data, sir?"

The general sneers, "Fool! We have been looking for the target for some time now! I naturally programmed all computers that, once his name was spoken, the individual would immediately be targeted and scanned. We have confirmation, it is the boy! We have a 67 percent match!"

Arbim again interrupts, "Sir, 67 percent?"

The general confirms, "Yes, the weapon has changed since we had searched for him on his home planet, perhaps genetic experimentation to conceal his identity. Nevertheless, our computers confirm that it is him! We now have all his genetic analysis, spectral scans, infrareds, everything you would need to find him. Do not make this more difficult than what it is!"

They fearfully reply, "Sir, yes, sir!"

The general concludes, "Upon your return, we will proceed to destroy the planet, so make it quick! At least we can obtain something to bring back to the master from this futile Ze'ev campaign!"

Arbim and Eser Shimon reply, "Sir, yes, sir!"

They run off into the small hallway. On either side of the hallway is an elevator. One of the elevator doors opens, and they enter. Moments later, they enter their private ammunition hangar, many levels up. Arbim and Eser Shimon proceed to strap on jetpacks and various weapons. As soon as they are equipped, they remotely open a small circular porthole far above them. The two robots fire their jetpacks and guide themselves out and down toward the planet below.

Meanwhile on Malak-Beth, as if on cue, as soon as Bridge had finished warning them of the true nature of Efazinok, the tanks mobilize. The cry of their gears howling in the night is horrifying, as almost two hundred tanks start toward the village. Defender glances at the tanks and then back at Vicky. She grabs her by the shoulder and entreats her, "You need to get to your people! I shall hold the tanks off!"

For a minute, Vicky stammers, but before she can say another word, Defender literally leaps into action, jumping some twenty meters toward the oncoming invasion. Defender points her weapon toward one of the tanks; miraculously, the weapon extends hundreds of meters. It goes straight through the first tank and then right through another. Then, seemingly effortlessly, Defender lifts both tanks off the ground, without the spear so much as bending. The tank tracks spin helplessly in the air as dirt and grass fall from them. Then she swings them around.

The sight of some hundred-plus tons of metal flying overhead causes Vicky to crouch defensively. The Ze'ev soldiers cower to the ground in fear; the warriors run for cover. Finally, after a 360-degree spin, Defender releases the two tanks into the line of other approaching tanks. The explosion is deafening, and the crash causes a domino effect. Five of the tanks explode immediately and are thrown back by the impact of the first two tanks.

A ball of metal and fire comes tumbling down the hill. To add to this destruction, as the shells inside the tanks catch fire, they explode! With her one action, Defender destroys more than forty tanks and temporarily halts the rest of the deployment of tanks from going up the hill. The remaining tanks scramble, trying to find alternate routes up the hill.

Moments later, Defender is back standing before Vicky and the Army Queen. Bridge has been laughing so hard the entire time she has to use Vicky's shoulder to hold herself up. Vicky tries to speak, but what she has just seen has taken away not only her breath but her words, as well. Finally, Vicky points a shaky finger at the spear in Defender's hand. She manages a hoarse whisper, "What, what is that?"

Defender holds it up. Then as if she were presenting an old friend, she states, "This? This is Efes, in your tongue, 'Zero Point.'"

Bridge once again brings Vicky back to reality; she chokes out one last enormous laugh. Then throwing herself totally on Vicky's shoulders, Bridge wipes away the tears running down her face. She exclaims, "Wow, that was great!"

Vicky recomposes herself; she straightens up. "That was amazing!" she states.

Vicky's mind is focused once again. She looks Defender in the eyes. "I need to get to my people."

Defender looks up. She states, "First, we need a ride!"

Defender looks at the Army Queen. "Can you handle this?"

The words from Defender's mouth seem more like a predestined confirmation than a question. The Army Queen lifts her sword by the hilt and places the blade in her other hand. She flashes a mischievous smile and confidently states, "Yes, yes, I can."

With that, Defender takes a few steps back. She looks up one last time at the warship above her, and then as she appeared before, she disappears! Like a star lighting the very night, she is pulled into the bright light, and then she is gone. No sooner after Defender leaves, the light still lingering in the atmosphere, the Army Queen cries out a loud battle cry! The cry reverberates throughout the plateau, down the hill, and off the trees of the forest. The sound revitalizes the warriors, they shout back the battle cry, and the battle is engaged that much more vigorously!

The tanks have already started to reform; some of them had begun to climb back up the hill, right over their own fallen tanks. The queen charges at the tanks!

The queen's blade slices the cannon on the closest tank. With her second strike, she slashes its tracks. The tank moves a few more meters before the large metal wheels dig into the ground and get stuck deep into the rich soil. The Army Queen, in blinding speed, moves on to the next tank. Again, she attacks the tracks; so hard is her strike that one of the tank's wheels breaks off. One by one she disables the tanks, occasionally removing the hatch from the tanks and disposing of the tank drivers. The Army Queen is phenomenal, but Vicky realizes that, before they leave, she has to find Private Rikes, and somehow they have to remove their fallen comrade Private Diamond. She refuses to leave them here! Vicky spies Eliana and reaches out to her. "Eliana, Eliana, I must find my comrade Private Rikes!"

Eliana nods. "Madam, fear not. In all the commotion, I forgot to tell you one of our older women is taking care of him. The boy brought him to her. He is unconscious, but otherwise, he is fine."

Vicky's eyes well up. Eliana, not knowing what to do, grabs Vicky by the shoulder; the two hug. Vicky regains her composure. "Eliana," she states, "take me to him."

"Yes, ma'am, follow me."

Like a bolt of lightning, Defender appears on the bridge of the third warship. The bright light startles the crew as they scramble to get weapons. Their efforts are futile, as Defender quickly slices through the Ze'ev personnel. The robot at the controls, General Nagid, removes his sidearm. He threatens Defender, "You shall not leave here alive."

Those are General Nagid's last words as Defender extends Zero Point, slicing Nagid straight through his head. The alarms blare throughout the ship. The piercing sound alerts the rest of the Ze'ev crew, and soldiers to rush to the bridge. Defender freezes in her tracks, but not because of the alarms or possible danger. Opening her hand, she concentrates.

Defender has a unique ability to control anything mechanical, like a puppeteer controlling a puppet. She does not need to know the complexity of the machinery. She can feel how it works, as if the machine were alive in her hands. Just as the soldiers are about to rush the bridge, Defender closes the blast doors, separating them from the rest of the ship. There is a bizarre, deadly silence aboard the bridge in contrast to the commotion on the other side of the blast doors. Defender concentrates even more deeply, accessing all the ship's controls.

Suddenly she fires the main rockets. The ship vibrates violently as Defender lifts it up and out of the atmosphere, into space. Then Defender quiets the rockets, and she then systematically proceeds to open all internal doors. The crew, uncertain about what is happening, wander about aimlessly. Meanwhile, the soldiers outside the bridge hasten to get blowtorches to cut through the blast doors that separate them from her. Then Defender opens all outside doors and hatches, and even the hangar door slowly opens like an enormous creature's gaping mouth. The great suction of empty space pulls everything not held down out into its void. Within moments, the entire warship crew is sucked out into space.

Defender holds Zero Point vertically; she then extends the weapon so that the bottom blade pierces the floor and the top pierces the roof. Holding on tightly, Defender raises the blast doors. The great suction pulls out all the fallen Ze'ev officials and General Nagid. Quickly the bridge is cleared; even most of the blood has been sucked out, leaving only long strands on the floor and walls. Defender seals back up all the outward doors and hatches and closes the hangar. She fires the rockets and slowly returns the warship back into Malak-Beth's atmosphere.

Meanwhile, the two robots, unaware of what has happened aboard their warship, have landed in search of the boy. They scan the courtyard. Arbim turns to Eser Shimon. He states, "The scans appear to be malfunctioning. I get a lock on the boy, then it disappears and reappears somewhere else."

Eser Shimon replies, "If we cannot find him, we will cause him to find us. Focus on the villagers, kill them! When he comes to save them, then we will capture him."

Arbim asks, "Do you think he will come out? He has been hiding all this time."

Eser Shimon replies, "It does not matter if he comes or not. Once everyone else is dead, the one that is left will be him! Besides, killing the villagers will be a bonus."

With unbridled conviction and hatred for all living creatures, save for their master, they raise their weapons and begin firing upon the warriors. The warriors are taken off guard; the weapons the robots fire are not bullets but energy blasts, and the robots' speed is almost a match for the warriors themselves! The robots' aim and precision are near perfect. Five warriors are down in less than half a minute. Luckily, even the robots' blasts are not enough to kill the warriors. However, they are enough to put them down for a few minutes until they heal. While they are down, a second or third shot may prove to be fatal, but their brothers will not allow this. When one warrior falls, he is quickly pulled to safety by another. The warriors have to dodge the robots' blasts and try to fight; this is extremely difficult for the men whose weapons are used mostly for close combat.

Soon the horrid stench of burnt flesh stains the air as the warriors fall before the might of the robots.

The Army Queen, however, is seemingly unaffected by their presence. She strolls up to Private Diamond. She looks upon his cold, fallen body with compassion. She raises her sword and then slams it down, seemingly mercilessly, through Diamond's back. Diamond's tormented body has been calling to her from the moment he arrived on Malak-Beth. When he fell, his corpse cried out to her in agony.

She speaks to him. Her words are like a melody, picked up by the wind and surrounding him. "What gives you strength? Do you think it is the mechanics or the weapons? No, Private Volt Diamond, your soul is your strength! Your caring, commitment … love. This allowed you to remain in control. The enchantment has bonded to your warmth, not this machine's coldness! You have the ability to gain control again. Realize that you are more than the metal, more than the machine, even more than the enchantment! Rise and truly become what you were supposed to be!"

The Army Queen removes her sword and backs away. The hole seals back up instantly. The queen smiles. Suddenly the great body of Private Diamond shakes. It begins to change. A shiny black leather-like skin covers his entire body. Air brutally spurts out from his nostrils, pushing away dirt. Diamond rises. His body, which was once robotic, is now muscle covered under what appears to be metallic black skin! His bull-like head is even more defined than before. His unique "star eyes" shine bright in the night sky. He grunts a sound only a beast can make.

Only for a second does he acknowledge the queen, then observing the chaos of the battlefield, he spies a tank approaching. Without giving a second thought, Diamond rams his massive head into the side of the tank! His left horn cuts a gaping hole through the metal. Then, with his muscular enormous body, he lifts his head and tosses the tank over his shoulder! Again, without hesitation, Diamond attacks another tank, jamming his massive head into the side, forcing it back over the side of the hill. The tank tumbles down, exploding and bursting into flames.

Diamond then takes notice of the two robots firing mercilessly against the warriors, their brutality and love of it nauseate him. Diamond releases a bone-chilling grunt. He attacks. Arbim does not see the attack until Diamond's horn is impaled deep into his chest plate. Diamond proceeds to lift the robot above his head and shake him violently, like a dog with a chew toy. Parts of Arbim's body fly off. Diamond grabs hold of him with his hand, ripping him from his horn. Arbim is torn to pieces as Diamond tosses his remains to the ground! Eser Shimon yells out, "Ethan Han, Bone Eater, you live? Then die again!"

With that, Eser Shimon takes out a second weapon and fires both weapons ferociously at Diamond. Diamond roars; however, the blasts bounce off his metal-like skin. Then Diamond reaches his left hand out, grasping an incoming tank as it rises over the hill. With just Diamond's hand, the tank is halted, its tracks digging futilely into the ground. Diamond's hand expands. The tank advances, and as it advances, it is absorbed into his hand. Diamond raises his other hand and points a threatening finger at Eser Shimon. The finger grows and turns into a tank cannon, then it is quickly followed by three other cannons. The four cannons rotate, firing shell after shell at Eser Shimon. Eser Shimon is instantly vaporized, the explosion causing a large hole in the ground where he stood.

The remaining Sheol fighters, hearing that he is alive, quickly change course and circle to make a pass at Diamond. They scream over their intercoms, "Ethan Han n'moht! Moht, moht! (Bone Eater is alive again! Kill him, kill him!)"

Diamond, with eyes on the incoming Sheol fighters, expands his hand, ejecting out the broken corpses of the two tank drivers. He holds their carcasses in his hand. Then from out of Diamond's back, rockets emerge. The rockets roar as Diamond rises to meet the incoming Sheol fighters. The lead fighter is close. Using the tank drivers' remains as a projectile, Diamond hurls them at the fighter. The pile slams into the fighter, knocking it off course and causing it to crash into the forest below. Diamond then raises his cannons, and in an impressive move, with cannons firing, he spins around in a 360-degree turn. In this single action, he takes out all ten fighters!

Ruth has joined Vicky to retrieve Private Rikes. Rikes is on a stretcher, and the villagers help Vicky to carry the fallen member of their team down toward the village. Vicky and Ruth pause to watch the awesome image, as Private Diamond disposes of the Sheol fighters. Vicky smiles and turns toward Ruth. Ruth smiles, her smile filled with joy and expanding everywhere! She gasps, "He lives!"

Vicky nods, "Yes, let's get Rikes to the courtyard. We have to go!"

With Diamond's aid, the tide of the battle is definitely turning for the people of Malak-Beth. In the courtyard, Vicky calls to Diamond on her communicator, "We have Rikes. Defender is getting us a ride back to our people. We have to depart soon."

Diamond lands in front of Vicky, Ruth, and Rikes. He reaches out toward Vicky. His hand opens up, and out of his hand comes a rifle. He hands the rifle to Vicky. Then out of the other hand, he hands her a belt strap with seven grenades. Vicky takes the items and smiles. She looks up at Diamond and states, "Well, while waiting for Defender, I might as well help the villagers."

Vicky flings the strap over her shoulder and rushes off into the battle. The rifle that Diamond gave Vicky is more than just formidable, dispensing bullets at amazing speeds. Vicky runs down the hill to the forest to aid the women. Just as Vicky runs out of ammunition, she hears a crash from behind her. A tree falls from the tracks of one of the few tanks remaining, which has decided to overrun the forest in an attempt to wipe out the women warriors. Without a second thought, Vicky is on top of the tank. She lifts the hatch just enough to fling one of the grenades inside. Holding the pin, which has a remote option, as she races to safety, she yells to the women in the forest, "Get down! Take cover, the tank is about to explode!"

The women quickly run for cover. Like all of Diamond's replicas, the grenades are enhanced, yielding four times the explosive power of her standard UPA grenades. Once Vicky is confident that she and the rest of the warriors are out of harm's way, she presses the remote ignition. The tank explodes into pieces. The force of the explosion takes out multiple trees, but the warriors are safe. Vicky rushes back up the hill toward the village.

Just then she notices that Bridge is still in the courtyard, wide-eyed, like a child watching fireworks. Vicky walks over to her. She asks Bridge, "We are getting ready to leave as soon as Defender finds us a ship. Are you coming with us?"

Bridge smiles, but it is not a genuine smile. Although she does appreciate her asking, she has no intentions on going with them. "No," she states, quite calmly. "You go on ahead. I'm not really a fighter. 'Sides, I have things to do."

Chapter 21

Brown is finally united with Sergeant Pierce; they place their injured on the remaining tanks as they proceed down the rocky road. Fortunately, the ground is dry, and for the past few minutes, it has been quiet. The scans indicate a large open area and an energy source straight ahead of them. They march slowly toward the energy source. Morale is low, but Brown can only hope that they will find answers, perhaps even safety and a way back, when they reach the energy source. His heart races as he wonders, what happened to his friends? Where is Jones? Where is Yang? He wonders if they will get back to the *Tiqu-Qi*. Right now, he directs his efforts to move forward. He must be their guiding path; he must push forward! How could he expect the others to follow if he himself feels lost?

Suddenly, Sergeant Pierce breaks the silence. "Sir, there is movement up ahead!"

Brown immediately kneels, lifting his fist. Pierce gives the command, "Halt!" The tanks' brakes squeak throughout the cavern. Pierce kneels beside Brown. Brown asks, "What is it?"

Pierce points forward. "Up ahead, sir. Just beyond the clearing, something's flying in. Fast multiple targets! Sir!"

Tank commander A1 yells out, "Sir, should I open fire? Sir!"

Pierce, annoyed, stands up. He turns toward the tank and yells, "No, you definitely should not open fire!"

Pierce looks at Brown and kneels again. In a voice almost a whisper, Pierce asks, "Sir, should we open fire?"

Brown taps his damaged visor, trying to get magnification. He quickly stands and turns toward the tank. He slams his palm against the tank two times. "No!" Brown commands.

He looks around at the troop and repeats, "No, stand down!"

Brown turns forward and gazes ahead.

Jones's squadron is in the air again. They, too, have discovered the energy source and are making their way toward it. Lieutenant Chu calls out to Jones, "Ma'am, up ahead in about one thousand meters is our best chance to land, just before the energy signature." Jones nods. "Make ready for our descent."

Chu replies, "Ma'am, yes, ma'am."

Chu gives the command. "Prepare for the descent, eight hundred meters!"

The remaining squadron replies, "Sir, yes, sir!"

Chu calls out to Jones once more, "Ma'am, life-forms detected, approximately 1,200 meters ahead."

Jones responds, "Let's hope they are ours. We could use a little good news."

Chu responds, "Roger that, ma'am!"

The fighters land at the edge of a large open area. The floor in this open area is amazingly smooth, with a glasslike shine to it. The entire section of the cavern is illuminated with an eerie glow. The source of the light is unknown; whether it is coming from the walls themselves or from some other source cannot be determined. The circular cavern has three large entry points. There is the tunnel that she and her squadron flew in, at the opposite end a second one, and to her immediate right, a third one. As the pilots open their cockpits and prepare to depart, Lieutenant Chu calls out, "Ma'am, what is that?"

In the very center of the cavern is a figure, what appears to be a person kneeling. The figure is too far away to be certain. Jones shakes her head. "I do not know."

There is something odd and mysterious about the figure. Jones feels a strange, uneasy sensation. Jones asks Chu, "Can you scan it?"

Chu sits back into the cockpit. He activates his ship's scanner, the best and fastest he can get his hands on. Chu calls out, "Ma'am, in that direction, I'm only picking up a powerful energy signature. But there are life-forms dead ahead, the same life-forms we picked up earlier. Look! They're at the other end of this cavern!"

Jones smiles wide, as at the other end she views Brown and what remains of his troop arriving. Then as Jones places her foot firmly on the ground, she notices that not only is the floor in this area of the cavern unusually smooth and shiny, but the color is also different. The floor is marbled, browns and whites swirled together. Again, a chill shoots up her spine; something is not right! She calls out to Chu, "Chu, can we get an analysis of the ground? Something is off."

Chu replies, "Ma'am, yes, ma'am!"

He quickly retrieves a handheld scanner from a compartment on the side of the ship.

At the other end of the chamber, Brown peers across the vast floor of the cavern; they spy Jones and her squadron. Sergeant Pierce asks, "Sir, is that—"

Brown nods. "Yes, that's our squadron."

Then sadness falls over Brown's heart, as he realizes that there are only a handful of ships left. He does not even entertain the thought as to whether Jones is one of the pilots still alive. He knows in his heart, that if any of them have survived, it was because of Jones!

Pierce, unemotionally states, "It seems they suffered loss also, sir."

Brown nods somberly. "Yes."

Sergeant Brack steps forward. His face is contorted in confusion. He points to the center and asks, "Sir, what is that? Is that a person?"

Brown, startled by the discovery, calls out to Sergeant Pierce, "Pierce! Find someone with a scanner, I want to know what that is."

Pierce looks over toward the object and freezes. His eyes grow wide; he falls into a trance-like state, "It's, it's a little girl…" he babbles.

Brown, puzzled by his comment, unsure if he heard him correctly, asks, "What? What did you say?"

Pierce snaps back to reality. He shakes his head trying to regain his thoughts, embarrassed by his outburst. He replies, "Sir, I'm sorry Sir! I don't know why I said that."

Then trying to redeem himself and to make some logical sense of what they are seeing, he asks, "Sir, do you think that it could be Dr. Long that we've been looking for?"

Brown shakes his head, "Not sure, go find me that scanner!"

Pierce straightens up, "Sir, yes Sir!"

He rushes off commanding a soldier with a scanner to come forward.

Chu states, "Ma'am, I'm sorry, ma'am! It's confusing, maybe I'm not reading this correctly. The scans can't get a scan!"

Jones frowns. "What does that mean?"

Chu replies, "Ma'am, sorry, it's the scans, they seem to be malfunctioning. And I asked Lee and he retrieved his scanner, and we're getting the same readings! Sometimes it reads normal organic rock, sometimes it's picking up energy, and sometimes it scans as if there's nothing there, or it can't find what it is! Ma'am, sorry, ma'am!"

Chu and Lee continue tinkering with the scanners. Jones looks at the ground once more and responds, "Humph."

As they move forward, Jones points toward the center and asks, "Lieutenant Chu, how about that?"

Chu responds, "Even with the handheld, all we are picking up is a strong, unidentifiable energy source. If that is a person, they have something very powerful in their possession, ma'am!"

Jones calls to Lee, "Lieutenant Lee, a moment."

Lee walks over. "Yes, ma'am."

Jones asks, "Can you do me a favor? Go pilot to pilot, assess their condition, and make a list to see who is missing." Her words drift off as it is hard to believe what has happened; just saying the words forces her to accept it.

Lee understands; he clears his throat and quietly confirms, "Ma'am, yes, ma'am."

He walks off to assess the pilots.

Meanwhile, on the opposite side of the cavern, Brown, Pierce, and Brack move forward to investigate. Brown tries his luck with his communicator. "Jones, is that you?"

Jones's lips break into a smile. "Brown, it is good to hear your rusty voice!"

Brown chuckles. "It's good to hear you too … Do you guys have any idea what that is in the center?"

Jones shakes her head. "Not yet. We are going in to investigate."

Brown replies, "Roger that. We'll meet you in the center … Any communications from the *Tiqu-Qi*?"

Jones replies, "No, the communicators are on a constant loop, searching for a signal, sending out a distress call. So far, no response."

Brown sighs. "Roger. Meet you in the middle."

Jones replies, "Roger, over and out."

Both sides make it about one hundred meters in, when a rumbling from the third tunnel causes concern. So loud is the noise that they can hear it through their helmets. Then they notice a light, growing brighter by the second, moving down the cavern. Brown's able men instinctively raise their weapons. Jones and her pilots remove their sidearms.

Shooting out from the tunnel is a shuttlecraft. The craft is smoking and sputtering out the back. When the pilot sees Brown and recognizes the troops, she settles down about twenty meters from them. Amazed, Brown looks at the shuttle then toward the cavern. Out from the cavern come running Yang and her troops. Noticing the two companies and finally feeling a small sense of safety, she calls out to her troops on open communications, "Halt!"

Her team is exhausted and barely able to stand when they finally stop. At such a short distance, the intercoms automatically connect; both Brown and Jones hear Yang give the command. Immediately they recognize her voice. Brown calls out on the communicator, "Yang, is that you?"

Yang responds, "Brown?"

Brown replies, "Yes, and Jones is here too!"

Jones calls out, "Ma'am, it is so good to hear your voice! When we get back, Lieutenant Young is going to be happy you made it out!"

Hopeful, Yang asks, "Have you had any word from Lieutenant Young?"

Jones shakes her head sorrowfully. "Not as yet, we've been down here. No word from her, but still, we are glad to see you!"

Yang responds, "Likewise."

Then curiously she asks, "What is?"

Brown responds, "We don't know, ma'am. We are on our way to find out."

Yang responds, "Let me assess my soldiers, and then we'll meet you there."

Brown and Jones both respond, "Roger that."

Brown's and Jones's teams' pace is about the same; however, Jones's team is slightly faster. Brown's visor has broken to the point that he can no longer use its magnification. At about 150 meters from the center, they get a better look at the figure. It does appear to be a person, a person in a white or grayish garment, kneeling, sitting up. The closer they get, the greater the details. After a few more meters, Sergeant Pierce's eyes open wide once again. Barely able to talk, he mumbles, "It, it, it is her!"

Brown looks at Pierce and then ahead. It is true; it does appear to be a young lady, definitely a minor, perhaps a teen. Jones becomes concerned; she opens her speaker so that the girl can hear her. Still some distance away, she calls out to her, "Miss, young lady, can you hear me? Are you okay? Do you understand me?"

There is no response. Jones picks up the pace and begins to trot toward the young lady. The other pilots look at one another and then follow suit, running behind Jones. Brown also picks up his pace, but at this point, he is barely able to walk, so the increase in his speed is barely noticeable. When they get even closer, they see the young lady more clearly: very pale, filthy, covered in dirt. She has long black hair to the ground. She is on her knees. She is wearing what appears to be some sort of toga; it probably was white at one time but now it is gray and stained. The girl looks battered and beaten, thin and frail, and she is crying bitterly! Then, the final thing they notice are her hands. Her hands are bony from malnutrition, and they are cuffed! Thick cuffs and chains run from each hand forward into the ground and from her ankles in the back, running in the opposite direction!

Jones cannot believe her eyes; tears fall down her face. She makes a mad dash toward the girl. The girl's eyes move in Jones's direction. The girl cries out, "No, no! Do not touch me! Do not touch me!"

At first, Jones does not comply; she does not slow up. She keeps her speed toward the girl. However, the girl cries out even louder, "No, DO NOT TOUCH ME!"

Jones takes a moment to pause; she waves her hands out in front trying to ease the tension. Now, they are only meters away from her. Her eyes are dark and large. Jones calls out to Brown, "Brown, we need a medic. We need some food and water!" Brown replies, "Roger, I'll see what we got."

He calls to Pierce, "Pierce, have someone check the tanks for any supplies."

Yang interrupts, "Brown, hold that. We should have all those things in the shuttle, we are checking right now. Jones, we will bring them to you."

Jones responds, "Yes, ma'am. Thank you, ma'am! Appreciate it."

Brown replies, "Roger, thank you, ma'am."

Jones turns her speaker back on to communicate with the girl. "My name is Jones…" She states, pointing her hand around her. "These are my friends, we are from Earth. We are here to help you. Do you have a name?"

Besides her constant waves of tears, the girl does not respond.

Jones continues, "Are you hurt?"

The girl's sobs become even deeper; just then, Brown and his men arrive. The girl cries out, "I'm hungry, so hungry!"

Jones, whose heart is breaking, cannot stop the stream of tears running down her face; however, she does try to hide the evidence of her sorrow in her voice. She calmly states, "Yes, we are getting food for you right now, but you need to let us come closer."

Jones slowly takes a few steps closer. Brown opens his channel. "Young lady, who did this to you?"

The young lady's crying eases, as she turns her direction to Brown, who is standing about ten meters directly in front of her. Her eyes look straight through him, and although he would not admit it, a chill runs down his spine. The girl asks, "Why are you here?" Her voice seems innocent and young.

Brown, for a moment, is taken off guard, then he responds, "We are here looking for someone, looking for something. But right now, we are here to help you."

The girl looks toward Jones. "Are you looking for something also?" she asks Jones. Jones replies, "Yes." Jones points all around once again. "We all are."

The girl asks, "Is it an energy source?"

A hush falls over everyone. Brown replies, "Yes, that is what we are looking for. Do you know anything about it?"

She glances at Brown then back at Jones. She states, "I have something for you."

The girl takes her bony hand from the ground, the severe malnutrition and the weight of the chains making it extremely difficult for her to move. Trembling, she reaches under her toga. She touches something, and in response to her touch, it lights up. She pulls out a small square box, only about three centimeters thick and a little longer than the palm of her hand. The box is a black frame with a white screen. The white screen is so bright it fills the entire cavern, to the point where they can barely see. They cover their eyes with their arms and look away. The girl places it upside down on the ground so that its light does not blind them.

Brown asks, "Girl, where did you get that?"

Jones turns to Lieutenants Chu and Lee. With her finger, she motions for them to scan the mysterious object. They nod, and both Chu and Lee turn their scans toward the device. The girl replies to Brown, "It was given to me to protect it."

Chu taps Jones's shoulder; she turns toward him. With astonishment, he exclaims, "Its energy signature is off the charts! This is definitely what we were looking for, what Dr. Long came down here to get. We cannot even define its nature, it emits gamma rays, x-rays, everything! We can't get a focus on it, it's spiking up and down!"

Jones frowns. "Is it giving off heat?"

Chu, caught off guard, states, "No, no, it's not. In fact, its temperature is"—he checks his scanner—"sixty-six degrees."

Meanwhile, Brown asks the girl, "Who—who gave you that to protect?"

The girl does not respond. Jones, with a hand out in front of her, calls to her, "We need to get that device, it's not safe."

The girl covers it with her long fingers and pulls it closer to herself. She hisses, "Nooo! I was given special ability to hold it, but only a true child of Efazinok can touch it."

Jones pauses and looks toward Brown. Brown straightens himself. "Well, we just happen to have one."

Brown turns toward Pierce. "Sergeant, bring forth Guide 1."

Pierce shouts the command, "Guide 1, forward!"

Lieutenant Taylor flies the shuttle off the ground and lands it mere meters from Brown's position. Brown turns to Pierce. Using a closed channel, he states, "In all this commotion, I almost forgot about him."

Remarkably, the shuttle has not been damaged throughout all the disastrous hardships that have befallen Brown's team. Brown commands, "Bring out the prisoner!"

Moments later, the side door opens. A cool fog escapes into the cavern. First, one guard exits, then when the chamber reopens, the gray alien emerges. Lastly, the second guard comes out. The two guards escort the alien creature to Brown. Brown looks at the gray alien. He asks, "Do you know this girl?"

The alien states, "She was not here when I was here."

The alien walks to the side of the girl. The alien takes a moment to consider her, then he walks toward her. Jones yells out, "Do not get too close, she does not want to be touched!"

The alien does not respond, he continues walking toward the girl. Brown, Jones, and their crew just look at one another, unsure of what to do. Jones takes her clues from the girl; she does not move. It would seem that she does not feel threatened, so Jones does not intervene; in fact, Jones even extends her open palm out toward Brown, indicating for him to hold. The two guards follow behind him, remaining at a distance but not relieving their aim. The girl never looks up directly at the alien. The alien squats down next to the girl. She then lifts the device and places it between the alien creature's arms. He turns without incident and walks toward Jones.

Amazed, there is a hush throughout the cavern; not one person can believe what has just happened or how easy it is for the alien to retrieve the device. The white screen powers down as soon as it is handed to the alien; it would seem that the device is reacting to the alien creature's touch. Jones asks, "What exactly is that device? Is it a battery, a weapon?"

The gray alien almost smiles. "This is not the device. This is merely the doorway to the device."

Curious, Brown and his two sergeants move closer. The alien creature looks toward Brown and then Jones. "Let me demonstrate."

He turns his face toward the device carefully balanced between his arms. The alien creature commands, "J, 1, 06!"

The device suddenly flashes like the flash from a camera then falls to the ground, tripling in size to the size of a small window. Jones immediately calls out, "Brown, Brown!"

Brown finally turns toward her. Jones's voice is intense; she asks, "Did you see that?"

Brown mumbles to himself, not knowing what to say. Of course, he saw what just happened, but obviously, there is more to what Jones saw or noticed than what he has. Jones continues, "Sound like some sort of code or alien coordinates."

Brown considers her observation and nods. "Yes, I think so!"

The screen on the device changes. The image is bright; it takes a moment or two for Jones's eyes to adjust to it. It appears to be a large space, lit by a cool white light. On a metal tripod sits a second device. This device seems ordinary. It is rectangular, similar in appearance to the first device. The frame is a grayish metal. It has four clasps, two on each of the longer sides. Each clasp has a belt attached to it. Although covered by the device, it seems that the straps are connected in the back, as if it were meant to be worn. Held within the metallic frame is a gray screen. Like the first device, there are no visible controls. Brown, Jones, and the two sergeants peer inside. Jones, who is closer to the alien creature, has the best view. Instinctively Jones asks, "What is that?"

Then surprisingly, quite uncustomary for the alien, he responds, not only a one-word answer or a quick sentence but something similar to a conversation. The creature states, "That is the power source you were seeking. It is an energy transferor, one of the original three Equalizer artifacts, created to protect the universe. It was imprisoned inside this pocket dimension. This exact spot is the only junction in the universe in which one could enter into the dimension. Only a child of Efazinok can retrieve the artifact."

Jones and the rest remain speechless as the gray alien being turns his head toward the device. Kneeling, he extends his restrained arms toward the portal. Jones steps back. She wonders to herself, *He may be a child of Efazinok, but his shackles are not! Will this portal allow those restraints to enter in? Should we even let him retrieve such a valuable asset?*

Brown wonders, "Can we trust him? Are we really letting him do this? Is there no other option?"

However, before they can react, the alien creature pushes his shackles through the portal. From Brown's vantage point, it seems as if he were pushing his arms right into the ground. However, from Jones's vantage point, she can see his arms entering the dimension.

Then suddenly the screen shuts off with his arms still in it. The alien hisses in pain, as the shackles and the parts of his arms that are still inside are chopped clean off from the rest of his body. He jerks back in agony; however, he is able to contain his emotions. Jones's overwhelming concern causes her to reach out toward him. She cries out, "Oh my! Are you—"

The alien, however, straightens up and shakes what remains of the shackles off from his arms. With the shackles gone, the remaining restraints fall to the ground with an echoing thump.

Jones again reaches out to comfort him; however, there is something holding her back. Brown is the first to notice; without the shackles, the alien's arms begin to grow back! Within seconds, he has both his hands. He victoriously opens and closes them repeatedly for the first time in three hundred years!

Jones, amazed, asks, "Are you okay?"

The alien creature returns to his eerie, arrogant silence. Brown does not like what he sees. Something in his stomach is turning; something is not right! He can sense it. Brown moves; he walks toward the alien creature. He firmly states, "All right, all right!"

He motions for the two guards to get closer. Then placing his palm up, he states, "I think before we do anything else, we need to dictate what happens next!"

Surprisingly, it is the girl who speaks up next. She turns toward Brown and asks, "Aren't you looking for your friend?"

Brown is taken aback for a moment. Brown mumbles to himself, "He's not really my friend!"

Jones calls out, "Dr. Long? Do you know where he is?"

The girl nods. "Yesss, I know where he is. He's here, he's been waiting for you."

Suddenly the lights in the cavern dim. The girl straightens up and opens her mouth. Her mouth continues to open, wider and wider, inhumanly wide and round! Finally, the mouth is larger than her entire body, with three rows of teeth circling inside her mouth. Her gums are brown and ragged, resembling undercooked meat. Her teeth are like pointed wooden pegs made from the bark of a tree. If that were not bad enough, if anyone lives through what is about to happen, the next image they see, they will never forget! Dr. Long's head and shoulders emerge from her mouth! Although covered in slime, scratched, and bleeding, it is definitely him, or what appears to be him! He cries out, "Help me! Help me!"

Those are his last words, as she swallows him back. Then the girl closes her mouth to about half the width. The soldiers instinctively lift their weapons, pointing at this creature that, moments ago, they felt tremendous sorrow for.

Brown, horrified, asks, "What are you?"

Earlier on Malak-Beth

Defender replies, "It is a planet of caverns, it is called Efazinok. It literally means 'dark cave.'"

Bridge lets out a sharp laugh. "Ha!"

Defender and Vicky look over at Bridge. Defender asks, "What?"

Vicky chimes in, "Bridge, please, if it is important, tell us. What do you know?"

Bridge takes in a deep breath and then smiles. "All right, all right," she says as she steps forward. "This planet, Efazinok, does not mean 'dark cave.' It literally means 'dark dimension' or 'dimension of hell'!" She points at Vicky. "Let me tell you what that place really is. Years ago, Doc made a horrific mistake and created a creature he couldn't control! He made a deal with the Dictator to hide her in the caverns where he grew up, in exchange for his help. However, she was so powerful she overtook the caverns and she became the caverns. The caverns themselves are part of her body, she is Efazinok! She has an uncontrollable, insatiable hunger. She has to continuously eat!"

Vicky, fearfully confused, asks, "Eat what?"

Bridge chuckles. "Why, people, of course. Soon after she was placed in the cavern, she ate all the cave people, all of the Dictator's people! Within minutes, she ate them all!"

Bridge firmly grabs Vicky's shoulder. "Seriously, if it's true that your people are there, she will consume them all! You have to go there now and save them, before it's too late!"

Efazinok now

The girl begins to salivate; thick white pus falls from off the teeth on top of her mouth down to her bottom teeth. Simultaneously the floor of the cavern becomes rubbery and unstable. Giant globs of white slime secrete from the roof of the cavern, falling onto the soldiers below. Brown yells out, "Fire! Any of you who have ammunition, fire!"

The soldiers attempt to fire, but to their horror, their guns have become chains, long, thick chains! The chains are cuffed around their wrists and extend outward into the ground. In panic, they pull back, trying to free themselves, but to no avail; the chains hold tight! The girl lowers her open mouth to the ground. The pus flows into her open mouth like the tide. She slowly raises her mouth from off the ground. Between the rows of brown teeth are long chains. They extend from deep in her throat, out her mouth, and into the ground before her. The sight is both unreal and horrifying! The soldiers yell out, "Brown, help us! We can't get these chains off!" Brown, however, is in the same predicament, trying with all his might to pull himself free.

Suddenly things go from horrifyingly bad to horrifyingly worse. As the chains in the girl's mouth begin to pull inward, so do the chains on the soldier's hands pull them forward! The soldiers are jerked into the white slime and are dragged slowly across the floor toward the girl. The tanks and fighters both begin to pitch to and fro as they start to sink into the ground.

For some reasons Jones does not yet understand, the area around her and the gray alien creature is not covered in slime, nor is the slime falling on them. Jones, with her sidearm in hand, is unsure what to do. Then out of her profile vision, she notices the gray alien creature, whom she has forgotten all about in the commotion. The screen on the device on the floor is open once again; the alien creature is reaching his hands into it. Inside the pocket dimension, nothing has changed, except the severed piece of the alien's shackles resting on the floor, just in front of the tripod. Jones turns toward him with her sidearm in hand. Jones sneers, "What are you doing? Do not move! We told you that we would retrieve the energy transferor together!"

The alien pauses for a moment. Just then, a chain from the girl's mouth shoots out toward Jones. As if it were alive, it wraps itself around Jones's arm and jerks her forward! Jones fights back; she grabs the chain with her other hand and pulls it with all her might! Seeing that it is impossible to pull her arm free, she tries a different tactic. She slowly, painfully, moves her hand to fire her sidearm toward the chain. The first try, she misses. She twists her arm for a better shot! Her teeth are clenched tight as Jones has to almost break her arm to get the right angle. With her second try, she is able to shoot the chain. The bullets spark as they hit the chain; finally, the chain breaks, and Jones is free! The remaining piece of chain still wrapped around her arm falls to the ground.

Panting for air, Jones turns toward the alien creature once again. Propping her injured arm up with her other hand, Jones aims her sidearm directly at the alien creature. The creature has not only retrieved the energy transferor but is also in the process of strapping it on his chest. The creature's body is changing; like air being pumped into a tire, his muscle mass is increasing. He no longer looks frail, but quite formidable! The creature mockingly asks, "Would not your efforts be better spent saving your comrade?"

Brown, for the most part, has managed to stay on his feet, using his massive muscles to pull against the chain. Another less-fortunate soldier is centimeters away from the girl's mouth! Brown, without concern for his own life, rushes forward to save his fallen friend. Brown slips in the slime but manages to reach out and to wrap his arms around the soldier's torso. Unable to get a footing, he tries his best to pull the soldier from the impending doom. Unfortunately, his efforts are futile; like a snake swallowing its prey, the girl's mouth stretches as it pulls the young man in! Brown quickly jumps back to his feet, but the chain around his wrists has already been pulled tight, and now he is even closer to the girl!

Jones has to divert her attention from the alien to Brown. She shoots her sidearm at the chain pulling Brown. The chains snap! The shackle breaks off as Brown falls back into the pus.

The alien uses the chaos as cover for his actions. He takes the device from the floor and whispers commands to it. The device responds and grows even larger, to the size of a door. The alien props the device onto the floor. It stands straight up on its own. The chain's speed increases. Brown and Jones feverishly try to save their people. Jones shoots their chains, as Brown pulls them free. However, as many as they save, the girl swallows twice as much. In addition to this, as soon as they are free, the chains shoot back up from the ground, entrapping them once again. Sometimes the chain snares their arm or their leg or even around their waist!

Brown and Jones call out, "Use your weapons! Shoot the chains!"

Those with any ammunition try their best, but the angle is difficult, and most of the bullets fly into the ground or into the air.

Jones, knowing that soon she will run out of ammunition, is frustrated. She decides to bring the fight to the girl. Jones fires at the girl. A barrage of bullets hits the girl; it seems to do little to nothing to her. The bullets sink into her flesh, but her skin closes back up immediately. However, her action does not go unnoticed by the girl, who, upon impact, shrieks a horrifying, bone-chilling wail! Instantly the ground rises, and a huge stalagmite rises from the ground, pushing upward into Jones. Fortunately, it does not impale her, but it does toss her almost ten meters. The impact causes Jones's helmet to fly off. Brown quickly rushes to her side. She is alive but in a great deal of pain. Jones refuses to give in to the pain, when there are others who need her. She grabs hold of Brown's arm and pulls herself off the ground. Brown stammers, "Are you—are you alright?"

Jones, without her helmet, can barely make out his muffled voice from inside his helmet. She understands what he said and nods. Brown, concerned, calls out, "We need to get you a helmet!"

However, Jones waves his request down. "No!" she cries out, loud enough for Brown to hear. "We must save as many as possible!"

Just then, a chain wraps around Brown's helmet, pulling him backward off his feet! Before Jones can respond, a chain wraps around her leg from the ankle almost all the way up her thigh. It yanks her down, pulling her into the slime! It seems that the more the girl consumes, the stronger and more aggressive she becomes!

Chapter 22

It would seem that all is lost; there is nothing more they can do! Within a few minutes, all of them will be gone, food for this monster! Then, all of a sudden, a roaring rumble from above shakes the cavern! Giant boulders fall to the ground. Even the alien creature pauses to consider the commotion from above. The noise also gains the attention of the girl. Distracted, the chains lose their tension and drop to the ground, giving the remaining soldiers a momentary rest. Then, a large circular hole appears in the roof of the cavern. The hole ascends many meters, all the way to the planet's surface. A bright burning light fills the hole.

Brown is able to remove the chains from his helmet, and while he and Jones watch in anticipation, he attempts to remove the chains from her leg, as well. Slowly descending the hole is a black Ze'ev shuttlecraft. The landing rockets flare more intensely as Private Rikes lands the shuttle mere meters away from the girl. The shuttle door opens, and Lieutenant Young jumps out. Jones and Brown both cry out in joy, "Lieutenant Young!"

Although warned, Vicky is horrified at what she sees. The entire cavern is frozen, all parties shocked at Vicky's intrusion onto the scene. The roar of engines cracks the silence as Private Diamond, with Ruth in his arms, flies down the hole. Diamond lands and places Ruth on the ground. Ruth runs to Vicky's side.

Malak-Beth

Bridge is tormented; should she speak, or should she remain quiet? Finally, she can no longer hold it in and blurts out, "There is one more thing!"

Defender impatiently turns toward her. Frustrated, she asks, "What! Just speak or do not speak!"

Vicky looks at Bridge. She pleads, "Please, tell us. We need to know whatever you can tell us."

Bridge screams, "Ahhh!" She shakes her head violently. Finally, she gives in, "Very well. Just be careful. The Dictator, he is dangerous! Ever since we found your dimension, he has planned out everything! He handpicked the entire crew. Everyone, except for you! You were the only one who was picked simply because you were the best qualified for the job."

With her hand facing upward, Bridge points at Vicky. She continues, as if she realized something, "You! You are the wild card!"

Vicky can take it no more; she grabs Bridge by the arm. "I do not understand, you said that he planned this whole thing. Our expedition, our being stranded, finding Malak-Beth?"

Bridge responds, "Yes, yes, and no! Stranded, yes! Expedition, definitely, yes! But here"—Bridge points downward—"no. Everything you've done, he has not planned! You're the one thing that he has no control over!"

Vicky, still confused, asks, "But how?"

Bridge points with her finger as if she were pointing to objects in front of her. She explains, "You see, he's able to control things, people's thoughts, their actions from far, far away, even across galaxies! He just has to find the people. They think that they're making their own decisions"—she waves her fingers back and forth—"but they're not!"

Defender responds, "That is why no one can remember what he looks like!"

Bridge puts her finger on her nose. "Exactly!"

Vicky, concerned, asks, "Tell me, who is the Dictator?"

Bridge's eyes open wide. "You haven't figured it out yet? He's been with you all this time."

Efazinok

Standing partially behind Vicky, like a frightened small child, Ruth points a finger at the gray alien creature. She waves her finger at him. "That's him!" she states. "He's the Dictator!"

Vicky turns to Diamond. She points to the little girl. "Diamond, kill that creature!" Diamond immediately raises his hand and transforms it into a five-barrel weapon! Suddenly, from nowhere, a large blackish-gray stone as wide as a house appears above Diamond's head! With unbelievable speed, it crashes into Diamond, pressing his body into the white pus below! The Dictator states, "Oh no, it would not be polite to interrupt her while she's eating."

Vicky looks toward the Ze'ev shuttle. "Rikes," she commands, "eliminate the creature with extreme prejudice."

The Dictator calls out to Vicky, "Oh no, Lieutenant Young, let her finish what she started. I promised her she could."

The Dictator raises the palm of his hand, and before Rikes can fire a single shot, a large rectangular wall of stone blocks his line of fire! Rikes fires, but the bullets bounce off the wall without even making a scratch!

Vicky turns toward the Dictator and sneers. She leaps into action toward him, but he simply smiles at her and walks through the doorway. On the other side of the doorway stand Commander Ripclaw and his second. Ripclaw's hand is extended to receive the Dictator. As soon as the Dictator enters, the screen turns black, and the device shrinks back to its original size. It then falls to the ground into the white ooze.

As soon as the device hits the ground, the creature seemingly comes back to life, as the girl once again pulls in on the chains! The remaining soldiers claw into the murky floor, trying to resist their impending death! With target one in the wind, Vicky changes her focus to target 2. Seeing that both Brown and Jones are free, she commands, "Brown, are the tanks active? See if you can get one to fire on the target!"

While running toward the half-sunken tanks, Brown replies, "Ma'am, yes, ma'am!" Brown hails the tank commanders. "Tank commanders, do any of you have a clean shot at the girl? Take it!"

Command A1 is more than willing to take the shot. He responds, "Sir, yes, sir!"

Quickly he moves his barrel around to line up with the creature and fires! The shot is wide; it hits the wall that separates the creature from the shuttle. The explosion lights up the cavern but has no effect whatsoever on the wall. However, the girl is angered! From out her mouth, she shoots a chain straight through the cavern, right into the tank's cannon! Before he knows what is happening, the chain wraps around Command A1's torso, and with a vengeance, she pulls him into the tank cannon. The force is so great it causes the tank cannon to buckle and crack and for the tank to be pulled free from the ground before the chain snaps.

Meanwhile, Vicky notices that Jones has lost her helmet but also concludes that Jones seems well enough to run. Quickly pressing her outward speaker, Vicky commands, "Jones, see if you can get to one of the fighters!"

Jones responds, "Ma'am, yes, ma'am!"

As Vicky dashes toward the girl, she has to dodge chain after chain, like a football player outfinessing the opposing team's defense to score a touchdown. Vicky commands Rikes, "Rikes, lift the shuttle. See if you can maneuver around that wall!" He also replies, "Ma'am, yes, ma'am!"

Brown dodges the chains three times; however, the third attempt to ensnare Brown is when the tank's shell explodes! Brown dives for cover into the ooze. Moments later, Brown looks up to witness the brutal demise of Command A1. Shaking his head in both anger and sadness, Brown is determined to move forward. He decides to use the ooze as camouflage and crawls through it toward the tanks.

Jones is even less fortunate; she does not get more than ten meters toward the fighters when a chain once again grabs her ankle. She fiercely fights against its hold, only for another chain to wrap around her arm.

Rikes has fired up the engine. As he attempts to pull the shuttle out from the slime, tentacles of rock reach out, grabbing hold of the ship! The rocky brown tentacles pull the shuttle back down hard. Rikes cries out to Vicky, "Lieutenant, Lieutenant! Something is holding down the ship! I am facing resistance!"

Vicky is still in the middle of dodging the chains and has made little progress toward the creature. She replies, "Try your best, soldier. Get that shuttle free!"

Rikes replies, "Ma'am, yes, ma'am!"

Vicky is horrified as she witnesses the creature swallowing two more helpless soldiers. However, this gives her an idea. Changing her trajectory, Vicky moves toward the front of the creature to make sure they have eye contact. While running, she removes the clips on all six of her grenades. She moves in closer than ever. This time, she allows one of the chains to get on her. However, at the last moment, just as the chain is about to wrap around her, she removes the grenade belt. Vicky allows the chain to wrap around the grenade belt. Instantly, the creature swallows it up before realizing what it swallowed. The creature pauses for a moment, then, like a cat with a hairball, tries to regurgitate the bombs. For the first time, the predator is panicking! With her mind totally distracted, all the chains fall off the soldiers, into the slime! The soldiers are momentarily free. Vicky yells out to Brown, "Everyone take cover! Take cover! Brown, let me know when everyone is safe!"

Brown hollers back, "Roger that, Lieutenant! Roger that!"

Fortunately, the Dictator has left two huge stone structures that are perfect for the soldiers to hide behind. Pain and exhaustion are replaced by hope! Those who can move did, and not only do they move, but any fallen soldier who cannot move somehow mustered the strength to lift them from the muck and mire and pull them to safety! Even Jones manages to make it to her fighters, dragging one of the pilots to safety. Another pilot miraculously has held on to the wheel of his fighter, unconscious from the strain. Jones is able to move him further back. Many of the soldiers call out to Brown, "Clear!"

However, he knows that some of them cannot even speak, nor is he sure that their communicators are working, so he eyes the situation from behind one of the tanks. Brown announces to Lieutenant Young, "Lieutenant, we're clear!"

Hiding behind a curve in the tunnel near the fighters, Vicky braces her back and presses the remote ignition!

Five minutes earlier

Aboard the *Tiqu-Qi*, Lieutenant Lin is insistent on the idea of saving his people. Captain Barr and the rest of the crew aboard the bridge are trying desperately to talk Lin out of it. Captain Barr, pointing to the screen, tries to reason with him. "Ye canny go oot thir, ye donna naw exactly whir they ur!"

Lin, standing away, trying to edge toward the door, is blocked by the massive Moses. He points his finger at the screen. "I can't leave our people out there! How many more explosions must we detect before we do something?"

Wei interjects, "Captain!"

Captain Reynolds tries his hand at reasoning with Lin. "It is true, Lieutenant, there are explosions, but we do not know exactly where they are! How are you going to find them?"

Wei interjects again, "Captain Reynolds, sir!"

Captain Reynolds continues, "It is madness! We need you here. We cannot have yet another person lost down there!"

Lin, eyeing Moses, warns, "I will get out. I need to go down there! Captain Barr, you must let me go!"

Captain Barr states, "I don't think—"

Wei stands from his seat and grabs Captain Reynolds by the arm and shakes it. Then, most uncharacteristically of him, he almost screams at the captain, "Captain Reynolds, sir!"

Captain Reynolds, Barr, and Lin all turn and ask, "What?"

Then they see it, the giant Ze'ev warship, more than twice the size of the *Tiqu-Qi/Liberty Crane*! Captain Reynolds stammers, "What?"

Wei blurts out, "Sir, it just appeared out of nowhere!"

Captain Reynolds commands, "Battle stations, Wei!"

Wei responds, "Sir, yes, sir!"

Captain Barr commands, "Lin, sound the alarm!"

Lin rushes to the controls. "Sir, yes, sir!"

Wei speaks over the intercom. "Battle stations, battle stations! This is not a drill! Battle stations!"

Lin presses the alarm; a piercing siren floods the entire ship.

Suddenly a message appears, scrolling across the main computer screen. Wei states, "Sirs, a message?"

Their eyes stare at the screen as Captain Reynolds reads, "Captain Reynolds, Captain Barr, Lieutenant Minor, this is … Lieutenant Young!"

Captain Reynolds turns pale with joy; a gasp escapes his lips. Clearing his throat, he turns to Wei. Wei is smiling, his eyes welling. Captain Reynolds commands, "Wei, Lin, stay alert!"

Lin and Wei both respond, "Sir, yes, sir!"

Captain Barr places a firm, comforting hand on Captain Reynolds's shoulder. He states, "The lass has returned!"

Captain Reynolds nods joyfully. He turns to Moses, who is trying to maintain his composure, holding on to the chairs for support, seemingly to have lost power in his legs. He tries not to cry, but his tears do not obey him. Moses exclaims, "Sir, she is alive!"

Captain Reynolds smiles. He commands Moses, "Moses, find Lieutenant Minor, on whatever assignment he is, and tell him Young is back!"

Moses nods. "Sir, yes, sir!"

Now

The creature is frantically trying to remove the bombs that she swallowed. Her arms have turned a dull grayish tint; they have grown long and thin. Her fingers alone have grown three times their normal length as she reaches into her throat, desperately trying to grab hold of the cluster of grenades. It would seem that, once the creature swallows something, it is hard for her to retrieve it. Her hands frantically pull out half-disintegrated limbs and body parts. Finally, one hand grabs hold of the chain, and she begins to pull it up. The slime shooting out of her mouth is thick and brown, like gravy.

Hiding behind a curve in the tunnel, near the fighters, Vicky braces her back and presses the remote ignition. It can be argued that, the moment before someone's demise, there is a sense that they know they are about to die. As the saying goes, "Their life flashes before their eyes." Perhaps it is fear; perhaps it is solace that the fight is finally over. Whatever it is, the creature's eyes widen for just that second, right before the explosion.

The explosion is enormous. Although it does flash across the cavern floor, most of the explosive force shoots upward through the tunnel Ruth had carved out in the roof of the cavern. It flows out into the Efazinok sky, like an angry volcano!

Aboard the *Tiqu-Qil Liberty Crane*, the sighting of the explosion causes a hush to fall over the bridge. Wei exclaims, "Oh my god!"

Captain Reynolds slaps down on Wei's shoulder. Pointing to the control panel, he commands, "Get on the communications, see if we can reach them! See if they survived that!"

Wei is pushing the buttons even before he responds, "Sir, yes, sir, on it!"

Meanwhile, in the cavern, the space is filled with smoke. Tiny bits of debris fall from the sky. As the smoke begins to clear, the center becomes visible. Where the creature was, there is a black crater, about a meter deep and three meters across. Vicky moves from her perch and looks around. She calls on her communicator, "Is everyone okay?"

One by one they respond; the first to reply is Jones, followed almost immediately by Brown. Soon, all those who can respond did, "Ma'am, yes, ma'am!"

For the first time since they entered the tunnels, their heads feel clear; although they feel beaten and exhausted, a fog has been lifted from their minds. Suddenly their communication link with the mothership is reestablished. Wei's voice is like music. "This is Wei from the *Tiqu-Qil Liberty Crane*, are you alright?"

Lieutenant Young replies, "Sir, it is good to hear your voice!"

The crew in the caverns are still on an open channel when they hear the cheers from the bridge. Vicky surveys the casualties and the state of their crew. Vicky calls Wei, "Sir, we need an extraction team and medics."

Vicky is unsure what else she should say. Captain Reynolds and Captain Barr look at each other. Captain Reynolds leans forward. "We're on it! We will send you everything we have!"

Vicky replies, "Sir, thank you, sir!"

Vicky then rushes her tired body toward Private Diamond, trapped under tons of solid grayish-black rock. She calls on a direct line to Private Diamond, "Private Diamond, what is your condition? Private Diamond—"

However, before she can repeat herself, Diamond sends her a text. She looks at her communicator. It reads, "I am pinned down! I cannot move!"

Vicky confidently states, "Do not worry, we will get you out!"

Ruth and Rikes are walking toward her. Vicky motions with her hand for Ruth to come quickly. They run over next to her. Ruth timidly asks, "Ma'am?"

Vicky, with her hand out like she was chopping the stone, asks Ruth, "Do you think you can cut away some of this rock?"

Ruth looks down, shaking her head doubtfully. "I'm not sure, ma'am. Did you see? Bullets, even the explosion, had no effect on it."

Vicky looks up, as if considering what she said. Then she looks over at Ruth and states, "But you are not bullets nor an explosion, you are something special, aren't you?"

Ruth almost smiles. "I guess so, ma'am."

Vicky motions to Rikes with her finger. "See if you can help guide her."

Rikes nods. "Yes, ma'am."

He kneels close to the ground. There is a space between the stone and the ground. Using the light on his wrist, Rikes is able to pinpoint where Private Diamond's body lies. He scoots over just slightly and then motions for Ruth to come join him. He directs her, "Ruth, right here, if you go straight down, you will not hit him." She straightens up. "I will try."

With her hand similar to the way Vicky had moments ago, Ruth focuses and forms a thin strand of acid from the ground up, just slightly higher than the stone. She extends the thin line, moving it forward. Slowly the line sinks deep into the stone. As Vicky suspected, her acid can cut through the stone; perhaps it is the only thing that can.

It takes about a full minute for Ruth to cut through the stone. Finally, when the acid reaches the other side, the piece of severed stone hits the ground with a large thud. The force of the stone falling throws out a cloud of dust in every direction. Now, with half the weight of the stone off Diamond's back, he is able to maneuver his arm under him. He pushes his back against the stone. As soon as Vicky realizes he is able to move, she commands, "Everyone clear out, give him space!"

Suspenseful moments pass as he uses his massive muscles to prop himself up. First onto one knee, and then he is able to push the stone up vertically. Finally, he walks out toward Vicky, none the worse for wear.

Chapter 23

Defender is barely able to control the giant warship through space. So right before Vicky and her crew depart, Defender tells Vicky that she will move it out of the atmosphere and fly it as fast as she can into that solar system's sun. She assures Vicky that they will see each other again. As for the cleanup, the lives of the crew are the top priority! Dr. Davis is put in charge, much to the resentment of Dr. Lanthrop. Shome organizes the entire ship as a giant hospital. She also prioritizes the injured in order of severity. Private Chang sets broken arms and legs. Then those who are able are given a crash course in first aid, and then they help others in worse condition.

The morale aboard the entire ship is very low. Not only are they stranded and not only do most feel that they will never see their families again, but they have 3,339 unaccounted for, presumed dead! They are their friends, comrades, and for some, even family members. Out of the crew who remain, over 1,000 are in the makeshift sick bay, and for over half of them, their lives hang in the balance.

On the planet, Sergeant Yang, with permission from Lieutenant Young and Lieutenant Minor, takes it upon herself to take a small team searching up and down the remaining tunnels for survivors. Sadly, even with the aid of Private Diamond and his advanced scans, they are unable to find any more survivors.

With the creature gone, the rock is just rock, and most of the tanks are soon able to pull themselves out. Using the tanks as tow trucks, they are able to pull most of the fighters out, as well. Besides low fuel, for the most part, the fighters' bodies are in good condition. The landing gear, however, which is sunk into the rock, has to be dug out. Some of the gear is in too deep and has to be removed totally before the fighters can be towed. Ruth is able to remove a small sliver from one of the two stone walls to study. Because of the sliver's dense nature, all preliminary tests have come back inconclusive. However, with all the injured, both Dr. Davis and Dr. Shome cannot give much time to analyze the sample. All that is known is that the stone is made of a material stronger than anything they have ever encountered.

The crew of the *Tiqu-Qi/Liberty Crane* have no time to mourn and no choice but to move forward. They all know that, as much horror and tragedy that had already befallen them, the worst part is still yet to come! Aboard the bridge, in the meeting room, are Lieutenant Young, Lieutenant Minor, Captain Reynolds, Captain Barr, Lieutenant Lin, Wei, Moses, and Rikes. After forty-five minutes of debriefing, the eight leaders have to decide what the next course of action is. Captain Reynolds sits with his fist on his chin, considering everything that has been heard. Frustrated, he states, "So we have all just been puppets!"

Captain Barr places his fingers on his forehead. He looks around and asks, "So whit ur we gunna do noo?"

Vicky sits back. She takes a breath and states, "We just have to pick a side!"

Epilogue

On the outer rim of the Milky Way, the magnificent woman of fire sits on her throne. Suddenly a strange sensation overcomes her, similar to the feeling one has when sleeping and is suddenly awakened. Although it cannot be described, it is unmistakable, perhaps a sixth sense telling her that someone else is there or warning her of danger. She looks around at the vastness of space and turns her head slightly to look over her shoulder. She spies something. Her eyes are amazing; she can see across star systems and spot a person on a planet hundreds of millions of kilometers away. She gasps. "You?"

Before she can say another word, a rip in the very fabric of space opens! An enormous vortex of a great black hole appears out of nowhere! Even with her great power, she cannot resist the insatiable gravitational force pulling on her. Within seconds, she is gone, and the hole closes as if nothing was ever there. Millions of kilometers away, standing on the moon of a nearby planet, a hand gently strokes a leather satchel hung over her shoulder. Bridge calmly states, "Don't worry, Dead Cat, everything will be alright."

www.ingramcontent.com/pod-product-compliance
Lightning Source LLC
LaVergne TN
LVHW091533060526
838200LV00036B/591